"*Many writers try to play it safe with the dreaded second novel. Many writers, but not all, as Chris Panatier took chances and delivered with his second book... Reminiscent of the well-loved* Hitchhikers Guide To The Galaxy, Stringers *delivers the laughs, with the jokes drawing on the author's clear love affair with the grotesque, with poignant moments peppered throughout. A highly enjoyable read with moments of real emotional honesty that deserves to reach a wide audience.*"
– Gabriela Houston, author of *The Second Bell*

"Stringers *is f*cking ridiculous in all the best ways. I haven't laughed this hard at anything EVER. In fact, to have this many laugh-out-loud moments should be illegal - there are nuggets of gold to be found on every page. Throw in a fun plot, characters who are rich and lively and incredibly funny in their own distinct ways, and a unique and engaging format (you'll see), and you've got yourself a joyous and exciting read. None of you are ready for this.*"
– Dan Hanks, author of *Swashbucklers* and *Captain Moxley and the Embers of the Empire*

"*Panatier finds the sweet spot between the social satire of The Coming of the Great White Handkerchief and the pathos of the farting, tap dancing aliens of the planet Margo. A tour de ridicule!*"
– R.W.W. Greene, author of *Twenty-Five to Life* and *The Light Years*

"*Wholly original. Ridiculously brilliant. Panatier's* Stringers *is filled with genuine characters, mind-boggling humor, and the raw and hysterical emotions of beings plucked from obscurity, sold to the highest bidders, and used to serve Universe altering purposes. Panatier's unconventional storytelling, combined with poetic sentences and a plethora of bug facts you never knew you needed, will keep you entertained until the very end. I can't recommend enough.*"
– Noelle Salazar, author of *The Flight Girls*

"*In a universe of sci-fi novels, Chris Panatier's* Stringers *inhabits a galaxy all its own. Equal parts hilarious, inventive, and action-packed, this absolute gem of a book delivers a riveting, poignant plot full of flawed, lovable characters. Come for the bug sex, stay for the jar of pickles.*"

– Ron Walters author of *Deep Dive*

"*Panatier's latest book is a riotous, interdimensional adventure with heart. Zany and erudite,* Stringers *reads like an SMBC comic that swallowed a whole series of* Red Dwarf, *veering from the unabashedly puerile to the profound by way of esoterica and galactic hijinks. With bug facts galore and a truly memorable jar of pickles, it has all the makings of a cult favourite. Panatier is one to watch.*"

– Calder Szewczak, author of *The Offset*

STRINGERS[1]

ANGRY ROBOT

1   By Chris Panatier

ANGRY ROBOT
An imprint of Watkins Media Ltd

Unit 11, Shepperton House
89 Shepperton Road
London N1 3DF
UK

angryrobotbooks.com
twitter.com/angryrobotbooks
The Universe takes you back

An Angry Robot paperback original, 2022

Cover by Kieryn Tyler
Edited by Gemma Creffield and Andrew Hook
Set in Meridien

This novel is entirely a work of fiction. Names, characters, places, and incidents are the products of the author's imagination or are used fictitiously. Any resemblance to actual events, locales, organizations or persons, living or dead, is entirely coincidental.

ISBN 978 0 85766 962 9
Ebook ISBN 978 0 85766 963 6

Printed and bound in the United Kingdom by TJ Books Ltd.

9 8 7 6 5 4 3 2 1

MIX
Paper from
responsible sources
FSC
www.fsc.org   FSC® C013056

For all the kids in the school principal's office.

Here lies Ben Sullivan. Died in space. Couldn't open the pickles.

CHAPTER ONE

Jim's in the store again. Jim doesn't buy shit.

"Morning Ben," said Jim.

I'd always liked Jim, but he'd never so much as flirted with a spool of 5x tippet.

"You going out today?" I asked, flipping the magnifier up from the brim of my cap.

"Yep," he answered, fingering some light-wire hooks on a rack.

"You know those are for sale, right? You can buy them with money and they become yours forever."

Jim didn't respond, ambling instead to another rack of fly-fishing goods he also wouldn't end up purchasing.

I knocked the magnifier back down and returned to wrapping a yellow midge.

"Hey," said Jim, just as I'd regained my focus. "What do you call that fly you made for Winston Hollymead? He won't shut up about it. He's throwing all these numbers at me that sound ludicrous. A twenty-five-pound, post-spawn striper? In the Pawnee?" He blew a raspberry. "Makes no sense."

I chuckled pretentiously at Jim's underestimation of my work. It made a lot of sense if you knew how to get un-horny fish to bite like I did. "The *Alpha-Boom-Train* isn't just for striper," I said with a shrug. "It'll work on any post-spawn perciform. They like bloodworms."

"I don't get you, kid."

"I'm twenty-nine."

"Alpha-Boom-Train? Flies ain't supposed to have names like that."

"Customers are supposed to buy things. What a paradox."

He directed a finger lazily in the direction of my fly-tying vise. "Need you to make me oneuh them boom trains then," he said, issuing an edict as if I were his personal river Sherpa.

"Sure thing, Jim," I answered. "Will you be paying for it or just putting it on layaway until the rapture?"

"I'll pay if it looks right," he said, heading out. He pushed the door open, then stopped, half-in, half-out, sending the electronic chime into a recursive death spiral. "How you know so much about spawning river fish, anyway? You ever even been out of Kansas?"

Now I could tell him the truth. I could explain the things I know – that my knowledge goes *way* beyond fish sex. I could tell him, for instance, that the flatworm *Macrostomum hystrix* reproduces by fucking itself in the head. It's called hermaphroditic traumatic insemination. I could tell him that the practice isn't isolated solely to hermaphrodite worms either. Sea slugs,[2] also hermaphrodites, fuck *each other* in the head. They do it with a two-pronged dong, one of which is called a 'penile stylet'. I could shock his system with the revelation that earwigs have two dicks.[3] Or take him on a tour of class Mammalia and into the dens of prairie voles, who are affectionate and monogamous with each other unless the male is drunk, in which case he pursues anonymous hookups. That dolphins will fuck

---

2   *Siphotperon* species 1 – *Oh, here we go, doing the scientific names showing-off thing.*

3   There's a trick-dick in the event of a broken penis.

literally anything. That porcupines flirt via golden shower. I could tell him these things I know, but then I might have to explain why I know them. And that I am unable to do. So, I answered his question with the simple truth. "I just know, Jim."

"That internet, then," he said, answering the question for himself. "See ya in a few days, kid."

I flipped down the magnifier. "Jim."

The truth is I was jealous of Jim. Of his obliviousness, his ability to step into the world from the shop and move on with his life, while mine never changed. Wherever I went, my brain came with, bringing along its innumerable tidbits of faunal knowledge which infected my every thought. There was no explanation and no apparent source. And it would have been completely useless if I didn't work in a fishing shop trying to figure out new ways to get post-coitus fish to bite at fake bug larvae.

I'm no fly-fishing fanatic. I'm just too distractable for any other job.

Every waking moment is a constant barrage of intrusive thoughts with even the most innocuous stimuli churning up commentary from deep within the folds of my brain.[4] *See?* I've tried training myself to think of it as background noise, but it's tough to tune out when your overactive brain is also an asshole.[5]

The door chimed again as if it were being strangled. Through the magnifier came a giant yellow blob that I immediately recognized as Patton, my never-employed stoner friend. He wasn't a stoner by choice – well, it was by choice, but it wasn't

---

4   Koalas and koala-like animals have smooth brains. A condition known as lissencephaly – *Kill me.*

5   I'm just a distilled version of you, buddy. Besides, assholes can be really useful. The giant California sea cucumber, *Apostichopus californicus*, eats *and* breathes through its butt.

just for getting high. Weed legitimately helped him function. Patton was the only person I'd ever met who got paranoid as a consequence of *not* being high. Also, weed is generally pollinated by wind, not by bees.

He struck a pose and pointed at me, suggesting a pop quiz. "In which Order will we find *D. sylvestris*?"

"I'm not doing this, dude."

"*Hymenoptera*," he said, proudly answering his own question.

"How long did you have to train your eight neurons to remember that?"

"A while," he said breezily, removing a blunt from within his hair somewhere.

"You can't smoke that in here."

"I know that." He sniffed it and returned it to his haybale.

In one of his many attempts to push me to broaden my horizons, Patton had tried to get me to audition for Jeopardy (R.I.P. Alex Trebeck), convinced I'd make a bazillion dollars. What he failed to appreciate was that the only way for me to win would be if every single category was natural science. I don't know jack about much else.

Okay, I also know a lot about clocks. Mainly watches. Ugh. This is so embarrassing.

If areas of knowledge were like college specializations, then entomology, with a focus on bug-sex, would have been my major, with a minor in time pieces.[6] Antiques, for the most part – anything older than about three decades. Imagine seeing a watch and having your head suddenly flooded with facts about said watch, while at the same time not giving two shits about the watch or the facts. A six-thousand-dollar Rolex that gains five seconds per day is said to be within tolerances. That's over a thousand dollars for every second it steals from the Universe. The NASA astronauts who landed on the moon were wearing Omega Speedmasters, all except

---

6   Horologics.

Neil Armstrong, who left his inside the lunar lander as a backup clock. Watches on display are almost always set at ten past ten or ten till two because the hands form a smiley-face, a subtle form of suggestion for the prospective buyer. Do I come from a family of watchmakers or antique dealers? Nope. I just know. And it's exhausting.

"Well if you won't do it, then at least train me, man," said Patton. "Be like my game-show *sensei*. Just put all your knowledge up here." He popped the side of his head with his palm.

"Plenty of room."

"I know, right? So, there's no excuse. Please dude? Winning gameshows is the only way for me to get enough cash to start my own Formula One racing team."

"No."

"When you off?"

"Seven."

"Want to get wings?" he asked.

"No, busy."

"Not research again. Come on, dude. Every night?"

"You know the drill," I said.

"It's Friday though. Friiiiiiiiday."

I gave him serious-guy face.

"Alright," he relented. "Roll over to my place in the morning. Aunt Lisa will make us chorizo empanadas and refried beans and we can play Simon."[7]

"Your Aunt Lisa microwaving frozen breakfast empanadas is not making breakfast. And I'll pass on the beans. But Simon is awesome. I'll be there."

"Yeah!" He reached around the counter and patted the

---

7   The original Simon was first marketed by Milton Bradley in 1978 and later on by Hasbro. The console has four colors: red, blue, yellow, and green, running clockwise from the upper right. The colors light up with a corresponding sound in a random sequence and each player's challenge is to repeat the combination exactly.

underside of that bit of my belly that hangs over my belt buckle.
I fired a palm into his sternum and he crashed satisfyingly into
a rack of indicators. "Duuuuuuude," he wheezed, accepting
my justice.

"No more fat slapping. Jesus Christ, man. Grow up."

He staggered away from the rack and smiled passively at the
door. "Okay bro, whatever you say. Hasta mañana."[8]

"Bye."

"See you tomorrow. Empanadas."

"Yeah, bye."

I needed to get to the library, but I also wanted to finish off
a fly I'd been tying – a Hutch's Penell – for one of the area's
best anglers, and possible future wife of me, Agatha Jensen.
It's used in the UK for catching coastal sea trout but it also
closely resembles the sedge-flies that the local bluegills, *Lepomis
macrochirus*, love to eat. When I started tying them a year ago,
the locals couldn't get enough and it kept the shop owner,
also named Jim – I call him "Owner Jim" – pretty happy. I
could do them in my sleep: size 4 hook, black 8/0 thread, a
red tippet, Peacock herl, zebra hackle and silver wire for the
rib. Fly fishermen were always looking for an angle (anglers,
right?) and this Penell had them shelving their Silver Sedges –
the traditional go-to when throwing loops for fish that go for
the caddis fly.

I tied in a white hackle feather, wrapped it with thread,
thickened the front of the hook to form the fly's "head" and
tapped a bead of glue at the top of the shank just under the eye.

After locking up the shop, I had thirty minutes until the
library closed, which was fine, because I already knew the
book I'd reserved was waiting for me. I jumped into the used
Subaru that I'd bought after graduating high school. At the
time I'd let Patton talk me into souping it up so we could race it
on weekends – an actuality that always seemed to get sidelined

---

8   Spanish – *Wow, really?*

by our full schedule of being stoned. Now I just had a car that sounded like a weed-eater in a port-a-potty. But it was fast and I got to the library in sixteen minutes, per my twenty-five dollar Timex brand digital wristwatch, which does not gain five seconds per day unlike a certain unnamed luxury brand performing "within tolerances."[9]

"Ben!"

"Ludlow the Librarian!" I said, miming the solo sword dance of Conan the Barbarian as played by Arnold Schwarzenegger. Ludlow was similar to a barbarian, if you replaced the muscles with nougat and the leather armor with black nail polish.

"I got your book right here. *Reserved for Ben*," he said, tapping a lacquered finger on a stickie note reading same.

"Oh, great. Thanks," I said, rolling up to the circulation desk.

Ludlow prepared to scan in the book, pausing first to consider the cover. He pulled his long, warlock-black hair behind an ear. I could see a question forming. Oh, here it comes. "You studying to become a psychiatrist, Ben?"

"Ah, no, Ludlow." I didn't have much more of an answer for him that I cared to give, though he was well aware of my borrowing history.

"Just a hobby, then? Remote viewing? Claircognizance?"

"Not so different from your weekly séances," I quipped. "You get up in all your customers' business?"

"Only if I think they might be performing witchcraft."

"Afraid you won't be invited?"

"I'm talking about," he lowered his voice, "*the occult*."

I stared at him incredulously. "Have you seen yourself, man?"

He recoiled with offense. "I'm a goth, Ben, not a Wiccan." He slid the book across the counter with a corpse-pale hand.

"I'll remember that for next time," I said, taking the book and tapping the side of my head.

---

9   It's Rolex – *I know!*

* * *

The car rumbled into the gravel drive at the house where I rented an above-garage apartment. I opened the driver's door to a thundering chorus of *Neotibiden linnei*[10] booming away like nature's own heavy metal string symphony. Although that's a bad analogy, because while crickets utilize stridulation for their song – the rubbing of one body part against another, a crude version of pulling a bow across strings – cicadas are percussionists, vibrating a membrane in their exoskeleton called a tymbal.

Yeah, so anyway, it was noisy outside.

I tossed the new book, *Harnessing Your Psychic Powers Part IV: Remote Viewing & Claircognizance*, onto a larger pile of similarly themed texts beside my desk and quietly hated on myself for possessing any of them. Taking in the collection, I began to appreciate the merit of Ludlow's witchcraft accusation. I even had a stack of religiously-themed candles on a nearby end table, though those had come with the apartment. Sure, I lit them from time to time, but for ambiance, not any ceremonial purposes.

On my way to the fridge, I paused at the giant LEGO sculpture that had risen from the surface of the coffee table in recent months. My parents had treated my moving out as their cue to begin a steady process of getting rid of anything I'd ever owned, including a massive tub of the plastic bricks. I'd planned to give them away, but started pressing them together one day, and soon, well. I found playing LEGOs to be a calming and cathartic exercise; and yes, I am almost thirty. What began as a mindless ad-libbing of pieces ballooned into a gargantuan living room monument that looked like one of those spiky naval mines set atop a golf tee. I reached down to the pile, grabbed a grey eight-by-two and a brown six-by-two, overlapped four of the studs,

---

10 Known to laypersons as cicadas.

and pressed them together with a satisfying *skritch*, then added the component to the ponderous hulk.

There was leftover kale and chicken hash in the fridge, which I warmed, doused in barbeque sauce, and devoured with a spatula as I snapped more LEGOS onto the art. I subscribed to the canceling-out method of eating, where you eat as much junk as you want, so long as you cancel it out with something healthy. I figured the kale would counter tomorrow's breakfast empanadas.

Holding the spatula between my teeth, I dragged my laptop over and tapped it to life.

So. Why was I burning through library cards checking out books on psychic phenomena? Why was I there almost every night and then on the internet for hours after that?

Well, it had to do with the bug fucking and the watches. As a child, tiny pieces of information would crystalize in my head before there was any way for me to have learned them. Déjà vu was one possibility, but I've had déjà vu and it isn't quite the right fit for my experience. You never actually *learn* anything from déjà vu. It's just the sense of vague recollection that fades almost as quickly as it comes. My experience was different. Repetitive. Verifiable. I knew things I had no business knowing. Male soapberry bugs, *Jadera haematoloma*, are absolute sex hounds, screwing for up to eleven days in one go just to ensure that other males don't inseminate the same female. What in the *National* goddamned *Geographic* fuck, right? No one should just *know* that.

My parents recognized early on that there was something weird happening. The second I could make words I began referencing obscure facts, the truth of which could be verified with a little research, but for which my knowledge had no basis. At first, they'd just assumed I was a focused listener. Maybe I'd heard someone drop an interesting nugget in line at the grocery store. Kids repeated stuff all the time. But as I crossed out of toddlerhood, the pattern settled in. Instead of the occasional, passing tact bomb, I might give a play-by-play of the mating habits of Brazilian bark lice, leaving out no detail. In between bites of mac n' cheese I'd let slip that the female actually has a dick that she uses to *scoop sperm* from the male bark lice's vagina. I remember my parents being in such awe of science that they'd not cared that I was blabbing about insect uglies at the dinner table.

So off I went to the pediatrician for the basic *is-this-kid-okay*[11] checkup, and on from there to the child psychologist. My parents explained to her that I was some sort of genius, but a few simple tests quickly dispelled that hypothesis. Unperturbed, they insisted on a full battery of IQ tests, which were conclusive: I was solidly average, entirely unremarkable. I was simply regurgitating information and terminology of unknown provenance. They went for a second opinion. My scores went down. I was a parrot, not a prodigy. Still, they wanted answers. So did I.

A barnacle of kale and chicken plunked the laptop's touchpad. I set the spatula down next to it and eased it back onboard with my pinky, then hoovered it up.

Together my parents explored every contrived and far-flung theory to explain my curious condition, going so far as to accuse me of reading books in secret. Sneaking off to read? I mean, do people do that? Certainly not me; I had video games to play and snacks to eat (which I then later cancelled out with different snacks).

There was a phase, thankfully brief, where my parents became quite manic in trying to answer the ultimate question. The house was filled with books on gifted children, from verifiable prodigies like Bobby Fischer[12] , Blaise Pascal,[13] and

---

11 No.

12 Youngest ever U.S. Chess Champion at age fourteen.

13 French inventor and mathematician, authored a treatise on projective geometry at age sixteen.

Maria Agnesi,[14] to the entirely paranormal – ghost possession by historical figures unwilling to cross the River Styx. They got into psychophony,[15] retrocognition,[16] transference,[17] claircognizance,[18] and of course, remote viewing.[19]

For an entire year, every horizontal surface of our downstairs was covered in crystals. The local news even did a story once. There I was, blithely regaling the weatherman with a credible, and detailed, description of grasshopper sex gear as he grinned nervously into the camera. The whirlwind of brief regional fame disappeared as quickly as it had arrived, and by fourth grade I was a local oddity that most people noted and then promptly forgot. The novelty wore off. One minute, you're blowing your teachers' minds, and the next they're sending you to the principal's office for offering to explain how liver flukes spread via sheep shit. It wasn't like I could help it. Holding in what my brain was spewing was a form of torture. My mind was a kettle under pressure and my mouth the spout.

Ultimately, my parents kept their sanity, resolving to accept the way I was. It wasn't like I had a disease or anything, just an interesting glitch in my wiring. A mutation maybe. It was a party-trick. Like being double-jointed or popping out an eyeball. They moved on.

I couldn't.

You can ignore another person if you want. Put on headphones, tell them to buzz off if they won't take the hint.

---

14 Wrote solutions to complex math problems in her sleep.

15 Spirit speaks through a medium (me, in this case).

16 Knowledge of a past event which was not learned or inferred.

17 How doctors say "possession".

18 Like omniscience, except with more incense.

19 Knowledge of something one cannot directly perceive. Also known as ESP, or extra-sensory perception – *Or the scientific term: "bullshit."*

Brains are different.[20] You're a captive audience to an unfiltered version of yourself. The "me" that occupies my cranium is a know-it-all jabberer. I'm trapped with someone who won't shut up. Like that guy in line at the coffee shop who wants to discuss his passion for latte foam art. Now imagine he's in your head, but instead of heart-doodles in bubbled milk, it's precision timepieces and the toothed vagina of the cabbage white butterfly.[21]

Sleep is my only respite, and even then the thoughts creep in.

I lit some of the candles, illuminating four different versions of white Jesus, then hopped on the internet to begin the evening's search. As I did every night.

Knowing what I know has never been a gift. And I was singularly driven by an obsession to find the cause. My life was a mad search for answers that occupied my time and attention, to the exclusion of nearly everything else. If a patient wakes up from surgery with a bit of gauze sewn into their arm, it sucks but at least they know how it got there. My condition had no explanation. It was too specific to be the result of chance or coincidence. It felt... purposeful – or planted. Like it was inserted into my head. It wasn't *mine*. And if the knowledge wasn't mine, was I even myself? Was I an experiment? Someone's project or toy? And to what end? I didn't know. That is why I searched so vigilantly.

Like I said: it isn't a gift. It's an invasion.

---

20 We *never* take the hint.
21 Just imagined it.

CHAPTER TWO

"Fuck this," said Naecia, tossing a bit of particle shielding across the floor of her dig. She'd rebuilt the machine a dozen times over, trying every configuration that presented itself, solved and re-solved every theoretical calculation, and experimented with every variation in materials she could get her hands on. Not only did it not work, she didn't even know exactly what she was building.

She looked up from the wreckage to check the time. Still a bit left until her shift on Vask's day-side surface began.

Her hands were sore from fabricating. Sorer than she got wrestling flanges and packing glands out on the pipe farm. She flexed and squeezed them, observed her sienna-purple skin brightening along the knuckles enough to show the fine craquelure that the planet's arid climate produced. She reached for her cup as she considered the build and swallowed down a fat gulp of scorching jha without checking the heat. "Ffffffffff," she hissed. Then, inexplicably took another drink while pondering the machine. Nothing was working. And would she even know what "working" looked like? "Shitfuck!"

Truth was, Naecia was probably going mad. Whether she was sleeping, resting in her dig, or out on shift, visions of the machine intruded into every corner of her life. It had become a compulsion that felt like a race against insanity: successfully

13

complete the build, stop going crazy. When she did that, the intrusions would surely, *hopefully*, cease and she could live out her life in peace. She longed to think about nothing.

In the meantime, there was the project.

Most things are designed and built with a purpose in mind. Naecia, though, was working backwards; she had been presented with a design (by her brain) and was tasked (by herself) with constructing a machine according to that design in order to learn what it did. Only once a section or component came together was she able to draw vague conclusions about its purpose. For instance, the use of heavy copper and carbon allotropes suggested an electromagnetic shielding – the type used to prevent interference when playing with subatomic particles. This allowed Naecia to conclude that she was building a device that interfaced with the physical world on a quantum level. To do what, she didn't know. Her brain was giving her contradictory information

This, of course, was a form of torture.

What she had been able to divine about the machine was as follows: firstly, it was a device with astronomical computational power. More than anyone could conceivably need for any practical application. She'd managed, through a variety of both legitimate and illegitimate channels, to obtain seventy-two quantum deep-circuit processors, for a total of over a quintillion high-stability superpositional bits, or enough quantum memory to hold the name of every star in the Universe, their elemental makeup, spin velocity, and favorite dessert.

Secondly – and this was the part that made her feel like her mind had genuinely cracked – the machine was supposed to move things from one place to another instantaneously. Some called this "quantum teleportation". Others called it im-fucking-possible.

To start, the machine was plainly not set up to move anything from one place to another, and, even if it was, the task was barred by science. In the end, the purpose of the machine as dictated by her mind (it's a teleporter!) was plainly contradicted by what it had told her to build (a calculator).

Naecia surmised it had something to do with entangled particles: sibling particles linked strongly enough to interact with each other even if separated by a great distance. Manipulate one, and the other reacts. This was not a revolutionary concept: entangled particles had been used for centuries in the Pangemic system to relay communications, i.e. dirty pictures; not people.

Following unsourced notions from one's brain wasn't exactly a scientific approach, but it was all she'd ever had. And she *felt* like the device was aimed at utilizing entanglements between local particles and those light years away in order to allow for faster than light travel (impossible). But in order to do that, it would have to *force* entanglements with distant particles – a truly revolutionary concept that also happened to be ludicrous as it violated every law of the Universe (double impossible). Entire volumes could be devoted to the myriad reasons why the idea failed, but volume one would undoubtedly be titled, *YOU WASTED YOUR LIFE TRYING TO BREAK PHYSICS – WHY?*

While Naecia's mind became more insistent as to the machine's purpose, the build itself remained stubborn. Over the years, she had run each stage of construction through the relevant databases and conducted searches through the Pangemic system's open access research libraries, to see if it matched with any other projects in the public domain. Coming up empty was disappointing, but not unexpected. To date, she'd built nothing more than a behemoth processor, without any idea what data was supposed to be processed. Or even how to input that data if she did. Amazing!

Before long, a cygment and a half had passed with her sitting in a fog of stalled ideas at the bottom of a yawning chasm in her understanding. She stood from the assembly on cramping legs and considered it blankly. How could such a complex hunk of equipment remain so utterly inert? It confounded her. A cube ot purchased and pilfered parts, capable thus far of generating only frustration.

She rubbed her eyes, grunted. Time for work. She drank down the rest of the jha, wheeled the machine over beside her sleeping nook, and draped it in a blanket. *What exactly am I doing?* she thought. *Hiding it?* She laughed. *No one could possibly know what it is, because not even I know what it is.* Yet it represented years of work, so here it was under a blanket, for anyone looking at it to say: *someone's trying to hide that.*

Time had gotten away from her. She gave her armpit a sniff and, not being too offended, opted out of rinsing and stepped into her work overalls. She looped her brother's puzzle amulet over her head, grabbed her helmet before locking up her dig and hopped on an underground vacuum shuttle along with the other pipefitters. In a quarter cygment, she arrived at the centralized power station on the surface, one of five thousand just like it dedicated to bringing power to the Dawn Ring: a thin, habitable band that ran longitudinally around the planet. The station was just inside the outermost edge of the Ring, where things started to get hot.

Naecia debarked and made the short walk to a second bank of magnetic shuttles, where smaller groups of pipefitters were ferried deep into the star-side territory. Once the shuttle had accelerated to cruising speed, the crews wordlessly donned special radiation suits made of a light, metal alloy-foam. "Light" was relative. It only meant the suits wouldn't crush you immediately. The hunched posture of the older workers suggested it took a little while.

The shuttle rocketed south, stopping along its route every few hundred mylics to let a worker out, with the most senior exiting first, at the highest – and least sweltering – latitudes. That was the way the union had set it up. Having only been with the crew for less than a hundred cycles-galactic, Naecia was dropped at a platform near the end of the line, over a thousand mylics from the central power station in the Dawn

Ring. She knew she'd appreciate the whole seniority thing once she'd been around a while, but right now it was a beating.

The only other person there was Embo Lial, another newish grunt, who, being done with his shift, stepped tiredly onto the shuttle with a nod and blasted back toward home.

The gridspace spread out before her was a star-baked yellow wasteland without shelter or water. Add to that the high pressure pipeworks and the landscape took on the feel of a place that was waiting to kill you. Naecia had to be vigilant – a feature of the job she welcomed. It allowed her to forget the stupid machine for a while.

She ran an integrity check on her starshield and customized helmet. Any pipefitters hailing from Scella, as she did, required modified headgear to make up for their slightly longer necks and respiratory requirements. A Scellan could breathe through their nose and mouth, but it was most efficiently, and comfortably, done through the small spiracles on either side of the neck just below the jawbone. Not wanting to trust anyone else with her life while out in the pipe fields, she'd done all her own mods, welding fresh metal-foam rings onto the neck opening and rerouting the inner vents so that they would be proximate to her preferred respiratory pathways. The icy surface of her home planet was a far cry from the crucible of Vask's day side.

She double-checked the suit, put on the helmet, and stepped from the small shuttle enclosure. Her starshield darkened immediately, preventing the nearby red dwarf from burning the eyes out of her head.

A crosshatch of pipe, the source of Vask's power generation capabilities, stretched to the horizon and beyond. Naecia went to the operator's lectern and lifted the protective panel to reveal a screen. Swiping away a scrim of dust, she brought it online and scrolled through various readings on things like radiation capacity, energy absorption efficiency, pressures, etcetera. She concluded that they were nominal, then ran through them again out of caution. When problems did crop up, it was usually as a result of wind, sandstorms, or solar flares, but nothing outside tolerances had registered during Embo's shift. She signed herself onto the grid and closed the panel. Data was one thing, but her job was to be the eyes – and hands, if it came to that – on the ground.

On the short side of the platform was the byceptor that Naecia and the other pipefitter-operators used to do their rounds. Ships or drones would be a quicker way to conduct field surveys, but hostile air conditions made airborne methods expensive and dangerous. Anyway, Naecia liked riding the 'ceptor. It was a chance to go fast and forget about things. A voice command released it from the platform's clamps and she muscled it forward to the narrow lane between the two giant grid pipes that marked the boundary between her section and the one just north.

She mounted up and bit lightly down on the inside of her cheeks, sending a chirp from her implanted com, which then paired with the 'ceptor. The vehicle's readings glowed into view on the lower third of her starshield's display. Power, good. Both wheels, good. Motor, good. Map, present.

She lifted her legs and accelerated into the grid like she'd been shot out of a valve at eight-thousand pressures per square meb. The ground was largely smooth, except for bumps here and there where the wind had carved tiny sand dunes. She careened toward the horizon, a tiny black dot trailed by an arcing tail of dust.

The grid was a colossal network of steam pipes, grouped into bundles then running on racks just above the surface. Here and there, they were suspended higher up to allow ingress and egress for observation and maintenance. Naecia altered her route each cycle – it was the best way to keep from getting complacent and losing focus. The pipes she oversaw operated at immense temperatures and pressures, which meant that there was no such thing as a minor failure, only catastrophic ones. Today she decided on a spiral pattern, careful to cover ground only once.

She tore down the westward corridor at full speed, imagining what the wind might feel like in her face, a sensation few had ever experienced. The atmosphere wouldn't allow it.

Even with its harsh climate Vask was at least a place where she'd been able to find work, which was more than she could say for the other worlds that orbited the dwarf star Pangema. Her family had fled Scella after civil war had erupted to determine control of the tiny, cold planet's limited resources, notably destroying most of them in the process. Her father was in the government and had been able to secure extrication for her mother, herself, and her younger brother, Aeshua. They were transferred to Drev, a large aqueous moon orbiting one of Pangema's fat gas giants, where they waited for her father. He never made it off Scella.

Their accounts were supposed to have been transferred to them on Drev, but it didn't happen. Back on Scella, a new government was formed, and its members stole from those who'd been part of the old government. Their mother managed to talk her way into one of the few jobs in Drev's recycler network while Naecia cared for Aeshua. Still, there wasn't enough to live on.

Before they'd fled Scella, her father made her promise to step into his shoes if something happened to him, to make it her responsibility to care for the family. At the time, she'd considered it just one of those things parents say to distract their children from the trauma of separation – to redirect their energy toward a long term task. Looking back, Naecia recognized that he knew he wasn't going to make it off the planet. She wished she'd understood that then. She might have made a point to remember his face. It was forgotten now. A sick irony as she had easy recall of so much that she'd never experienced at all.

Naecia had affixed her name to every job posting that she

could and one day it was called. Pipefitter. Off planet. Along with droves of others, she accepted the post and emigrated to the seared badlands of Vask to work energy generation, hoping to make enough to send back to support her family. She hadn't brought much with her on account of the cost of extra mass – just some clothes and the toy amulet Aeshua had forced her to take. At the time she'd wanted him to keep it. Now she was glad he'd gotten his way.

Fitting pipes together, how hard could that be? she remembered thinking. That was one severed finger – the middle digit on her left hand – and three shirt sizes ago. The work was grueling, but for some reason her body had taken to it. She'd added muscle like a rutting brymlack on a torpgrub diet.

A yellow alert flashed in the base of her starshield. A valve error at the southwestern corner of her territory – literally the farthest possible point from her current location. "Define the error," she said.

The warning icon bounced, then unfolded to provide more detail. A pressure warning. Not terribly alarming. Valve safeties were triple-redundant. Her job would be to get a visual on the bypass valves on either side of the troublesome equipment to make sure they were reading accurately. To say it was dangerous work was putting it lightly. If the bypass valves weren't closed all the way, the valve maintenance team could be cut clean in half by superheated steam when they went to pull out the malfunctioning unit. Naecia headed to the distant end of the western stretch and then made south for the bad valve. She called it in.

HyRope: I have a pressure warning on valve zero by zero.
Home: We aren't showing.
HyRope: Calibrate then. I have valve zero by six thousand forty at ninety-one percent, valve zero by seven thousand forty at eighty-seven percent. Do you show same?
Home: We have those, HyRope. Nothing below three thousand

longitude, nothing west of two thousand latitude. Seems the
stratosat for that segment is offline.
HyRope: A flare?
Home: Negative. We're moving another over, but it will take
some time. Advise when you have visual.
HyRope: Yep.

Naecia flew along the eastern boundary toward the southern
horizon, checking for new alerts, but saw none. Whatever
the pressure issue was, the problematic valve wasn't affecting
down-line equipment. Yet.

Repairing a single bad unit was a straightforward problem
and wouldn't have any measurable impact on the overall
power output from a grid with forty-nine million other valves.
If it led to a failure cascade, then they'd be in trouble.

The rows blurred by, seven thousand of them in the space of
ten or eleven cyclets.

Even before row zero was discernable on the horizon,
Naecia saw the problem. A geyser of steam, blasting straight
up. It wasn't a pressure problem. It was a breach.

HyRope: The valve is completely blown!
Home: Shutting down lines zero by zero through zero by one.
HyRope: Thank you Home. I'm just five out.

Naecia accelerated the byceptor and checked her display.
"Show me the pressure gradient," she said, but the icon failed
to respond. "Repeat, valve zero by zero." The icon remained
yellow. It should have changed to a breach warning. "Clear
cache. Reconnect." Her eyes flicked down to the status as
the icons cycled through a soft reboot. Finally, three red bars
appeared where the alert had been. No connection. Satellite
issues. "Reconnect."

She let the 'ceptor coast to a halt ten rows shy of the blown
valve. The geyser rose high over the field into the red light

of Pangema, making it seem like magma rather than vapor. Home's attempt to shut down the lines hadn't taken.

HyRope: Home, retry line shutdown, zero by zero through zero by one, grid nine hundred.

Naecia sighed, then rounded on the valve from the upwind side in order to get closer. "Optical zoom, right side, times ten," she said. She left-eyed the troublesome valve, then once she'd found it, swapped eyes to the magnified portion of her starshield.

The valve came into focus – that is, what was left of it. The short length of pipe between the body of the valve itself and the access flange on top was cleanly shorn away.

Impossible.

Catastrophic failures like this would come at the weakest point: the flange, not the valve body. And if it did, it wouldn't be a clean cut. This was sabotage.

"Area scan," she said, momentarily forgetting the loss of connection with the grid's orbiting stratosat. Static crackled back. "Shit." She panned the landscape. Nobody.

HyRope: HyRope to Home. Com with grid nine-hundred is still down. Valve has been… cut?
Home: Ent– the–
HyRope: Repeat?

Static.

"Fuck."

The entire grid would slowly drop in efficiency if it couldn't be closed or bypassed. Doing the shutdown manually was the only remaining option, and not an easy one at that. She spun the byceptor and raced down the line a safe distance to the nearest bypass valve. She jumped off and pried its integrated shut-off lever until it locked into place. With all of her weight behind it, the metal arm moved tediously forward. Being seldom, if ever, used and crusted in dust, it had nearly seized. She ducked underneath to the opposite side and pulled the stubborn lever backward with a series of bouncing yanks.

Her spiracles were sucking open and closed from the exertion. She released the arm and stood back to catch her breath. The flow had only partially abated. Steam continued blasting skyward where it evaporated under the gaze of Pangema's burning eye.

The plume darkened as a shadow materialized in the geyser's bloom.

CHAPTER THREE

I navigated to a secure search engine and slid Clay Dean's *A World of Flies* from the shelf above my desk. I had brought it home from Jim's shop a few months back just for the hell of it, thinking maybe I'd pick up a tip or two. I'd flipped through it for any obscure tidbits on fish behavior that might up my fly-tying game, but quickly found that there wasn't anything written on its pages that I didn't already know.

I turned to the chapter on Strathspey flies where I kept my research list. Jumping off points for my nightly dives generally fell under one of the following topics, and quickly devolved from there.

cryptomnesia
spirit possession
multiple personalities as a result of forgotten trauma
recovered memories
confabulation
strategic retrieval account theory
revelation
frontal lobe damage
source amnesia
Jamais vu
transferred psychography
phenomenology

And so on.

You think those sound nuts? At my lowest I've dug into "past-life regression", the ultra-kook theory that one person can recover memories from past incarnations. As in, *reincarnation*.

The most famous case, and the one that kicked off the whole past-life regression movement involved a housewife named Virginia Tighe who believed she possessed the memories of a 19th-century Irish woman named Bridey Murphy. I was rooting for Virginia as I did my research because, as insane as it sounded, it might have provided an explanation for me. Maybe I had PLR too. But, like everything else, it turned out to be bullshit. Virginia had grown up living next door to an Irish lady who was of similar age and station to Murphy, and was indeed named "Bridie Murphy Corkell". Experts explained it as a straightforward case of cryptomnesia, where a person mistakes a forgotten memory as something new and original. It was back to the drawing board for me.

My stomach grumbled, reminding me that it had yet to receive dessert.

I leaned back in my chair toward LEGO-Kong and opened a grey panel framed in clear-amber singles, remembering that I'd left a stack of Thin Mints inside it while playing Simon with Patton the other week. I retrieved them and pawed three or four into my mouth, then began my work in earnest. The upcoming search terms on my list:

dream transference
fugue states
drive-by hypnosis
wakeful inception

I scoffed. First at the list and then at myself. I'd searched them all a dozen times, returning to them every few months to check for anything new. It was a sad state. I had ventured beyond the realm of science and into a zone of pure speculation and fantasy. My evenings were a slow crawl along the perimeter of the dark web among self-identified warlocks and thaumaturges, the legitimately insane, and support communities for "space hamsters" who claim to have been probed by aliens – or who, in most cases, were looking to become probed. To each their own.

I spent a few minutes on the first search term, running through ten or so pages of hits, but it was the same old garbage I'd seen before. Sadly, most of the entries were from lonely people *hoping* to have an extra-normal experience rather than seeking answers for them. Sometimes I felt contempt for them. Other times I couldn't explain why I was any different. Loneliness doesn't discriminate.

I closed the tab and dropped my hands from the keyboard in disgust. Disgust at myself for getting to this point, scavenging the dregs of the web in the hope that I might stumble upon an answer, unable to quit until I did. It was like having a thorn in my brain. It had to stop. I had to make it stop. I pushed away some darker notions with a trio of cookies.

I opened a new tab and headed to a particularly marginal forum hoping to find something that might spark a new angle.

The site itself was pretty shady, allegedly focused on abnormal psychology only with no actual psychologists present. Plenty of abnormal opinions, though. I clicked through to a sub forum entitled *Déjà Who?*

Déjà Who? was the place devoted to the myriad phenomena involving the intersection of the present by past lives, future lives, other people's lives, imaginary lives, or hallucinated lives. It was never so fruitful as it was entertaining.

Most of the thread titles were purple, meaning that no new posts had been made since I'd last checked the site a few weeks back. One, though, was blue. Right at the top. I went to the kitchen for more cookies. Returning to my seat, I tapped the link and lifted a cookie column from the package, tonguing one off the top for energy. The page rendered and the new post appeared. It was by a user called EarthrBro_99.

I am hoping to find someone who can help me understand... myself. It's weird to say it out loud, or to type it, but here goes: I know things I shouldn't know – I can't figure out how I know them. They feel like memories, but they aren't. Or they aren't mine, anyway. My brain is just constantly serving up crazy facts that I never learned. It's mainly this odd pairing of geology and history of burlesque. Yet, I don't have any experience in either of these areas. Ask me anything about either topic and I can answer it without Googling. What is the chief amphibole mineral found in the Murphy Belt? Easy: anthophyllite. Burlesque was invented as a way of making fun of "high class" entertainment like opera. Comes from the Italian word burlesco, which means "a joke". Who cares, right? Like I said, I have no idea how I know this! Oh, I also sometimes get a whiff of super detailed dog show competition knowledge. Did you know that in order to compete at the highest levels, a beagle must show a "cheerful" disposition while a poodle must appear to be "proud"? I own a fucking cat! Anyone?

I read the message again. Again. And again. Each time my heart pounded harder, faster. Pensively, I devoured more cookies. It was like *I'd* written it, only with the knowledge bases swapped out. I flicked the mousepad and quickly skimmed the responses for anything on point, but it was the same old guesswork and amateur pseudo analysis as always, with the usual trolls sprinkled throughout.

The cookies formed a delectable paste in my mouth as I tapped the user profile for EarthrBro_99. For the first time in years of searching, someone else had described my experience to a T. They seemed legit. If so, it meant I wasn't alone.

I feverishly composed a multi-paragraph direct message on my own situation, quickly realized it was a little hot and heavy, and decided to back off a bit. *Start slowly, Ben.* One sentence at a time.

>O)))<<Flyguy: Hey man, saw your thread in deja who. I have the same thing.

I hit ENTER and slid another cookie from my hand like it was a PEZ dispenser. A response popped up before I could even crunch down.

EarthrBro_99: Are you trolling me?
>O)))<<Flyguy: Trolling you? Are you trolling me? Lol.
EarthrBro_99: No.
>O)))<<Flyguy: Me neither.
>O)))<<Flyguy: How long have you had this thing going on?
EarthrBro_99: Whole life.
>O)))<<Flyguy: Same. Ever since I could remember.
EarthrBro_99: You know about geology and Burlesque and dog shows like me?
>O)))<<Flyguy: Ha, not really, man. For me it's like any type of natural science. Fauna. Bug reproduction is big. Also, antique watches. Dumb shit like that...
EarthrBro_99: Anything else?

I allowed my hands to slide from the keyboard and swished my tongue around to get all the cookie glue.

There *was* something else. Another thing I knew. A thing I'd never disclosed to anyone besides Patton. I'd researched it, ransacked the stacks of human knowledge on the internet and in books, only to come up dry. They said nothing about this other thing. I deposited another cookie and pondered an answer.

EarthrBro_99: ???
>O)))<<Flyguy: Nah, nothing else.
EarthrBro_99: Oh.

>O)))<<Flyguy: What?

EarthrBro_99: Nothing. I guess we are all just different. With different sets of weird junk in our heads. I was hoping to find someone who had some knowledge of this other thing like me. I just wanted to make sure I shared with the right person. Someone in the EXACT same situation as me. Anyway, have a nice life.

>O)))<<Flyguy: Wait wait! How can you say that we're not the same?

EarthrBro_99: You didn't mention the Chime.

I shotgunned the screen in cookie crumbs, then doubled over beside my desk, hacking out the rest of the bits I'd aspirated into my trash bin. When the episode passed, I gathered myself and shook the computer over the garbage then wiped the screen with the cuff of my flannel.

Okay. *The Chime.* Where to start?

Here's what I know: The Chime has something to do with the Note of Jecca. Except I haven't got a clue what the Note is, or what it has to do with Jecca, or who or what Jecca is. But I understand that the Chime, whatever it might be, is important. Central to somebody's existence. I know that like I know everything else. It is a source of meaning and identity, not merely symbolic like a totem or a sacred place. Its cultural significance is important, but secondary to its purpose. The Chime is powerful. The Chime is life for some, death for others. And I know where it is.

Kind of.

See, my brain has tiers. On the first tier, I'm a natural sciences savant specializing in insect romance. That knowledge is broad, detailed, and clear to me. Then on the next level down are the watches. I know a lot about those, but my range of knowledge is spottier – and in some cases ambiguous when compared to the bug stuff. Where my ability to call up natural science facts is quick and effortless, I have to press a little harder to get the watch stuff to the forefront. Then there is this third thing, even further down, the Chime. It exists behind a veil of shadow and confusion, but that it exists is certain.

Growing up, I never spoke to anyone about the Chime. The other stuff was crazy sounding enough, but at least it was grounded in reality. This Chime business was of a different character. The kind of crazy that gets you institutionalized. I knew with every cell of my being, that the Chime and the "Note of Jecca" were just as real as a Rolex Reference 4113 Split Second Chronograph[22] or a water boatman's musical penis.[23] I knew these things existed just as I knew anything else existed. I could almost describe them, but there was a fogginess to my understanding and recall that I didn't get with the watches or the bugs. It was as if I was having to *remember* them from farther back. Tangible, but distant.

Every day since I'd learned to use a computer as a kid, I had searched for answers. "The Chime" was frustratingly non-specific, but I'd nevertheless waded through thousands of pages of search results ranging from faerie lore to jewelry to dating advice, while always coming up empty. "Note of Jecca" on the other hand, was highly specific, and had never returned a single result. I had tapped it into the search box every day for the last two decades and never received so much as the whiff of an answer.

I knew where the Chime was, though I lacked the understanding or vocabulary to describe its location. Or even to give the name of the place where it was hidden. But it *was* hidden. And I felt like I could find it once I was situated in its milieu.[24]

I flicked a crumb from the shift key and typed.

>O)))<<Flyguy: Yeah. I know about the Chime.
EarthrBro_99: K.

---

22 Only twelve ever made.

23 *Micronecta scholtzi*. World's Loudest Penis, Guinness World Records, current champion.

24 Now that's a four-dollar word – *You made me use it.*

>O)))<<Flyguy: Seriously.

EarthrBro_99: Are you fucking with me?

>O)))<<Flyguy: No.

EarthrBro_99: Do you know what it is?

>O)))<<Flyguy: No idea.

EarthrBro_99: Well I do.

CHAPTER FOUR

A ship pushed through the geyser. Slow. Watchful. Looming. Slate in color, like the nightside of Vask, all manner of weapons and equipment bristling across its top.

Naecia's hands fell away from the valve. "The fuuu–"

It wasn't a Vaski ship. Nor was it Scellan or Drevian or any other variant she'd ever seen in the Pangemic system. She leapt onto the byceptor and blasted westward, away from the craft along row zero.

HyRope: Home!

No response.

HyRope: There's a ship out here. Do you know about it?

No response.

The ship followed patiently, tracking at pace. After trailing for some time, it leisurely overtook her position and spun to face her while continuing to fly backward. Naecia braked, pivoted ninety degrees, and accelerated up the rows of grid nine hundred. Even if she could make it back to the platform and summon an emergency shuttle, she doubted the ship would simply hang around so she might escape, assuming it was there for her.

Heat alert. She was taking the 'ceptor beyond its limit. A glance back. The ship righted its lateral movement and casually turned to follow. No doubt, she was its target. Oddly, her curiosity as to why tamped her panic.

Naecia called through the com again and again. It was all dead. She even tried her implant, which would only be good locally. Nobody.

When the ship carried overhead again, Naecia turned once more, this time heading East toward grid nine-zero-one. Perhaps its stratosat wouldn't be down and she could hail Home and warn them. More heat warnings sprang onto the display.

She raced down the rows and crossed column zero. Grid nine-zero-one lay in the distance, on the far side of a wide plain. She darted across. The ship banked smoothly, again overtaking and rotating toward her, as if waiting for the right moment to pounce. Her suit was burning up. Its cooling system was tied to the 'ceptor. Sweat pooled inside the forearms and ran down her legs. Nobody was built for the unchecked climate of Vask, least of all a Scellan. A person could last ten or fifteen cyclets in a powerless suit. Twenty in the shade. Another alert. She didn't let up. Her only hope was to reach the next grid and reconnect with Home.

The ship made its move, speeding ahead to just outside the nine-zero-one border where it slowed to a stationary hover.

She keyed the com even though her starshield showed no connection.

HyRope: Home? Home? Home? Answer please. Unidentified ship at null zone between nine hundred and zero-one. Answer please. Home?

Out in front, the vessel descended. Naecia steered wide. As she drew alongside it, the 'ceptor died and she rattled off a chain of choice Drevian expletives before sliding off and running full pelt toward the neighboring grid.

HyRope: Home, come in! Home–

She attempted to hurdle a pipe at the grid's boundary and an energy pulse caught her midair, slinging her up and over a large junction rack and into the dirt, knocking the wind from her lungs. She lay still, her spiracles held open in a frozen cry for air. She gasped, feeling her starshield for fractures.

HyRope: Home?

Static.

Home: HyRope – lost – repeat – transmiss – ping – Home –

HyRope: Grid nine-zero-one. She struggled to fill her chest. *Unidentified ship. Hostile. Warning.*

Home: We lost you HyRope – over grid – back to nine hundred – check –

The signal died. Then the suit died. Even the hot air that had been blowing on her spiracles ceased. Lack of air wasn't the issue. It would be the heat that killed her.

Feeling her body beginning to cook, she wrenched herself up the rack for a glimpse. The ship was five hundred paces away.

She pinged Home again. Nothing.

She took another look over the rack. A single, helmeted figure had come to stand in the shadow of the ship, motionless except for what looked like a... gown? Naecia dropped to the dirt and bellycrawled to the next line of pipe, then without looking back, quickly wrestled herself over and into the next column. The farther inside nine-zero-one that she got, perhaps the closer she'd be to a functioning stratosat.

HyRope: HyRope to Home, do you hear me? HyRope to Home. Danger. Hostile ship. Landed. HyRope to Home!

"Naecia."

She froze. It was a new voice. Clear. Calm. And coming through her implant, not her helmet.

"Naecia HyRope. I know you can hear me." It was a beautiful voice, thick and confident. "There is no need for you to acknowledge, only to listen."

Naecia was listening. Lying still. Breathing hot, stale air. Mind racing but still listening.

"My name is Asog Arrohauk. I am the captain of the *Knell* – the ship in front of you. You might have noticed it. Big, imposing."

"What do you want?" Naecia whispered.

"Only access to the gifts of your mind."

"Who are you?"

"A prospector of ideas," said Arrohauk. "I help people understand who they are."

The stifling air was clouding her perception. Naecia tried to clear her head. "And who is it you think I am?"

"You are a *Stringer*, Naecia," she said.

"No thanks," answered Naecia, continuing her desperate sun-dragon belly crawl over the parched ground, not knowing or caring what the term meant.

"I'm afraid that what you have is too valuable for me to pass up." This was punctuated by the muted sound of a shot being fired.

Naecia grunted. "What do I have that is so valuable?"

"Hindsight."

A small cylinder thumped into the dirt just off her shoulder.

CHAPTER FIVE

I gasped a little, careful this time not to breathe cookie crumbs into my lungs. Was it as simple as asking him to explain? I didn't want to screw this up.

>O)))<<Flyguy: Can you tell me what it is? The Chime?
>O)))<<Flyguy: What is it?
>O)))<<Flyguy: ?
>O)))<<Flyguy: Dude.

I sat there and waited. A minute went by (*eons* in internet-reply-time). Then another. After five more minutes, I broke open a second column of cookies. I'm usually a one-cookie-column-a-night guy, but all bets are off if I get stressed out. I refreshed the screen. He finally responded.

EarthrBro_99: I won't say it on here.
>O)))<<Flyguy: Why?
EarthrBro_99: Too dangerous.
>O)))<<Flyguy: You can't just throw it out there that you know what the Chime is and then not tell me. Guarantee you whoever you're afraid of isn't hanging out in the Deja Who sub forum of this stupid website.
EarthrBro_99: I'll tell you. But only in person.

>O)))<<Flyguy: Not even by phone?
EarthrBro_99: Can't.
>O)))<<Flyguy: Why?

No answer.

Now I was starting to see the angles. The classic catfish move. Someone poses as someone else online in order to lure a mark out into the real world and defraud them. As the possible catch, I was sniffing a fat wad of stink-bait.

At the same time, we had a shared experience defined by obscure knowledge of a mysterious item. I had never posted about the Chime online alongside anything that could identify me. Never as Flyguy. So it wasn't like he could have targeted me. He wasn't asking for money or favors.[25] Couldn't be kidnapping, because I had no money and no one I know could pay a ransom. So that only left murder, really. But why go through all the effort to target someone like me if that's the play?

>O)))<<Flyguy: Where do you live?
EarthrBro_99: Long haul trucking. I live everywhere, nowhere. You?
>O)))<<Flyguy: Central Kansas.
EarthrBro_99: I-70 is my east-west.
>O)))<<Flyguy: Is that like your route?
EarthrBro_99: Yeah. I should be through there in four days or so. If you can get near Junction City, Salina, Hays, Colby, or somewhere close, we can meet up and I'll give you the low down on the Chime.
>O)))<<Flyguy: Why do you even care if I know the truth?
EarthrBro_99: Tbh I don't, really. I just want to meet another one. I've been searching for years. Maybe we

---

25 Yet.

put our heads together and figure out what's what.
Some common experience. I don't know.
\>O)))\<\<Flyguy: I feel the same way.
EarthrBro_99: I'll dm you when and where. Over and out.

I hammered out a few excited responses and deleted them, as
that seemed a tad aggressive for the sensibilities of a long-haul
trucker. Didn't want to spook my new friend.

I cycled up and read the chat over once more, then deleted
the entries, and logged out. EarthrBro had advised discretion.
Best to follow suit.

Exactly four days later I got a direct message while working at
the shop.

EarthrBro_99: Susank. Tonight. Between 2-3am. Gravel lot
by the big grain silo south side of street. Sorry couldn't
do earlier, that's just when I'll be passing through.

Susank. Half an hour from me here in Great Bend, but it
wasn't on I-70 either. About twenty miles south of it. I stared
at the message as two coequal thoughts fired my synapses.
One was that Susank would definitely be the place to go if you
wanted to keep things on the downlow. I'd driven through
while scouting creeks. It had one cross street, a stop sign, and
no gas station. The second thing that came to mind was that
it was also a perfect spot to get kidnapped or murdered, or
kidnap-murdered. So, on the one hand, I might learn the truth
about myself. On the other, I might end up a deviant trucker's
DIY taxidermied sex mannequin.[26]

I spied Jim, back in the store, absentmindedly spinning a
rack. "Helpya find something, Jim?"

---

26 I'd pay to see that.

"Negatory."

"You know you're in the salt-water section, right Jim?" I said. "'Cause that watch you're wearing ain't a diver."

Jim grimaced, glancing down at the hunk of scrap-metal on his wrist. "The guy said it was."

"The guy was lying. The humidity in my bathroom would rust out that hunk of pig iron."

"So now you're a watch expert?"

"Always have been, Jim."

He put his hand in his pocket, concealing the watch, and scrunched his face. "Anyways, we're in the early stages of the trip. Just plannin'."

"Does the plan involve spending any money in here?"

Jim looked at me with something that resembled sanctimony. "Yeah. I am," he said. "You finish that Alpha-male Boom Train?"

I snorted. "*Alpha-Boom-Train*, Jim." I reached over and grabbed the custom fly, held it up for him to see.

His eyes brightened and he zombie-shuffled toward the front, hands scrounging in his pockets. "How much?"

"Thirty-five."

His face went redder than a crested macaque's ass.[27] "Thirty!"

"Jiiiiiim," I said, drawing the word out. "I said thirty-five."

"No way I'm paying that."

"I'll sell you a box of sparkle worms from the kids rack for six instead if you want to be a cheap-ass. I thought you wanted to catch big boy fish."

"What'd Winston pay?"

"A million dollars. This one is thirty-five."

That put him over. Face red and puffed with anger, he headed for the door. "You got a lot of G-D nerve, kid."

"Did you just say 'G-D'? I think we found the alpha male."

---

27 One of your more promiscuous primates, with arguably redder, and more tumescent bottoms, even than baboons.

He was gone.

Truth was, I could sell the fly online for a whole lot more than thirty-five bucks. It was brilliant and beautifully crafted. It was just that out here in the middle of nowhere folks were cheap – even the fly fishermen, who'd take out a second mortgage if they thought it would get them a few more strikes. Didn't matter what you were selling. If they could get a reasonable facsimile made of Styrofoam and asbestos at the dollar place, you'd lose the sale. I'd sell it online for real money later. I wrapped it in a baggie and shoved it into a pocket.

The door kicked open. Patton. I glanced at my watch. Eleven a.m. He was up early.

"Ahoy, matey!"

"It's nearly lunchtime," I said. "Did you bring me a snack?"

"Hey, slow down *bromine*, I just got here." He grinned and looked around. "What was your question?"

"Did. You. Bring. Me. A. Snack?"

"Oh, no. Sorry. Aunt Lisa and I were baked all morning. We went deep in this marathon Simon sesh and – *hey* are those real shark teeth?" He flicked one of the cheesy necklaces Owner Jim insisted on offering for sale.

"No."

"Aw."

"Take one. It's yours."

"Really?" he said, slipping one from the display, legitimately happier than I'd ever seen him.

"No one else has ever bought one. You'll be a trendsetter."

He threw it on, considered his reflection.

"So, look," I said. "I'm going out to Susank tonight."

"Susank? What the fffffuuuuuuck? Why?"

It was possible I had sent Patton's brain into a flat spin, which is fair because no one would ever willingly go to Susank for any reason. "Patton, you're right, but listen: you know my uh…" I tapped my head, "my *thing*?"

"Yeah."

"Well, I met this trucker on the internet, and he–"

"You," – and Patton did finger air quotes here – *"met this trucker on the internet?"*

"Fair," I said. "But look: it was on one of the abnormal psychology forums. *Déjà Who.* He described the exact same thing I got. He's dog shows and like, burlesque and geology though."

"Burlesque. *Mrow.*" He feathered his fingers in a mock cat-claw.

"I'm telling you, he described it perfectly."

"Ben? Newsflash: those are just words. Anyone could make something up like that for some reason. Troll you. Get close to you. Eat your face."

"Yeah, but it wasn't like this guy approached me. He put it out there publicly. *I* approached *him*."

"Probably exactly like he planned it. You're gonna get *Chainsaw Massacre*'d." He mimed a big Leatherface chainsaw sweep, complete with sound effects. "Nice knowing you. Thanks for the necklace."

"Can you just listen for a second?"

"If you're going to become a skinsuit, I hope you're his size at least."

"Patton: he knows about the Chime. *He* brought it up." Patton was the only other person who I'd ever told about it.

"Whoa."

"Yeah. So, he's being just as secretive about it as I have during my entire life. He'll only discuss it in person."

"In Susank."

"Yeah, it is a bit... middle of nowhere."

"It's a bit Children of the fuckin' Corn, Ben," said Patton. Then, leaning in, "What time do we leave?"

I walked around the counter and took him by the shoulders. "You're my oldest–"

"Only."

"Only friend." I cracked up. He'd always had a bead on my funny bone. It also happened to be true. "I have to do this alone – *he* wants to do it alone. That's the whole point. I can't show up with a sidekick."

"Demoted from only-friend to sidekick. Wow."

"Come on. You of all people should understand. You're the *only* one who understands."

Patton fiddled with the ersatz shark-tooth and scratched his patchy stubble. Then he took *me* by the shoulders, and in a shockingly serious – and sober – voice, said, "You're not going alone to meet a forum-posting trucker sociopath at the grain silo in Susank. End of debate. I'll hide in the car. This is non-negotiable."

He was unflinchingly loyal. I couldn't say no to the guy.

"Fine. But you actually do have to hide yourself."

He pulled the shark's tooth up and kissed it. "Awesome. You buy the snacks."

"Sure."

"What weapons are you bringing?"

"Weapons?"

"Nunchaku or throwing stars?" he asked, wielding a pair of phantom chuka.

"Yeah, no," I said. "Look, I'll put the rods in the car and we can throw some loops when the sun comes up. Make a whole thing of it."

"What's the guy's name?"

I grimaced a bit. "Earther bro underscore ninety-nine."

Patton surrender-frowned like a parent who'd finally had to accept that their kid was an idiot. "You realize that I'm the guy who's gonna keep you out of the pit in that trucker's basement, right? He probably asked you to moisturize ahead of time, didn't he?"

"He did, actually," I said. "Been getting moist all day."

Patton headed to the door. "Going to bed now, dude." Making it nearly one wakeful hour for Patton.

"See you tonight," I said.

* * *

When the shop closed, I headed back home. Patton had the right idea, getting some sleep ahead of time. If I tried to push through until three a.m., I'd be a zombie.[28] I set my watch alarm and laid down.

It was dark outside when I was awakened by my own snoring. I squeezed the button on the side of my watch in order to backlight the numbers using Timex's proprietary Indiglo® technology. Just after midnight.

Unsure what theories Earthrbro_99 and I might discuss, I collected my notes from *A World of Flies* and a pile of my top reference books, all of which I stuffed into a shopping bag and set by the door.

Out on the porch I ate a carrot snack to cancel out an earlier candy bar snack while the cicadas sang. I took a moment to reflect on the many choices I'd made in my life, up to and including what might end up being the most consequential: the conscious decision to rendezvous with a possibly insane skinsuit-wearing trucker at a remote crossroads in the middle of the night. Every single detail of this scenario screamed *Don't do it!* My bubbling gut issued the same warning, telegraphing the identical message over and over to my dumb brain: *This ends poorly.*

But that's why we have brains: to provide us with rationales for overriding our instincts and gut reactions. All that stuff

---

28 Which is a very real thing. The insect world is riddled with parasites that take control of a host's brain, causing them to act against their best interests. The Costa Rican wasp *Hymenoepimecis argyraphaga* lays its eggs inside orb spiders. The hatched larva injects a toxin that causes the spider to spin a web specifically tailored to support the larva's cocoon. Once finished, the little wasp grub devours the spider and takes up residence inside the custom house it forced the spider to build.

served us well when we were still hunter-gatherers, when reliance on our fight or flight impulse was essential to avoiding the inside of some megafauna's stomach. We still have that primitive coding that controls our basic functions, from breathing and balance, to running from predators. It's often dubbed the "reptilian brain", because it is found in physical structures that we share with reptiles.[29] It is reliable, but compulsive – doesn't get nuance. Good for basic survival stuff. After millions of years, humans evolved higher order thinking, which allows us to consider those reptilian impulses and ignore them. Like I'm doing right now.

Regardless of the danger, I had to know the truth. Decades of wondering, researching, and little else. Year after year, it had been the first thing I thought about in the morning and the last thing at night. It was a form of paralysis, arresting all of the other things I might have done with my life if I hadn't been so single-minded about solving the mystery of my jumbled psyche.

I couldn't fathom living out my years without answers. I was desperate. Enough to override the small downside risk of becoming a flesh Muppet for a pervert trucker. If I didn't go, I'd always wonder. And the regret would join desperation in consuming me, like the wasp larva that devours the spider.

---

29 The basal ganglia.

CHAPTER SIX

Who selects a full-sized jar of dill pickles as their snack? Patton, that's who. And he wasn't even eating them. Just warming them in his crotch for later.

"What?" he said, noticing my side-eye. "You want one?"

"I mean, I might have taken one before, but now they're the same temperature as your balls."

"Temperature is temperature, Ben."

"Yeah, but now it will be impossible to eat one without thinking *oh this is the exact same temperature as Patton's balls; a balmy ninety-three degrees.*"[30]

Patton shrugged. "Some people might not think that's such a bad thing."

I twisted in my seat, looking away from the road, exclaiming, "Who?"

"People." He sat quietly for a few seconds, then presented a baggie from inside his jacket. "Shrooms?"

"Not right now."

"Aunt Lisa's personal stuff."

"Aunt Lisa is going to federal prison one of these days, you know that, right?"

---

30 Actual human ball temperature – *Why do we know that?* – Let's ask the trucker.

Patton scoffed. "You underestimate Aunt Lisa. She's a pro. Her grow operation is untraceable. Underground. Literally. Some say it was an old fallout shelter or missile silo or something. Come on." He took one out of the bag and stuck it under my nose.

"No!" I said, slapping it onto the floor.

"Dude!" said Patton. He retrieved it and blew it off.

I tried to put some calm into my voice. "...Not yet anyway. Not until we've got flies in the water."

Patton could drive me absolutely nuts sometimes, but he was, without exaggeration, the reason I had survived middle school. As a student I'd had an impossible time holding back the never-ending avalanche of facts that overwhelmed my defenses, and I never knew what would be next out of my mouth. A kid who asked to trade lunches might receive a short lecture on *Ariolimax dolichophallus*, banana slugs who often trade and eat each other's penises for lunch. Show and tell was, predictably, always a whole event. It was annoying. *I* was annoying. A constant and reliable irritant, unfailingly bringing things back to the science of bug fuckery. Not only did it drive away any other kids who might have become my friends in different circumstances, but I was actively disliked. And I couldn't argue with them. I didn't like me either.

It came to a head in the seventh grade, when I found myself cornered in the locker room by resident meathead Donnie Robautham, who had decided to shut me up once and for all. Even then, while stuffed into a pair of emerald green polyester shorts and under threat of violence, I was unable to exercise even the slightest restraint, taking the opportunity to explain to him that while the silverback gorilla might be physically unmatched within a troop of apes, they still had baby dicks.

Patton, who had come looking for a quiet place to smoke some herbs from his parents' spice drawer, happened upon me getting my ass whipped. He blindsided Donnie and then went crazy, jumping around and screaming like he'd snorted angel dust. Having already done substantial damage to me and probably not wanting to test the waters of a possibly methamphetamine-fueled berzerker, Donnie retreated.

And that's how I met Patton. For some reason my trivial fact-vomit never bothered him. Sure, he wouldn't let go of the fantasy that we could get rich winning Jeopardy or joining a traveling curiosities sideshow, but more than anything Patton just wanted me to feel better. Whether it was hanging out playing marathon games of Simon, dragging me to the fishing stitch, or lighting different chemicals on fire and then inviting me to inhale the smoke, he tried anything that might mitigate my brain's ceaseless bombardment via factual nuggets. The guy genuinely cared. He wanted relief for me at least as much as I did. I very quickly learned he was the type of person who – if he wasn't napping – would dive into traffic for a stranger just as much as his best friend. I don't know where it came from, really. Hanging out as kids, I hardly ever saw his parents and neither, really, did he. The few times they passed through the house while I was over, they were distant and cold. Somehow, he came out of childhood being nothing like them. As an adult, he was warm and caring, if a little directionless – something I understood. Maybe it was his way of setting things right, rebalancing the Universe with kindness and the support of a zealous drug habit.

The Subaru flew down a two-lane road headed north to Susank. It was dark as hell with no streetlights or moon – an ideal setting if one was, indeed, planning an abduction. We turned from 281 onto 190, also a two-laner. A quarter mile up and through a stop sign was a big silo on the right with a large gravel staging area for the grain transports that came through. There were three old trucks parked next to the silo that looked like they'd come with the town. Earthrbro_99 obviously hadn't arrived yet.

We parked and I shut off the engine. Dark and quiet all around. "You stay in the car like we agreed," I said, stepping out. Patton fidgeted with nervous anticipation but remained buckled. I walked around the front of the car to surveil the lot. Nothing.

Patton rolled down the passenger window, the frost of his breath illuminated by Susank's lone streetlight.

"You're supposed to be hiding," I hissed.

Ignoring me, he held out the pickles. "Wanna crack these open?" Big, dumb grin. "It's cold out and they're warm."

"Ehgh, no." I tried not to gag and took a wide step away from the car. "You think he's in one of those?" I asked in the direction of the prehistoric eighteen-wheelers.

"The only thing inside those are the bones of his other victims." Patton scooched down in his seat and almost out of view.

He was right – not about the bones, I hoped, but the age of the trucks. The tires were flat, many of the windows were broken. We were early. A shiver went down my back. It wasn't the cold. I looked over to Patton, eyes wide. "What the hell am I doing?"

"I don't really know, Ben," he answered, peeking over the sill. "We did the pros and cons. It was pretty much all cons."

"Fuck it," I said. "Let's go."

"Yes, *let's*." A new voice. From somewhere behind me.

I spun around. Patton untangled himself from the seatbelt and jumped out of the car, pickles clutched tight to his chest.

A figure emerged from behind a giant propane tank near the corn field. Definitely not a trucker. A deduction I made based on their iridescent space armor.

"What the fuuuck?" whispered Patton.

The figure walked toward us. A metallic voice came from behind a glistening, crisply-edged helmet, "Which one of you rudimentary lifeforms is Flyguy?"

"Holy fuck," I said, hanging my head. I'd been lured to a corn field by a space LARPer.[31]

"That's Earthrbro?"

"Come on, Patton," I said, turning back for the Subaru.

---

31 LARP. Live Action Role Playing. Best known for the foam swords and shields variant, in which elaborately costumed grown-ups battle for dominion over city parks.

And then there was no more Subaru. Well, it was there, only now it was flying over the road and smashing through the concrete wall of a grain silo on the distant side with a thundering crash.

I found myself embracing Patton as he clutched the pickles between us.

"Is this thing on?" said the figure, tapping the chin of his facemask and clearing his throat. "*I said*, which of you is the Flyguy?"

"I am!" shouted Patton.

I pushed him to arm's length. "What are you doing? Shut up!"

The figure came to a halt maybe twenty feet away, gleaming invincibly. In the light of the gravel lot, he looked pretty convincing. "Disclose the identity of the Flyguy," he said, assuming an imperious tone, "or be maimed." A mechanical arm emerged from his back. At the terminal end was a small node which I suspected was a tool for maiming.

I thrusted a finger at Patton. "You be quiet." His foolish loyalty was drowning his judgment. Then to the figure: "I'm Flyguy."

"Don't be stupid," Patton interrupted, stepping boldly in front of me. "*Run*," he hissed below his breath. "*I'm* Flyguy, he announced, "but you can call me Patton. And this is my friend Ben who just gave me a ride here. He knows nothing of our rendezvous and is not worth your time. He will be leaving now. I'm the one you want. *I* know about the Chime."

"Stop this!" I insisted. Then to the figure: "I told *him* about the Chime!"

The shiny helmet pivoted back and forth between us.

"Ben, you're an awesome friend," said Patton. "But don't do this for me."

"What are *you* doing?" I exclaimed.

"Your love for each other is at once adorable and nauseating," said Earthrbro, approaching. "But I don't have time for it. I'll take both of you."

"Wait! Stop!" I said, then to Patton, "You, shut up. Shut up now!" Nervously, I stepped forward. "I'm Flyguy. This," – I wanted to say "brain parasite survivor" – "this *person* is Patton. He's nobody. I'm who you want. We spoke on the *Déjà Who?* forum. You told me your special knowledge was dog shows and geology. I'm your guy. Please leave him alone."

"I told *you* about all that, Ben," said Patton with surprising conviction. "Stop this nonsense. You're a great friend, and I appreciate it. But you forgot *burlesque*. Earthrbro knows burlesque." He turned to the figure. "Leave my friend here. I'm your guy. Let's vamos."

I grabbed him by the jacket and shook him. "You fucking idiot! Shut up! It's me he wants, don't do this!"

A pulse of light flickered over our heads from somewhere in the corn field. I turned just in time to see the top of the grain silo into which the Subaru had been deposited, sliding off like it'd been sliced with a Ginsu. It plummeted down, shaking the ground. Whatever had come from the corn had sliced straight through it. Shock and awe stuff. Patton froze. The pickle jar thumped to the gravel and somehow didn't break.

"Follow me," said Earthrbro. "The two of you. Or I dial this down and put the next one through an arm or an ass cheek." Across the road in Susank, house lights blinked on. "Or you can wait for the locals to rush over with their pitchforks and muskets and begin shooting. I'm confident the friendly fire will eventually get one of you." The figure turned for the corn field. "This way, Fly*guys*."

"Where are you taking us?" asked Patton.

The shining helmet twisted only slightly in our direction. "Does it matter?"

"Yes!" I answered.

"Not to me," said Earthrbro, heading into the crop rows. "Follow. Don't make me pull you."

Seething, I looked over at Patton. "What the fuck was that all about just now?"

"I'm not letting you go alone."

"What do you plan to do, when whoever-this-is finds out you're faking, Patton? What do you think happens then?"

"What happens to *you* when they find out you're *not* faking, Ben?" He walked past me toward the edge of the field.

"Where'd he go?" I said as we pushed into the corn, beginning to think maybe we could make a run for it.

"Keep walking," came the answer from up ahead.

"He's parked out here?" asked Patton.

"Maybe he drove a combine."

We came to a clearing. Patton stopped. "That doesn't look like a combine, Ben."

He wasn't wrong. The LARPer had a spaceship. Calmly, I gave the order to run.

We sprinted back toward the road, crashing out from the crop line screaming to the people emerging from their homes. Patton stopped like he'd hit an invisible wall and slammed hard to the gravel. I got a little further, then came down right after him, my wind knocked out.

Patton rolled back and forth, mumbling about broken ribs while I wheezed. We were then pulled back across the lot like roped calves, dragged by the thinnest of lashes around our ankles. I flailed about, struggling to free myself. Patton, meanwhile, pulled out the baggie of mushrooms and stuffed them all into his mouth, then played dead.

I wrenched forward, digging my fingers under the wire or cable that was cinched tight around my legs. My lone ab quickly gave out and I flopped backward just as I slid past the pickles. I shot my arms out like a giant squid[32] and snatched them up as we disappeared beyond the crop line.

We came to a stop at the feet of the figure. He looked down at us, then nudged Patton with a foot. "I can fish too, Flyguys.

---

32 Giant squid arms, of which there are eight, not to be confused with squid tentacles, of which there are two, or the squid penis, of which there is one, but the longest of all squid appendages when erect.

Do you wish to walk under your own power or be dragged the rest of the way? It doesn't matter to me."

I pushed up, yanking a few crusty corn leaves from my pants. "We'll walk."

The figure released our bindings with a gesture, then turned away with a flourish. "Brilliant."

We returned to the spot that we'd come to before: a flattened crop circle with a spaceship in the center of it. *"Earthrbro,"* I grumbled, shaking my head, and feeling like a goddamned idiot. Common sense, my reptile mind, and even Patton, had all said it would be kidnapping or murder, maybe both. A doleful chuckle escaped my lips. *One down.*

The ship was easily a hundred yards across. Thick in the middle and thinner out at the edges, or wings, or whatever they were; sleek and just low enough to be entirely missed from the road at night. It looked like a fat stealth bomber, crimped upward in the middle so it sat above the corn tassels. "Who are you?" I called. "And what is the Chime?" No answer. "Hey!"

A ramp lowered from the belly of the ship. Earthrbro stopped, and I briefly marveled at his intricate, almost biological armor, reminiscent of a jewel beetle.[33] I tried again: "You said you know what the Chime is," I said. "Tell me."

"Yes, I'd like to know as well," insisted Patton, still playing the part, even as he surely began to hallucinate.

The figure shifted his weight from one hip to the other, then shrugged, "I don't know."

"What?" I said, thinking I'd misheard. Then, realizing I hadn't, "Wait – What! Mother*fucker*!" I yelled, jumping up and down and stomping the corn.

Voices drifted over from the gravel lot. Flashlight beams swept through the dark.

"Better come with," said Earthrbro. "The townsfolk will be here soon. In my experience, this doesn't end well for them

---

33 Family *Buprestidae.*

if they get close." He turned back and headed up the ramp, saying, "I only know that the Scythin want the one who knows about the Chime. That's *Flyguy* – whichever one of you that is." The articulated arm gestured to each of us accusingly, as expressive as a hand on a wrist.

"We don't know anything about it!" announced Patton, trying to stay in the flow, but becoming increasingly distracted by something flitting about his head that only he could see.

"After what they paid me to get you, you better."

"Paid?" I cried. "You're a bounty hunter?"

"I try to avoid labeling people."

The Susank brigade had assembled and could be heard crashing through the corn. I wondered how pitchforks would fare against space lasers.

"Oh, they sound angry," said Earthrbro. "Hold on." He pointed a finger to the hull of the ship and then mimed an arcing motion toward the corn. The ship launched something that looked like an ascending firework over the crop, where it bloomed into a colorful, luminescent dome, then dissipated.

"Whoa!" exclaimed Patton, as he entered the spirit world.

All the flashlights went dead. "Did you just kill them?" I yelled.

"An electromag pulse accompanied by a light show is usually sufficient to scare off the natives. They should be impressed enough to leave now," said Earthrbro casually. "Oh, look, there they go. Buh-bye!"

The voices receded. *Thanks for the valiant rescue effort, fellow humans.*

"Enough dawdling," said the bounty hunter with a pirouette. "The Scythin only need your brain. I'm free to shoot your legs off if need be."

As we were compelled up the ramp under the threat of having our legs shot off, something dawned on me. Insectoid Boba Fett here had said that I was valuable because of the Chime. He didn't know what it was, but the money was real enough to make him run a four-day catfishing scam in hopes of hooking me. Someone – these Scythin – wanted it. *The Chime was real.* Under the circumstances, that was oddly validating.

We reached the top of the ramp and it closed behind us.

"Whoa," said Patton, whose pupils had opened wide enough to see the future.

I didn't know what I was expecting but this wasn't it. The inside of the ship was gorgeous. Like the command deck of an oil-prince's yacht rolling out of St. Thomas. All gleaming surfaces – some of which looked like polished wood. Supple chairs covered in… *leather?* I'd thought bounty hunters only flew shit boxes.

Earthrbro curtsied. "Welcome aboard the *Silent Child.*"

One feature immediately stood out from the rest. Set off to the side, was a long, black, well, *coffin* was the only word to describe it. Thigh height, it was maybe ten feet long, with a glass top and metal walls that flared out at the bottom where it was secured to the floor. A few lights blinked along its length.

"That where you sleep?" I asked.

"Fucking space vampires," mumbled Patton.

"I don't require sleep," answered Earthrbro, punching some icons on a screen.

I was still putting everything together. "You set a trap on *Déjà Who,*" I said, more to myself than anyone, and feeling dumber by the second. *Unbelievable.* It wasn't a trap I was ever guaranteed to see, much less fall into, but it was there if I swam by. This *bounty hunter* had simply gone to a place where someone like me would be expected to go, dropped a hook in the water and waited. And just like a catfish, I'd swallowed the bait. Do catfish hate themselves when they realize they've been had?[34]

My cheeks went hot with all the emotions. Anger, despair, fear. Abyssal lament. Self-loathing. "You just, what, went to the library and posted that thread?"

"No, no. This thing has internet," he said, twirling a shining

---

34 Unlikely. However, the channel catfish, *Ictalurus punctatus*, can remember a human voice for longer than five years! Wow!

finger up toward the ceiling. "Your planet's technological robber-barons have flooded its thermosphere with communications satellites. So that's what I used to do my web surfing and our little conversation after you slid into my DMs. Anyway, the funny part is that I still needed you to show yourself. Even once I'd hacked your account, none of your registration information was legitimate. You used an anonymous ISP routed through servers on four continents. Telltale giveaway for a porn addiction. I had to flush you out into the open, you dirty little space herpe."

"It's not *just* for porn!" proclaimed Patton, surfacing from his trip and still trying to make himself a plausible me. "I know the Chime is important. I didn't want my research to be traceable." He flung his hands out to the sides, then slapped his legs. "So much for that!"

I was about to shout him down again but realized the shifting dynamic. Now that we were captured, we both had to insist on being Flyguy as long as we could keep it up. Otherwise, Patton risked being sold off as a probing dummy.

Something else didn't make sense to me. "Why wait four days to meet us once we took your bait?"

Earthrbro placed hands onto narrow hips as casually as someone considering a used car. "I couldn't risk spooking you. It would have been super suspicious if I'd said that I just happened to be in your tiny little town in the middle of nowhere – or would you still have come? I had to 'get' here. *Lol* – that's what I say at this point, correct? Lol?"[35]

"Oh no, he knows lol, Ben," said an increasingly agitated Patton.

"Besides," Earthrbro continued, strutting across the floor like a supermodel, "I used the time to digest a wide selection of your planet's strange and mostly unintelligible media. I really like that Michael Jackson. Good people, him." He did a little spin onto tiptoes just like the King of Pop.

---

35 Internet colloquialism for "laugh out loud" – *Try this one: STFU.*

Suddenly I had tunnel vision. My brain was cramping. The entire situation was so utterly ludicrous that I wondered if I was dissociating, having an episode, falling into shock. A single, terrible choice had irreversibly changed the course of my life. I'd agreed to meet with a stranger from the internet and had gotten myself kidnapped into space along with my best friend.

Patton and I stood there dumbly as Earthrbro walked to a sleekly crafted cabinet, almost like a wardrobe, running up the opposite wall. It was made of the same iridescent, shell-like material as his armor. The doors opened and Earthrbro backed into it. The armor cracked open along invisible seams and was pulled apart, then into the cabinet, leaving the figure in considerably less threatening clothing. Tight and... form fitting? *Wait a second – Earthrbro was fit.* Then the helmet lifted off last and I heard myself exclaim something like *Jesus Fuck.*

"Not what you were expecting?" asked Earthrbro.

No. Not at all. A space vampire would be preferable to this. But nothing about the world was what I expected anymore. I just shrugged, mumbling something as I considered his "face".

"The travel is a bitch on my looks, Flyguy," he laughed, as slavers of translucent goop dribbled down from rows of jagged and glassy teeth. He had pupil-less eyes in roughly humanoid orientation, and tiny nose slits to go along with the meth-mouth of a female angler fish.[36]

"Wha... what–" I couldn't form a full question just yet.

"Can you believe it," he exclaimed. "This was a design

---

36 You know the ones. Little light up lure on a stick coming out of its forehead. Attracts tiny fish with shiny bauble, eats tiny fish with nasty teeth. I say female angler fish only because you wouldn't recognize the male. Males of the species are tiny and not long lived, unless they attach to a female. They release an enzyme that dissolves its mouth and the female's skin, fusing them together. Then, anytime the female wants to spawn, she nudges the attached sperm bag.

choice! I guess this is what happens when people are built rather than born."

"You're a robot?" asked Patton. "I knew it!"

The hideous face grinned and I could tell we were about to get a philosophical speech on the Nature of Things.

"What is a robot but a series of parts assembled?" said the possible-robot.

"Robots aren't alive," Patton answered smartly.

"Maybe not in Kansas, Flyguy," he – or it – said. "*Robot* is an archaic term reserved for non-sentient task-oriented programs or builds. I am fully biological rather than mechanical. Still assembled, though. A special order. A bespoke individual, and very much sentient. Very much alive." The teeth dissolved away and the face morphed into something vaguely humanlike, wrapped in tight, pearlescent skin. Still not human, but undeniably less harsh on the eyes than before. *Almost* attractive. And suddenly not so bro-like.

Just as I began to wonder if maybe this flesh robot was a girl, I reminded myself that Earthrbro might be biologically diverse when it came to sex. There were thousands of examples on Earth. Some species have no sex at all, while others have the ability to switch sides. And some can even be both at the same time.[37]

The ghostly eyes narrowed. "Are you confused, Flyguy?"

"No, I–"

"Oh, how sweet. Look at you. You're trying to figure out *What I Am*," proclaimed the figure in a bold, radio announcer's voice and clapping along to each word. "You humans love to wedge things into your narrow categories, don't you? Everyone has to be a *this* or a *that*."

"But I wasn't–"

"You were."

---

37 Gyandromorphism. Seen in zebra finches, snakes, lizards, locusts, lobsters, and ants, among many others.

"Well, a little. I was just – you were Earth*bro*!"

"I can assume any of the outward signs of human or galactic biological sexes – of which there are considerably more than just two. Doing so is essential for sneaking into people's confidence in order to snatch them up – but I have no sexual or gender designations of my own as I am uncategorizable. So, I am just me. Aptat," said Aptat, grinning brightly. "Any apparent conformity I might express that seems consistent with your species' largely obsolete notions of sex or gender is purely coincidental, and you would do very well to leave your Earthly prejudices here on, you know, Earth."

"I'm not prejudiced!"

Aptat looked me up and down as if searching for flecks of prejudice. "Hmmph," they said. "We'll see."

"You're a fucking kidnapper!"

"Categories, Ben," Aptat said, ticking a finger.

"What are you going to do to us?" I asked.

"Much of that will be up to you. But for now," they said with a gesture, "you go into holding until I can transfer you to the Scythin." Another grin and blink of vacant eyes.

"Holding?" Patton squeaked as two cylinder-shaped glass enclosures emerged from the metal flooring.

"Prisoners go into prison cells, Flyguy," said Aptat, gesturing politely for Patton to enter his cylinder, which he readily did.

"No, wait," I said, panicking, trying to get more information. "Where–"

"I'm really very busy now, Flyguy," said Aptat, backing me into the chamber. "And a word of advice: behave yourselves. I don't normally excavate the merchandise, but I will if you give me or any of the others any trouble."

"Others?"

"And you can keep those. In case you get hungry."

I looked down to realize that I was very tightly hugging Patton's jar of pickles like it was my baby.

The glass on the cylinders closed around us and we began

our descent. It was cold, but the pickles, as Patton had earlier noted, were warm.

The world had altered so drastically that I was unable to process it. Twenty minutes before, I had been driving the Subaru, anticipating the chance to finally get answers. Now, I was cuddling a jar of pickles on a bounty hunter's spaceship, and all I could think about was the temperature of my best friend's balls.

CHAPTER SEVEN

It was dark, of course. And why wouldn't it be? Was Aptat, the flesh-bound living robot, going to leave us here like cave creatures until our eyes grew bulbous and Golem-round and I – *oh, there's the lights.*

They came up slowly, in the warm spectrum of yellow – not the flickering fluorescents that cast everything into sick greens and greys that you'd expect in a prison setting. The others that Aptat had mentioned were down here too, all sitting in the bases of their single-occupancy glass chambers, like a galactic menagerie, passively considering us. Being the only obvious humans in the bunch, I would have considered us too. Most of our fellow captives seemed to have legs and arms in roughly human proportions, excepting an extra limb here or there. No blob creatures or tentacle people. Not so much as a pseudopod from where I was standing.

Near the top of each beaker-shaped chamber was an electronic display. Words – I think – rotated across them in different languages. Not like French, German, or Chinese. Like space languages. But no Klingon.[38]

Apart from Patton and I, there were five others.

The beaker-like chambers were organized into a cluster of

---

38 *tlhIngan Hol* to Klingons. *Heghlu'meH QaQ jajvam!*

seven not dissimilar from a wasp's brood comb,[39] except that they didn't share walls. It was seven individual cells suspended in a hexagonal pattern with one in the middle: me. Far below us was a large cargo hold. Various boxes and pieces of equipment were secured into tracks on the floor.

Patton was up and pounding on the walls, though I couldn't hear his protestations. It was like watching TV with the sound off. God only knows where his mind was by this point.

I was less in shock about being surrounded by actual aliens and probably more surprised at my lack of shock. Rather than recoiling in fear at the sight of them, I was intrigued. My brain had already begun churning, horny for science.

These other five were a brilliant example of convergent evolution, the phenomenon whereby different species evolve in a similar fashion even in total isolation from each other.[40] It suggested that these prisoners came from places with environments not terribly dissimilar from Earth, giving further weight to a panspermic origin story of life in the galaxy, which was the theory that life has a common source or sources, distributed via meteors. Basically.

A loud clank rang from somewhere above us and the cluster of chambers descended as one from the ceiling, then tilted to forty-five degrees, causing everyone to slump back against the curving glass walls of their cells, including me. I clutched the jar of pickles to my chest as one would an infant and crouched. The other prisoners casually reclined as I fidgeted, terrified the glass holding me in would break. Patton was belly-down in his cylinder like a squirrel cooling its nuts on the sidewalk.[41] My ears popped. A pair of eyes caught mine.

---

39 Where non-honey producing flying insects of the order *Hymenoptera* put their babies.

40 Also known as homoplasy – *I'm indulging you, right now. Don't push it.*

41 It's called 'heat dumping' when a squirrel does it – *It's called tripping balls when Patton does it.*

This one was lying on their back, hands fondling some contraption on a chain necklace, eyebrows raised like my mom used to do when giving me a few seconds to give up on some bullshit I was into. Their skin was sweet potato purple and they had small holes on the sides of their neck that opened and closed like a stingray's spiracles. They put their hands out in an earnest sort of *chill-out* gesture, then, in one smooth motion, moved their fingers to their eyes then out to a point straight ahead. If I didn't know better, I'd say this alien was trying to give me some advice.

Acceleration smashed me against the glass. My stomach felt like it was pinched against my backbone as the force pulled me up from my squat. My lungs struggled against the pressure. *Isn't this how people get embolisms and stroke out?*[42] *Surely Aptat wouldn't do anything to endanger their valuable cargo, right?*

The pod holding the chambers swiveled on a gimbal somewhere above, keeping us in line with the vector of the ship. While I assumed that was to prevent us from tumbling around inside our test tubes like laundry, the entire assembly still swung wildly from one side to the other. The feeling was like that carnival ride with the spinning swings that fly out to the sides, only with unpredictable direction changes, taken without any notice. I worked my diaphragm, forcing air into my chest to keep from blacking out. I turned my head to check on Patton just as the ship maneuvered suddenly to one side. A change in momentum registered deep in my guts.

And the inside of my chamber was promptly covered in vomit. At first I didn't know where it'd come from. I hadn't even felt nauseous. The gimbal swung us back the other way and the yellow-pink slurry swirled with the motion, coating the inner surface in a chunk-studded bile glaze. Through a bit of unmarred glass, I saw the others laughing, except for Patton, who seemed fine despite having eaten enough mushrooms to send an elephant to Narnia.

---

42 Yes.

The smell was awful. My clothes wicked the warm liquid to my skin. I tried not to breathe. I shouldn't have eaten that convenience store hotdog.[43]

Somehow, though, the shock of sopping in barf brought with it a clarity of vision. What had I done with myself? How did I get here? It was selfishness, wasn't it? All of those years spent searching for the cause of my unbidden gift rather than *using it*. There was so much in my head. Maybe instead of crafting locally renowned fish flies, I should have gone into medicine or zoology to find a cure for cancer or prevent the next pandemic. My parents had certainly tried to get me to see the bigger picture, to view my condition through the lens of opportunity rather than as a personal burden. A chance to contribute to the world, to help others. Now I could only see my current situation through the lens of comeuppance for my self-centeredness. Soaking in my own ejecta after abduction by a meat robot.

The pod spun again and I yodeled out another volley. I groaned miserably, resigned to it. Being vomit-covered had a way of amplifying guilt. For a lazy, pathetic, self-absorbed life. For allowing my only friend to get wrapped up in it as well. "I'm sorry," I mumbled to the pickle jar – *Patton's* pickle jar. "I'm sorry," I sobbed, twisting my head to get a glimpse of him through the chunks. "I'm sorry. I'm sorry. I'm sorry." He was too blindly loyal to feel bad for himself. I wished he could hear me, my definitely-not-a-sidekick, only friend.

We traveled like this for I don't know how long. Eventually, my stomach went dry and I could no longer smell the vomit, my olfactory receptors having been chemically singed away by whatever preservatives they put in hotdogs with infinite shelf-lives. Thankfully, the acceleration had eased and breathing

---

43 Four. You had four convenience store hotdogs. *Quatro.*

became less of a chore, with the pressure just enough to keep us all down on the glass without floating around.

A few peep holes were left in the film on the interior surface of my cell. My neighbor on one side was a becloaked individual with a face that looked as though most of it had been sanded away and then polished, not terribly unlike the deep-sea faceless cusk, *Typhlonus nasus,* only this person had beady little eyes. They seemed content to stare up at the top of their cell and hadn't really looked my way. I turned to the other side and tried to find the prisoner from whom I'd received the previous non-verbal communiqué but they were obscured behind the puke curtain. Pickles sat against my stomach, uncomplaining, my fingers interlaced beneath.

In the tubes to either side of Patton were a pair of prisoners I could see. One wore a purple and orange cloak and looked like a monk who'd just returned from a monthlong bender and now appeared to be meditating... or crying. The other was a gigantic, nectarine-colored pro-wrestler. That was the only way to describe them.

"I've never seen the merchandise so defile itself." It was Aptat, their voice piped into my chamber.

"Do none of these other people have stomachs?" I asked, because that is a thing. Platypuses have no stomachs, so maybe I'd ended up in prison with a bunch of their egg-laying, semi-aquatic stellar relatives. And Patton.

"Oh, I don't know. Some of them, probably. "Ke'xatt there beside you has the same basic digestive anatomy as an Earthbound ruminant."[44]

"You're a shitty driver," I said. "The mess is your fault."

Aptat chuckled. "I have a reputation for delivering cargo in the same state as when I obtained it. Can't say that for all stringhunters. You're lucky I'm the one that nabbed you."

"Stringhunters?"

---

44 Mammals with sectioned stomachs. Cows, for example.

"Your buyers will want you in good condition," said Aptat, ignoring my question. "Stand away from the glass, please." The chamber was still tilted at an angle. "I can't." Almost immediately, the entire pod shifted, the gimbal bringing it flat to the ceiling with the chambers perpendicular to it, allowing everyone to stand again.

As soon as I was away from the side, a thick, pink liquid flowed down from the top, coating the inside surface. It was like being inside a blood vessel. I don't like blood, and my stomach, already strained, convulsed weakly. The fluid moved quickly down the walls, leaving the glass clean behind it, then drained out the bottom. I glanced up to see Aptat looking down through a hole, their face still in a pleasant – relatively speaking – non-predatorial fish configuration.

"Put this on. I don't need you further spreading any more of your juices about my ship." They dropped a tiny black cube into the chamber and the portal above closed. The voice remained. "Remove your soiled clothing and place it through the door at the base." Between my feet was the outline of a small, arm's-width porthole.

I glanced over to Patton, who'd managed to keep his convenience store meal – beef taquitos – on the inside. He smiled, gave a little wave and a supportive thumbs up. That he was even conscious was a feat as wild as our abduction.

I kind of wished that Aptat had waited to clean away my privacy screen. The prisoners, including Smooth Face next to me, seemed suddenly interested in my costume swap. I picked up the little black box and rotated it in my hands. It was solid, smaller than a Rubik's Cube. Spinning it in my hands like a squirrel preparing to devour into an acorn, I was totally lost on how this was supposed to be clothing. "Uh, what is this?" I asked.

"Wearable body bag," said Aptat through the intercom.

"Body bag?"

"It has the advantage of keeping your fluids from leaking

out," they said. "I don't have clothes just laying around for when people befoul themselves. You'll have to make do."

I found a small starter tab on the outside of the cube similar to the loose bit of cellophane on a pack of gum or cigarettes, and gave it a yank. The thing popped open, sending out a billow of black fabric. The material was light and airy, riding the currents within my chamber. I plucked it from the float, barely able to feel it. It was as if chiffon were engineered to a tenth of its weight. Not only was it tissue-thin, but it didn't look sized for humans who lived by the food-cancelation method of dieting. There was no way it could be stretched over my body without bursting. Suddenly I had the terrifying image of it splitting up my middle with my belly puffing out like dough from an exploded biscuit canister.

"Uh, do you have anything larger?" I asked. "Something maybe in the husky range?"

"It will adapt to a certain extent. Make it work."

I didn't like undressing in front of other people. It'd been a thing for me ever since the Donnie Robautham era of gym class. Stretching those emerald green shorts up over my hairless thighs to the jeers of my classmates, some of whom already had full mustaches and neck beards, had built in some trauma.

I set Pickles gently down and clutched the space chiffon to my middle, trying to work up the courage to begin. I glanced over at the neck-hole person, who stood with arms patiently crossed. They lifted a hand and did a get-on-with-it finger twirl. *Oh my god.*

I didn't feel like getting naked in front of these people but escaping the rancid clothes was the stronger urge. "Fuck it," I muttered, yanking my shirt up and over my head and tossing it. I sucked in my belly out of habit, but then, how were these people to know I wasn't anything but the ideal physical specimen by the standards of Earth? At that thought, I relaxed and let my belly go free, but kept my biceps low-key flexed.

I played with the shadowy fabric – what ended up being two garments with roughly the same dimensions as kitchen trash bags – looking for arm and neck openings. What was I supposed to do? Sit in one and asphyxiate myself with the other? I glanced over to Neck Holes, who grinned with amusement and shrugged.

I put the first bag over my head and pulled it down with my hands. Despite its airy feel, the stuff was strong, but with constant pressure it gave and my head emerged through the top. I repeated the same process with my arms, which stretched to fit, but did not break through the material. Then, with me fully inside, it all contracted, shrinking down until it was skin-tight over every inch of my top half. Only my face was left exposed.

I shed my shoes, socks and jeans. I didn't want to do the underwear, but like the rest of my outfit, it was sopping.[45] Quickly, I rolled them down my legs, doing a dance to get them off my feet, then held the second bag open and stepped in, pulling it up over my waist. As with the "shirt," the material flexed and gave. I could feel it adjusting to the contours of my body. It went snug just below the shirt portion, muffin-topping my middle. I tried to hike them higher to no avail. I gave up and considered my reflection in the glass. An outer-space sausage-goth stared back. Comeuppance, no doubt, for my ribbing of Ludlow the Librarian.

Ugh. I slid down the glass into a cross-legged sit and pulled Pickles to the center.

"Those nanites are *struggling*," giggled Aptat through the intercom. It cut out, clipping off what sounded like an attempt to rein in more laughter, then came back on. Cleared throat. "Ahem. Place the desecrated clothing into the excrement port." A clank, and the door in the base popped open.

Excrement port? "Will I get these back?"

"Do I look like the space laundry? Put them in the hole, Ben."

I pushed my shirt down through it and was about to do

---

45 *And* cold. *Wink* – *It's your dick too, man.*

the same with my jeans, but held back when I felt a bump in one of the pockets. I reached in. The *Alpha-Boom-Train* fly I'd made for Cheap Jim. There it was in all its glory. I palmed it and pressed the jeans through. Upon shutting the portal, there came a flash of light and the faint scent of vomit smoke wafted up from it. My shoes and socks were in decent shape. I put them back on.

And that's when the song *Pretty Young Thing*, by Michael Jackson, began playing.

"What are you doing?" I cried.

"This is *P.Y.T*, Ben, *Pretty Young Thing*, by Michael Jackson," said Aptat through the system.

"I know that!"

"Do you know it was his sixth Top 10 hit from the *Thriller* album?"

"I hate this song and I hate Michael Jackson!" I screamed, covering my ears. "Do you even know what he did?"

"I know he made Platinum records, Ben. I figured it might make you feel more at home while you ate."

"Hell no! Wait – did you say 'ate'?"

"Yes. Good news. It's food time."

An object fell from above, hitting Pickles on the lid with a clunk. Inside neighboring chambers, the others collected their rations. It seemed mildly familiar, a thick breakfast-bar style puck of something, almost pemmican-like.[46] I gave a sniff. Nutty, bland, unobjectionable. The scent was enough to wake something in my stomach, which, being newly emptied, roared to life. I dove in, biting off a fat chunk. *Oh, that's dense.* Like trying to chew a mouthful of Tootsie Rolls.

---

46 Pemmican was an undeniably genius life-saving food eaten by Indigenous Americans. It is a mixture of dried meat from whatever game was available, usually buffalo, elk, or deer, beat into a powder and then mixed into rendered fat along with regional berries – *I don't want to know what's in space pemmican.*

The food, tasteless though it was, settled me, fortifying my constitution. I stood up, feeling it was time to shout about my rights. "Hey!" I yelled over the blaring chorus to the song. "Tell me where we're going! Who are you selling me to?" I screamed a whole host of other questions, interspersed with increasingly strong language and a few insults. I got into a good flow, too, delivering a real oratorical barrage of righteousness, when Aptat interrupted:

"About thirty gilleys from Earth," they answered as the song mercifully ended. "That's where we're going."

"Gilley?"

"Galactic Light Year. G-L-Y. *Gilley*," said Aptat. "It's a unit derived as the average time it takes the innermost stars to orbit the black hole your scientists refer to as Sagittarius-A, but is more widely known as–"

"Thirty light years!" I screamed.

"It's more like, twenty-six point something Earth Light Years, but yes."

I groaned and slumped against the glass. "Hey?" I asked.

"Yes, Ben?"

"Why do we understand each other? Does everyone in outer space speak English?"

"Only when we want to insult someone's intelligence," said Aptat, chortling at their own joke. "The shortish, longish answer to your question is that bulkspace-traveling species have evolved to the point where languages can be largely deduced from a few key elements like alphabet size, subject-verb arrangement, and basic phonemes. Picking up English for me would be like you figuring out which one of your toes is itchy. It takes a little bit of investigation, but once you've found it, you know you've got it."

"So, your answer is that you're really smart?"

"Mmm-hmm."

"How do I understand you, then?" I asked.

"I'm speaking English."

"Ah."

"But even if I wasn't, I put a course of eavesdropping nanites into the food."

"You put nanites in the food? Like – like little robots?"

"Yes, Ben, like little robots. It beats a fish in the ear."

"Hey, Aptat?"

"Yes, Ben?"

"Fuck you."

"You'll thank me later when you can understand what your eventual owners are saying. You've had a long day, Flyguy. Go to sleep."

"Sleep? I don't even know what's happening! You can't do this to people!" I pressed my back to the cell and began kicking the opposite wall, pounding it with the soles of my shoes over and over. *Thud, thud, thud.* I screamed, even past when my voice broke. *Thud, thud, thud.* My breath went ragged as my assault waned. I turned around and pressed my face to the wall, lightly bounced my forehead. Then again, a little harder.

"Whoa there," said Aptat. "You've had your tantrum and that's understandable, but your brain is mine." A mist descended from the upper circumference of the cell. "Sleep now, Flyguy. There will be a time, not too far off, when you will look back on your stay here with great fondness."

CHAPTER EIGHT

I slept eventually. Or I think I did. My awareness booted up when the lights returned and it only seemed natural to conclude that sleep must have happened. Whatever depth of slumber I experienced had been somewhere within the vacuous strata of nothingness that lives below where you dream, leaving my mind an oily swirl. I perceived a low vibration in my gut. Vigilance, perhaps. Fear. Panic. All of the above. The farther we got from Earth, the more real it became.

I tapped the Indiglo® button on my Timex. Yep. I'd slept alright. For thirty-seven hours.

I considered the Boom-Train, still in my hand. Being a last vestige of my life back home, I was attached to it, thankful now that Cheap Jim had been so cheap. The wearable body bag didn't come with pockets so I tried to put the hook through a strap-hole in my watch, but it just fell out.

I caressed my earlobe, felt the tiny scar in the center of it. Junior year of high school, I'd found myself in a fit of lust over Agatha Jensen, who at the time tended toward the bad boy aesthetic. Figuring to raise my game, I'd gotten a two-for-one deal on a kanji tattoo and an ear piercing the summer before senior year. I'd hit campus for the fall semester with a diamond stud and jorts to ensure that the ankle ink was on display. Agatha never paid it any notice, which in retrospect, was for the better. That way I didn't have to explain what it meant.[47]

I pressed again at the scar in my earlobe, then brought the tiny hook to it, touching the skin. Didn't feel so bad. I pressed harder. Still, not too bad. *Screw it.* I gritted my teeth and pressed the hook into the flesh until it popped. Pain came, but it was worth it. I pulled it through until the body of the fly hung directly below my ear. *Who's the bad boy now, Agatha Jensen?*[48]

The others rose from their drug-induced slumbers around the same time. Our pods gimballed. We swung to the opposite orientation from when we had first launched, and my inner ear registered deceleration.[49] When the lateral inertia ceased, the pods returned to their vertical positions and I was lightly pressed into the base, the welcome return of downward-pulling gravity. Our chambers rotated around the center axis of the pod, clanking loudly when centered. Right as I began to ask myself what would happen next, Patton's chamber began to ascend. It pushed up through the floor until he disappeared.

This was bad. It had to be an interrogation, right? Patton was not a strategic thinker. Clearly, Aptat had figured this out. If there are checkers players and chess players, Patton is eating the pieces. He's a pleaser – a disposition that would work to his disadvantage under cross-examination by an alien bounty hunter.

My anxiety was allayed when after a few minutes the

---

47 It meant "Warrior"! You got a tattoo that means *"warrior"* in a language you don't even speak! Ohmygod. Let me repeat: you got – *ENOUGH!*

48 Still not you, dick-knuckle.

49 For vertebrates, the sense of balance, acceleration, and gravity comes from tiny fluid-filled pockets in the inner ear called the saccule and the utricle, which contain tiny hairs that sense the movement of little crystals that float around as we move. The message from the hairs travels through the vestibular nerve to the brain.

chamber descended. Patton smiled widely to which I raised my eyebrows in question. His response was an enthusiastic thumbs up. *Oh, god what did he do up there?*

Clank. My turn.

When I ascended to the main deck of the *Silent Child*, Aptat was there waiting in casual black yoga pajamas, their face configured in what you might call *koi pond chic*. They gestured to my chamber, causing a gap to open in the glass between us.

"How do you feel today, Flyguy?"

"My name is Ben."

"And how do you feel?"

"*Fuck you* is how I feel. Is this a joke?"

"That's all understandable. But no, this is no joke." They held a large black ring in one hand. I eyeballed it. Aptat acknowledged the item, pivoting it almost like a tambourine. "I need to measure your coherence."

"My what?"

"The degree to which you are yourself," Aptat said, twirling the ring around three manicured(?) fingers. "This will be necessary for you going forward. Knowing your baseline could save your life. You'll just have to trust me."

"Trust you? *Earthrbro_99?*" I snorted. "No. Fuck off."

"If I can't evaluate your resting coherence, then you are worthless to me... and to your buyers."

"Good."

"Not good, Ben. Bad. I don't return spoiled cargo to where I found it. I dump it. I'm all about that hustle, Ben. And mass is money."

"You mean, you'd like, throw me out an airlock?"

"Do you know what it feels like to die in space?" Their voice was cordial, not threatening. I realized it didn't have to be. The concept was enough.

I shook my head.

"It's tortuous, but mercifully fast. All of the gas in your body rapidly expands and the liquid on your eyes, mouth, and skin boils off, vaporizing in seconds. Then you pass out and asphyxiate. It goes faster if you hold your breath, but I recommend against it as doing so makes your lungs explode. So. Do you acquiesce to a painless coherence assessment or shall we proceed to the airlock?"

I said nothing.

"Good, Ben. Smart choice," they said. "When I ask how you are feeling, it's not because I care about you personally or because I'm being friendly. It is because I need accurate information. So. Do you feel mostly normal? Like yourself?"

I eye-checked my space goth costume. "I guess."

"Brilliant." They held up the ring. "This is called an axon diadem. It will give me data for your neural efficiency, synaptic integrity, etcetera, etcetera." They pulled the ring along its circumference, changing its dimensions, then placed it atop their own head. "You wear it like this. Nothing physically invasive. Not painful. But necessary. And it is better than dying alone in space."

I shrugged. "Whatever."

"Hmm." Aptat glanced at my head and adjusted the circlet. They pulled it to a large circumference, which gave me feelings about my head size. "Step forward." I obeyed and Aptat gently placed it so that it settled just over my ears and across my forehead like I was a little space prince. They opened a palm, over which an ethereal holographic display rendered in aqua and orange, akin to a hospital-style readout with bars and lines jumping around, along with symbols and figures changing in sync with their corresponding graphic displays.

"Just answer or respond to my stimulus in whatever way feels natural. I am making a record of your 'self' at a moment in time. This will give me your resting coherence. There are no right or wrong answers. Honesty is the only prerequisite. Are you ready?"

"I guess."

"Okay then, let's begin: Name?"

"Ben Sullivan."

"Place of origin?"

"Great Bend, Kansas, United States, Earth. *Fucker.*"

"Your earliest memory?"

"Distracted."

"Lying on the ground, looking up at the sky."

"What am I supposed to say?"

"First thing that comes to mind. It's not about the substance of the answers. I may repeat questions to measure variability. Just go with it. So: Lying on the ground, looking at the sky."

"Insignificant."

"Parents."

"Disappointed."

"Dreams."

"Sometimes."

"Life."

"Wasted."

"Life."

"Regret."

"Wonderous.   Joyous.   Pallid.   Neutral.   Indecision. Magnificent."

"Indecision."

"Fire or Ice?"

"Neither."

"You are walking on a beach."

"Never been to one."

"Purpose?"

"I don't know."

"A terrifying thing," they said, more quickly now.

"Dying in space."

"A terrifying thing." Faster.

"Dying in space alone."

"Your first memory." Faster.

"Waking from a nap."

"Your first memory."

"*I said*, waking from a nap."

"Your first memory!"

"Dawn!"

"Your first memory!"

"I said–" but stopped as something else came to mind. "Hearing my mother sing to me. In the morning."

"Again. Your first memory."

"Mom singing after I wake up in the morning."

"What is the song?"

"Four and twenty blackbirds baked in a pie."

"Baked in a pie?"

"In a pie."

"A pie."

"A pie!"

"A pie?"

"When the pie was opened the birds began to sing."

"How was it opened?"

"Its petals unfold."

"Petals?"

"Petals like a flower."

"A flower?"

"Like the Bloom of God."

Aptat's eyes snapped up from the display. "The Bloom of God, huh? That's one I haven't heard before," they said, reaching out for the diadem and lifting it from my head.

"It's part of the song."

"Seems incongruent, but whatever you say," said Aptat. "Anyhow, I've got what I need."

"What the hell did one minute of free-association tell you?"

"It showed me who you are, Ben. It's how I know that you're *Flyguy* and your friend is not. Also, I told him this thing is a lie detector and he readily came clean. Can't say I didn't suspect it already. He's an awful liar."

"Uh…" I groaned.

Aptat gave me a chummy pat on the shoulder. "Don't worry, Ben. I won't be throwing him out of an airlock."

Oddly, I felt they were telling the truth.

"After all, you have great affinity for him. The Scythin might be able to use that."

"What–?"

But Aptat swiped at the air, shutting the glass and pinching my voice to silence.

CHAPTER NINE

I couldn't look at Patton. He would read the guilt on my face and know immediately that something was wrong. He was perceptive like that. Not a lot of book learning in him, but a very high emotional IQ. I couldn't tell him that his poorly conceived attempt to conceal the true identity of *Flyguy* had lasted a grand total of a day and a half. And what good would it have done if we could talk, anyway? To be able to tell him that he's "leverage"?

Then, nothing happened. Days passed. Day-night cycles as dictated by lights on, lights off, lasted a little over thirty hours. I wondered where the timing of it originated. Another rotating planet that wasn't Earth, most likely. This overlapped my own twenty-four-hour cycle, which had an unsettling, and surreal, effect. Sometimes I slept under lights. Other times I woke and sat in the dark for hours, flashing the Indiglo® on my Timex for entertainment. My grasp on the passing of time was slipping even if the watch gave me the numbers. What were readings for date and time if they weren't anchored to something perceptible? Absent the rising or setting sun, the temperature changes that signaled the passing of night or the end of the day, or driving down and opening Jim's shop, the concept of *days* decohered. Days. *Days.* I thought the word and spoke it again and again until it sounded foreign. What were "days" anymore but a reference point for the rotation of a newly irrelevant planet? Time, undefinable and fluid, passed. I slept. Woke. Ate the pemmican. Daydreamed of microwave empanadas and playing Simon.

Unable to pursue the food-cancellation method of eating, my body bag quickly began to fit more comfortably, so that was a silver lining.

Of all the prisoners, it was Patton who had unquestionably adjusted best. He kept a simple routine: meditation and chanting (which no one, thankfully, could hear), then pemmican breakfast followed by his version of "calisthenics" and finally, a little doze. He tried to engage the others in games – which of course, didn't work. Unphased by these failed attempts, he was currently on a unilateral charades kick, acting out who knows what without accounting for the fact that hypothetical guesses from participants (there were none) would have to be delivered back to him in charades he would then have to guess – using charades. Eventually, I rescued him from the solo endeavor and we settled on a manual version of Simon, using hand placement on the glass of our chambers to stand in for the colored quadrants. Two for each hand, one up one down. *Red, blue, yellow, green.* And there we commenced slapping out combos and patterns that the other had to repeat. It wasn't so bad, actually.

We had just concluded a marathon session of Prison Simon when the ship decelerated. I glanced over at Neck Holes and noticed that the electronic display on the glass of their chamber was now legible to me. *Huh.* The language nanites in the food had been legit. The glowing text read as follows:

IDENTIFICATION DESIGNATION: SC 004-1547
PLACE OF ORIGIN: SCELLA, PANGEMIC SYSTEM
COORD: a29130y23042
PLACE OF ACQUISITION: VASK, PANGEMIC
SYSTEM COORD: a09483y59238

DATE OF ACQUISITION: 13,812,027,000.33.34
SPECIES: SCELLANIC APEX
SEX SPECTRUM, IF ANY: PARTHENOGENIC
FEMALE
GENDER SPECTRUM, IF ANY: FEMININE
NAME, IF ANY: NAECIA HYROPE

She was rubbing her face and seemed fixated on the ceiling above her, perhaps waiting on some communication from Aptat through the hatch. Gone was what I had taken for her breezy disposition during our arrival. She fidgeted nervously. But it wasn't just her. The others were up and moving around too. On the other side of me, Smooth Face – the one Aptat had referred to as Ke'xatt, and who, according to the electronic display, was a quinary Amorphous Trendallian from the planet Tr4 – was standing in their cell, less animated but seeming just as intent on whatever was happening. I could almost smell the glucocorticoids, or whatever hormone Amorphous Trendallians exuded when in a state of alarm. My own pulse quickened in kind.[50] It would have been good to know why we were all panicking.

The pod rotated slowly around its axis before locking into place, then ascended.

The smell of fear is a thing, and it was bleeding out in a sour musk from my apocrine glands.[51] We arrived on the main deck. There was Aptat, wearing the fancy bug armor again, along with three large, and vicious looking, uh... I wasn't sure.

They looked like my idea of legit bounty hunters, or space pirates, all smarmy and leathery and strappy and long hair-y. It might not have been hair at all, but the effect was the same.

---

50 Also known as a "sympathy reaction", experiments in rats have found this empathy behavior to center within the cingulate cortex with the firing of mirror neurons – *Yeah, we get it.*

51 Which humans share with dogs, cats, and horses.

They were thickly-muscled and wore equipment that looked like scuba rebreathers over the bottom of their faces. Their tiny yellow eyes shone out from deep pits in grey faces coated in horny toad skin. A trunk – might as well have been a treasure chest – sat at their feet. I prayed these weren't my new owners.

The walls of each chamber opened just a crack, allowing the discussion between the space toads and Aptat to filter through.

"–fresh, unscrambled." It was the middle amphibio-pirate speaking, and judging by the small, and apparently unironic, crown atop their head, they seemed to be leader of the trio.

"Let's dispense with the prattle, Princess," said Aptat dismissively. "You know mine are always treated well."

The crowned one – a Princess? – shook her head, less an answer and more of a reaction, like she was trying to ignore the offense she'd taken at Aptat's derisive tone. A ridge of well-worn armor rose along her spine from the shoulders down, like a dog raising its hackles.[52] Unbothered by or oblivious to the display, Aptat sashayed over to the first chamber and flicked the glass with a shiny finger, making it ring.

Inside was a waifish creature with a small, round, chinless head. Two pairs of arms were folded across their chest in a calm, ministerial pose, as if awaiting instructions. "This here is Ghuxch-hexer-chchch,"[53] said Aptat. "He has access to business accounts all over Lealum and its respective satellites. Some sort of ex-bookkeeper to a water-skimming syndicate that was wiped out by a rival organization. I've run the numbers and they check out, so I'm guessing if you drill downcord far enough you'll get those passcodes – pays for himself with only a modicum of effort on your part." Aptat rubbed their thumb against fingers. "He's seventeen thousand registered guush or forty-five unregistered."

Holy shit, Aptat was selling us. *Right now.*

---

52 Piloerection – *You said erection.*
53 Gesundheit.

"It's the bookkeepers who always seem to live," said the crowned one with a sneer. "Craven little sewer blats. What else have you got?"

Aptat moved to the chamber next to mine, punching a thumb to the glass. Smooth-Face, the Amorphous Trendallian. "Former navigational engineer for the *Vaporglance*."

"The *Vaporglance*?" exclaimed the crowned one.

"Ah, so you know it," continued Aptat. "Ke'xatt here is just an encyclopedia of information on the ship's last days. I've obviously done my due diligence and what they know goes months beyond the end date of the public logs, right up to when Captain Queva murdered the crew and hid the ship. You Vortu are big on salvage, yes?"

She approached the chamber and eyed Ke'xatt. "How much?"

"For you, Dekies..." Aptat hesitated theatrically, "...twelve thousand."

The Princess – Dekies – laughed heartily enough that her compatriots were forced to join in. Then they all stopped abruptly. "You sold us a fuel steward from the *Vaporglance* the last time we swam these filaments, or do you not remember your prior swindles?"

"*Swindles*, please," scoffed Aptat. "Let's not throw insults. The risk of a fruitless Stringer is the gambler's plight. If I recall, he *was*, in fact, the fuel steward for the *Vaporglance*. Don't burden me with your grievances on sinking a shaft only to find it barren. What did I charge for the steward?"

"Twelve."

"Then I should be demanding more for the navigational officer," said Aptat, straightening from the chamber. "Nevertheless, the loss is mine, I've already named a price and I will stand by it."

"What else do you have?"

I tried to shrink into the shirt of my body bag.

Grimacing, Aptat proceeded across the pod to the chambers

on either side of Patton. The first was the habitual meditator and crier in the purple and orange robes.

"This is Izairis," said Aptat. "She is what I would consider an actualized Stringer, needing no further excavation. Her priors include a master forger and code breaker. Indeed, her skills were used to acquire several of these other Stringers. Think about that, my friends. An instantaneous return on investment."

Dekies just snorted. Aptat took the hint and went on to the pro-wrestler, a colossus called Oush-Sadicet Ciksever from the Maqueni star system. Aptat explained that Oush was a theoretical weapons architect, but he looked to me like he'd been kidnapped right from *Friday Night Fights*. He was comically muscled and spray-tan orange, with a shimmering blonde mullet that cascaded over his bulging trapezius like a waterfall caught in the setting sun.

Dekies passed over him without saying much and stopped at the fifth chamber. Neck Holes. She looked her up and down, even tapped on the glass as if she were a fish in an aquarium. Then slowly, she turned her attention back to Patton. *No no no.*

"Not for sale," said Aptat.

Whew.

"And that one?" said Dekies pointing at me. I glanced around innocently.

"Same," said Aptat.

"Why not?" Dekies asked, giving Patton a closer inspection. Then, twisting to Aptat, "You mined them already, didn't you? What do they know?"

"Keep your next slander in your throat, lest I open it, Princess," growled Aptat, before continuing along pleasantly, "You know my reputation. I don't mine the product, which explains the prices. I'm just a good listener, a patient and tireless connoisseur of opportunity. Willing to lay low until fortune presents itself. Maybe if you were a better listener, you wouldn't have to employ stringhunters."

"How much for the pair?"

"You don't even know what they've got," said Aptat. "It doesn't matter anyway – they're already sold."

"Pre-sold Stringers? Now that's something you don't see. Either you've got a fat milk gumplin with a loose purse on the hook or these two are sure things." Dekies squared on Patton, looking him right in the eyes. Patton backed to the far side, smiling nervously like he'd just shat himself. Maybe he had. "I'll beat whatever price they're paying you."

"Very bold, Dekies, and I do appreciate your overtures, but I must again respectfully decline," said Aptat. "They're bound for the *Timelance*."

Dekies said nothing for a breath. "The Scythin bought these?"

"Indeed."

Dekies backed away from Patton like he was a holy relic.

What the hell was a *Timelance*?

"Shall we continue with the others, then?" asked Aptat.

Dekies reluctantly turned back to Neck Holes. "What of this one?"

"The jewel of my *unsold* inventory. She's on a divided cord."

"You lie."

"You know I don't."

"Divided cord. How can you say that..." asked Dekies, stalking the circumference of her chamber, "...if you don't 'mine your cargo'?"

"I acquired her from another stringhunter who'd already put her under a number of times, during which she'd made considerable progress in accessing the theories of her priors. I have the readings if you wish to consult them."

"Which stringhunter?"

"Asog Arrohauk. The *Knell*."

"The *Knell*?" Dekies exclaimed. "The *Knell* was found clipped into pieces just outside of the Erath Conjunction. You stole her."

"You have qualms, suddenly?" exclaimed Aptat. "Besides,

I didn't steal her. The *Knell* did. With the help of that one, there," sweeping a hand toward Izairis, "they siphoned the signal from my transception cone while I was surveilling Vask. They stole *my* information and simply got to her before I did. I paid a price for my patience, but I took her back. I'm sure you understand."

"And her downcord coherence, if she's been under? Near zero by now?"

"The *Knell*'s log had her priors at forty, forty, and fifteen, proceeding down-cord. Not bad, I'd say."

Something subtle about Dekies' body language said the pirate princess was impressed with these numbers. I didn't understand them, but as homework grades, they sounded low.

"Three priors, two on the cord at the same time. How?"

"Twin sisters, apparently," said Aptat. "Sharing a few threads of the same string. If you've ever been around twins, it wouldn't surprise you. This one is worth the asking price for those alone," said Aptat, letting the tension build. Dekies remained quiet, waiting to hear the reveal. "She is called Naecia HyRope.[54] And *she* can build a cheat drive."

Dekies barked a laugh that echoed across the deck, again egging her cohorts to join in. "Now I know you are lying! How many of these others did you lie about?"

"I do not lie."

"The cheat drive is a myth," Dekies scoffed. "If that's what she had, you wouldn't be selling, you'd be shopping for your own galaxy."

Unperturbed, Aptat continued, "Her research transmissions over time were enough to convince me that she is on the same cord as *two* Pangean mathematicians – the aforementioned twin sisters – who had made the secret pursuit of such a drive their lives' work–"

---

54 Sounds like *Nay*-shuh High-rope – *Yeah, I heard. We use the same set of ears.*

"Why don't we all have cheat drives then? Did you say *twin mathematicians?*"

"I did. They died of an accidental depressurization during a test. This is what happens when you work in secret and then die suddenly. All is lost. Fortunately, for you, dear buyer, these two were Stringers and Naecia is their subsequent," said Aptat. "A thermodynamics engineer by training, she has been trying to replicate their progress for near half her life, and is close to accessing the full theory – which I surmise resides down the cord in that third prior. Nevertheless, what she had managed to assemble on her own by the time I acquired her was a stellar age beyond what anyone living has been able to construct to date. For us, the cheat drive is a myth. Not so for her. I'll show you." Aptat gestured to the floor and a cube of steel ascended from the cargo hold. The top panel opened and the sides thereafter folded away.

My eyes flicked to Naecia, who was pressed to the glass like a parent whose child was on the other side, just out of reach, and for the first time, I heard her voice. She yelled, "You have it!"

"Of course I have it," said Aptat. "The *Knell* was listening, but not for as long as me. Your public systems research queries were too specific for a hypothetical machine and so I easily surmised that you'd built a prototype. I simply retrieved it after you had – *ahem* – moved on from Vask and before Captain Arrohauk had any idea you'd actually constructed the thing. I almost didn't find it under that blanket."

Naecia was fixated on the piece of equipment, which to me looked like nothing more than stacks of something arranged in a roughly cubical shape. Sticking out of the top of each stack were some metal prongs wound in multiple layers of wire. Below all that were four squat columns wrapped in brushed steel.

Dekies was struggling to hold her long ears flat.[55] Eyes

---

55 The forward movement of the pinna, or outer part of the ears,

flicking between Naecia and Aptat five or six times, it was clear she wanted her. Finally, "Okay. How much?"

"Two-hundred thousand. *Registered.*"

"Two-hundred. Registered. You're joking! You could retire on that!" Dekies forced a laugh. She couldn't hide her interest, though, as the bloodshot yellow eyes again flashed to Naecia.

Aptat was reading the same cues that I was. They shook their head and said, "The number is fair for what is being sold. And I'll throw in the prototype. You've brought enough guush, I presume."

"Of course we have," growled Dekies. "I'm one of only sixteen hundred Vortu Princesses."

That sounded like a lot of princesses to me.

"Yes, I understand," said Aptat, "but are you a buyer?"

"If what you say is true," said Dekies, "I agree. She's worth every last billet. But – I want to... verify."

Aptat blew a raspberry from inside the helmet. "*Thatssss* a big ask. Like I said, she was mined on the *Knell*. I have the logs. That should be good enough. Stringers get fragile, you know."

"You have the prototype," said Dekies. "If she was that close to solving it, you'd keep her for yourself. I want to verify that you aren't selling me a brain case full of Zuthian bowel pudding."

"Mm, delicious." Aptat gestured to the prototype. "I'm a stringhunter, not a theoretical engineer; otherwise, maybe I would hold on to her." They spun back to Dekies, clicking heels. "Must say, I haven't known Vortu to be so... *timid*. But if that's the way you want to do things."

"It is."

Aptat motioned toward Naecia's chamber, and the glass slid wide enough for her to step out of it. "You break, you buy, Dekies."

---

being a dead giveaway, or tell, for genuine interest. At least in horses – *Thanks for that. I'll let you know when we meet some space horses.*

Dekies said, "Is your neural dredge calibrated?"

I straightened inside my chamber. *Did someone say – *neural dredge*?*[56]

Aptat gestured to the black coffin in the corner. "Always."

Dekies marched over, seizing Naecia powerfully by the arm. "If she's half what you say she is, I don't care if she takes a little damage."

"You will *kill* me," protested Naecia, yanking her arm away. Dekies quickly reassumed her grip and pulled Naecia effortlessly to the far side of the room, where the dredge awaited. The Vortu princess pressed something and the clear lid folded open into segments. Etched into the glass were ruler-like markings down the length and width.

She released Naecia. "Get in."

Naecia pushed the Vortu away and darted to the side. Dekies thrust a palm into Naecia's chest, ragdolling her backward over the lip and into the contraption. Patton and I shared a terrified glance. Dekies lowered the lid. Aptat didn't object, though they visibly stiffened at the coarse treatment of their merch.

A barrage of fists and knees emanated from the dredge as only the softest of thuds. Dekies leaned casually on the edge of the thing, pointed down at Naecia through the glass. "If you don't volunteer to take the visual, I'll introduce anxiolysin – nasty side effects on that. Your choice, brain-bank."

The pounding stopped. I put a little pressure on the gap of my chamber to see if I could get out – to accomplish what, I didn't know. But the glass was immovable.

"Bring me proof that you have access to that third prior and the session will end," said Dekies, punching some icons on the interface. An orange glow ebbed from inside and began slowly flashing. The light intensified as it strobed – a vitrine full of fireworks.

Then the character of the light changed. The flashing fell out

---

56 Yeah, can you find out what that is?

of pattern until it was no longer following any sort of rhythm. I watched, rapt, wondering just what was happening. None of what Dekies or Aptat had said helped me understand.

"Brilliant," said Dekies. "She's on the cord."

Aptat nodded. "I see it."

Patterns appeared on the inner surface of the glass. Some only for a nanosecond, others for longer. They moved while new patterns quickened elsewhere. This occurred independently in spots, while in others the patterns merged or were merely positioned nearby like layered puzzles formed of light. The relationship between Naecia and the patterns had a feeling of call and response. She interacted with some shapes and ignored others. And while at first both the shapes and their movements seemed random, it took on a distinctly autonomous feel, as if Naecia was controlling the overall direction of... whatever she was doing. A large spot on the glass remained in near constant illumination as shapes were moved there, while the area directly over her face rendered and faded more quickly. Every now and then, a shape would be moved down the glass to join the others.

This went on for ten, twenty, forty minutes, at least. My grasp on time was more tenuous than it had been before. I could only imagine what being inside the dredge must have felt like. My own eyes burnt from lack of blinking even though Naecia was the one plugged into the thing. Then the light went out.

Aptat rushed to the dredge.

"Cursed Stringers!" bellowed Dekies, hitting a command on the side and punching the display below it. Aptat went tense and assumed a wide, vigilant stance as the dredge powered down. From my vantage point I could see the articulated arm pop free from its housing between Aptat's shoulder blades.

The lid opened in sections and Dekies pulled Naecia out. She was conscious, barely, eyes unfocused. Limp. Instinctively, I looked to the spiracles just under her ears to gauge the strength of her breathing. In underwater animals, they become languid, failing to fully open and close when death is near. Hers still cycled powerfully. She was stunned; worn out, but not dying – if the clues I was taking from her space physiology correlated at all with the creatures of Earth.

My face was shoved into the vertical opening in my chamber, hands pressed to the glass on either side. Dekies dragged Naecia back to her cell, propping her into a seated position against the glass, and then returned to the dredge. On the upturned lid was a complex network of shapes colored in the heat-orange of dying embers. It was a jumble to me, meaningless, indistinguishable from any other random assortment of geometrical vomit.

Dekies folded the lid down and considered it. Shaking her crowned head, she said, "Three distinct separations here."

"Exactly what you asked for," said Aptat. "Proof she can reach the third prior. That's where the secret lies."

"Ah, but she slipped the cord."

"And held on." Aptat walked to Naecia's chamber, lecturing Dekies. "You can't control anamnesis.[57] It goes where it goes. Let us hope – for the sake of your bank account – that she didn't hit the Fray." Aptat knelt. "What did you learn down there, Naecia?"

One hand grasping her necklace, she slumped against the glass of her chamber, watery eyes blurring out at some vague spot only she could see. Aptat took hold of her wrist, gently, imploring her to surface.

After a moment, they let go and stood. "I hope she recovers. But it's no longer my concern is it?"

"Did she hit the Fray?" asked Dekies.

"No. But she came close. Deepest I've seen." Aptat glanced back to Naecia, then to Dekies, and shrugged. "A risk you willingly took."

Dekies jutted her chin, forcing the rebreather out like a

---

57 You hear that? – *I sure did.*

second mouth. "Who could have known she'd be so weak? Sixty is what we will pay," said the Vortu, pointing imperiously at Aptat. "And that, only because we have a business relationship. I believe she possesses what knowledge you say, but the odds are even that we don't retrieve it before her mind collapses."

Aptat sneered. "You knew the price. You set the intensity of the dredge."

Dekies shrugged. "Sixty is what we brought." Then, sweeping a hand over the trunk. "It's all registered. Take it. That's a fine haul for you. Or – we can kill you, take her, and keep the guush. What do you say?"[58]

"I'd say you're a cheat."

Dekies laughed, "I'd say I'm more a... connoisseur of opportunity."

Aptat crossed their arms, shook their head. "They warned me about doing so much business with Vortu, and especially their infamous princesses. 'A time will come when their greed will outstrip their sense', 'they will take advantage of your good will', 'they are no more than marauders and thieves'. But being so magnanimous as I am, I announced that I don't pass up business, nor do I judge based on hearsay. I told them that the Vortu are plentiful across the Dasma Arm and were always buying – a reliable influx of guush even in times of depressed markets. I lectured them, arrogantly announcing that until somebody crosses me personally, I will always give the benefit of the doubt. Something about it being my gift to the Universe in return for it unburdening me from my own chains."

"That's a lie," said Dekies. "You had no such conversations."

"No, I did not," answered Aptat, giving me a cheeky wink. "But if I had, that's definitely what I would have said."

Aptat turned to face me directly, mere feet away. I sucked in a breath. Behind, Dekies and the other two squared themselves

---

58 I'd say shit just got real.

to the bounty hunter. Aptat's helmet closed over their face. "My fictional colleagues were right," said the metallic voice. "And now *I* have to take a loss for my show of good faith."

The Vortu drew down.

"Guns," I muttered.

Before I could flinch, Aptat's articulated arm had spun once around, producing three short hisses in quick succession. A crown went flying, and the Vortu delegation collapsed, their weapons firing aimlessly. Somewhere, Patton hooted.

Aptat came within inches of my face, which I had anxiously wedged into the gap in the glass. The seams of their shining helmet came apart, exposing a friendly version of the stringhunter's piscine visage. "Did I get them?"

I glanced again over their shoulder and nodded stupidly.

"Hmm, good," they grunted. "But this will shit my reputation."

CHAPTER TEN

I exchanged a distressed glance with Patton as Aptat skipped between the chambers spitting colorful curses. Two prisoners, Ke'xatt and Ghuxch-hexer-chchch, were no longer standing. Aptat opened the shattered glass of their chambers and dragged them out, checked vital signs, then let loose another round of expletives. The Vortu's stray rounds had found soft targets.

Unable to help the deceased, Aptat flew to Naecia next. Her eyes bumped open. Aptat unsnapped a piece of armor from around their neck, a thin ring of black – I quickly realized it was the axon diadem – pulled it to shape and set it on Naecia's head.

Aptat summoned the holographic readings just as they had done with me, and made some adjustments, moving little bars up and down like tuning a stereo, eyes flicking between it and Naecia. More adjustments, additional readouts. Another look. One more tap.

Naecia sat up – nearly springing awake – eyes wide like she'd received a shot of adrenaline, then slumped again, groaning and holding her head. Aptat helped steady her. "Naecia. Sit, sit."

She pushed herself up slowly, blinked her eyes while regaining her equilibrium. Aptat lowered their voice and began speaking, quietly, privately. The pacing of the exchange was that of the coherence test I was given. I hoped she was okay. I remembered what Aptat had said about useless mass. I wasn't ready to see someone get dumped into the void. I'd become invested in the welfare of this stranger. I didn't know her, but we were all in the shit now. It's not like I wouldn't have empathized with anyone who had just undergone the apparent torture that Naecia had... but she seemed just as alone as I would have been without Patton. So I was suddenly, deeply concerned for her. Or maybe I was projecting. *Just because I'm fragile doesn't mean she is.*

Aptat ran through the test and stood away, leaving the diadem in place – I hoped it was just to keep her monitored. I let out a lungful of air, realizing I'd been holding it. Aptat gestured to the rest of the chambers, closing them. I stared in disbelief as the glass on my own chamber slid closed like it was in slow motion. After all of that, I was going back down without any chance to understand what I'd just seen?

I shoved my arm through the opening. "No!"

Aptat whipped their hand into a "halt" position, pausing the glass. The other chambers continued down.

"Idiot," said Aptat. "That would have sliced through your arm like a yorp sausage if I hadn't stopped it. What do you want? I'm a little busy right now, what with my latest negotiation going to holes and two of my merch full of them."

The three other chambers with still-living prisoners – excepting Naecia's – sunk into the floor. Patton wore a puppy-dog's lament as we were separated. I turned back to Aptat. "Dekies said *anamnesis*," I said. "I know that word."

"What about it?"

"Is that what I have?" I swallowed nervously, not sure I wanted the true answer, not believing I was going to say it out loud. "Memories of a previous life?"

"*Lives*," said Aptat. "And call it what you like, but yes." A sweep of the arm over the gleaming floor. "Same as all the others."

"All of them?"

"Hmm-mm. Well, except for your friend. He's the only normal one here."

There it was. The answer. Suddenly, my whole life leading to this point made sense. I wasn't crazy, I was just... possessed?

"I'm Virginia Tighe," I said.

"That means nothing to me. Explain."

With my arm still stuck between the glass, I said, "Past life regression. Virginia Tighe swore that she had the memories of this dead lady named Bridey Murphy. She knew all this stuff about Murphy's life that she had no business knowing. They discredited her because it came out that she'd grown up next door to another Irish immigrant much like Murphy. I'm who she thought she was."

"Congratulations on getting closure," said Aptat with increased agitation. "Now please withdraw your arm before I liquify it."

"No." My voice cracked. My eyes filled – which caught me off guard. "No." Maybe it was the years of wondering, never knowing. Of doing nothing more with my life aside from searching. Wanting an answer had become my purpose. Now that I had it, a thousand more questions spawned in its wake. "I want to know why. Why am I like this? You owe me that much. I saved you."

Aptat tilted their head and displayed a skeptical grin. "That's debatable – Dekies was girding for a fight. And even if hypothetically your warning did give me a teeny, tiny, little advantage, you saved yourself as well. The last place you'd want to be is in a Vortu slave dungeon. Let's call it even."

"No," I grumbled, trying to force more of my flesh through the narrow gap. I managed to get a calf and some belly through. Now I probably did look like an exploded can of biscuit dough. "You explain. You tell me what I am. Why I'm like this."

"Pathetic," said Aptat with a lazy sweep of the hand, opening my chamber all the way, causing me to stumble out and nearly trip to the floor. "But fine. You are a *Stringer*, Ben. Someone with access to your downcord priors. But it isn't reincarnation."

"Downcord?"

Aptat stepped casually over one of the Vortu sprawled on the floor on the way to the captain's chair at the ship's sleek console. They slumped into it with a dramatic sigh. "Sentience… self-awareness – whatever you want to call it, is just another form of matter. All around us, in fact. Ubiquitous." A twirl of finger. "Your scientists have speculated on a substance they cannot yet see, giving it mysterious names like dark or exotic matter, polaritons, quasiparticles, "background" particles. They hypothesize and infer its existence but haven't actually observed it. They will at some point, and once they do, it will be generations before they gain any understanding of what it actually *is*. Eventually, maybe, humankind – if it lasts long enough – will learn the truth." A series of finger taps called up a holographic display from the console, a three-dimensional closeup that looked vaguely like the inside of a sponge, with densely concentrated areas adjacent to empty vacuoles. "This is the *Oblivion Fray*."

"Mm-hmm." *I don't understand.* "Which is…"

"The raw material of consciousness. Everything is matter these days."

I poked my hand into the hologram and gave it a stir. "That stuff is… consciousness?"

"As I said, the raw stock from which consciousness arises."

"And it's everywhere?"

"Everywhere."

"Why haven't we run into it? Why don't the planets get caught in it?"

"You're fortunate I'm a conversationalist," said Aptat. "So. Not all matter works that way – even your scientists understand this. 'Matter' is mostly nothingness. There's more distance between the nucleus of an atom and its orbiting electrons than you think. If your eyeball was a nucleus, then the electrons would be about three kilometers away. With all of that empty space, other types of matter can pass right through and you'd never know. This is the character of *Fray*. Think of it as a web of fleece from which you would spin a thread, and from that thread you might braid a cord. Your consciousness – what you perceive as your subjective experience, is like a length of that cord."

Aptat paused to see if I was following. I didn't say anything as I wasn't exactly sure if I was or not.[59]

"The universe, while not itself technically *aware*, does respond to stimuli," Aptat continued. "There is a point in the development of some beings when the capacity for consciousness emerges. It is at this moment that bits of the Fray coalesce into strands and those strands become threads. A trillion threads twist to become a single cord that will run through your mind for the duration of your life. At death, the cord unravels, the threads come apart, the strands dissolve, and all is absorbed back into the Fray. A new life comes along, another cord is spun. Each length belongs to a single sentient individual."

"Unless it doesn't," I said.

"Unless it doesn't," said Aptat with an affirming nod.

"But why does it sometimes fail to unravel?"

"I may have the body of a god," they said, sweeping a hand over their toned chest, torso and legs, "but alas, I don't possess the mind of one."

"So, if a person dies and the cord doesn't unravel back into the Fray..."

"What is the saying on Earth?" said Aptat. "*Nature abhors a vacuum?* That rope of twine will eventually find its way into a life capable of hosting sentience. And that individual will continue along the same cord as their predecessors. Like you."

---

59 Not.

"But how–"

"Let me try to put it in terms you can better understand. Imagine there was a person – we'll call him 'Uncle Jed' – who discovers oil on his property while shooting at some food–"

"Wait? Uncle Jed? Shooting at some food? Are you talking about *The Beverly Hillbillies*, that old TV sitcom?"

"I had four days to kill in Earth's orbit while you foundered into my web. I consumed a great deal of your media at an astronomical framerate, much of which only further confused me about humankind. You have a strange obsession with the geographical orientation of 'real housewives'. What is it with them? Are they regional magistrates of some sort? Is Earth plagued by imposter housewives?"

"I never watch those shows."[60]

"Anyway. Now imagine that Uncle Jed sells the property where he found the oil, buys gold with the proceeds, buries it, then dies before he can tell anyone. Now, nobody will ever know about it."

"Right," I said. "Unless he's a... Stringer."

"Correct," Aptat said. "Thirty years after Uncle Jed goes to the big whiskey barrel in the sky, let's say there's another Stringer, a small-town banker who needs money after a run on the bank... uh, call him George Bailey."

"Really? *It's a Wonderful Life*?"

"Did you want me to continue explaining?" Aptat waited to see if I was done interrupting. I was. "So, George finally gets tired of the visions he's been having of a bright red Black Tupelo tree.[61] He sees it clearly in his mind. It's a hundred paces behind an abandoned gas station on the outskirts of Hill Valley, a place he's never been. He closes the bank and drives down from Bedford Falls, finds the boarded-up filling station, hops out of his car and walks around back. His heart skips a beat

---

60 Lie.

61 *Nyssa sylvatica*.

when he sees the flaming red leaves and he knows it's a Black Tupelo because he's googled it so many times. He burrows into the earth and a few minutes later he's pulling the dirt-covered lid from a priceless find. Unrelated legally to Uncle Jed, George ends up being the only beneficiary of the dead hillbilly's estate! Because, in a way, they are related!" Aptat exclaimed. "It means George can save the bank, now, Ben. Merry Christmas."

I nodded, happy for the overwrought explanation to be done. "I get it."

"The reality, of course, is that the great majority of Stringers aren't privy to the location of some hillbilly's riches – most of the knowledge they have is mundane because most people's lives are mundane. And more often than not, they die without, any understanding of their condition. We stringhunters seek out those few who possess a form of treasure far more valuable than Jed's gold: secrets. Nobody dies without them and most are worthless, but some... some will fetch a lot of guush, Ben. Scavenging the galaxy for Stringers is how we find information that would otherwise be lost to the eternity of death. Get it?"

"Like stealing someone's mail," I mumbled. Mostly it's cable bills and coupon books and unwanted catalogues, but sometimes it's a card from granny with a cold hundred dollars folded neatly inside.[62] Mostly it's junk, but sometimes you get Uncle Jed and his gold. I had too many questions. "Does the Fray, like, go into animals?"

"Yes, if their brains are developed enough, it seems to. But by degree," Aptat continued. "The more advanced the lifeform, the more threads in the cord that reaches out. It is why you would never find yourself occupying the same string as an animal with only rudimentary awareness. Some are so basic that the Fray devotes only a few strands, while those that operate completely by instinct, without any subjective

---

62 Five, if it's your granny.

awareness of their perceptions, seem to be ignored by the Fray altogether."

My brain was galloping along now. Some animals were obvious candidates. Dolphins, whales, cephalopods, the great apes, cows, grey parrots, dogs, corvids, elephants, pigs, and cats. Even some insects displayed considerable intelligence like bees, ants, and Ludlow the Librarian.

I thought about the sea squirt, an adorable little hermaphrodite chordate, the larvae of which float around the ocean looking for a place to attach so they can begin filter feeding. When they finally settle down, they no longer need their cerebral ganglion – a primitive little brain – and so they eat it.[63] Does the sea squirt enjoy some basic level of consciousness before devouring its brain? Does the Fray reach out during the larval phase and then unravel when the brain is consumed? These are important questions.

"We don't fully understand the intricacies of how the Fray functions, but what is clear is that as you live, your experiences imprint upon the cord, leaving behind a partial record of your life. Some things make clearer impressions – intense experiences or strong beliefs tend to leave deeper marks. This is why you don't have access to the whole house, so to speak, of your priors. Only the most important rooms will have been preserved, and even then, not completely. This is what I mean when I talk about downcord coherence: the measure of what a given Stringer can actually perceive of those prior lives."

"Well, my guy had a whole bunch of rooms devoted to bug nuts. So, one of my past incarnations was an insect perv."

"*No*," Aptat said, standing from the captain's chair, making it spin. "This is *not* reincarnation. Those downcord lives were *not* you. Your consciousness is not a continuation of theirs – it was simply the next in line. You get to visit their house, stand in a room or two. You never lived there. You merely occupy

---

63 Autocannibalism. May explain Patton.

the same string of matter that bestows consciousness. *You are a product of your own biology and genetic code*, not the cord. The cord grants awareness, not individuality, nor does it influence the innate traits of 'you-ness'."

"Okay, fine. It's not reincarnation," I said, taken aback by Aptat's sudden adamance.

"The situation of reincarnation would be your identity and your consciousness moving from one corporeal habitation to the next. That's not this."

"Yeah, I get it."

"Being on a cord that failed to come apart when it should have, grants you the gift of *retroception* – 'hindsight' to some. Access to a portion of what your priors knew."

"And look where it's gotten me," I scoffed. "What a gift."

"Point taken," said Aptat.

"So you hunt us… Stringers."

"Hard to call it hunting, really. Most of you have been screaming about it for your entire lives. I only listen."

I stared flatly.

"You Stringers devote so much energy to making queries, trying to understand why you are the way you are. Eventually a signal gets out."

"I didn't send any signals."

Aptat rolled their pupil-less eyes. "Earth is radio bright, Ben. It's been shooting unintentional electronic information out from its surface at the speed of light for a few hundred years."

"What does that have to do with me?"

"Well, you've been a busy little source of signal yourself – asking the internet about the Chime for decades, I'll guess. Anyone out here with an open ear could hear you. *What is the Chime? Why don't I know what the Chime is? Is the Chime a weapon? Is the Chime a religious icon?* Did you ask those questions, Ben?"

"Maybe."

"You did, because I heard you ask those questions a few years after you asked them. Anyone listening, even casually, for messages like those you sent would have heard them. Like me."

"All my searches?" *Gulp.*

"You have some interesting tastes and proclivities," said Aptat, surrendering their hands. "No worries, this is a judgment – free zone."

"So when I tried to learn about the Chime–"

"You were like a giant homing beacon shouting 'HERE I AM. I AM A STRINGER. I KNOW WHERE YOUR IMPORTANT CHIME IS. PLEASE COME AND KIDNAP ME'." They laughed. "You didn't use your real name and location, so it took me a while to narrow down your geographic location based on your active hours and the occasional reference to some uniquely regional item, usually something about a fish. I made my post on *Déjà Who* at a time when I figured you'd see it. And, well, you bit."

"So you're a scavenger, not a bounty hunter."

"I never claimed to be," Aptat said. "But it's still a roll of the dice. The amount and quality of knowledge possessed from Stringer to Stringer varies wildly. Some are sources of vast knowledge – several lives worth, with good coherence, while others are limited. The neural dredge," they thumbed in the direction of the space coffin that Naecia had been forced into, "can be useful to coax more of that buried knowledge to the surface – perhaps open the doors to a few more rooms. Brains are potential treasure-troves, but they have flimsy walls. Sometimes the ceiling falls in. Trying to get at that treasure can be dangerous..." eyes flicking to Naecia, "as you've seen. The more time spent downcord, the more familiar it will feel, the greater the chance that the silt of past lives gets churned into the current. It's one of the reasons I rarely dredge the cargo. You spend enough time in someone else's home, you start to think you live there. You come back up, unsure of who you really are. You risk decohering from your present state."

"Is that what happened to Naecia?"

"No. She wasn't down long enough. Though the dredge allows us to see the depth of her descent and the demarcations between priors, it can't display exactly what she is visualizing. That remains in her mind. But I surmise she was chasing a memory and slipped the cord – dropped onto the lower reaches of a distant prior. The farther down you go, the closer you come to the bottom, where the cord meets back up with the Fray."

Naecia was curled in peaceful slumber against the wall of her chamber, still wearing the diadem, feet sticking out the open gap in the glass. "Is she going to be okay?" I asked.

"She came close to the Fray, but her coherence is nominal now. Her mind was simply overtaxed, I think, by everything that happened."

"What happens if you go all the way down?"

Aptat turned back to the display, spun the image with a gesture. After a long enough pause, I realized they weren't planning to answer the question. "What happens," I asked again, this time with some grain in my voice, "if you hit the Fray?"

Aptat waved the hologram away. "Evanescence, disaggregation. *Oblivion*." Then swiveling to face me, "The Universe takes you back, Ben."

CHAPTER ELEVEN
THE INSTRUMENT MAKER

The woman sat inside a small shop, her large, deer-like eyes shining thoughtfully as she flicked a thin strand of wood with a fore-digit while bending it around a mold. *Plink. Plink-plink-plinnnngg.* There it was, the sound she'd been listening for.

She held the wood in place while reaching for a clamp with her other hand, knocking some unfinished blanks to the ground along with a pile of tacks. Unphased, she dabbed the pieces with glue, checked the sound once more – *pling* – and tightened the clamp. With the component ready for curing, she hung it on a peg alongside a row of more than two hundred just like it and allowed herself a moment to appreciate all the hard work. A quick smile, just for her, and she was on to the next task.

The Instrument Maker had been the one to fashion ukelaklavas for Odvella since before it was even considered a place. Now it was a good-sized town, with plenty of other able artisans up to the task if she wasn't, but she was, and no one trusted anyone else with the music. She'd built the music for more Processions than anyone, having done it five times during her life, which was a momentous feat for an event so rare. People didn't come from all around to hear the Processions played on someone else's ukelavs. They wanted to hear hers. Three hundred and one of the instruments were required, each representing a separate segment of the moons' journey to apex.

This was to be her final time building the music that would guide the moons along their way. After she was gone, someone else would continue the tradition, but it would never again sound like it had sounded when played on her instruments and set to her arrangement. It would be gone, living only in the memories of those who had heard it. Some thought that was sad. Others, the Instrument Maker included, thought that was what made each era so special.

CHAPTER TWELVE

Naecia stirred in her chamber, moaning out off-key notes. "Ah, good," said Aptat. They trotted over but stopped halfway and turned to me. "Back to your cell, Ben. I think my 'debt' has been paid."

I was reluctant to leave the co-captain's chair I'd been sitting in – it was paradise compared to the ass-beating of the floor inside my cylinder.

The ship lurched.

Aptat looked frantically around.

"What was that?" I asked.

Another shudder, and then sudden acceleration. I slipped from the chair and flopped to my stomach, slid across the floor just missing the pods, and slammed feet-first into the wall on the opposite side. The ship entered a steep bank and the stack of dead Vortu plowed into me like a string of pungent grass carp[64] left in the sun too long. "Are we under attack?"

Aptat was back up, staring at the ceiling. "Princess Dekies' sortie ship – it's still docked with us. It has remotely engaged." They clicked across to the ship's console. Something about the suit allowed them to walk without slipping under the acceleration. "Control is disabled. They've altered our course."

---

64 *Ctenopharyngodon idella.*

"What does that mean?" I asked.

"It means they broke through the security protocols. They have my ship!"

Aptat flicked through screen after screen tapping and punching. "Dock is locked down," they muttered to themselves. "Were they planning this all along?"

I struggled to free myself from beneath the fragrant bodies, finally wrenching my legs clear of one especially ripe fellow, then crawled toward freedom. I angled myself over Dekies last. The rebreather facemask thing had been knocked off, leaving the nose and lower half of her face exposed. Words flashed in my head like a neon sign. *Rhinolophus paradoxolophus.* Dekies looked like a Bourret's horseshoe bat. The entire middle of her face was dominated by an elaborate nose structure, which in *paradoxolophus* assumed a flower-like form, with two large petal-shaped growths layered over two more "petals" set just above the mouth, orchid-like. If the lessons of evolutionary physiology carried over to space people, it probably meant that Vortu used sonar to see in the dark.

A small light flashed on the inner surface of Dekies' facemask apparatus.

"Ben. Chamber," said Aptat at my loitering.

"Sure, but there's a... thing," I said, pointing to Dekies. "Little light. Flashing."

Aptat strode over and flipped the mask around, then tore it away from the housing and crushed it with one hand, quenching the light.

"What was that?" I asked, still not in my chamber.

"They were transmitting the whole time!" they said, tossing the scrunched tech into a distant wall where it shattered. They went to the console and brought up a holographic map and expanded the view out over the floor. "They're bringing us right to them."

I scurried into my chamber. Pickles lay on its side, unharmed. I pulled the jar close. "Can you, like, detach their ship?"

"No. They've locked me out of everything except for life support and basic functionality. We're slaved to the sortie vessel, which I'm guessing is under the control of this new ship, here." They pointed to an icon on the hologram, far away, out in space. "That is a Vortu cruiser, registered name: *Terror's Glaive*. So long as the sortie is docked, I can't do anything." They worked the unresponsive controls. "Ben!" said Aptat. "Get out of the chamber!"

"You told me to get in my chamb—"

"Shut up!" Aptat opened a panel, typed something into it, and yanked a lever. "I have good news and I have not terrible news." The main console split apart at the center and the sides began to separate. "The good news for you is that you're disembarking the *Silent Child*, which means you will not be available for murdering when the Vortu arrive. The not terrible news is that the Scythin are convinced of the authenticity of your mental treasures and do not require you to be dredged ahead of time."

I feel like I'm being dredged right now. "Wait, you're selling me?"

"You're already sold, Ben." The console continued to drift apart, exposing a sleek black craft, tapered at the end like a torpedo.

Panic swelled inside my tightening chest. "What's that?"

"A Scythin voidscull. Your ride. Departure time: now."

They gestured to the floor. Patton's chamber ascended.

A dribble of ice ran down my spine. "The Vortu didn't lock it down too?" I asked, trying to delay, slow things up.

"Escape modules are always blockaded. The sortie can't see it. Get in."

"Get in? Now?"

"Now!"

The conical rear of the voidscull cantered upward and the outer shell split in two, with each half folding up against the body and revealing a slightly larger than Ben-sized hole.

"Will they dredge me?" I said, still not out of my chamber.

"It's the only way to retrieve everything you know, so yes I imagine they will."

"Keep us here," I said. "You dredge me. You can just tell them what you find."

"I'm not immune to the circumstances of your plight, Ben. But I wouldn't know how to calibrate the dredge to coax out what it is the Scythin want. And chances are neither of us would understand what comes out of you. The Scythin are... different. Plus, as I've said, they've already paid me. It's done."

I glanced to Naecia, who was alert inside her cell. If the Vortu were coming for the *Silent Child* and they already knew what she had downcord, her prospects were pretty poor.

"Ben!" said Aptal again, urgent. "There's no time."

Clutching Pickles, I stepped out as Patton's chamber locked into place.

A flick of the wrist. "Into the voidscull. Now, Ben." The articulated arm sprang up from their shoulder.

"Where are we going?" asked Patton casually, like maybe it's to the grocery store.

"If you shoot me," I said, "then you'll have nothing to give the Scythin."

"I'm not going to shoot *you*." The arm swung toward Patton. "Get in. Now."

I went across the floor and crawled into the craft. Patton followed. It was small, barely wide enough for the two of us to lie shoulder to shoulder and only enough headroom to sit. I popped my head back out. "Can you beat the Vortu?"

"Unlikely."

Naecia was watching all of this from her chamber. "What happens–" I began.

"Get all the way inside the scull, Ben."

The fairings started to close, with only a moment to back myself in and avoid having a body part clipped off. "What happens when I find the Chime?" I yelled as the view pinched away. "Will they send us home?"

Naecia's head snapped to us, eyes wide. She burst from her chamber as we were folded into darkness.

There was nothing now. No light. No sound from outside.

"Ben?" said Patton.

"Yeah?"

"Just wanted to make sure you were still in here."

The voidscull pitched downward and my stomach swam into my throat. It felt untethered from the *Silent Child*, and I visualized the tiny craft with us inside, launching away from it. All of the things which should have brought mortal fear – shooting through space inside a suppository, knowing that my brain was set to be drilled when we reached our destination, the prospect that we were unlikely to ever return home – I observed as if they were happening to someone else. What terrified me in that moment was something else: the image of Naecia as she had erupted from her cell, and the expression she wore, now burnt in my mind's eye. The face of someone who had just heard the world was ending.

CHAPTER THIRTEEN

Naecia stumbled from her chamber. "No! No! No!"

Aptat had already engaged the voidscull, sending it below decks and then out from the ship. Naecia flew to the console as quickly as she could, and leaned upon it, casting blindly over the controls. "You have to bring him back!"

"It's autonomous," said Aptat, casually. "And I have bigger problems."

"That Earth man said he was trying to find the Chime!"

"Yes, that's why the Scythin wanted him," said Aptat. "Back to your chamber, now. It's like I'm running a kennel for orphaned plorgies in here."

Naecia sat down right on the floor. "You idiot."

"Back in your chamber," said Aptat, weaponry taking aim. "Now."

"Go ahead," she said. "We're all dead anyway, thanks to you."

Aptat's expression was of one who had missed the punchline to a joke. "Explain."

"If the Earth man leads them to the Chime, then everything is gone."

"*Gone?*"

Naecia's teeth creaked from the pressure of clenching. She glared at the stringhunter. "Do you not know what the Chime actually does?"

"I've heard the same rumors as everyone else. A nihilistic weapon, a magical relic that can wipe out galaxies. Tales no doubt designed by one stringhunter to dissuade other stringhunters from pursuing candidates who might be able to find it. Misinformation is commonplace when valuable Stringers are floating about. It isn't the first time someone has played the galactocalypse card." They paused, placing hands on hips, then tilted their head thoughtfully. "Okay. So? What is it you think the Chime does?"

"Creates a cold spot, a big one."

"And why would one want to create a cold spot?"

Naecia shrugged her shoulders mockingly.

"You think it's to force a dimensional handshake?"

"What else?" she said.

"Hmm."

"Everything dead in a million gilley radius, gone," she said. "Existence. Gone."

"*Nullibiety*," said Aptat, describing the condition in a word. "That's all very scary. Sounds a bit far-fetched, though, drawing dimensions together. Do you know what isn't far-fetched? The Vortu, on their way to kill us. Literally right now."

Naecia shook her head in disgust. "The crew of the *Knell* were hunting for Stringers with knowledge of the Chime too."

"Unsurprising. Every stringhunter in the Dasma Arm has been looking for that Stringer since the Scythin put out the offer. I'm the one that found him."

"And apparently the only one who didn't fully understand what you were looking for. Captain Arrohauk knew what the Chime was. She had proof. Scoped images of the *Timelance* at Arusne."

"Arusne is a supervoid that formed three billion years ago."

"Well," said Naecia, "three billion and one years ago, the Scythin were sitting right in the middle of it. If you had managed to salvage the scope logs from the *Knell* you could see it for yourself."

"No need," said Aptat, sweeping through menus on the console. "Arrohauk transmitted the images to our network. We'd all seen, and promptly ignored them." The display came up showing a macrograph of pure black space labeled with specific coordinates. A second image taken at the same coordinates showed a robust starfield. The only difference was the timestamp. The second image had been captured several years earlier. Then there was a third image, taken at the same time as the second, at the same coordinates, only magnified by a few billion times. At its center was the Scythin ship, a wickedly spindle-shaped awl of black. Asog Arrohauk had referred to it as the *Timelance*, after what she believed to be its purpose: lancing spacetime.

Naecia shot back to her feet. "You *have* the images?" she exclaimed. "And you still handed over the Stringer?"

"You must be new to stringhunter subterfuge. Anytime we're chasing down a new lead, we're working just as hard to throw the competition off the scent. These macrographs are no different. Easily faked."

"Well, they're not faked!" her voice cracked. "Captain Arrohauk would have shown you on the scopes herself if you hadn't killed her."

"Sympathy for your captor?" said Aptat, approaching. "That's one I'll have to ponder."

"At least she was hunting to kill."

Aptat barked a laugh. "To kill who? The Stringer? His cord would only have requickened in some other unfortunate. Someone was going to find Ben – or whoever landed on the cord after him – and sell them to the Scythin. Better for me to profit now than allow the benefit to pass to another of my ilk down the line."

Ugh, lightheaded again. Naecia wavered. "You can count all the guush you want. If the Scythin get that Chime, you'll be just as dead as the rest of us."

"Well, bright side: you'll be able to stop worrying about the Chime when the Vortu turn us to dust," said Aptat, finger-tapping to the words on Naecia's shoulder. "Back to your chamber."

"And when will they be doing that?" she said.

"Four cygies give or take. Sooner if they decide to fire the *Child*'s engines."

Naecia stepped into her chamber and waited to be sealed and sent below.

Aptat hesitated for a moment before closing the glass. "Tell me: would you rather that I turn off your air supply or space your chamber when the Vortu arrive?"

"You're not going to fight them?"

Aptat laughed grandly. "What fight I can manage with no ability to maneuver and limited access to the ship's systems. I will make my best personal stand." They clicked heels and mimed a sword twirl. "You're the one with a choice. I'll do it for the three of you who remain. Or, if you choose to stay in your chambers, alive and well for your kidnappers when they arrive, I suppose that's an option as well."

Naecia turned a shoulder at the non-choice and the chamber descended.

Silence magnified the pounding headache. It was worse than a hangover from an after-shift party spent drinking pipe spirits back on Vask. She'd long since given up on returning home to the steam fields or to her family on Drev, but had always been able to take comfort in an imagined homecoming. Now if – *when* – the Earth man gave up the Chime, the entire Pangemic system and the galaxy it called home, would cease to exist anywhere.

The arrival of nausea was an unpleasant companion to the headache. Of course, she'd choke on it rather than decorate her chamber as the Earth man had. She condemned his weakness. With any luck, the trait ran deep, and the Scythin dredge would do to him what should have already been done. With any luck, it would melt his brain before he spilled.

CHAPTER FOURTEEN

I had never considered myself claustrophobic, but being trapped inside a roughly sarcophagus-sized space-kayak was enough to bring the phobia forward. Did this thing even have an air supply or were we stuck with whatever was in here when we departed? My mind jumped to Loricifera, a phylum of sediment – dwelling microorganisms that can live in anoxic environments. How fitting to daydream on such a thing as we suffocated.

"I'm glad you got the pickles," said Patton from beside me in the dark. He reached over and caressed the lid. "I liked the protein bars fine, but they made me gassy. I'm glad to be out of that fart jar."

"Give it time," I said. "This thing is smaller and there are two of us."

Distracting myself from the disorienting dark and strange alterations in momentum, I explained to Patton everything I'd learned from Aptat. He took it all in relative stride, including that no one believed that he was me and that he'd likely end up getting tortured if I didn't give freely of whatever treasures my mind possessed.

The interior became lambent, exposing black spans of something stretching from wall to wall, weblike. I reached out and touched one, expecting it to give, but found it inflexible.

There had been nothing like this on *Silent Child*. That ship was – and I feel the use of this word odd under the circumstances – *conventional*. Expected. Regular old spaceship stuff. This though... different.

The lights dimmed and rose as before, with the black material shifting along the walls. It must have been softening or liquifying and then resolidifying. The strands processed toward us, changing orientation each time the lights strobed. One strand pulled down across our shins, another across our laps. A biomechanical seatbelt?

"Just like a rollercoaster! Wee!" Patton crowed, shooting his arms up in amusement park form, only to have one of the strands force them back down against his sides. "Ow."

Several others swayed into position at about chest height, then pulled across our chests and foreheads, effectively sealing us to the structure of the voidscull. I couldn't turn my neck. "Rollercoaster, huh?"

I held Pickles with my thighs. Inhaled, exhaled. "Breathe. I think we're supposed to–"

And then it was like we were catapulted, launched. Shot from a gun. Fast. Like skin-of-face-stretching-backward kind of fast.

Acceleration can kill, you know. The human body can only handle about nine longitudinal g's – nine times Earth's gravity – before the heart can't pump blood to your brain. Fourteen lateral g's will tear your organs loose. Naturally, this is the type of information I am privy to as an expert in the watches worn by pilots experiencing heavy forces during maneuvers. Swiss watchmaker IWC,[65] for instance, builds its best timepieces to withstand around seven sustained g's.

Point being, the g's were getting up there and even though the voidscull was dark again, I guessed that if the lights came

---

65 International Watch Company – *Boring name, exciting watches* – You should trademark that.

up, we'd be seeing them through a rapidly constricting tunnel as we struggled to stay awake. Our mass was pressed into the wall and floor. The acceleration was unrelenting. Patton made some gurgling noises just as my own throat constricted. Exhalations hissed out in short bursts through my teeth. We had reached the human limit.[66] The darkness in the scull merged with the darkness in my head. And after that, there was nothing.

My senses were numb – or, actually, absent. I couldn't tell if my eyes were open or closed. "Patton?"

No answer.

"Patton!" The strands of material were still present but had loosened enough for me to shift. I put my arm out, able only to reach his wrist. I grabbed it and shook. He mumbled. Thank god. I squeezed Pickles and placed my hand on top, reassuringly, as if it were the head of a small dog. I traced about the edge of the lid with my finger pads, feeling the dimples that would mock would-be pickle jar openers. "Patton?"

"Yeah."

"You okay?"

"I think," he mumbled. "Hungry."

"Same."

"Pickle me."

My mouth flooded with saliva. "Yeah, of course," I answered. It felt like days since the last bit of space pemmican. I visualized the act of opening the pickle jar and the great reward and briny snap of that first juicy bite. I whispered an apology to Pickles. Its time had come to do what pickles must do.

The lid might as well have been welded on. I wrenched at it from beneath my restraints to no avail, then leaned to the side

---

66 As opposed to the tardigrade limit, which is closer to sixteen-thousand g's. Those microscopic abominations were built for survival – *At what point do brains undergo liquefaction? Asking for a friend.*

and tried to tap the edge of the lid on the floor. My hands felt insubstantial and weak, against which Pickles easily resisted. My situation strained the absurd: trapped inside a space-laxative while wearing a repurposed body bag, and unable to access our only food source. I was the punchline to somebody's joke. *Here lies Ben Sullivan. Died in space. Couldn't open the pickles.*

"Give 'em here," said Patton. "Bigger hands."

Happy to surrender the task, I lifted Pickles over my lap, which was tough with my wrists barely mobile, and set them down between us. I edged them toward Patton with a finger, while he simultaneously tried to reach them. Eventually, they came to rest at a point of limbo between us, a quarter inch from anyone's fingertips in snack food purgatory. Taunting us.

Patton lurched toward them only to gag himself on a restraint.

The strand of whatever that ran across my lap pressed painfully against my bladder. Distraction over other things had blunted the sensation, but now it was coming through full strength. This was going to be a problem.[67] "Hey!" I cried out to no one. "I need to pee!"

Our tethers released, with each of the strands melting back into the walls. Simultaneously, however, the places where my body contacted the floor and wall softened, and I was absorbed into the structure of the scull itself. Struggling only made it worse – as if we were in quicksand – and I was soon embedded. Same with Patton. Only my face, top of my legs and arms above the wrist remained above the surface. More dim lights.

"It's carbonite!" Patton squealed.

---

67 Interestingly, bladder size has little effect on duration of urination. Most animals take twenty-one seconds to relieve themselves. A beagle will take the same amount of time to pee as an elephant, who carries a five-gallon bladder – *Now I have to pee even worse! Ahhhhhh! –* Me too! Aaaahhhhh!

"Not a real thing," I grunted, still hopelessly squirming.

The ceiling appeared to bow at the center and the material gathered into bulge. Then it drew long, stretching toward the floor, forming an eel-like appendage.

"What is that?" squealed Patton.

The head of the eel descended and a bead of blue light shone from its tapered tip, first onto the jar of pickles, also embedded in the floor, then directly onto my crotch.

"Whoa, what are you doing?" Arms hobbled, I flippered my hands at it. "Stop that."

"Oh, no!" cried Patton. "It's trying to get your dick, man!"

The eyeless eel *looked* me in the face, then traced up over my belly and chest, coming to rest just inches from my nose. The blue light began to pulse. Slowly, quickly, slowly, quickly, slowly—

CHAPTER FIFTEEN

The Vortu. The Chime. The Vortu. The Chime. Two independent sources of impending death. One local, one galactic. Even with the very real possibility of her own impending death by the local one, Naecia's mind was distracted by the Earth man, who according to his now-empty cell was called "Ben". It was Ben who threatened the lives of everyone she cared about, namely her mother and brother back on Drev, because he didn't understand the world-ending potential of the object he would soon be tasked to find.

Stewing over their predicament, Naecia slid around the tiny metal panels of Aeshua's puzzle amulet. She wasn't trying to solve it – it was a pleasant distraction that reminded her of home. In fact, she was consciously trying to keep it unsolved. Solving it would be like ending the chapter of a story, her family's story. The trinket was her last remaining physical connection to those she loved, a conduit to them, and while she played at it, she was keen for it to remain unfinished. She lolled her head to the side and made eye contact with Oush, who floated in the neighboring cell. In exercising remote dominion over the ship, the Vortu Cruiser *Terror's Glaive* had shut down the gravity generator.

"Hey," she said. They were able speak freely now. Aptat had opened communications between their cells, so the captive

Stringers could brainstorm together, and had promised their freedom if they devised a way to defend the *Silent Child* against the coming assault. They weren't entirely sure whether to believe their captor or not, but what choice was there? It had been over three cygies. So far, no plausible solutions had yet been presented that would prevent their demise. They had one more cygie before the Vortu arrived.

Oush was in the midst of reviewing the ship's equipment manifest and didn't so much move his head as shift the mobile eyes in his orange face to different locales within it. "What news, Naecia?"

Even though they'd been prisoners together on the *Knell*, Oush, Izairis, and Naecia had never before been permitted to speak. Their introductions were nevertheless brief – even after so long in confinement, Oush wasn't a huge talker. The little Naecia had learned was that he had been a "grappling-thespian" near a shipbuilding station at Apho Scion, one of a triumvirate of planets orbiting Stru, a yellow star nine gilleys from Pangema. According to him, he'd been a natural at the craft of faux pugilism and quite the local celebrity due to his size, dramatic timing, and ability to bleed out of his face on command. He'd been abducted in the middle of a scripted bout where his persona, a heel named The Bolide, was about to perform his hugely popular signature move – a bombastic elbow drop titled *The Re-Entry*. He'd climbed a gantry, whipped the fans into a frenzy, and leapt. He never landed.

Asog Arrohauk had been ready, simply scooping him out of the air with a capture drone. Apparently, when he wasn't showboating in front of sellout crowds, he'd been researching his mysterious knack for unconventional weaponry and Arrohauk had sniffed the signal.

Naecia grunted, scrolling through the ship's design schematics on a data pad. "Not much here. Aptat really decked this thing out when they designed it, though. Poshest setup you ever saw. Two entirely separate living quarters. Two! On a long-range ship?"

"A lot of extra weight," said Oush. "Nice defense system, though. Too bad it's locked out."

"Yeah, I saw that," Naecia answered.

"Well, they put all the guush into weapons and décor because the encryption sentinels are crotchwater." It was Izairis, who occupied the chamber directly across from Naecia and spent most of her time looking depressed. Izairis intrigued Naecia, in no small part because she was a nun.

She'd come from a system that Naecia had never heard of, where one entire planet served as the religious and spiritual center for all the others. After years of fruitlessly searching for something that would explain the intrusive thoughts that pushed her to grifting and forging and criminal schemes, she'd taken up the cloth as a last resort in order to purify her mind. It was there at the convent that she'd accidentally fallen in love with several of her cohorts, chief among them, kind Sister Nezlin.

Lovesickness aside, Izairis had taken her service seriously, hoping that with enough time and devotion, she would be cured of the unwanted machinations that plagued her every thought. Aside from eating and doing chores about the convent grounds, Izairis prayed and meditated in solitude; that she might wake one day with a mind clear of nefarious plans, and free of lust for her sisters in faith. The way she told it, she had been on a meditation bender in the woods when Asog Arrohauk had appeared in her trademark space gown. Believing at first that she had accidentally summoned Lantharaptus, the Vixen God of Salvation (Arrohauk was a looker), Izairis offered to place herself into service of the deity. Delighted by her quarry's vulnerable state of mind, Arrohauk played along, escorting the smitten nun back to the *Knell*. By the time Izairis realized that she'd been had, it was too late.

Faced with captivity, Izairis quickly became despondent. With her eyes no longer clouded by the illusion that religion would save her, her love for Sister Nezlin only hardened the farther away she got, and her faith collapsed along with her heart. She did not eat or drink. Realizing that the captured nun was prepared to die, Arrohauk proposed a mutually beneficial arrangement: Izairis use her hidden talents for bludgeoning security protocols to assist in the acquisition of additional Stringers, and she would return Izairis to her home in the space of one galactic year. Strangely, she'd found Arrohauk's proposal to be sincere. Especially once the stringhunter had explained the larger picture – that she was trying to find a particular Stringer, one who held the secret that could destroy all that they knew.

After that, Izairis surrendered to her mind, and repeated trips into the dredge while on the *Knell* had focused her skills considerably. It was Izairis's code-replication ability that had helped Arrohauk get through the security protocols of Apho Scion to nab Oush during his staged combat matinee. She'd been forced to do it, of course, but that didn't mean there hadn't been hard feelings. Oush rarely spoke directly to her.

Izairis also confessed that she'd played a roll in Naecia's abduction. Once Arrohauk had detected Naecia's research transmissions, Izairis had been the one who hacked her work schedule so that the *Knell* could chase her down over the Vaski steam fields. Naecia found herself surprisingly ambivalent at hearing the truth. She supposed she would have done the same, and Arrohauk was coming for her one way or another. Naecia actually empathized with the little nun's situation. She stood to be returned to those she loved until Aptat had come along and murdered her ticket home.

Not all of their priors knew weapons or ciphers, or physics-shattering space travel. Not everyone was considered so special. Izairis had a second prior, down below the forger, some type of mop weaver. That was it. A weaver of mops. Oush's second-deep was a boblet shepherd. Boblets, apparently, were small, roundish, six-legged oinkers, bred in order to guard the perimeters of livestock farms on some distant planet. Naecia had probed for more but Oush maintained there was nothing else there. Just memories of these tiny gruntlings that could gang-devour a would-be predator in the blink of an eye. That was the thing: being a Stringer didn't mean that everyone who came before was onto some great mystery. Why couldn't Naecia have been one of those, occupying the same cord as mop weavers or boblet shepherds?

She pushed her lament aside and retrained her focus. Izairis had said something about encryption sentinels. "What about them?" Naecia asked.

Izairis, who had reengaged at the prospect of freedom, gestured derisively to the display on her access pad. "Well, you'd think they would have thought about bottlenecking the network connections at the dock so nobody could hammer down the security protocols and slave the ship to a parasitic shuttle!"

Naecia wasn't super keen on the lingo but she got the point. "So, no way to get through it?"

"Locked out is locked out, Naecia."

"Oush? Do you see anything we might repurpose to construct a relativistic jet gun or a geometric laser?"

Oush rolled his eyes. "Those aren't real things, Naecia."

"You're the one with the theoretical weapons architect lurking in there somewhere. Are any of those theories worth a shit?" She was tense. Time was running out.

"You don't have to raise your voice," said Izairis, covering her ear nubs with hanks of purple robe.

"No, I actually do. Between us we have access to nine brains and haven't come up with anything resembling a viable solution."

Izairis crossed her arms and glared. "Seven brains. I don't think Oush's boblet farmer or my basket weaver are destined to contribute much."

Even with all the brains, there wasn't a lot they could work with. *Silent Child* had been tied to the Vortu sortie, which itself was under the control of an approaching cruiser. They needed to either crack the sortie and retake control or find a way to kill the oncoming marauders.

"Anyone got a Vortu downcord?" Naecia grumbled rhetorically.

She rage-scrolled through the ship's schematics. The sortie had taken near full control of the *Silent Child*. They needed to figure out a way to defend the defenseless. Getting rid of the sortie was the most obvious solution, except that they couldn't access the airlock to reach it and the dock's emergency charges used to remove unwanted or dangerous vessels were, of course, also under lockdown.

Naecia continued through the submenus, swiping back and forth, growling. "Oush!" she called. "What menu was environmental?"

Oush shifted his eyes across his face. It looked like a chore. Naecia wondered why he didn't just turn his entire head.

"Hull," he said.

"Right!" *Right.* She scrolled to the menu for *Silent Child*'s hull. Submenus included anything attendant to the hull, whether externally or between its inner and outer shells. Structural integrity, electrical, flight surfaces, locks, air circulation and filtration systems. There were stability and equilibrium readings for housings through which the ship's nine – *wow, nine* – dilaceration cannons ran. Worthlessly inoperative at the moment. After that came the fire suppression system, hydraulic fluid transport, and the critical steam system utilized by the attitudinal thrusters. *Hmm.*

"Aptat!" she called.

They patched through after a beat. "Naecia. Did you solve quantum transport?"

"Not yet. It's too cold down here to think. Do the Vortu have control of environmental?"

"Standby." A pause. "Let me know if you feel a change."

"What are you doing, Naecia?" asked Izairis.

"Making it more comfortable."

Naecia grinned as a current of warm air bathed her face. As with most void-bound ships, active heating requirements were low because the warmth generated by onboard activities had nowhere to escape. Components and people created heat which had to be actively dumped into space as radiation. Naecia suspected that such low demands meant that any environmental heating requirements would likely be set up to pull from the critical steam. Warm air meant the steam was actively circulating even though the ship was not currently utilizing its pitch, yaw, and roll thrusters.

She selected the sub-submenu for the steam system map and navigated to a macro showing the entirety of the *Silent Child*. The sortie was up top, connected to the docking ring just aft of the ship's center of mass. She zoomed in and found four thruster hubs just behind the ring. Thrusters meant critical steam and that meant pipes.

"Okay, okay," she said, canting her head to call to the deck above. "Turn it off."

Aptat came through. "Thought you said turn it on?"

"Turn if off now. I don't need it anymore."

"Explain."

"I need you to let me out."

CHAPTER SIXTEEN

There was an unfamiliar character to my stirring. It didn't feel like waking from slumber as much as I imagined it did emerging from a coma. My eyelids were like chainmail and my jaw was glued shut. A rapid deceleration pressed me forward, stretching the sore muscles of my neck and back. And then, it seemed, we'd stopped moving.

The wall and floor began to shift, like they'd been waiting for me to reach some baseline wakefulness before I could be regurgitated. The blue-eyed cyclops eel was gone. Or maybe it was slithering around in the dark, just off my skin. I felt myself contracting inward. I didn't have to pee anymore. Maybe it was just a harmless space catheter: a piss eel.

Patton was still embedded in the floor of the scull and didn't stir when I shook him. He was breathing, though.

My eyes felt small, weak. Atrophy takes a long time, right?[68] Still, it was tough to tell in the black. I felt around for Pickles. When I didn't immediately find him,[69] I sprawled across the floor, stretching my arms and legs like a four-armed starfish

---

68 Eye shrinkage can be caused by regressive evolution. Take for instance the Mexican tetra, a brilliant example of eye loss due to – *Stop. This isn't regressive evolution. It was a long nap.*

69 Him? So he's a boy now. A *real*, Pickle boy.

blindly reaching for a crumb.[70] My middle finger grazed the lid. Weakly, I pushed to all-fours, trying to right myself. My arms failed and I slipped to the side. I fell hard but shielded the jar, allowing my shoulder to take the brunt. *That hurt more than it should have.*

Still on my side, I latched my fingers around the jar and dragged it protectively into my chest.

"Patton! Wake up!" I said over my desiccated vocal cords, while struggling to sit straight. I coughed bitterly. The amount of effort it took to remain steady was exhausting and my breath came ragged. I felt insubstantial, ghostlike. "Patton!" Apparently still under the piss eel's spell, he didn't answer.

There was now a collar around my neck. Metal, or something like it. I gave it a yank, but it didn't budge. I ran my hand down my chest towards my belly, but there was only empty space where I'd previously kept my energy stores. The flat expanse that had become my stomach felt like somebody else's. Some sort of rubber material had replaced the body bag loaner. Had we been changed in our sleep? I felt at Patton. He was garbed in the same stuff.

Then I felt something else. "Oh God," I whispered as my hands settled upon a bundle of tubes erupting from the place where my belly button should be. I made a sound that rivaled the cry of a howler monkey.[71]

---

70 Not actually blind, and definitely not fish. These crustaceans have tiny, simple eyes on the tip of each arm that can resolve about two-hundred pixels worth of visual information. Good for searching for your home rock, so long as it isn't more than about three feet away – *Enough with the fish eyes!* – Again, not actually a fish.

71 Genus *Allouatta*. People like to throw "howler monkey" around, but it is actually the loudest land animal in the world, their trademark call enabled by an enlarged hyoid bone at the top of the throat. Only the blue whale is louder – *And yes, all of this actually goes through my*

"Patton! Wake up," I pleaded while bumbling with the tubes, groaning miserably every time I touched them. They didn't hurt, surprisingly, but their presence made me want to retch. "Patton?" I reached over in the dark, one finger extended bravely out to where I guessed Patton's stomach was, skin crawling at the expectation of coming into contact with AAAAAH HE'S GOT THEM TOO! FUCKING GROSS! I wiped my finger across my rubber suit and continued to scream.

"Ben?"

"Patton!" I said, "Oh god, I'm glad you're awake. Listen to me: Don't move. We have tubes coming out of our stomachs, okay? But don't touch them, it's disgusting!"

"What?" he asked blearily. And even though it was pitch black I knew he was doing it. He shrieked.

"I told you not to touch them!"

The floor started to change again. I slipped down into a divot that, growing wider, became a shallow dish. Patton slid in after me, leaving the two of us flopping around like fish in an empty bowl. As the dish elongated, the floor gradually pulled out from under us, and in the space of seconds we went from sitting on the floor of the voidscull to a new surface. I squeezed Pickles snugly to me, summoned my strength, and felt around on my hands and knees, belly tubes slapping side-to-side like protracted udders.[72]

Ever so dimly, light returned to the space, searing my pupils. Patton moaned. I slapped my hands over my eyes and squeezed tightly enough to *hear*.[73] How long had we been

---

head as I'm squealing.

72 Joke all you want, but udder and teat health are important for all ruminants. Sounds like you've got keratinized corns on yours. Consult your veterinarian for treatment.

73 In animals there is a small muscle in the ear called the tensor tympani that is triggered by a tendon that adjusts when the eyes

under? *Under.* It felt like we'd come up from anesthesia.

The voidscull was changing once more. I squinted just enough to take in basic information; light and dark, big shapes but no details – like a starfish. The walls stretched and skewed like hands under fabric. Then they expanded upward, the space transforming into a room tall enough to stand. I immediately tried to, if only to prove I still could. The lower portion of the wall was solid and I used it as a brace, pushing carefully, gingerly, upright, like a child just learning. The walls continued to stretch higher still. What had been the voidscull was now... not.

The black walls brightened, forcing my eyes shut again. I held my breath and slowly reopened them. It was like an illusion, as the source of light was ambiguous, making it impossible to tell if it was passing through from the outside or radiating from within the walls themselves. Black faded to grey to muted light blue in a gradient that ran from opaque to translucent. Maybe it wasn't the light that was changing at all, but the walls, allowing whatever illumination was beyond to filter in.

That's when I noticed what we were wearing.

Patton screeched. I would have too but couldn't get any air into my lungs. There was no other way to put it: we were in gimp suits. Gleaming. Slick. Something like space-latex. Full-body rigs, just without hoods or zippers. I tried fishing a finger underneath at the wrist, but it was sealed to my skin – like I'd been dipped in liquid that had hardened around me. It didn't stretch and wouldn't tear. We struggled futilely, then just stood there, staring at each other in shocked surrender.

"My nipples feel like they've been sanded off," Patton moaned miserably.

Our eyes drew down the tubes onto our opposite's stomach.

They hung limply like severed umbilici, prompting such a visceral disgust that I immediately wanted to tear them out. Patton bayed sorrowfully.

---

are squeezed shut. Like cats.

I took hold of the tubes and shut my eyes, but something stopped me from carrying through. How had we been eating? Eating... and – *oh no*. I felt around toward the back, slowly crawling my fingers along a cheek. Yep. There was one in my ass. My eyes teared up. I flapped my hands in revulsion and howled like a pistol shrimp.[74]

Resigned, Patton reached around for the inevitable, and nodded in somber affirmation. He brought his own butt tube around to the front and held it tenderly like a tail that'd been up the vacuum cleaner. "Have we been pooping through these, Ben?"

"I think so."

"Oh, god."

To top it all off, our odor was biblical.

I began to think wistfully about our initial abduction. Who was it who said, *only worry about the things you can control?*[75] I tried to stay calm, filing away the stench, captivity, the unbidden butt stuff into the Things I Can't Control drawer. Can't say it helped.

The walls continued their oleaginous transformation into a twisted and organic non-shape. The material, membrane-like but strong, brightened further, and for the first time there was a sense of a world on the other side. Motion. Ambiguous forms slipping apart and congealing. *Life.* We'd arrived someplace new.

"Patton, you see that?"

He moaned in the affirmative.

I struggled to stand again, using my hands for stabilization, and pressed my eyes to the wall to see what lurked just beyond. One of the shadows came close, its outline sharpening until it was just outside. Then more shadows gathered, obfuscating the first, undiscernible. Their shapes were similar

---

74 *Alpheus frontalis.*

75 Your mom.

and then different, changing. There was an organization to the movements, coordination.

It suddenly exploded to triple its original size, then doubled again, and again. It was dynamic, expanding and contracting every few seconds, akin to the watery dance of *Deepstaria enigmatica*.[76] Except, where *enigmatica* move gracefully, the thing on the other side of the wall altered forms with lightning speed, defying any logic of the world that I understood. The closest analog would have been an octopus, with its ability to quickly occupy volumes that seem impossible given its size. This, though, was no cephalopod.

The voidscull – or what had once been – drew farther upward, pulling the walls with it like spans of chewed gum. Hundreds of feet up. An opening appeared there, as if we were inside the tightly wound bloom of a moonflower looking through to the sky. But here there was no sky. We were inside of a breathtaking structure and directly beneath the apex of a great vaulted rotunda. Sinuous spans of black material radiated from the center, sweeping in gentle arcs toward the perimeter of the room, where they ascended out of view.

Near the top edges of the membrane walls, the frosted blue faded away and became clear, and this transformation slowly processed downward. The thing was still on the other side of the once-voidscull's blurry skin directly in front of me. Undulating. Breaking apart and reforming. Innumerable individual pieces making up the whole. Only shape and movement translated through the membrane walls. Though not for long.

I was really squeezing Pickles.

I watched the morphing torrent of silhouettes outside and felt my mind running through its catalogue of Earth's biota in a breakneck effort to make familiar what wasn't.[77]

---

76 Famously shapeshifting jellyfish of the family *Ulmaridae*.

77 *Cervus camelopardalis* (giraffe)-*Psychrolutes marcidus* (blobfish)-*Troglodytes gorilla* (gorilla)-*Formica rufa* (forest ant)-*Chalcosoma*

"Hold me," said Patton.

I held my breath instead as the walls around us finally turned clear.

Have you ever seen something so unfathomable that you stared at it mouth agape? Like for real. Were you ever actually confronted by something so stunning that you only realized later that your jaw had fallen open? Because this is what happened. I froze in this state for an unknowable amount of time, aware on a subconscious level that slack-jawed paralysis was the best my body could offer in the face of the ineffable.

And fear? Fear, I think, must be reserved for those things we can comprehend. Whatever seeds of fear which were sowed by my lizard brain didn't quicken. And perhaps that was because what stood before me simply could not be real. What is not real cannot threaten you. Right? I saw it from a perspective removed from myself, watching in awe at this... entity. I should have been shrieking at my imminent demise and pee-soaked like a reasonable person – like Patton was literally right now. Yet there I stood, silently contemplating what was by any definition, a *monster*.

---

atlas (Atlas beetle)-*Hippopotamus amphibious* (just what it sounds like)-*Architeuthis dux* (giant squid)-*Pelecanus onocrotalus* (you guessed it: pelican).

CHAPTER SEVENTEEN

"Let you out?" laughed Aptat.

"Yeah," answered Naecia. "I think I know how to kill the sortie."

"Explain."

"I need to get out and move around some. If you want to know how to regain control of *Child*, you'll let me float around a bit, stretch." She glanced over at Oush, who rolled his wandering eyes.

"It won't work," said Izairis.

The pod of chambers rotated and Naecia's began to ascend. She grinned shit-eatingly at the other two.

Aptat was waiting when she came up through the floor and they gestured the glass aside. "Wait," they said, before she could push herself out. "We are within a cygie of rendezvous. Disclose your solution first. Then have your little float."

Naecia glanced around the deck. Aptat had been busy. Components lay strapped to the floor in piles, some neatly arranged, others tossed aside like scrap. "This ship," said Naecia, casting a finger casually about, "it's built for two. Is that just in case you find the right flesh construct to settle down with, or–" the words died in her throat as Aptat seized her by it.

The stringhunter inspected Naecia's face as she struggled for breath – their powerful grasp collapsing her spiracles. "Is that uncomfortable?" they asked, stepping inside the chamber and pressing her against the glass in back.

Naecia grabbed at Aptat's arm and sputtered through her teeth.

Aptat said, "There is a dynamic here you fail to appreciate. Until we are all dead, we don't occupy the same spot in the hierarchy. Do you understand that?"

Aptat released her and turned away, leaving her on the float. She held her neck and swore she'd kill them if she ever got out of this.

"Now," Aptat sighed, "tell me this solution of yours."

She swallowed the pain, trying to keep it from showing on her face. She needed the stringhunter to cooperate. She cleared her throat, businesslike. "I need to get into the hull," she said pointing to the ceiling above. "Up near the docking ring."

"Why?"

"Because I can kill the sortie."

"How?"

She swallowed down more of the pain. "Hopefully I can damage it enough to make it inoperable, but I might also blow it up."

"Which is it?"

"I don't know," she said with a touch of defiance. "We'll have to see."

"You're going to do this damage with what? The electrical systems won't allow tool adjunction. Dock charges are inaccessible."

"I don't need electrical. And I'll make my own explosives."

"Explain."

"Environmental taps the propulsion system for heat. The propulsion system is supercritical water."

Aptat was inscrutable.

"Supercritical is nearly plasma. Surely you know that."

"And you're going to do what with it?"

"I'm going to open the system beneath the sortie and dice it."

"Back in your chamber."

"Listen to me," Naecia said, pushing tentatively forward. "If I can direct a jet of supercritical through the outer hull and into the sortie, it will either – depending on the shape of the plume, which I can't really control – bore a hole into it or cut it in half. Or possibly blow up and take the sortie with it."

"And destroy this ship!"

"It won't destroy the *whole* ship. There's a deck between us and the docking ring, right?" She stretched her neck. "Then even if something catastrophic happens, you can just seal the third deck."

"This is a very interesting strategy. One small problem though. The space between hulls is under vacuum. Normally, I could fill it with atmosphere, but the menus that would allow me to do so are currently disabled. Alas." Aptat drew a circle. "Have your float and return to your chamber."

"You don't have any voidsuits?"

"No. It's only me and Stringers here. There's never been an occasion when anyone other than myself would need to go outside."

Naecia blinked condescendingly.

"Yes, obviously, now would be one of those occasions," they admitted. "Bad timing. Chamber."

Naecia tightened her lips in frustration and pulled back toward her cell, but stopped short, her gaze having fallen upon the vault on the wall which housed Aptat's extravagant armor when not being worn. "What about that?" she asked, drawing a finger up and down at Aptat's body like a paintbrush. "That's capable in vacuum, isn't it?"

"My carapace?"

"Yes. Your…" shaking a hand at it, "carapace."

"It is, but–"

"Problem solved."

"We are integrated – *I* am integrated with the suit. You wouldn't have any augmented movement or tools. Just baseline functions."

"Would it keep me from dying?"

"Life support, yes. But I don't think it would fit."

"No doubt I'm thicker," she said, squeezing a hand to show off a muscled forearm. "I'll make it work."

"I'd rather–"

"Rather what?" Naecia closed in on Aptat, eyes narrowed. "Do you know what we've come up with down there; all nine plus consciences brainstorming for three full cygies with almost no sleep? *Fuck all.* Unless you count boblet breeding techniques. If you want a chance at unhitching the *Silent Child* from that sortie, you'll let me play dress up."

A furrow formed in the pearlescent skin of Aptat's otherwise smooth brow.

"Or maybe you already know steam systems," Naecia added breezily.

"And why couldn't I go and do it myself, under your tutelage?" asked Aptat.

"Balancing pressures is more art than science – a delicate operation, even if you know what you're doing. But yeah, you should go for it," she bluffed, "give it a try."

Aptat was inscrutable.

Naecia made one last push to make her point. "You'd trust me to tell you which valves to open and which to close? Because an open line in the wrong place would go through you and your carapace like a parallax beam through slarp butter. On second thought, I like that idea." She floated into her chamber and crossed her arms, prepared to go back down, but knowing she wouldn't have to.

Aptat looked on with obvious discomfort as Naecia smiled brightly from inside the suit.

"It's only a bit tight, but it's light," she said, stomping and flapping her arms. She flexed the suit's armored fingers into fists, which was awkward for her left hand. The suit had all its fingers, but she didn't, which left the middle digit sticking petulantly upright. "Well, that's a bit annoying." She pushed it down with her other hand, only to watch it spring up again. "Whatever."

"You won't have power augments," said Aptat.

"I can move fine. Why would I need augmented movement?"

"For fighting, fleeing, lifting," answered Aptat. "Try not to blow yourself up. I'll need that back to fight the Vortu after your plan fails."

Naecia answered Aptat's pessimism with a carefree shrug, even though she felt anything but indifferent. She wasn't about to let the stringhunter see her sweat. She kicked over to the control console. The armor was snug around her muscled arms and thighs, but it was otherwise comfortable and far less stiff than it looked. She would have killed for a suit so light and flexible in the pipe fields of Vask.

"How will you do it?" asked Aptat.

"I don't know yet. The pipes will tell me." Familiar now with the *Silent Child*'s menu, Naecia navigated quickly to the environmental tab, then to the sub menu with the liquids transport map. She cleared everything from the display, leaving behind only the piping schematic – a densely packed web of twisted metal that followed the rough shape of the ship.

She focused the schematic on the docking ring and the four attitudinal thrusters close by. All manner of valves studded each length of pipe, designed to maintain the delicate equilibrium of the near plasmatic vapor inside. The veins that fed the thrusters ran under the skin of the outer hull and beneath the parasitic ship docked above it. She selected each of the lines and brought up their equipment lists and service histories. "Ah. Uh-hmm." Looking up at the ceiling, she traced the lines somewhere in the guts of the ship overhead. "One, two, three," she said, counting out the imagined equipment. "That one."

"What are you doing?"

Naecia pointed to a spot. "I need access to the hull above deck three, at about this orientation. Show me the closest access point – do you have a tool pod?"

"On the third deck," said Aptat.

"Oh, before we go."

"What?"

"Free the others."

Aptat coughed like something had tickled their throat. "I already promised everyone their freedom if your plan works."

"Promises aren't worth much when you're the one sitting in a cell. You wouldn't understand."

"You'd be surprised."

"What guarantee do we have that you'll hold your end?" Naecia asked.

"You have my wo–"

"Don't say your word," she interjected. "When I go into that hull, I'll be imprisoned again – effectively your hostage. And you," she said, "will be mine. You release the others, but code the doors behind me. Your security will be ensured."

"Lock you in?"

"Oush and Izairis won't kill you while you have the code to get me out, but they will kill you if you refuse to free me."

"You assume a lot about the loyalty of others."

"I suppose if I'm wrong, we both die. What other choice do we have? I'm not going up there until you agree."

"Agreed."

Aptat summoned Oush and Izairis from below. Naecia explained the arrangement and they assented. Aptat was at their mercy until Naecia returned safely. In exchange, she would go into the hull and be locked inside with a code only Aptat knew.

Naecia followed the stringhunter to the third deck, which housed the living quarters and galley. The rooms were buttressed together and each had a door that opened onto the communal area. One was presumably Aptat's. Questions whirled over the other, but she dared not ask for fear of repeat strangulation.

Aptat unclipped a standard tool pod from the wall. "Obviously you'll not be able to use the powered components, but it has all the standard manual pieces."

Naecia took it, put her arms through the straps and tightened them, bringing the pod snug to her chest where tools could easily be accessed. "A magmafier would be nice."

"Oh, the suit has one," said Aptat, reaching over and tapping a small node just over Naecia's wrist joint. "It's useless to you, of course."

"Thanks," she answered sarcastically. "How do I get up there?"

Aptat indicated an access door at floor level across the galley. They kicked over and took handholds on the wall.

"When the helmet closes, you'll begin receiving life support."

"And how do I–"

"The tab below your chin," Aptat said. Then, tapping a slider on the collar, "Lock it here."

Naecia found the tab and chinned it, closing the helmet's four segments over her face, then locked it down by throat-slashing a slider across her neck. "How long do I have?" Her voice had taken on a reflective, metallic tone.

"It will keep you for an entire cygie, though I'm confident you'll slice yourself into pieces long before you have to worry about life support."

"You're very negative," she said.

"I'm a realist."

"I'm gonna go now and try to save us all."

"I'll lock you inside."

"You'll open it again when I finish?"

Aptat grinned. "Of course."

CHAPTER EIGHTEEN
THE INSTRUMENT MAKER

There was another joy to announce that happened to coincide with the Procession of the Moons. The Instrument Maker had been granted permission by the High Imperial Council of Knowers and Sayers to reproduce. The good news had spread quickly, with the space outside of her small shop piling up with notes of well-wishes and gifts. Tidy, hand-carved boxes, candles, perfumed scarves, dyhydranthium bulbs, homemade sweets, and exotic selections of rare teas and incense.

The townspeople hoped the blessing of reproduction bestowed upon the Instrument Maker might mean a stripling or two with even half of her talent who might grow up to build ukelaklavas and arrange the music which could only be played upon them. They might then be graced by at least some remnant of the numinous sound the Instrument Maker had produced during her lifetime. For now, though, they were just delighted to see what sound this year's Procession would bring.

She shared in their joy, more so over the simple prospect of becoming a mother than the thought that any of her children might follow in her footsteps. She hoped for that, of course, but it was not the reason she had sought leave of the High Imperial Council to spawn. She'd known that she wanted to raise children longer than she'd known she wanted to build ukelaklavas, which was saying something.

Nevertheless, there was a harmonious intersection that the bearing of children would have with her craft. Only children could play the ukelaklava. Its size, delicate construction, and pitch requirements made it wholly unsuitable for a fully grown Quileg. An adult could try; they could pluck the notes and bend the tonal arm, but it would sound blunted and clunky, whereas in the hands of a well-practiced child, it shouted to the heavens. And maybe one day, hers too would lift the instrument and call down the sky with a chord.

CHAPTER NINETEEN

All of my senses were devoted to the thing before me. I did not breathe – rather, I hovered in the space between the last breath and the possibility that I would never take another; the inflection point every human being pushes through twenty thousand times a day, until the one time they inevitably don't. Would this be the last breath I took? I was so rapt by the thing that I didn't dwell on it. If I died now, so be it. All that mattered was the monster.

Patton – remarkably – was still screaming.

My mind returned to me slowly like a thaw. I exhaled.

The screaming strained to a wheeze as Patton used up the remaining oxygen in his lungs. I took the moment to pat him on the shoulder and offer reassurance. "It's not going to hurt us, Patton. It kept us alive."

"Why did it keep me alive, Ben?"

I didn't have an answer for that.

The thing swelled up from a sea of itself, a great anvil-headed leviathan breeching to observe the world beyond the surface. It was colossal. The size of a battleship. Dark, almost black. No, wait, not exactly. Subtle waves of color coursed across its surface like an octopus in deep purples and blues. Eyeless, it watched us as we watched it. It lived as one, and yet was made of discrete parts, which also seemed alive; each moving independently of the whole while keeping its place in it – like cells. They were armored and scale-like, but heterogenous in shape, size, and motility. It was an individual and a colony – both *it* and *they* at once.[78]

Then it collapsed. Innumerable pieces poured to the ground like sand and scattered. They spread out around the newly transformed voidscull enclosure, rippling and frenetic; forming and dispersing, then congealing again. A new shape emerged, encircling us, but at a distance this time. It coalesced rapidly – near instantly – into a sculptural ring, studded with small projections. The speed at which these pieces moved was... I want to say, *impossible*. I spun around, trying to take it all in. It was huge, hundreds of feet in diameter. Fin-like structures erupted upward from the body of the ring, almost like spikes on a crown, their tips changing from black to violet, to hot pink. Pulsing. The fins tilted slowly inward toward the center of the ring, their points angling slowly down, down, toward our enclosure.

Cold overwhelmed me. Existential cold; the chill of death. I couldn't feel my hands. And I couldn't look away.

Sweat streamed down from my armpits. The sharpened fins continued their downward tilt. Was this some great device, the Scythin's version of the neural dredge, that would hollow my brain and dissect it for its secrets? Anticipation built as the points took aim. A trapped animal, I panicked, spinning in circles, making strained pleas for mercy that froze at my lips. My core plummeted to ice. The display was a trespass, a finger that reached into the weft of my soul to pluck an uncanny chord.

My heart froze solid, halting my breath, and everything around me –

---

78 Pyrosomes are large underwater colonies of tiny invertebrates known as zooids that join together to form large, shapeshifting blobs.

Patton, the enclosure, the megastructure, the great living sculpture – were obliterated by a burst of light. There was nothing but cold then, and a whiteness that was just as much nothingness as the purest black. Within this nothingness an image flashed. A great, devouring mouth that filled my heart with awe. I was being shown something I recognized but could hardly describe. A thing that transcended existence; a glimpse of... *perfection*.

I was seated against the wall when my vision returned to a very close view of Patton's face. "I thought you shorted out, man." He went in for a hug. I let him. "What was that?"

I was exhausted. My breath came short. But I knew the answer. I looked him in the eyes. "The Bloom of God," I said.

He looked at me quizzically. "The what?"

My mind was frazzled. "Uh," I said, "You know, from the nursery song, *Sing a song of six pence, pocket full of rye?*"

"There's nothing about a bloom of god in that song, Ben."

"Sure there is," I said, trying to place the lyrics. "The pie opens and then it goes on that...*the birds began to sing*...uh... *wasn't that a dainty dish...*" my voice trailed off. I couldn't find it.

The ring was still there outside the enclosure, the fins ascending slowly back to their original, skyward positions. The bright colors at their apices darkened to indigo and then slate. I must have only been out for a millisecond, but it was long enough. I never wanted to feel that again. Perhaps Patton was right – maybe I had shorted out, suffered some kind of trauma-induced syncope. I wrapped my arms around my chest to recover from the penetrating cold, only to realize that I was perfectly warm.

The ring reverberated and fell apart. The mass moved again, herdlike, but... coordinated, as with birds in murmuration.[79]

---

79 Coordinated flocking activity wherein birds, most famously, starlings, take on shapes in the sky. In 1986 Craig Reynolds developed a

There was an unavoidable *presence* when the group was assembled, that went beyond the stunning visual display. A sentient swarm. Mass consciousness. Communion.

Tendrils formed of smaller, corpuscular units – *I can't help but think of them as boids now* – reached out from the swirling whole and slithered toward our enclosure. Individual cells ranging in size from grapefruit to suitcase circulated in and around these curious extensions, filling spaces vacated by others that were absorbed back into the swarm.

Upon reaching the outer walls, the tendrils moved curiously, changing the vantage of their inspection while still shifting, morphing. Colors in every hue pulsed up from the gentle tips. These creatures had some sort of chromatophore analog that allowed them to change color almost as quickly as they altered their shape. Unsure how to respond, I approached the clear membrane and pressed my hand to it – a gesture of peace and kindness as one does in a movie. I held it there nervously, allowing a tendril to tenderly consider it. Patton did the same and was ignored.

This massive creature exuded tremendous power, and was surely able to – if it wished – crush our enclosure, and us inside, with the slightest of gestures. I was scared, but told myself that if it wanted us dead, it wouldn't have sprung for custom bondage suits with feeding tubes and butt plumbing.

The tentacle retreated from the glass, turned bright green, and stared. It didn't have eyes exactly, but you *know* when you're being stared at. Then all at once, the entire swarm ceased its performance and simply fell apart. The uncountable boids skittered across the floor and into piles that dotted the massive expanse before us. Then all at once, the piles rose from the ground, congealing into large, humanoid individuals

---

program that simulated the flocking behavior of birds called "Boids", using computer generated "bird-oid objects" shortened to "boid." Also, a shot at New Yorker pronunciation of the key word.

– thousands of them – that then strode into the strange mist at the periphery of the enormous rotunda.

All but one.

It stood patiently as boids finalized their positions in its body. The assembled creature was a biped. Big, powerful. The outer boids formed layers of darkly armored plates. The way it was put together suggested that it could take any form it wanted, so diverse and varied were its building blocks. It *was* just like building blocks, actually, only sleeker and spacier. And alive. Perhaps its present configuration was just a mimic. A costume.

It stalked forward.

Patton backed smartly away from the membrane. "They're gonna kill me as soon as they realize I'm not you. Tell him I'm your emotional support animal."

The thing stopped just outside the wall and leaned in toward my face on the other side. Its broad, flattened head sat featurelessly atop neckless shoulders. The boids were integrated like puzzle pieces, with some variation in hue between them from black to dark grey. The outer edges on some boids were worn and ashy – this, I assumed was their default coloration. Breaking all of it up was a prong of shining, unmarred metal embedded in the center of its chest.

Seams ran smoothly across every surface where the boids met, and those on the "face" began to shift and move, opening and closing. Small moments of color burst outward wherever they moved, fading quickly. A slit pulled across the top of its face and from it came the lowest note I have ever heard.[80] Then four smaller holes opened just below the first, playing a chord in the slightly higher register of a woodwind instrument, almost as if it was tuning itself. It bled air slowly through these

---

80 Humpback whales sing songs to each other in frequencies often too low for any human to hear, which is good because they rarely shut up, singing for up to twenty-three hours in one go.

holes, and I heard the sound of a voice – *my* voice – mimicked perfectly inside the breathy whisper.

"Is it talking to you?" asked Patton.

"Yes."

"What's it saying?"

I watched different-shaped channels and holes form and fade through several cycles, listening to the faraway voice that traveled over the wind. Then it stopped. Patton asked again. I turned to him and answered.

"It says 'welcome back'."

CHAPTER TWENTY

Naecia unfolded the locking mechanism on the access hatch to the hull space. Taking hold of the handle, she used her weight to yank it down and break the seal. Atmosphere from the third deck blasted by her and she quickly slipped inside. Aptat closed the hatch and coded it shut.

It was like being inside a massive mechanical body, stuffed with alloyed veins and arteries carrying the *Silent Child*'s vital fluids, keeping it alive. The hull space followed the contours of the ship's middle section, which was roughly dome shaped. The equipment she had to access was at the apex of this dome and just beyond toward the opposite side. She pulled herself along by the hands. The hardest part about working in zero gravity was remembering to hold on and not to push off anything too forcefully, lest she wind up helplessly suspended and unable to get back down. She started up the hull's arc, crawling over layers of pipes and conduit. These were systems she knew and understood, and familiarity brought comfort. The tool pod strapped to her chest shifted back and forth as she went, and she checked it with a hand as one might a child in swaddling.

Near the hull's crown she shuffled sideways to where the dorsal thrusters were mounted in the outer shell, then traced the supply lines back from each of those to the docking ring.

"How are you progressing?" asked Aptat through the suit's com.

"I'm below the dock now."

An airlock ran between the dock on the outside of the *Child* and the inner hull, creating enough space for her to stand. She weaved in between the structural supports below the dock to the other side of the airlock passage, where the critical steam piping continued down to the fore side of the ship. Here, the hull space opened dramatically to allow for the massive power generators that supplied the forward-mounted dilaceration cannons.

Naecia located the run of pipe that she'd keyed on from the schematic. She withdrew a simple spanner from the tool pod and moved along.

A shift in momentum yanked her suddenly aft, but she managed to wedge a forearm between pipes to keep from shooting back down the slope of the inner hull. Acceleration gravity.

"Aptat?"

"I'm here. Are you hurt?"

"Not yet. What happened?"

"They've fired our engines. Wondering if we did something to tip them off. Is it looking workable?"

"When do they get here?"

"Soon."

"How soon?"

"You need to hurry."

Great. The intercept was imminent.

She scaled down the pipe rack, trying to stay focused on the task and ignore the approaching threat. "This will go in three steps," she said. "First, I'm going to close the upstream supply to the four thrusters, bottle-necking the pressure. Then I'll empty the packing gland on the key downstream valve below the thruster that I want to destroy. I'll return to the upstream shut-off valve and open it back up. All of that pressure will overwhelm the downstream valve below the thruster. Either the whole thing will blow or it will vent through the gland on top. If I'm not melted, I'll crawl back down to the conjunction of decks two and three and manually adjust the bypass valve there so the entire system doesn't bleed out into space. If you do regain control of the ship, remember that you won't have upward pitch. Got it?"

"No upward pitch means no downward pitch either. If I fire the ventral thrusters we'll somersault forever."

"Yeah, which is why I'll try to get back and lock down the sabotaged valve once the job is done, so you'll get three of the four back."

The added acceleration made everything more difficult. She tugged herself to the ship's fore, up to the main shut-off valve for the bank of thrusters, and unfolded the lever that controlled the aperture of the big gate valve.

"Quickly, Naecia."

It was larger than she was. She slid the lever out from the flange assembly and wrenched it downward. It slammed all the way open and her hands slipped off. She'd overestimated how difficult it would be. Having lost her hold, she tumbled back over the hull's arc, and right past the valve she needed to sabotage. She ping-ponged between pipes and equipment, finally crashing into the bulkhead back down at the second level with a force that would have killed her had she not been in Aptat's indestructible suit. It still hurt, though. A lot.

"Is it done?"

Naecia groaned. "Uh… no."

"Are you injured?"

"I lost my grip. I'll be okay. But…" she winced, her chest tightening. "I need to go back up and open the packing gland on the thruster valve."

She repeated the trek up the hull's backbone, unable to take a full breath for the pain in her ribs. She reached the valve, stuck the spanner through an eyehole at the top and spun it round. Dodging a small jet of leftover steam as the packing gland came loose, she wheeled the spanner until the gland popped all of the way out, removed the few metallic rings inside, and reassembled the valve. She quickly scuttled by, then slid back down toward the big shutoff valve. "How much time to do we have?"

"Not much, Naecia. I have visual on their deceleration burn. If you can get rid of that sortie, now would be the time."

"Yeah. Out." She half wondered if Aptat would simply leave her in the hull if she succeeded in blowing the sortie. Probably not, now that she occupied their prized armor. She was practically wearing a second hostage. She ducked under the lever so it sat atop her shoulder. "Ready?"

"They're here. Do it."

She burst upward, opening the full flow of critical steam downstream. Even lacking instruments, she sensed the pressures skyrocketing. The sabotaged valve lasted barely a moment before blowing. The hull space blinked and the shock hurled her backward through the works. She caught a support and held on, then flipped violently to the other side as the ship decelerated.

"Naecia, check in."

"I'm here," she said. "The valve blew. Pretty sure the sortie is gone."

"It took the dock and the top half of the hull with it."

"Opportunity cost," she responded. "Do you have control of the ship?"

"Yes, but I need that steam back on."

"I'm making my way to the cut-off now." Steam was venting through the blown line causing the *Child* to flip. She crawled hand over hand. "Where are the Vortu?"

"Just above us. Hurry."

The thruster valve had blown clean off, leaving an open pipe elbow aimed straight up to where the sortie and the dock had once been, now erupting into the void. She scrambled to the cut-off, swung out the control lever and tried to pull it down. With no gravity, she had no weight to counterbalance her effort. Thinking quick, she flipped upside-down, bracing her feet on the inner surface of the outer hull. She reached overhead, took hold of the lever, and pushed it slowly down until the plume cut out.

Something thumped the hull just under her feet.

CHAPTER TWENTY-ONE

"*'Welcome back'?* What does that mean, Ben?"

The humanoid thing shifted its "head" as a wave of openings presented upon the "face". More whispers. I had to turn an ear to the sound. It was like trying to hear someone calling over the wind from across a field. Only, I was the one doing the calling. Cree-py.

"What now?" asked Patton.

I cleared my throat. "It just keeps saying the same thing over and over," I answered. "'Save us.'"

"From what?"

"No idea. Okay," I said, addressing the monster, "I want to save you. How do I do that?" The creature stood motionless. I scrambled to come up with something that might invite some information in return. "If you could—"

It turned away.

"I'll help you!" I broke into a fit of coughing. I turned to Patton. "I don't know what's going on. They want me to save them and I don't have any clue how I'm supposed to do that."

He grimaced and shook his head. "They're gonna probe it out of you, man."

"I hope not." It went without saying that in an alien situation we'd always naturally assumed it would be him getting probed.

Our enclosure was a monolith in the center of the giant

rotunda. Light came from above somewhere, illuminating the area that immediately surrounded it, but not all the way to the perimeter of the colossal space. The farthest walls were the color of twilight, against which the ever-present mist was tucked. I pressed my face to the membrane again.

Tiny vortices spun out from the churning fog. Occasionally the veil broke and a cycle of creation and dissolution presented itself between burps of dense vapor. Tumbling boids assumed form and shape, with some appearing in random configurations and others as fully assembled biped individuals. Then, as if linked by some internal sense of timing, the behemoth congealed from the masses, plowing through cloud like a rolling black wave. At one moment powerful and coursing, the next spilling apart and submerging.

I palmed my way around our enclosure, watching this process repeat itself again and again. The creature boiled through the dusky light while cycling through other-worldly color schemes, trying on new forms and discarding them just as quickly. Then it stopped, and the thick vapor rotated away its inertia.

I'd lost track of how long I'd been watching. The muscles in my legs burnt. I needed to eat. I needed to go number two.

A new figure approached from the mist. This one was smaller than the earlier individual, but still considerably taller than me. It might have been the same one for all I knew, just reconfigured, though that wasn't the vibe I was getting. It even walked differently from the first. The way the boids fit together gave it unique contours and features, which seemed to confer a sense of individuality. It also had the metal prong thing embedded in its thorax region, but the shape was different. A horizontal gap opened along the bottom of its head and it spoke, my voice, again, carried on the wind.

Save us, it said.

I shrugged. "Look–"

Then, with the volume and force of a locomotive's horn, it

roared, sending me cowering to the ground. When it stopped, I opened my eyes and gingerly removed my palms from my ears. A new message came then, barely audible, now that my attention was total. *Gone is the Bloom of God.*

"Okay… How do you get it back?"

Like a breeze that sifts through reeds, the creature answered, *Find the Chime, the Note of Jecca.*

I put my hands out beseechingly, stood slowly, spoke quietly, "I will do everything I can to help you find what you are looking for." I glanced to Patton, who cradled Pickles. "But… we really have to go to the bathroom. We need to eat and drink. Maybe if we had some food, I'd be able to think more clearly. Do you guys do that? Eat and drink?" I mouthed my words, over-enunciating them like my mom when she tells her housekeepers to *"por favor no necessario dust the Precious Moments figurines."*

Seams on either side of the creature's shovel-like head pulled apart, creating a pair of almond-shaped openings. *Eyes* – or more accurately, eye analogs. I had no way of telling if they served a purpose beyond providing me with a more familiar interface with which to communicate. It "looked" down at me, and then back toward a phalanx of individuals who had coalesced and now loomed in the haze.

A section of the membrane around us melted, creating an opening. I backed away. Patton sat straight down on his butt tube.

The figure stomped heavily into our space and knelt, then reached for my umbilicals, lifting them with a finger-thing. It tapped the floor. Two small holes opened from which pairs of black tubing flopped out beside my feet.

Eyes – the only label that came to mind for them – gestured for me to connect the ends.

What were they, feeding tubes, maybe? "Which one is which? Are they food or water or… or–" Eyes brushed me aside, then pointed to the longest tube at my stomach and presented the rightmost floor tube, then mimed pushing them together. Next, they directed a thick finger toward my behind, picked up the left floor tube and pointed to a glyph on the floor. I didn't understand it, but guessed it was Scythin for *shitter*.

They thrust the left tube closer and pointed at my ass again.

"I got it, I got it," I said, trying to keep my eye on the tube since it was inconveniently identical to the first. "Right goes with right, left goes with ass. Got that, Patton?" God forbid we crossed the tubes.

Eyes dropped the tube, and then turned to go.

"Hey!" I said, grasping at the bundle of smaller tubes protruding from my belly button. "What are these for?"

A whisper came as Eyes left the enclosure for the mists.

"What'd they say?" asked Patton.

"Ugh," I groaned. "'Research'."

I urgently needed to go. I snatched up the left tube, praying I'd correctly understood the Scythin, and slipped it over the anal chute. Then, in the penultimate moment, I held back, worried on its narrow diameter and ability to accept what I had on offer. Though the prospect of catastrophic equipment failure loomed, I could fight no longer. I took the ultimate leap of faith and relaxed.

Relief came like a cool breeze and I flopped onto my side, eyes glazing as I looked toward the fog from where alien legions watched me crap into a hose.

"It works?" asked Patton, shuffling along the floor and grabbing the second set of tubes.

I moaned pleasurably. When I finished, I'm pretty sure the tube ran through a bidet protocol.

Business complete and awash in nature's afterglow, I snatched up the rightmost tube, thinking it had to be food, and pressed it onto my belly hose.

Well, it was certainly something.

It was heroin – no – it was heroin cut with fireworks and soaked in gasoline.

I was transported somewhere else. Soaring over infinite fields of culinary pleasures like the God of Cakes. I tasted – and *felt* – every flavor I knew – and many I didn't, in a strange duality of experience. Tastes were perceived all at once, and individually. There were flavors I didn't understand, indescribable except by color – and even by *emotion*. Lime green and citrus orange chroma pinged my taste buds as delicious, joyous, penetrating sours, followed by the semi-sweet melancholy of robin's egg blue, curious sugared avocado purple, and ecstasy-flavored cheesecake-filling pink. There was a distinctly sexual pleasure to the experience that cycled tantrically through energetic peaks and cooling lulls. For hours or minutes, I couldn't say.[81]

Filled to bursting, I was treated to soothing gulps of water.

Somewhere Patton moaned. Maybe he'd found his way onto the food tube... or the poop tube. They were both great.

---

81 Bepenised female cave bugs of the genus *Neotrogla* routinely have sex for seventy hours straight.

CHAPTER TWENTY-TWO

The ship decelerated and Aptat's voice came through the com. "I've reset security parameters. They won't be able to get into the systems again. Dilaceration cannons are charging."

Naecia had maneuvered behind a screen of pipes where they converged at the bulkhead. "Aptat, run a scan. They're on the hull."

"Impossible! You blew the dock!"

"Run the scan!" she screamed, already knowing what it would show. "They can come through the breach."

Aptat cursed through the com. "Six of them. Sneaky shits. They must have debarked the *Glaive* while it was back-burning. Hold tight, I'll spin them off."

The inner hull lit with light beams.

"Too late."

"What do you mean?" asked Aptat.

"They're inside," she whispered, even though the hull space was in vacuum and no one would hear her. "Must have blown a bigger hole than I thought."

"Do they know you're there?" said Aptat.

"Not yet, but they will soon enough." The lights spread out.

"Good."

"Good?" she asked, shocked.

"You mentioned a com implant," said Aptat. "What is it?"

"Pangemic standard local receiver, the minimum."

"Can you send a chirp?"

"Vortu will hear it," said Naecia.

"I have to be able to access your com if I'm going to occupy the carapace."

"What are you talking about?"

"The suit's vault has a calibration link that I use to adjust its tolerances. I am going to broadcast myself to your com and see if the suit responds."

"I don't need anyone else in my head."

"I won't be in your mind. I'll only be using your com to transmit my neural signature. I have to be *inside* the carapace for it to have any augmented functionality."

"You're going to broadcast your brain waves from inside my brain in order to talk to your suit."

"Exactly!"

"Great."

"Chirp to pair the systems, Naecia."

"But the Vortu."

"This will give us weapons."

"Fine." She bit lightly down on the inside of each cheek simultaneously, firing a single chirp from the com hub sitting on the surface of her auditory cortex.

The light beams atop the hull immediately swung in her direction.

"They heard it, Aptat," she said, trying to crawl around the perimeter to put some distance between them.

"I'm in," said Aptat.

The voice was now coming from inside her brain instead of the helmet. *Yay.*

"I'm playing hide and seek," said Naecia. "What can you do?"

"I've got your location and the visor's visual feed. Do you have power augment?"

She hadn't noticed any difference, but she also hadn't done

anything that had necessitated exertion in the last few seconds. "Hold on." She reached over to a bit of redundant pipe bracket and snapped it like a stick of jha spice. "Wow, okay. Augments work."

"That's good. Vortu don't have power armor."

Naecia had rounded the fore side of the *Silent Child* along the deck line. The lights were following. "They're coming up, Aptat."

"You're faster than they are now, and you know the schematics. Use those advantages to evade them. I'm trying to get the melee limb to talk to me."

Naecia rounded the front of the craft, trusting the armor to help her jump obstacles and scale larger equipment. She still had to work to move, but it was like having another person contributing their strength to hers, halving her effort. She glanced up the arc. Predictably, the Vortu had split from each other, figuring to pinch her from the sides and neutralizing her speed advantage. It would only hasten her capture now. "You should hurry up, I'm out of space to move." She turned up the hull between the two groups closing in from either side. Sparks erupted all around as she went. "They're shooting."

"I can see. The carapace will protect you from most of that."

Just as Aptat said it, an impact pushed her flat to the inner hull. A strike of pain radiated from her back.

"See?" said Aptat. "Direct hit. You're fine. Keep going."

Naecia grunted. "They're gaining."

"Deploying melee."

A flame erupted from the node at her wrist, spraying fire into a compressor housing that reflected back into her facemask. "That's the magmafier!" she yelled.

"Apologies. I'm having difficulty translating commands through your antiquated hardware."

Naecia crawled ahead. She still had the tool pod, maybe she could bludgeon them with a spanner.

A pair of Vortu stood at the crest of the inner hull, which meant four coming up behind. They fired a burst as soon as she darted from cover, taking several shots to the ribs. The force knocked her sideways, but the armor adjusted to help her regain control, and she was off just as quickly, leaping into a tangle of equipment before they had a chance to fire again. She skipped through the web of conduit and structural skeleton, digging into the tool pod for something she might use. Her hands touched upon a thick handle. A long, heavy, radial pipe cutter.

"ETA on that melee thing?" The magmafier node fired again. "Stop that!"

The flame signaled her position and another barrage lit through the hull.

"Are you trying to get me killed?"

"In almost any other context, yes, I would be. Your com is glitchy."

Keeping to the shadows and hoping Aptat could hold the magmafier in check, she rounded quickly on the pair at the apex of the arc. Placing herself between the remains of the air lock and a capacitor for one of the dilaceration cannons, she eased up behind them. Directly above was a field of stars where the outer hull had once been. Flame erupted again from the magmafier. She thrust herself at the pair and swiped at them with the plume of fire. The first one dove away from the flames and she brought down the pipe cutter with double her regular strength upon the second, crushing the Vortu's helmet and head inside. She reoriented the flames on the first Vortu just in time for the magmafier to go cold. "Aptat!" she screamed as the Vortu unleashed a close-range volley.

The shot sent her spinning through the vacuum. "Fffffuuuuuuuuu–" she slammed into a girding, righted herself, and pushed off just as another round of fire pierced the outer hull. A shot to the hip sent her into a corkscrew. The armor had protected her from being holed but that was about it. The many impacts had taken their toll. She felt like she'd been pulped.

"I have the melee limb, Naecia. Get me visual."

But she was in free float now, having only barely gotten herself away from the last round of fire. And she was corkscrewing again. "I–" her breath was short.

"I cannot help you unless I can orient the limb to the target!" Aptat cried from inside her brain. "Naecia!"

There was nothing she could do on the drift. No way to orient herself until she made contact with something to grab or push. The Vortu had figured out she was defenseless and were climbing up the inner hull as she tried and missed getting a hold. Another volley came at her from below, striking her feet and ankles, imparting horizontal spin. The engineer in her wondered exactly what the suit was made of. The rest of her was trying not to lose consciousness from spin on double axes.

She tried to focus on one point each time she came around to see it, so as not to pass out. "Aptat," she groaned, lightheaded. "Can you fire the magmafier on my mark?"

"Yes, I can do that. I have the correct triggers set now."

The remaining Vortu had closed and were waiting for her to complete her trip across the open space. Naecia counted out the rotations to get the timing down, accounting for the delay between herself and Aptat. "I need two separate bursts on *two* and then *one*, got it?"

"Got it."

Naecia angled her arm with the magmafier node to the side, opposite the direction of her current spin. "Six, five, four, three, TWO!"

The node fired a short burst, immediately halting the horizontal rotation. "ONE!" she yelled, bending her arm next to her body as it flared the second time, stopping the roll and bringing her face-to-face with the hijackers. They reached for her.

The limb fired and the Vortu went limp. One second, they were on the cusp of capturing her, and the next they were dead, their blood suffusing the hull space in shining, yellow-black spheres. Naecia's breath hitched in her throat.

"Naecia?"

The voice was more background noise as she felt the full weight of her exhaustion. Aptat called through again. She answered this time. "I'm here," she said, still drifting. "I'm here."

She settled eventually on the smooth arc of the inner hull and decided to lay there and breathe for a bit. Or forever.

CHAPTER TWENTY-THREE

My dreams were as vivid as the meal I'd just transfused – and certainly a consequence of it. In them were every imaginable pleasure and feeling. From flying on a unicorn, to *being* a unicorn, to doing things unicorns do to each other when one unicorn surprises the other by doing the dishes. Some sensations I recognized, some were fully alien, some hybrid. I sensed in these dreams not just my own happiness, but the shared joy of those around me, overwhelming and enveloping me in their rapture.

I came to and righted myself against the chorionic wall of the enclosure. Dead to the world, Patton wore a contented grin. With him still out, I figured I'd just hook up the tube and have breakfast.

Stomach empty and taste buds aching, I searched for the tubes in the floor, trying to coax them out from their compartment. I cleared my throat, filled my chest, and – feeling imbued with unique powers ordained by the tube food – pounded the floor with both my fists.

No tube.

"Patton, wake up."

My beard itched. Wait. *I have a beard?*

I hadn't shaved in the time since our kidnapping and so already had a rugged sort of cattle rancher look going, but this was down to my clavicles. Six inches of new beard in one night? *What the hell was in that shit?*

"Patton!" I yelled. There was a big yellow tuft below his chin. A neckbeard. He looked like a Himalayan marmot. "Wake up!"

Patton came to and laughed when he saw me. I raised my eyebrows expectantly and waited for him to check himself. "Ah!" he screeched. "But we weren't asleep for long, right?"

I checked my Timex, which was, miraculously, still on my wrist. "Yeah. Like a solid ten hours."

We both looked to our belly tubes. It had to be the narco-food.

I stunk. We stunk. Hungry again, thirsty, disgusting. I could feel patches of enflamed skin developing in my armpits and the top of my crack but couldn't access them for scratching. *Five stars for food, no stars for accommodations. Two-point-five stars overall. Would not recommend.*

A big section of the wall melted away, and there was Eyes standing on the other side of it. Different shaped holes opened across their face. Ripples of color passed over their visage. *Come,* they whispered in my own voice.

I stood up, wobbly. My stomach cramped. "Can you give us some more to eat first?" I asked.

Come.

I stepped from the enclosure and the membrane drew quickly closed behind me before I could offer Patton a parting salutation.

I followed Eyes across the huge expanse of floor toward the rotunda's distant perimeter. Shuffling closely behind my escort, the divisions between the boid units that made their body were better discerned. Most remained in place, but sometimes moved independently of the larger being. They were generally dark in color, with lighter, mottled areas near the edges. Displays of color seemed to come at random and with no apparent stimulus. An expanding circle of indigo across their back. A stripe of magenta down an arm from the shoulder.

"So, uh, where are we headed?" I asked lightly.

No answer.

The perimeter of the room was considerably farther than I'd estimated from inside the enclosure. We traveled for several minutes before reaching the misty boundary. I looked back toward the center of the vast room to the distant nodule of membrane that housed Patton. From where I was it looked like a curled up dead leaf made of glass, thin enough to see the veins. Or a chrysalis.

The mist parted to allow us through. I could hear boids skittering and Scythin moving just beyond my view. Here and there, the dark edges of their bodies emerged only to disappear a second later.

We came out the other side at a convergence between the big center rotunda and a series of connected spherical chambers that ringed it. These rooms were large and empty, with only the curving walls having any distinctive character. As with the rest of the ship they were strangely organic. Long black fibers like those that had secured me and Patton to the walls of the voidscull were the default construction material. In some places they provided structure. In others, they assumed darkly beautiful patterns and macabre filigree.

Eyes turned into the fourth or fifth sphere chamber and led me down a labyrinthine series of passages. My feet were freezing. My stomach grumbled. My hands shook. All I could think about was the tube food. I *craved* it. "How about some more food, eh?"

Eyes gave me a look. I think.

We stopped outside of a large door, scrawled with all sorts of Scythin ornamentation. Eyes pressed their hand to it and fibers of material slithered over the back, swaddling it in glossy black.

"What is this?" I asked.

The door began to come apart and Eyes spoke the answer. *Jecca's room.*

CHAPTER TWENTY-FOUR

Naecia rested on the inner hull. She'd burned through her oxygen stores like an unchecked flare and was still undergoing the dual effort of both catching her breath and processing what had just happened.

It wasn't until perhaps the ninth or tenth time that Aptat com'd her that she even realized she was being hailed. "– seriously you need to respond," they said. "I held up my end and your friends are getting antsy."

"Hello?" she croaked.

"Oh, there you are," said Aptat. "Hear that, guys? She's fine."

"Are there any more Vortu?" she asked.

"No. Looks like this was a two-ship job. Once you get down here, I'll throw on the suit and run over to the *Terror's Glaive* parked nearby. See if there's anything I can… borrow."

Naecia grunted.

Aptat asked, "Are you injured?"

"It feels like every bone in my body is broken."

Aptat chuckled some. "That's the carapace. It's indestructible, but it'll make you feel it. Can you bring yourself down?"

"I think so," she groaned.

"Good because we don't have any more suits. I'll stay connected so you have augmented power. I've already coded the hull portal open. All you have to do is get there and let yourself out. Somehow you burnt through most of the air supply. So, take your time, but also speed up so you don't suffocate."

"Have to bypass the open valve."

"Make it quick."

Naecia really did feel like her bones had been pounded to dust, while every muscle was drawn and sore. Gravity had been restored to the ship and she managed the slow slog up to the blown valve where she closed its dedicated supply line, then slid down to the cut-off for the bank of thrusters and reopened it. Job complete, she rounded the circumference of the deck, trying her best to dodge floating orbs of Vortu ichor. By the time she reached the bulkhead at the deck junction, she was well oiled in it. Not her problem. Maybe the suit's storage vault had a steam cleaner.

She reached the portal, drew down the lever, and with some measure of surprise, found it unlocked as Aptat had promised. Quickly she opened it and pushed through the rush of atmosphere, then closed it.

"Move along." The voice was coming from the suit's com again. Aptat had graciously abandoned her implant.

"On my way," she said. Naecia stood where she was and thought. If only she could control the suit. She'd kill Aptat and take control of the ship. Retrieve her mother and Aeshua from Drev, then run as far away from the Dasma Arm as possible; maybe far enough away by the time Earth man found the Chime for the Scythin. It was a nice fantasy. There would be no escape if the Chime was recovered.

"Hang on," said Aptat. "The *Terror's Glaive* is firing up."

"What?"

"Seems the Vortu left someone behind just in case. I'm guessing they've gathered that their boarding party was neutralized. Move quickly."

Naecia took the lift down to the second deck where she

rushed out. The ship lurched. Aptat was strapped in at the ship's console. "Find somewhere to secure yourself!"

The others had retreated into their chambers. Naecia rushed into her own and braced against the glass.

The ship came around and the holographic display showed the *Terror's Glaive* pouring headlong. The *Silent Child* was fleeing, backward. "You can't outrun them with the fore thrusters!" Naecia exclaimed.

"Yes, Captain," chided Aptat.

The cruiser fired and the *Child* took a direct hit. Naecia cried into the helmet's com, "What are you doing?"

"Way-ting," sang the stringhunter.

"For what?" she screamed.

Oush called out, "Those are flay guns!"

The Vortu fired again and the ship took damage. Aptat spun in their chair, back to the display. Smug expression on their face.

"What?" asked Naecia, confused.

Then the *Glaive* was in pieces, deader than dust. In the fraction of a moment, it went from being whole to sliced like birthday bread. The dilaceration cannon had fired its nine planar lasers, dividing the ship into ten equal parts, which now quietly followed the *Silent Child*.

Naecia drew the helmet latch across her neck and chinned the inner tab, opening the helmet into quarters. She met Aptat's gaze.

"Nine cannons leave no doubt," sighed the stringhunter.

Naecia breathed out a sigh as well. The relief felt contagious.

"We'll visit each of the pieces so any salvageable bits can be collected," said Aptat. "Afterward, we can take the *Child* to the scavenger's swap meet on Dzilugra. Since I can no longer sell you to anyone, I'll need the guush."

"You'll split it with us," Oush interjected, emerging from his chamber.

"Of course," said Aptat. "We will split the proceeds evenly and get you each on your way. Agreed?"

"No!" said Naecia. "What are you all talking about? We have to go after the Earth man. If he helps the Scythin find the Chime, there won't be anyone to sell salvage to. And there won't be any of us left to sell it." Oush and Izairis drooped noticeably. They'd also come from the *Knell*, so they understood. "I would love to get rich on Vortu salvage. I haven't seen my family in years. But we have to get to the Chime before the Scythin do."

"Need I remind you that the Scythin already *have* the Earth man?" said Aptat. "If indeed the Chime is designed to force dimensional contact and galaxy-wide destruction as you say, then the most prudent course of action is to *loot that ship*," they pointed to the image of the carved-up cruiser floating in space, "and flee the Dasma Arm as quickly as possible."

Izairis nodded. Oush raised a golden eyebrow.

Naecia was disgusted. They were flirting with extinction. "You guys were on the *Knell*. How can you even consider doing anything but going after the Earth man?"

"Well," said Aptat, wryly, "you posit trying to chase down the Scythin and re-abduct Ben in order to kill him, after first, I presume, chemically wiping his brain. That seems, ahem, far-fetched. I think there is a much more direct answer to our conundrum; a way to ensure our escape from whatever void is wrought by the Chime." A quick upward gesture and the floor began moving. "You build me a cheat drive."

"That is mine," she snarled as the prototype ascended. "You stole that from me."

"I feel more like it was abandoned. Salvage, if you will." They grinned.

Naecia's voice shook. "I was abducted."

"Nevertheless, you weren't coming back for it. And you know what they say? Possession is nine-tenths of the law." A chuckle. "And I guess out here, in the absence of law, it's more like ten-tenths."

The drive was her life's work. "*I* went into the hull space. *I* destroyed the sortie. *I* saved this ship. You owe me."

"You saved yourself too; don't forget that. And now seems a good time to ask: what is this fantasy ledger to which everyone keeps referring where people are owed favors for taking actions no one asked them to take? The Earth man did the same thing and I humored him. I'm done playing these games of credit earned for selfish acts. I owe you nothing."

Now it was clear. Naecia had been playing fair in a game where fairness was irrelevant. She glared at Aptat, sized them up. The stringhunter was strong, but weaponless. And it was Naecia who wore the protective carapace now – even if it lacked its lethal functionality. She'd never have this advantage again. She reached into the toolkit, still affixed to her chest, and withdrew a weighty bolt driver.

"Don't do it," warned Aptat. "We were just starting to get along. I was thinking about inviting you to my book club."

Naecia lit across the floor.

"Come on then!" Aptat laughed as if they were summoning a pet. "That's it!" Then, unflinching, they rattled off three words as Naecia neared. *"Aureate Cicatrix. Disassemble."*

The armor exploded from around her body like a broken shell, clattering to the floor in pieces. She tripped and stumbled forward. Aptat caught her by the neck. Again.

"Oops," said Aptat, as their face morphed into a terrifying configuration, bearing long crystalline teeth and tiny, angry eyes. A low, click-clicking growl burbled in their throat. They lifted her upright then squeezed. "You fool. You utter fool."

Naecia's spiracles fluttered. She gritted her teeth, feeling the sting of the stringhunter's words because they were true.

"Your neck keeps finding ways to end up in my grasp. Why is that?" said Aptat, flicking the amulet hanging below her chin. "And what is this, anyway? You're always playing with it. Some bauble imbued by sentiment and nostalgia?"

"Don't... you," she hissed, barely able to force words, "touch... it."

"Here is what will happen. You are going to complete the

cheat drive while I salvage that cruiser. Then, we are going to take a trip to some other galaxy in the cluster. I'll even let you pick the destination." They released her and she collapsed to the floor, hands to neck. "Cheat drive or no, the next time I will crush your throat and watch you die."

Naecia cried. She didn't want to. But it was the only thing left. She wasn't going to work on the cheat drive only to have it used – should she actually be successful – to escape the Dasma Arm knowing her family, her home, and everyone she'd ever known would be destroyed when the Earth man finally delivered the Chime to the Scythin. Aptat might as well just kill her now, and she was about to say so.

Oush cleared his throat from behind. "Oops."

Naecia twisted around as the clementine giant gathered Aptat's helmet and chest plate from the floor.

The violet skin around Aptat's mouth quivered angrily. "Those are mine."

Oush's orange face seemed to brighten. "A wise barrister once remarked that possession is ten-tenths of the law" he said, wrapping the armor in his steampipe arms. "But, if you think you can come and... *reestablish possession*, well, you can try, I guess."

Aptat's face was monstrous rage.

Oush went on, "I'm not about to run only to end up dead anyway. Besides, everyone we know is here. I plan to get back to them one day. We go after the Earth man. Now."

"And there are some nuns on Sobliel I want to see again," said Izairis.

"So," Oush said, "once we've solved the problem of the Earth man, you may have your precious shell back."

Aptat laughed, but it was defensive and choked. "He is too far gone. Scythin tech carves bulkspace like nothing I've ever seen. The *Child* is fast, but my bulk drives are comically outmatched."

Naecia knew all about bulkspace even before she'd first

experienced it on the *Knell*. It was a layer of nothingness sandwiched between dimensions that presented a way to get from one place to another at what seemed like superluminal speeds. The bulk created a shortcut between two points in the conventional universe, allowing one to reemerge at a spot further than light would have traveled in the same amount of time, but without actually traveling faster than light while inside the bulk. It wasn't surprising that the Scythin's mastery of it exceeded conventional technology, considering they were extra dimensional. But even the fastest bulkspace drives were standing still compared with instantaneous transport.

"I'm sorry," Aptat continued, "but there is no way for us to reach them."

Naecia plodded across the floor and sat onto the rim of neural dredge. "Put me back in."

CHAPTER TWENTY-FIVE

The door's filamentous structure pulled wide. Eyes stomped inside and I followed, the door reforming behind us. The room was mostly dark, but as we trudged in dull violet lights came up along the perimeter, giving the space size and dimension. Atop a plinth in the center were a pair of neural dredges, sat side-by-side like the outdoor bathtubs in pharmaceutical commercials advertising boner pills.

"His and hers?" I joked.

Eyes repeated my words airily back to me, *hisandhers*.

That I was going to be dredged was hardly a shock. Given the highly advanced nature of Scythin technology, I guess I'd expected them to have fancier, and maybe less traumatizing, equipment. The fact that they'd just gone down to the dredge store and bought a couple of dredges was kind of a let-down.

Save us. Gone is the Bloom of God. Find the Chime, the Note of Jecca. Eat nectar.

Nectar. Okay. I find the Chime, they get the Bloom of God, I get more tube food – er, nectar. Saliva poured into my mouth. "Easy," I blustered, heart pounding. "Put me in."

Eyes opened the dredge. Inside, the floor was set at a decline toward the head portion. They made an expectant gesture and I climbed in and sat down. "So, how do I work this thing?" I dodged the lid as it closed over me.

I hadn't been wrong in thinking of the dredge as a coffin. It was snug to my shoulders and legs, making it difficult to shift. Naecia had been inside Aptat's dredge for less than an hour. I could do that. I wondered if she was still alive, what she was up to right now. I also thought about nectar and how I wanted more of it shoved up my tube.

The lid sparkled with light. First in glowing orange, then green and blue, almost like a vintage computer showing off its handful of colors while booting up.

A shape appeared. A simple, two-dimensional rectangle, outlined in blue. It disappeared. Then new shapes appeared. They had the illusion of being projected onto the lid, though there was no source. Maybe they weren't actually on the lid at all, but in my mind. I shut my eyes. Yep. Still there – just less vibrant. Ugh. Maybe they were in both places.

The shapes flashed randomly, one after another. Simple circles, squares, and triangles soon gave way to intricate and asymmetrical polygons. They appeared by themselves and also in sets, yet there was no discernable relationship for those that were paired. No rhythm or cycle to the order in which they came and went.

Sometimes an image reappeared soon after it had faded. Curiously, new images often flashed in a position that seemed to "fit" with the previous image, only to dissolve away a second later. Other times a new puzzle piece would appear directly over where the previous shape had just been. It was all too confusing, and all too fast. Briefly, I wondered if it would induce a seizure.[82]

"Slow it down," I said, not knowing if Eyes was still in the room. "I can't even look at these. I don't understand." I was huffing air like I'd run sprints.[83]

---

82 Probably. Flickering light is often seen as a trigger in canines with seizure disorders.

83 You have literally never run a sprint.

There was no answer from Eyes, just more lights. Patterns and lineations strobed one after another – just as I'd seen with Naecia. I tried to make sense of it. A migraine pierced my skull. Tears streamed into my ear holes. What was I supposed to do? I played games with my vision, latching onto a figure and tracing its outline before it went away, or following a shape as it scrolled across the lid, whether back and forth or up and down, or diagonal or randomly about.

I tried to relax my mind, and picked a shape to follow as it made its drunken way around the lid. I was right on it, and began almost anticipating which way it would turn. I felt I *knew* where it was going to move. This went on for a short time before I realized that I was no longer following the movements of this puzzle piece – I had gained control of it.

I traced my eyes slowly toward the upper left portion of the lid as other shapes came and went, careful not to let go of the piece I'd taken hold of. I brought it to a spot in the corner and thought consciously about letting go. It worked. When I averted my eyes, it stayed put.

After a few seconds it disappeared like the others. I selected a new one. A neon blue rectangle. I *willed* myself to be in control of it, and then I was. I tossed it around the area of the lid with my eyeballs, not feeling any lag whatsoever between the snapping of my eyes back and forth and the responsiveness of the shape. It was like a projection of my mind. I settled the piece directly above my face. And then, locking my eyes straight up, I *thought* about putting it into the upper left corner. The shape obeyed. My eyes hadn't budged, and yet I could see the piece moving to the designated spot through my periphery. Amid this lucid trance, a link had formed between myself and the dredge in some kind of mind-meld.

My consciousness occupied a new space now, halfway in and halfway out of my body – reaching into the language of this machine and communicating with it. I wasn't observing a light show, *I was* the light show.

One thing I couldn't do was to persuade the images to stick around. They were fleeting, with most blinking out of existence in under a second. Others might last for five or ten seconds before fading away, with only the brief afterimages burnt onto my retinas. They were adding up, overloading the rods and cones inside my eye. I tried blinking them away.

For a brief instant, one of the residual images hung over a new shape that flashed on the glass, and for a millisecond I saw them together. The next pattern appeared and I let it blur into the afterimage of the previous. They fit.

I began to understand. Not the why, or what, but the how. Layered upon each other, the images formed a more complete picture. To see it, though, I had to hold onto the image even after it was gone. I had to focus on some parts and ignore others – to train myself to compartmentalize the afterimages for recall while allowing others to fade. The thought occurred that this would be much easier with a schizochroal compound eye.[84]

Wiping away the headache tears and refocusing on the display, I stared at a figure and then applied its afterimage to the next, then repeated this again and again. The phenomenon continued. The shapes were made more complete when combined with the afterimage of the one that had come before. They weren't always oriented correctly, but I could rotate the newer images on the glass until they fit with the previous. Suddenly the shapes were larger, understandable as components. It felt like a breakthrough.

But a breakthrough of what? I was combining shapes to build a larger picture that I couldn't keep in my head longer than a few seconds. *Thousands* of figures appeared and disappeared. I built small units of two, and sometimes three, by combining

---

84 A type of eye had by the Strepsiptera order of parasitic insects (known to practice *both* hypodermic insemination and hemocelous viviparity (super gross)) that allows the gathering and processing of hundreds of separate images.

an image on the glass with one of the dual units I'd just built with the afterimages, only to have it dissipate seconds later. I just didn't have the RAM.[85] In fact, my whole system was overloading. I'd lost all concept of time. Ugh. Suddenly, I needed out.

I shut my eyes to break the connection with the dredge, but even in the blackness of my mind, I could see the patterns dancing vividly overhead. It was still connected to my brain. I needed to decouple. Images flew onto the glass, stuffing my visual cortex. I lost control. My mind was a runaway conveyor belt, a thousand car pileup.

I barfed. Straight up in the air like Old Reliable. The geyser sprayed the lid then returned to my face, where it aspirated into my lungs. I coughed and hacked against the breathed-in watery puke. The canopy lifted away.

"I threw up in my eyes!"

The Scythin reached in and effortlessly lifted me out.

Save us. Gone is the Bloom of God.

"I don't even understand how this thing works yet!" I gagged, dragging my fingers over my eyelids, trying to blink them clear.

The dredge is a mirror.

"Of what?" I said, getting one eye open and fighting the urge to boot again.

Read the reflections for the Note of Jecca.

"The shapes?"

Imprints reflected for you to see.

"I don't recognize anything being shown to me."

You will.

"There's a million reflections down there. How am supposed to keep track of all that? I don't even know what it is."

---

85 Random Access Memory, a computer's "working memory" that dictates how many tasks it can handle at a given time – *I apparently still have enough RAM for you to keep talking.*

Nectar. They grabbed me by the arm and pushed me toward the door.

"*Oh,*" I said, feeling my heartrate spike and a rush of blood to the face. "Yes, the nectar will help." Suddenly, I couldn't have cared less that my head was covered in vomit. The only thought now was of having my tummy tube reconnected to the holy source.

After a long walk, we approached the enclosure. The membrane opened enough for me to step inside – along with a friendly push from Eyes. Patton was slumped against it on the opposite side, arm wrapped loosely around Pickles. He ticked his chin and smiled weakly. "Hey man," he croaked. "I can't get these open."

"You didn't eat?"

"No, man."

"What about the tubes?" I asked.

"No tubes, I tried."

He didn't look good. Worse off than me, even with a skim-coat of chunder. His skin was grey. His straw-colored hair was filthy and matted. I couldn't delineate the boundary between it and his neck beard. Strangely, I recognized that seeing him like this should have caused me far more consternation than it did. And knowing that it didn't should have been another red flag. But I ignored all of it. I just didn't care that much. I needed nectar.

Eyes was still at the entrance. "Hey, I'm hungry," I said. Then remembered to add, "My friend Patton is hungry too."

The Scythin ignored me.

I went to Pickles and wrenched at the lid. The bones in my wrists seemed small and fragile. "God-fucking-dammit!" I exclaimed, straining to no avail.

Eyes came in and summoned the tubes.

"Ah," I proclaimed, feeling a great coolness wash over me. I abandoned Pickles and scuttled over like a piglet called to the teat. I squeezed the nectar tube onto my belly pipe and forgot everything of the world thereafter.

CHAPTER TWENTY-SIX
THE INSTRUMENT MAKER

It had taken her nearly all of the season's prime phase to get the rehearsal space prepared exactly as it needed to be. The performance would take place outside, of course, but a carefully balanced sound space was required if she was to discern the smallest divergences in tone produced by the ukelaklavas or those who had been selected to play them.

Taking her place at the head of the heavily draped room, she gazed out over three hundred and one chairs set in concentric semi-circles, and the bright-eyed children who sat patiently in them. They were among the most technically skilled children Odvella had to offer, but, more importantly, those the Instrument Maker had judged to hold the greatest depth of emotional connection to the music. The selection process had been long and tedious, but necessary. It hadn't been enough to play the piece perfectly – she had to feel each child's dual beating hearts translated through the notes.

"You will play only the exposition today," she announced. "The carriage notes from usbed esbed minor. We will repeat until it is perfect." She raised her hands and the nascent orchestra brought their instruments to ready stance. "Remember, children, I want to hear your voices in every note."

She brought her arms slowly up while counting down, watched the players inhale their tiny chests full of breath, and at the apex of her sweeping gesture, spread her fore-digits and initiated a second countdown, this one slower than the first. At zero, she pronounced her fists to the room and the music boomed.

A sustained note, held as long as her arms remained aloft. Then, at the expiration of her own internal count, she swept them slowly down, bringing the children with her. They drew their sliffbarque bows across the strings while bending the instruments' tonal arms. The sound was like a sledge carrying thunder that slid from the heavens to the liquid core of the planet below.

She ended the exposition with an abbreviated flourish of the hands. The children relaxed, lowering the instruments to rest against their thighs.

"Good," she said, proud of where they'd started. "And again."

CHAPTER TWENTY-SEVEN

Hitting the dredge yet again, going deeper than ever before, was a serious risk and without any assurance of finding answers. Aptat had actually tried talking Naecia out of it, and for her own sake – on that point the stringhunter's words had seemed genuine. It was still possible to make a run for it. There was always a chance that the Earth man wouldn't be able to find the Chime. Naecia, of course, declined the invitation to flee, as Aptat surely knew she would.

In a perverse sort of way, she welcomed another go at the dredge. If only to try to find the final pieces for the drive, to bridge the gap between notion and reality, to get closure for the thing that had tormented her since she could remember. Doodling schematics rather than paying attention during school, building replicas before she had any idea what they were. The same little rig crafted over and over again, with its processor stacks, shielded chambers and conduit, left around the family's dwellings. Never knowing what it was or how to make it work, the pursuit had been hollow – her entire life spent trying not just to understand *how*, but *why* and *what*.

The dredge on the *Knell* had shed some light. Every trip seemed to loosen what was imprinted on the cord, dislodging concepts and ideas that drifted to the surface even after she was out of the box. Calculations, algorithms, theories, materials, suggestions. It was while on the *Knell* that she had made strides in producing an interface with the physical world so the machine could actually gather and process data on a subatomic level. At the same time her mind had become even more insistent that this computer she was building was an engine – a drive – that could push them across the universe in the blink of an eye.

Which was still a problem. A big problem. Everything it proposed to do was impossible, hemmed in on all sides by the unbreakable laws of physics, including the king of them all, the absolute prohibition against anything moving faster than the speed of light. That's why they'd called it a cheat drive, it broke the laws of the Universe. Naecia couldn't bridge the gap between what the machine purported to do and the rules it had to abide by. The physical world simply prevented the feats the machine seemed both destined to achieve and ill-equipped to perform.

But she had seen something new when Dekies had forced her into the dredge. An abyssal reflection, an imprint of something poignant enough for her brain to latch onto and briefly observe. It was what had halted her descent when she'd slipped the cord, keeping her shy of the Oblivion Fray. She'd only caught a glimpse inside, but it had been enough. There was a woman. A *human* woman whose secret had been lost with her death. And that was who she had to find.

So, with Oush dressed in Aptat's helmet – tightly – and Izairis wearing the stringhunter's fancy chest plate cuirass, Naecia laid back into the dredge.

Getting on the cord wasn't difficult. Depth was controlled by the state of her mind, and she understood that two particular factors, familiarity and acknowledgement, would coax up the reflections that were most buried. Familiarity was the recognition of reflections that she'd seen before as they were displayed. But it was the registering and cataloguing of that reflection which seemed to quash the brain's desire to continue presenting it inside the dredge. Like digging a hole, an unacknowledged reflection was a shovelful of dirt dumped back in. Seeing it and processing it meant the dirt would be tossed aside, outside the hole, permitting the spade to plow deeper. As each subsequent trip into the dredge meant fewer reflections that had to be seen and appreciated for the first time, the dives went deeper. And this time she knew what she was looking for.

The most recent of Naecia's priors, of course, were the twin sister mathematicians. When they weren't arguing, they were building their revolutionary stacking algorithm, and Naccia was tapping into the thread of consciousness that ran through them both. It was that bit of math that had allowed her to build a machine with the ability to process and organize unfathomable quantities of data at mind-boggling speed. Yet the sisters had been unable to get beyond that point.

They had built their own machine with its algorithm in an attempt to bridge the gap between the theories of their first prior –Naecia's third – and the realization of instantaneous transport. What those theories had been, however, Naecia didn't know. They weren't accessible to her. Either it wasn't on the shared strands of memory that she could see, or the theories had not imprinted when the twins learned them.

Naecia thought she understood why. Usually, if a person's experience of an event was poignant enough, at least some information about that event was preserved. But if the concepts allowing for instantaneous travel had been acquired passively – like the twins simply perceiving thoughts that bubbled up from their own priors – rather than as a reward for scientific inquiry, they might not have been etched into the record of their consciousness for Naecia to see.

Yet, even armed with the theories that had spurred them on to develop the math and build their own machine, the twins couldn't make it go. The last reflection Naecia had seen from them was a catastrophic depressurization before running a test. She could feel their horror, their disbelief as they realized they would die because of something so trivial as a faulty seal in an airlock. And everything they'd known or learned had disappeared into the vacuum with them – that is, until Naecia came along. As a Stringer, she made salvage of abandoned memories. She had rescued their algorithm, but she needed more.

Reflections poured in, smaller details of the twins' lives that had yet to be acknowledged. She blinked afterimages of the raw data together, creating moments that churned into view, making the conscious effort to truly see and understand each one in order to make room for further descent. It was a brutal task to witness the private moments of strangers. To see and *feel* their joy, their pain, their successes and failures in spans of forced voyeurism – remaining ever vigilant to keep them separate from her own.

Acknowledgment of the imprints brought them closer to her own personhood, making them seem like her own memories, gathering into piles and crowding out those that were genuinely hers, weighing down the life she carried with her beyond the dredge. It was a chore, keeping so many selves separate.

She made quick – but deliberate – work of the reflections that obscured the third prior. Pushing aside reflections before fully acknowledging them had caused her to slip before.

Then the reflections ceased. Her back felt cold – it was a familiar feeling now, a sign she was approaching the Fray. She evened out her breath and waited. Finally, like a distant light drawing near, a single shape glowed into being on the glass. The reflection she'd seen before. A circle. Tilting it sideways, it had the form of a pillar, with a long center column and rings at the terminal ends. She pulled it close and began processing through the cross-sections of memory.

The human was here. Her image reflected from a wall of steel showed her to be tall and lithe with short, scruffy blonde hair, and a casual manner. Dressed in some type of animal skin coat trimmed in fur and baggy pants, she was standing inside a cavernous metal room with one end of it open to a wide expanse of blue sky. She stood alongside a shiny, primitive-looking flight craft.

The scene faded and Naecia shifted the reflection to the next imprint. The woman was now lying awake in bed, her mind bombarded by numbers, fuel allocations, checkpoints, and maps of a great ocean. There were many imprints just like this. The woman was entirely preoccupied. She seemed to be preparing for a journey.

In the following vignette she was joined by a second woman. Young looking, much like the first, but shorter. She had a strong face and long, dark brown hair, neatly pulled back. They stood together in an office crowded with books and stacks of papers before a large, black panel affixed to one of the walls. The first woman watched as the other scratched out notations with a dusty white cylinder that dropped crumbs as she went. Naecia paused the scene and pulled the writing close:

Thought Mass, Ideas Have Weight: Protoparticles: Ubiquitously Entangled – Chiral – Obey No Cloning

Further down the panel, beyond a great jumble of math, were a pair of large, translucent films. One looked like an archaic x-ray image of a human head, showing the skull and neck. Passing through it were lines in a gradient that resembled the force lines of a magnetic field. The other picture was a rudimentary negative, shown in black on white, of a random starfield with the same lines flowing through it as the first image.

A laughably simple diagram was scribbled on the last panel. A lone stick figure with a helmet and tiny goggles drawn on. Above it was scratched a letter: E. An arrow was drawn from the E. character to a box labeled *Capacitor*, with another arrow leading from the box to a sketch of the craft Naecia had seen in the prior reflection. This was labeled *Electra 10*.

The pair spoke quietly, closely, none of it audible. They went back over the notations and diagrams together before the new woman took up a felted block and used it to quickly rub away everything that had been written. They left the room together, shutting the door behind them. On the door was a name. *Cecelia Payne-Gaposchkin*.

The scene ended. Naecia's mind was frazzled by this point. Time had a way of slowing while down in the dredge as information uptake skyrocketed. She pulled up another sliver of the past; the final cross-section of the circular shape. Her throat burned as stomach acid burbled upward. If she surfaced now, she knew she wouldn't have the strength to go back.

E. piloted the *Electra 10* through the dead of night. There was a new person with her, a young man. A flexible grid of gold wire covered the contours of the cabin. The man considered a paper navigational chart. He tapped at a clock in the instrument panel and folded away the chart. They spoke to each other.

Naecia could hear her own breathing, somewhere distant. The walls of self were wearing thin. She couldn't stay down much longer.

E. nodded and then gave an instruction to her navigator, after which he took the yoke. E. leaned back and shut her eyes.

And that was it. The scene ended.

The Fray put off an eerie green aurora from somewhere below. Exhausted, Naecia pressed her mind back up the cord, toward the reflections of the twins, but her momentum stalled. She willed herself back to the present, like being underwater and kicking for the surface not knowing if you have enough air to make it. The Fray pulled on her consciousness like a magnet, beckoning her to rest, to become one with it forever. She ignored the sensation, walling off her thoughts and thinking only about waking up in the dredge. A pinprick of light in the distance steadily dilated. She tried to hold her mind together as the mouth of the tunnel widened. The blackness dissolved away and so did the light. And at the end, there was Aptat. *Aptat?*

The lid opened and the dredge spun down. "Did you survive?" asked the stringhunter cheerfully.

Naecia wanted to tell them what she'd seen but the room was spinning. Teeth chattered. Icy tremors danced down her spine. She blinked her eyes and rubbed her face, opened her mouth.

"Slow down," said Aptat. "Just relax."

Naecia grunted, trying to warm her throat. Then, after cycling her breath to slow everything down, she rasped, "They weren't trying to break physics. They were trying to go around it."

CHAPTER TWENTY-EIGHT[86]

86 A shrimp's heart is in its head. The jellyfish *Turritopsis nutricula* is immortal. Orangutans are shitty climbers – near half of them have fractured bones from falling out of trees. Ghost crabs growl at enemies by grinding the teeth in their stomachs. Bottlenose dolphins call each other by name by mimicking whistles. Slugs have four noses. An octopus has three hearts and nine brains. Ninety-nine percent of those bottlenose dolphins from earlier are righties (which means they are constantly turning left). Lots of animals vote. African buffalo, *Syncerus caffer*, vote on things like travel preference, but only females are enfranchised. Narwhal "horns" are really teeth that grow through the skin, that they use not for stabbing other animals, but rather to "bop" fish on the head, stunning them before eating. Some sharks glow in the dark. Male ghost sharks have retractable dicks on their heads. Many animals – like dogs, hummingbirds, and scrub jays – have semantic memory, which allows them to sense the passing of time... and anticipate when an event is upcoming. Watches are non-sentient machines that display the time according to a prescribed interval system. The Rolex Deep Sea Special was tested at the bottom of the Mariana Trench, home to comb jellies, the adorable Dumbo octopus, the tiny, bioluminescent hatchetfish *Argyropelecus gigas,* and the black seadevil anglerfish, a.k.a., Aptat. The tick-tock of a grandfather clock pendulum is considerably slower than the

tick-tick of a wristwatch, which is usually about eight per second. Quartz watches only lose about a minute per year. Kangaroos can't fart. Flies buzz in the key of F. Under all that light-reflective, translucent fur, polar bears are black. Mormon crickets ejaculate up to 27% of their body weight, equivalent to 47.25 pounds of semen for a 175 pound human.

CHAPTER TWENTY-NINE

I sprang up from something. Not sleep. You couldn't call it sleep. More like a fever-dream from inside David Attenborough's[87] brain after an acid-trip. Of course, that would mean he had a real thing for dirty bug sex. I banished the thought.

Dreams that included bits and pieces of my strange knowledge were nothing new – they'd been a part of my life since I could remember. But now the dam had broken. For however long I'd been asleep, the imagery and understanding of those prior lives poured in, churned up no doubt by my time in the dredge paired with a strong assist from the space drugs. But even amid the flood of downcord memories that had been knocked loose by my first session in the machine, there had been nothing in the maelstrom about the Chime. Nothing I could discern, anyway.

Still, I felt fucking GREAT.

I rubbed my eyes and tried to sit up but conked my head on the glassy lid of the dredge. There was Eyes on the other side, looking down.

Save us. Gone is the Bloom of God. You will find the Chime, the Note of Jecca.

Right. Not done yet. Do the stuff, get the drugs.

----

87 Famous naturalist and broadcaster; UK national treasure.

I launched into the session, tracing the figures and shapes – the reflections, as Eyes had called them – as I'd done the first time. I remembered to pay attention to the afterimages left on my retinae and to overlay them with new images as they were presented. It was easier to govern the second time around – the nectar regimen wasn't just for kicks – and soon I was building out little layered structures of two, three, and four images before they disappeared. The reflections came more quickly, and my ability to accept or ignore them advanced in sync. That said, if these were the reflections of prior thought, I was still at a loss for what they represented. They were just two-dimensional shapes. Unless one of my priors was a geometrician, I couldn't translate them into understandable ideas.

I plowed through piles of imagery, layering some, moving them into holding areas on the lid until they faded a few seconds later, tossing others immediately. This went on for an eternity with little progress. It was like a videogame where I'd reached the end of the map but hadn't won the quest. Based upon years of training across numerous gaming consoles, I knew that there was always another angle. You had to go back and find it; the magical gem that opened a gate to a new realm.

Controlling the pieces with my eyes – and my mind I guess – I rotated them clockwise and counterclockwise like the dial on a safe, as if there might be a combination to unlock a deeper level. I tried moving them in distinct patterns across the glass. Reflections reappeared at a faster rate, convincing me that I was stuck on level one. There had to be some type of code.[88]

A crescent shape appeared. I wiped it over the glass, side-to-side, up and down. How could something so simple represent an idea, or even the part of an idea? Maybe the good stuff is written on the back, *lol.*

Hold the fuck on.

---

88 Did you try Up, Up, Down, Down, Left, Right, Left, Right, B, A, Select, Start?

Rather than rotating the reflection on the two-dimensional plane in which I'd been working, I rolled it along the third axis, tilting it to the side. It wasn't two dimensional at all. From below I'd never suspected that they had depth, but oh did they. Just tilting the crescent showed it to be far taller than it was wide or long. I assumed it was just a feature of the display, but it seemed to climb straight up from the top of the coffin.

Every shape had depth in this third dimension. This had to be where the data was stored. I reached up with my eyes and pulled the pieces toward me, allowing the lid to transect their cross sections – another revelation: I could push them away or pull them close. Each one was a unique building block, made up of thousands of layers. Every reflection was, in reality, a stack of wafer-thin units – like *glimmers* of the larger thought.

Eyes is gonna be so proud. I can just taste the nectar.

An asymmetrical gear-shaped reflection came next, and I quickly flipped it to the side in order to understand how many layers it had. Thousands probably, though it didn't hold as many wafers as the crescent. I pulled the shape toward me, exposing a cross-section maybe halfway through it on the lid of the dredge. The layer itself was engraved, or etched, and still frustratingly unintelligible. The piece disappeared.

The edges of my brain were getting fuzzy.

Ignoring that, I took hold of a new piece – an easy semi-circle that looked like Ms Pacman, and selected a layer to examine. I counted three deep and set it across the lid, staring at its neon glow until it disappeared. Then, with the afterimage still fresh, I dismissed a handful of new shapes until I found the one that paired with the Pacman shape and scrolled to the third layer, then blinked the afterimage over it. A notion, a memory, a glimmer – suddenly unlocked.

A scene unfolded of a childhood. A mother as seen through the eyes of her son, sitting on the bank of a creek. The mother is holding something and speaking to the boy – to me, unsettlingly, as the child. It is as if I'm eavesdropping, but there is no sound beyond murmurs. This mother's face is crystalline. Every muscle an expression of unconditional love. I swallowed hard, having to remind myself that she is gazing upon her son, not me. They peer together through a magnifying glass at something in the dirt – a group of pill bugs – and the moment passes for the two of them. The mother is not my mother. The child is not me.

The image fractures and dissolves like a frame of melting celluloid. Gasping, I scattered the incoming reflections to the side, breaking my trance, and called to be let out, wiping my tear-streaked face.

The lid opened. Eyes pulled me up and out, considered me. *Gone is the Bloom of God.*

My hands shook and my teeth chattered all the way back to the enclosure. Seeing the memory of another human being played before me like a home movie was terrifying. I was a trespasser to someone's most sacred moments. An interloper of nostalgia.

The trauma, though, was tamped some by my anticipation of nectar. I was like a kid on Christmas Eve, anxious to tear open a big box of narcotics. Once inside the cell, I scrambled for the center where the food tube would emerge and deliver the essence of life. Patton was against the wall, clutching Pickles, zoned out.

"What's the matter with you?" I asked.

His eyes barely opened.

"Come get some nectar," I said.

He smiled weakly. "I don't get nectar, Ben."

Eyes came in and gestured toward the floor where a small panel opened. I giggled in anticipation. "Patton! Food!" I said.

Nectar is for the one who seeks the Chime, the Note of Jecca, said Eyes, handing me my tube.

"What's he eat, then?" I asked, only half focused on the question as I pushed the tube to my umbilicus.

Eyes made a gesture and an elliptical panel opened in the floor. A shining black spine bowed upward from the hole and slithered mechanically from it. My first thought was *it's the piss eel*. Remembering the blinking blue light and the forced hibernation, I panicked, and scrambled clumsily away.

This time the eel had no eye, just a hollow, scoop-shaped appendage at the head. It slithered over to Patton, and a lumpy slop the consistency of mucous-soaked oatmeal poured out of it. Patton scooted up and began to eat from it.

I watched him lap the gruel from the food eel's face. It wasn't ideal, but this was the way it had to be. Nectar was for people who were doing important work. He wasn't going to find the Chime or the Note of Jecca and bring back the Bloom of God to save the Scythin.

I was.

CHAPTER THIRTY

"Who's 'they'?" asked Aptat.

"My third prior," Naecia said, sitting upright in the dredge. "Let me..." Her head pounded and she laid back down. "Just for a bit." Her mind felt like it had been dilacerated on three axes. Hands on face and eyes still closed, she mumbled. "She's a human. An aircraft pilot. From long ago."

"You're on the cord with a human?" exclaimed Aptat, incredulously. "Then we are assuredly doomed and should delay no further. Time to run."

"*E*. The woman. She was working with a scientist. A physicist or astronomer, I think. Cecelia Payne-Gaposchkin."

Aptat swooped extravagantly to the ship's console. "I had the *Child* copy Earth's archives while I was catfishing Ben. *Child?* Standby for query. Naecia – say that name again."

"Cecelia Payne-Gaposchkin."

The display showed an entry which Aptat read aloud. "British American astronomer and astrophysicist, Harvard College Observatory. Noted for over three million spectral observations, including correctly determining the composition of the Sun and other stellar bodies, where her male contemporaries had failed. Widely published. Was not promoted to full professor until 1956, despite surpassing the accomplishments of many of her male colleagues in years prior. Some of her most important discoveries were later attributed to men."

"Well, seems that's universal," said Izairis.

Naecia shifted, aching. "Probably why they were working in secret. Testing a theory they didn't want stolen, maybe?"

"What theory?" asked Aptat.

"She had these pictures. Spectrographs of a human head next to a starfield." Naecia looked up, brow furrowed. "I think she'd found a way to observe the Oblivion Fray."

Aptat made a face. "Doubtful. But even assuming she'd determined the spectral range, humans don't understand the character of the Fray."

"I think maybe *she* did," said Naecia. "She'd written something: *Ideas have weight*. She used the term 'Thought mass'. What else could she have been talking about?"

"Even so, that's no more than we already know about it."

Izairis and Oush had come up around the Dredge. Oush offered a hand and Naecia felt stable enough to take it and step out.

Aptat was lost in thought, then asked, "So maybe a human stumbled upon the Fray. How does that get us to a cheat drive?"

"It doesn't. But perhaps it bridges the gap between what I've built and what it's supposed to do."

"Explain."

"Our thinking has been walled in by the confines of conventional matter. First of all, it's not entangled by nature. When we communicate via entanglement, we create the sibling particles and carry them through bulkspace to distant points where they'll be useful. Entanglement communication is 'faster-than-light' but only once we've set the particles in place using subluminal transportation. If, hypothetically, you could use entanglement as a means of transport, you'd have to follow the same procedure. Your origin and destination would be limited by wherever you placed the members of the pair. And that's all restrained by the laws of physics. You could only go where you'd placed them."

"Like setting out communications beacons across Dasma," said Izairis. "You'd need the infrastructure first, then you could jump from one place to the next."

"Hypothetically," said Aptat.

Naecia settled gingerly onto the rim of the dredge. "If one was going to play within the rules of the universe as we know it, yes, you'd be limited by the location of the space ports you'd set up. Payne-Gaposchkin wasn't trying to break those rules," she said, feeling her understanding of what she'd seen crystalizing. "She hypothesized that the substance of the Fray was *already* entangled. Ubiquitously. A great blanket of material waiting to be triggered. And why not? It is the raw matter of consciousness. It may not itself be *aware*, but it is already connected – conscious in the sense that Fray particles stand ready to talk to each other. Input data in any one place creates output somewhere else. If it's already entangled, there's no transmission so there's no delay. It's instant."

The others exchanged dubious glances.

"And your machine makes that connection?" asked Izairis.

"No," answered Naecia. "I think the machine is a… a camera."

"Explain. And quickly," said Aptat. "Because none of this is making me want to run away any less."

Naecia paused to think through what she was going to say. Her own understanding of what she had pieced together was taking shape in real time. "Think of it as a hyper-advanced tomographic imager. Only instead of imaging body tissues or geological formations or mechanical structures, it's imaging the subatomic particles making up the atoms for whatever is being transported. Quantum tomography. For any theoretical transportation of matter from one place to another, the information for that matter has to be faithfully catalogued so it can be reproduced exactly. I think the machine does that. It records the objects to be transmitted at a particle level."

"Did you say reproduced?" asked Oush, his orange face blanching some.

"That's how you don't violate the rule against light speed travel. You're not moving something from one place to another. You're just copying it and then rebuilding it elsewhere," said Naecia. "These women discovered the fabricator."

"The machine is a replicator of some type?" asked Izairis.

Naecia answered, "No, the machine only aggregates the data. The Fray does the replication."

"Okay, *replication*? So, there would be two of us?" asked Oush.

"*No cloning*," said Naecia. "Sorry – er, another rule of physics. Basically, when it comes to conventional entanglement, remember, you're dealing with connected particles of opposite spin. So, in 'turning on' the destination particles, the original set is automatically sort of 'turned off'. By nature, you'd never end up with two. Payne-Gaposchkin hypothesized that what we call the Oblivion Fray worked the same way. The original is erased. You're one of a kind, Oush. There won't be two of you."

"We get murdered?" exclaimed Izairis.

"Okay!" said Aptat, clapping hands. "You've clearly decohered." They took the axon diadem from around their neck and propped it on Naecia's head.

"Izairis," said Naecia, now wearing the black circlet but largely ignoring it. "Look: there is nothing special about our constituent parts. If they are reproduced exactly, does it matter if the original ceases to be?"

"I sort of feel that it does, yeah," said Izairis.

Oush removed Aptat's helmet from his head and tucked it below an arm. "So, you send data through the Fray to some distant location via entanglement: a spaceship, let's say. You've got the data. How do you get the spaceship?"

"I don't think that's very complicated, actually. All matter is made of the same panel of subparticles. It's all in the arrangement. Payne suggested the Fray was formed of protoparticles – like balls of clay that can become any number of things based on the input of outside information. It makes sense. The Fray is the raw material of consciousness, but it isn't yet a thought, right? So, the machine catalogues the matter, that data is transferred to the end point via entanglement, and then reproduced. Think of it as a trillion, trillion, trillion dials being turned in one place, which instantly turns sibling dials somewhere else."

Aptat flipped through the holographic readings for Naecia's coherence. "How, exactly, does the machine tell the Fray what to replicate?"

"Uh," said Naecia, absentmindedly adjusting the diadem, "it doesn't. The machine isn't conscious. It can't interface with the Fray. It has to communicate the data through something that is."

"Meaning?" asked Oush.

"A person has to be the hub – the link."

"So, all you have to do is think of something and an exact copy will be created somewhere?" Oush doubled over laughing. "I'm starting to agree with the space parasite. Let's run."

Naecia sidestepped the criticism. She understood things now. "If, theoretically, you had the capacity to catalogue and record the position and spin of every single particle making up that something and hold it in your head, then yes, I believe you could 'think it' into existence. But because you – because all of us – lack that capacity, the answer is no. Something far more capable than our minds has to do that. It's an immense amount of computation – and that's where the machine comes in. But our consciousness serves as the access point. We're the gateway."

"How did these primitive humans achieve it then?" said Aptat, scrolling through readings. "I spent four days immersed in their technosphere. Mostly they just care about taking pictures of themselves and asking other people to endorse those pictures. Even today, they couldn't do what you say they did generations earlier."

"Oh, there's no way they achieved it," said Naecia. "They had no means of cataloguing the subatomic makeup of the *Electra* craft or its occupants. They'd wrapped it all in wire. I believe they were experimenting – attempting to gather their data with some type of rudimentary interferometer in the form of a highly conductive antenna. Perhaps a basic form of quantum illumination. They understood the Fray but lacked the means to gather and communicate the necessary data."

"And how did their experiment turn out?"

"I don't know," she answered. "I only had the one moment. That was it. Maybe the twins saw more than I did, but it was enough for them to write the stacking algorithm and conduct tests. Maybe they would have been the first to successfully move mass if they hadn't been killed."

"For the purpose of my next question, let's assume all of this works," said Aptat. "How does one navigate? Is there a separate map machine or does one just wish upon a star?"

"Sort of that, yes."

"This is insanity," said Oush. "Like that time I agreed to a title bout with Phlegmula of Smeglax. She's still champion."

"So long as it is sufficiently specific, I believe that the operator just – yeah, thinks it. We're dealing with the Fray. It would make sense that thought is its language."

Aptat approached Naecia and gingerly removed the diadem as if the slightest touch would deflate her brain.

"What does it say?" she asked.

Aptat did a quick check of the readings. "It's fine," they answered. "Carry on."

"Fine? What does that mean?"

The stringhunter contemplated the diadem, then brightened. "You have nearly eighty-one percent remaining coherence. Better than I'd expected, to be honest."

"Eighty-one?"

"You might have left some of yourself behind, but only a small portion."

"Nineteen percent!"

"You have a big personality! It's barely noticeable. Your coherence was bleeding down. I'd say you're lucky. The diadem stanched the evanescing."

"What does that mean?"

"In practical terms," said Aptat, "I think it means you shouldn't ever go back into the dredge. And your recall for trivia when playing boardgames is going to suffer. Beyond that, we'll just have to see."

"Once the machine has catalogued all of the data," said Oush, "how do you get it all into your head so you can think it into the Oblivion Fray?"

Naecia was still trying to cope with the news that she was roughly twenty percent less the person she'd been before, even though she'd gone into the dredge prepared to lose one hundred percent, if it came to that. She addressed Oush, "You'd need an interface." She gestured for the axon diadem, which Aptat surrendered. "Something like this."

Izairis raised an eyebrow.

"Well," said Aptat. "It seems that you have much research and development still left to be done, and you are welcome to continue your work as we run away. Time to go now. All in favor?"

Oush and Izairis sheepishly raised their hands.

Naccia made no attempt to argue with them. She stepped carefully over to the outline of the cargo slot on the floor and turned to Aptat. "Bring it up, please."

Aptat gestured and the compartment containing the machine ascended. Naecia knelt and pointed to the base. "I need caridianite," she said. "Ovimine will do if you don't have it."

"For what?"

"Hyperconductive alloys. To get the data inside the stacks from here," she pointed to the machine, "to here." She swiveled the diadem, then made a show of setting it back onto her head. "I don't need a lot of it."

"You're asking me if I happen to have rare element allotropes lying around?" said Aptat.

"Yes please."

"I do not." Big toothy grin. "But I know who will. Hmm... if only we had access to the undefended ruins of a pirate space cruiser."

Naecia saw the angle. "*They* have it?"

"They do," interjected Oush. "Vortu flay guns are lined with it. It's how they're able to cycle so rapidly."

"He's right," said Aptat. "Flay guns."

"Go," Naecia said. "Get your salvage. You get me my wire. I'll work on the..." She stopped shy of using the term that everyone had repeated. *Cheat drive.* It wasn't correct. They weren't cheating anything, just swapping places. "Switch Drive."

"Switch Drive, hmm?" said Aptat. "I see no harm in it. If you can't get it working shortly after my return from the *Glaive*, we run. All agreed?"

Oush and Izairis agreed. And what choice did Naecia have? "Fine."

Aptat shrugged. "But, *oh*," they added in a low, almost sultry, voice, "I'll need my carapace returned so I can do the salvaging."

Oush balanced the helmet atop his head. Izairis, who had seemed comfortable in the armored cuirass, visibly tightened.

"You will," said Naecia, seeing it for the gambit it was. "You get to have your carapace."

"What are you talking about? No!" Izairis interjected. "If they have the suit, they can do whatever they want to us; imprison us again, run away rather than go for the Chime!"

"No, no," said Naecia, drawing a big circle over the room. "Aptat will put the three of us on the ship's note and transmit it to the Velpha Registry. *Then* we will return the carapace."

"You—" Aptat scoffed. "You want me to make you *co-owners* of my ship? The *Silent Child*? This ship we are in right now?"

"No, not co-owners," answered Naecia. "Owners. But only while you're wearing a suit that you can use to rob and kill us with. It's no secret that you'd rather be solo at this point. This way, your ship would become the property of our next-of-kin and/or designated heirs in the event of our untimely deaths." She smiled innocently.

"I'm not signing over the ship–"

"And," Naecia continued, "we will send a follow-up communiquery reporting it stolen, so that it will be locked down should you enter any port in the Dasma Arm after murdering us. When you return from the *Glaive* and have placed the suit back into our custody, we will execute documentation bequeathing the ship back to you, which will then be transmitted to Velpha, effectively canceling the prior transaction." She grinned. Oush and Izairis looked adequately impressed. It was at least eighty-one percent of a good idea.

Aptat raised the eyebrow-less skin above their eye. "If you escape from all of this alive, you should consider a second career in organized crime." They crossed the floor to the ship's console. "Follow."

The Stringers gathered as Aptat brought up the ship's note, which held all of its fundamental identifying information as well as make, class, capacity, reactor-engine type, and title history. Aptat opened the deed tab and dragged over the Stringers' profiles. "There. Happy to get something for nothing?"

"You're literally a slave-trader," said Izairis, exasperated.

"Point taken. Nevertheless."

Naecia highlighted Aptat's own profile at the head of the deed. "Delete."

"You want to divest me of any interest in the ship?"

"You won't be permanently divested of anything if you come back from the salvage run – with my caridianite – and don't murder us."

"And what is to keep you all from running once I'm off the ship?"

"I need those coils before the Switch Drive will actually do any switching. We will also need weapons. Oh, and voidsuits for our assault on the *Timelance*. So you should make that part of your salvage efforts too."

"An assault on the *Timelance*, eh?" Aptat chuckled. "And how would we get onboard? Pose as neural dredge sales representatives?"

"I have an idea about that, but it won't matter if you don't go and get what we need."

Aptat grumbled petulantly and deleted their profile from the ship's note, then dispatched the update to the Registry at Velpha. "There. Now. My helmet and cuirass."

Naecia looked over to the nun-forger Izairis. "Are we good?"

"It's legitimate," she said. "The ship is ours."

Naecia nodded to Oush, who presented the helmet. "I was starting to enjoy that," he said. Izairis surrendered the chest piece.

Naecia placed a navigational and communications lock on the ship. "I suppose you could still murder us," she said. "But if you do, you'll be on the float and with no com."

Aptat smiled genuinely as they pulled down the helmet. "If attacking the *Timelance* doesn't work out, we *should* partner up. Your cunning, my good looks."

"But we'd be dead," observed Oush.

Aptat cold-eyed him. "That's the joke."

CHAPTER THIRTY-ONE

I began to adjust to the dredge, moving quickly through the reflections, locking onto the patterns like a transmission dropping into gear. They began to seem more familiar, understandable, and... *natural*. As for my quest for the Chime, well, all the dredge had really managed to do was make Mr Bug-butts and Mr Rolex all the more accessible, with so much time down the cord knocking their reflections loose.

The churn did bring about new reflections from further down. In a way, this was progress. In another it was a devastating dead end. They were blank – data free. Just empty shapes without the layers containing tiny glimmers of life that Bugs and Watches had produced. How can you imprint something with no data?

Each day, Eyes retrieved me from the enclosure and we made the trip to the dredge. I began to recognize many of the other boid-made Scythin individuals, especially the ones with the metal prongs embedded in their chests. There were twenty-six of these curiously adorned individuals. They were given wide berth by the other Scythin, as if they were special in some way that I hadn't been able to discern – though I observed no hierarchical behavior beyond this formal deference. The Twenty-Six, as I came to think of them, were the only ones permitted to go near me, though only Eyes ever did.

I tried to make sense of the societal arrangement in the only way I knew how, which was to compare them to an insect analog. There was no direct comparison to any Earth species, but there were similarities, especially to *Azteca constructor*, ants whose colonies have multiple queens.[89] So I took to thinking of the Twenty-Six as Scythin queens even though I had no clue if they had sexual categories or genders, never saw one lay an egg, or don a crown. Nevertheless, as no two were alike, I named them. And likely not in a way befitting their office.

In addition to Eyes, there was Foot-head, Spike, Darth Vaper, Dirty Sanchez, Skinny-fat, Cha-cha, Front-butt, Xenodwarf, Cold-cuts, Lizard-Chief, Anubis, Kraken, Taint Viking, The Deech, Space Goat, The Big Woman, Scrungent, Sans Serif, Dan Hanks, Cheeks McGee, Senator Graham, Cock Wraith, Uncle Jerry, Karen, and finally, Millipedo, on account of this one preferred a "top half" configuration – just a torso with arms and head – carried about on a small boid-army of legs like a member of *Diplopoda*. The similarities ended there, hopefully.[90]

Back on the cord, I tossed aside familiar reflections that the machine pulled up. For Mr Bugs, it always started with his childhood. Walks near a pond with his mother, crawling into tangles of root and down along the bank, looking for new animals to inspect. Perhaps his mother was a teacher or a scientist. It was obvious that she had imparted her wonder and curiosity onto him as a child. After that, there wasn't much more about his personal life I could gather. Every reflection was stacked with

---

89 Phenomenon known as pleometrosis.

90 Male millipedes inject sperm through a pair of modified legs called gonopods – *File under "stuff I wish I didn't know."* – Sorry, Ben, that file is full.

glimmers of his own work – obsessive research, no surprise, focused mainly on the intricacies of bug junk.[91] Not sure that's what mom was going for.

There was even less about Mr Watches the person. Nearly all of his imprints were of things. He must have found them incredibly interesting for them to take precedence over actual life events. I wondered, sadly, if he'd even had life events. He seemed a solitary person with the one hobby and that was it. Not a single reflection, hardly a glimmer of any other people. No spouse, no kids, no family. Not even a cat. Imprints were largely of time spent alone, reading about antiques and rarities, pulling old timepieces down from a cabinet, inspecting them, then going to bed. No life beyond his obsession.[92]

These were very different people, except for one distinct similarity. They shared an imprint with each other – and with me. They knew about the Chime and the Note of Jecca. Both were plenty obsessed with them, and both put in hours upon hours in libraries trying to understand the things haunting their minds. They never got anywhere, of course. Having come years before me, neither had the internet – which explained why I was the one picked up by a bounty hunter.

A blank reflection appeared. A long span with heavy ends and crenellations down the middle length. Neon blue, with a glowing amber cap-piece. I caught it and flipped it around as I had with similar polygons a thousand times before, then pulled it through the lid on the third axis to check the glimmers. These were supposed to be imprints from a life lived. If I'd learned anything at all from Bugs and Watches, it was that only the most important things made an impression enough to imprint the cord. You can't form an imprint of nothing, and yet these were empty. A malfunction in the dredge? A malfunction in the third prior?

---

91 The *ins* and *outs* if you will. I'll be here all week.
92 Remind you of anyone?

I set the reflection to the side and caught the next as it traced across on the glass. I blinked the afterimage of the previous shape over it and flopped it around until I found an orientation that made sense. The two fit, like so many of the others. They had structure, completeness. But still no data. Nothing came of the glimmers even when the slices were overlayed. I tossed the pair and tried with another. I created couplings that had a quality of *wholeness*, yet they remained substantively empty. No scenes presented themselves. Nothing of the life of the person whose memories I now perceived.

I called them up more quickly, finding pairs, connecting them into larger components. With a heavy nectar habit and so many hours inside the machine, I retained the afterimages in greater detail than before, and began to lay pairs over pairs, soon discovering that those fit together too. Even as I lost touch with the components I'd built, I grasped upon a general understanding of a larger, but still data-free, structure.

It was sort of like Wheel of Fortune, where a contestant tries to guess a word or phrase while only being presented with some of the letters. The patterns and shapes displayed by the dredge was like being given a few of the letters to the larger puzzle. Early on, I didn't understand what they meant or how they fit together. But over time they began to make sense. I was able to delineate how reflections were organized to form coherent groups – what would be the actual "words" on the gameshow. I came to think of these groups as modules.

Take, for example, the word "abduction." At first, I needed the dredge to give me every "letter" in order to know the word. But now, with more time on the cord, I was adept at deducing the word without all the "letters". I could look at a whole series of patterns and have one for every "letter" but the "o", and guess the word, or module. Once I knew the reflection – or "letter" – that I needed to complete the "word", so to speak, I could call it up and complete the piece.

Soon, it got to the point that I no longer required every single reflection to complete the larger module. A few shapes – or "letters" – were often enough to dictate what the word would be. As I required fewer pieces, my work was easier, faster, and more intuitive. It's that intuition part that finally breaks my game show analogy.[93]

Because now I understood the arrangement of each module before I had enough reflections to logically deduce it. It was akin to solving a Wheel of Fortune puzzle with only a few letters showing and guessing it right every time. I could look at a nine-letter word starting with A and ending with N, and know right away the answer was "abduction", which shouldn't be possible. Technically, it could be antimycin, addiction, afternoon, agitation, animation, antivenin, apportion, adulation, adoration, accordion, amphibian, ascension, accretion. So how did I know the module spelled "abduction" with only two of the patterns in place? There was no explanation beyond my drug-enhanced intuition, and what is the explanation for the intuition itself? Maybe it's just another type of undiscovered matter.

I had a feel for what I was building, and with each new piece the picture became clearer, allowing me to purposefully call up reflections I'd never seen on the dredge lid, but knew to exist somewhere down the cord.

Speedily, I layered afterimages of stacked pairs upon new reflections that appeared, taking mental snapshots of the resulting modules and then fitting them to subsequent groupings. Like memorizing words to form a sentence, then sentences to form a paragraph, and paragraphs to form a page; my mind had reached the limit of visual recall.[94] I looked upon the page I had built, just before it dissolved, and finally understood what I was seeing.

Blueprints.

---

93 Keep your day job, Vanna.
94 I've reached the limit of your analogies.

The blank reflections I'd been ignoring *were* the data.

The reflections weren't coming from Mr Bugs or Mr Watches – this was genuine content from Mystery Contestant Number Three, the one who held the secret of the Chime's location and the key to resurrecting the Bloom of God. And here they were, handing over the map. Sort of.

I refocused and dove back in, creating modules from fragments to build pages – so to speak – of a larger thing. Soon I had two pages, and then three.[95] Then one page would fade away, forgotten. The process was a lot like playing Simon, actually, except instead of having to remember sequences of colors and tones, I was remembering shapes and orientations. I built more, working to outpace what my memory dumped.

Soon I had enough to construct entire sections into discrete segments, or chunks of the build, and hold them in my expanded short-term memory.

All of those late nights playing Simon with Patton had trained me for this very moment. Though, in fairness, I think the space-drugs helped.

Back in the enclosure it was nectar time. A rush of blood spread across my chest and head in anticipation, and I could actually feel my eyes dilating.

Tired from a long day of trying to restore the Bloom of God to its rightful owners, I rolled over and reached for the tube. Patton was there too, laying on his side, right where I'd left him that "morning" with Pickles.

His eyes were slivers. "Ben?" he mumbled.

He looked like shit shat sideways. We both looked like shit, but even though it had been a while since I'd consulted a mirror, there was no way I was pacing Patton's level of

---

95 And then a chapter and then a book, we get it.

defilement. Dark circles had formed around his eyes almost like bruises in purple, yellow, and green.

"Hey buddy," I said, yanking the tube to the wall of the enclosure so I could sit upright while I shot up. "You don't look so hot."

"I don't feel good."

Well, he wouldn't, would he?

"Ben? Do you think you could lend me the food tube? For just a minute or two?" he asked. "I'm pretty sure the food eel is just serving our own recycled shit." He laughed sadly.

Pathetic. Trying to soften me up with bad jokes. I was surprised they were feeding him at all to be honest. He wasn't even a Stringer. What could he offer? I propped myself against the side of the enclosure, tubes in either hand. "Man, you know I would, it's just that nectar is for saviors, and I need the vitamins and minerals in this to help me with my dredging." I used my nicest voice for all of this and continued, "What if I don't get enough nutrition because I gave some nectar to you and the dredge scrambles my brain? Also, I really think it's against the rules to share the food tube." Ugh, this was all so depressing. "Eat Pickles if you want something different. Just break it open, I don't care."

"We promised each other we'd save Pickles until we escaped or one of us died," he said.

"That was your weird idea and I absolve you," I said, making the sign of the cross and then pushing the tubes together. "Don't blame me for being hungry when you refuse to eat the food that they give you."

"I do eat the food, Ben, it's just—"

The nectar hit me like I'd been punched in the face through a paper sack full of fairy dust. My consciousness quickly scrolled up and out of view. All I heard of Patton was more self-pity about how the slop from the food eel gave him the runs.

CHAPTER THIRTY-TWO

Aptat made for the remnants of *Terror's Glaive* immediately, taking with them a small squadron of drones and a giant space net filled with more nets into which they would place whatever salvage they could cut out of it. Even though it had been sliced into ten pieces, the Vortu cruiser was a larger ship than the *Silent Child* and would have plenty of treasure left intact.

Oush sat at the console watching a visual of the *Glaive* as Aptat flew around, ~~excising~~ cutting out various components with the magmafier. The coupling of the powerful carapace to the stringhunter's mind and body allowed Aptat to work with exceptional efficiency and speed. Naecia watched with a mixture of awe and jealousy. What she could do with a fully functional suit like that.

She broke from the display and went back to working on the Switch. Before Aptat had crossed over to the *Glaive*, she'd made them break down the operation of the axon diadem. It was an exceptional piece of tech. Like a comprehensive implant, capable of parsing and cataloguing thought. With a few tweaks, it was easily modified, converting it from a transmitter into a junction. Eventually, she got the Switch talking to it, so that it would be able to receive the accumulated data and dump it into her mind while she tried to commune with the Fray. The only thing left was to connect them all together into one circuit.

"How much do you want?" called Aptat through the com.

Naecia removed the diadem and looked over Izairis' shoulder at the console display. "What did you find?" she said.

"Old Princess Dekies was an accomplished marauder. Makes us look that much better for taking them out," answered Aptat. "The *Glaive*, my merry crew of psychological anomalies, is a fecund trove brimming with treasures. Industrious little thieves, these Vortu were. Weapons, data cells, antiquities, stolen tech, food... probably. Don't know if we want that, really. Oh, and tell HyRope there's plenty of raw caridianite *and* any other precious elements she's keen on. I'll gather an assortment. Might keep some of it myself to wear as jewelry."

"Just the caridianite for me," said Naecia.

"Done and done," said Aptat. "Naturally, I'll bring this back to the ship myself when the rest of the salvaging is complete. Ciao."

"Ciao?" asked Izairis.

Oush shrugged.

Naecia would have preferred to just get the stuff in hand, but Aptat obviously understood the concept of insurance. It was theoretically possible that they'd abandon the stringhunter if they got what they needed. In fact, it was probably what they *should* do if presented with the chance. Aptat was, after all, a self-interested, kidnapping piece of space garbage. Still, Naecia had made a deal and the thought of betrayal... she wasn't wired for it.

"Open bay one, please, if you would, fledgling owners of the *Silent Child*," said Aptat mockingly.

"Bay one opening," answered Oush.

Aptat attached a drone to one of the bulging nets and pushed it out from the cruiser. "This batch has a rack of universal power cells, a squadron of short-range probes, some Khatisi religious iconography – wait until you see that, *I mean, wow*, and a case of genuine, variable-aperture Vortu blunderbusses. Never played with anything like those. Oh, and voidsuits, too.

Will probably be a little baggy on you lot, well, maybe not big Oush." The drone pulled the cargo across the vacuum, leaving it inside a stall in bay one, then returned to Aptat for the next load.

Naecia dug back into the Switch, hardwiring it to the ship's main power. It was the first time she was able to bring the machine fully online. Before now, she'd never had access to the immense energy required for its operation. After the connection was made, she checked the fidelity of the quantum processors on a small display and made some micro-adjustments to the particle shielding. She then ran through the aggregation and cataloguing script that she'd gotten courtesy of the twin mathematicians. It was the machine's heart; what it would use to bundle data for something to be transferred. In this case, the *Silent Child* and everyone in it.

Aptat remained on the *Glaive* for nearly half a cygie, excitedly filling more than twenty nets with salvage, while noisily regaling them through the com about every little bauble they'd found, like a child discovering a cache of gifts ahead of the Aphelion Festival. They dispatched the final drone, the one Naecia had been waiting for, and began a final sweep. She watched the drone's signature anxiously as it made its way over.

"Whoa, look at this," said Aptat. "Those cheap bastards!"

Oush switched from the macro visual of the *Glaive* over to the stringhunter's POV camera, and everyone pressed in around the display. The dilaceration cannon had sliced away a portion of the *Glaive*'s inner hull, exposing a compartment into which arm-sized metallic bars were set. None of them – probably even including Aptat – had ever seen so much guush in one place. Naecia's own mental discipline faltered as she swam into fantasies about what she could do with money like that.

Aptat yanked a pair of the billets free and turned them over, exposing red embossments crossing the base of each pewter-colored ingot like a ribbon. "And it's registered. All of it."

Excitement spread among the observers like a pheromone. Oush picked up Izairis, who, looking stunned, nearly disappeared in his massive embrace. Naecia, too, was swept up in the revelry. An equal share of that type of money could take care of her family for ten lifetimes. It was virtually unspendable. Aptat dragged a cargo box close and began filling it. "We'll need to do a second trip," they said, plucking the bars. "I'll get more hard boxes from the *Child* to hold all of this." A high pitch squelch filled the transmission. "Welp. That's a booby trap."

Aptat kicked off from the ship and hit the suit's thrusters. "Come on, come on, come on!"

The display bled white. A moment later, a shockwave hit the *Child* and hyper-accelerated debris punched holes in the ship. A piece burst though one side of the deck and exited through a display screen just over Naecia's shoulder.

"Depressurizing!" screamed Izairis.

Oush quickly navigated the ship's menu. "There!" he said. "Foam!"

Naecia watched the inbound hole fill with an expanding grey sludge. She rushed to a display that was still working and gazed upon the empty starfield. "Is it gone, is it gone?"

Oush manually narrowed the visual field to the *Glaive's* prior location. A few bits of detritus floated about. The rest had been ejected into space with the explosion. Oush tapped the com. "Aptat, can you hear me? Are you there?" He repeated it again. "Aptat–"

Silence.

"Oh no," said Naecia, thinking about the caridianite, the money, and the stringhunter, in that order.

"Send a ping," said Izairis, tapping the command.

There was an answer. "Hello. You have reached Aptat. I'm sorry I can't come to the com right now. If you leave your name, locator ID, and – *yeah* I'm here."

Naecia elbowed Izairis aside. "Where? You're not on the scope. Where is the drone with the caridianite?"

"Thank you for your concern, Naecia, I too am well after just being blown up in space." Pause. "I am currently tumbling outbound at eight thousand *mylics per cygment.* Fortunately for me, I suppose, I share the same approximate vector as the drone carrying your rare elements. You may come and retrieve us both now."

CHAPTER THIRTY-THREE
THE INSTRUMENT MAKER

She leaned in, tilting one of her aural ridges toward the Ukelaklava's sound cavity, as the young Quileg who held it stared up at her. "Bend it here," she said, just barely touching the instrument's tonal arm. Then sliding her fore-digit up the arm almost imperceptibly, said, "Not here. Do you see the difference?" The child nodded and rearranged his grasp on the instrument.

The Instrument Maker smiled and knelt while the other three hundred members of her fledgling orchestra looked on. She preferred to stand while giving instruction, but the new life quickening in her belly forced more frequent breaks. "Kodoah?"

The child raised his large, cervid eyes.

"The instrument is too sensitive to be played by fingers alone. Muscles are clumsy and inexact, no matter how small. You must allow your hearts to guide your body. Allow yourself to feel the music and your fingers will fall upon the right spot. Hearts lead, body follows, right Kodoah?" Seeing the tiniest gesture of affirmation from the child, she moved his fore-digits back to the improper position. "So. Do not think to adjust your grip to find the correct tone. I want your hearts to find it. Do you understand?"

Nod.

The Instrument Maker stood, hind limbs crackling. "Good. You know the music now. Every note, every count, every nuance. If you truly feel it in your hearts, then you will be able to find it no matter where your hand is on the instrument." She reached down and twisted a single peg on the ukelav, taking it completely out of tune. "Now, show me."

The child looked down upon the instrument as if it had been hammered into splinters.

"The notes are still there, Kodoah. If the music is truly within you, you will find the notes even though they are hidden."

The child studied her face, shut his eyes, then reset his grasp on the ukelaklava and placed his sliffbarque bow evenly upon the strings and tonal arm. He exhaled and drew the bow downward, releasing a whining note so incongruous with the music as to seem intentionally terrible. He blinked up at her.

"Go ahead."

He reset, closed eyes again, pressed the tonal arm so far down toward the body of the instrument that they nearly touched. A confident stroke and a single note sprang from the ukelav. Pure and powerful. The first note of the arrangement. Then the next. And the next. Through wild alterations in the positioning of the tonal arm, he found the music, stroking the notes one after another, bending them together, letting his hearts lead the way.

The Instrument Maker stepped back and addressed the room with her eyes. She held a single fore-digit aloft. When Kodoah reached the end of the first measure, she gave the signal and the air boomed as three hundred others fell in to joined him.

CHAPTER THIRTY-FOUR

We didn't see a lot of the old China White down in Great Bend, Kansas, so heroin was just my best guess. Weed and shrooms were about the limit of my experience, and nectar was not those. A few of the old guys from the shop sprinkled crystal methamphetamines into their Big Gulps to get a leg up on each other as they competed for the most productive fishing stitches before the ass crack of dawn every day. Meth. Big Gulps. That's a real thing people do.

Nectar was heroin *plus* shrooms *plus* steroids... and probably a dash of meth. Enough narcotic and psychedelic firepower to blow my brain's restrictor plate clean off. You know how they say that humans only use ten percent of their brain?[96] Well, now I was using all of it. Exhilarating, but also terrifying. Like at any moment my skull might spring a leak and annihilate a star.

Down the cord, I was able to park exponentially more pieces of the build in my short-term memory, retaining enough to see entire segments of structure that by this point comprised thousands of reflections. I spent longer inside. Being on the cord was the only time I didn't suffer from withdrawal. I think that was planned.

---

96 A myth, of course, but that still hurts, man. You and I were pushing eleven, twelve percent.

I was no longer fitting pieces together and wondering what to do with them, I was *constructing*. Reflections became pairs, pairs layered on other pairs and became modules, modules matched and layered became chunks. Chunks grew into clusters that together formed sections. I soon realized that the blueprints weren't for a machine or a ship. They were of a location. A place. A place I'd seen before. In my living room. The LEGO monument from the coffee table. Not the LEGO version, of course. That was merely a crude translation of the thing I was assembling in the dredge, but there was no doubt they were the same. Patton and I sat on the couch for hours snapping pieces together, never thinking about what the thing was other than a way to pass the time while stoned. Thinking back, I must have known all along that it was more than that, because after he would go home or pass out, I routinely undid all of his work. His pieces didn't fit the plan that I didn't know existed. Something in my subconscious had been trying to push through.

The structure began to crystalize. Nothing about the fragments or their conglomerated forms provided any concrete information about what they were, but context of location, shape, orientation, size, etcetera, allowed me to deduce the function of the various sections I built. Some were operational units – where the orders and signals came from. I knew this based on their positions and the deduced functions of surrounding areas. This wasn't some autonomous blob. It was a place for people – or someone. There were common areas and living quarters, energy generation, propulsion, climate management, transportation. Some were weapons. I built them up and understood their *purpose* even when nothing about the designs explained how they worked.

A city was the only thing it could be. Roughly spherical, and immense at that.[97] It had something *like* buildings, tens

---

97 So, the Death Star – *A spherical city is not a novel concept.* Star Wars

of thousands of them, each many times taller than Earth's skyscrapers. And they didn't sit on foundations. They were joined together, forming the body of the studded sphere itself, with a hollow core made of open space.

Was this where the Scythin lived?

I could see almost all of it at once now, and yet reflections kept coming. I had to build it out. Every detail. And even though I held exponentially more information than any human mind before me, it was getting hard to keep it organized. Even the performance-enhancing properties of the space crank was limited by my basic physiology.

I improvised an organizational system. I divided the sphere into four quadrants, or slices, and assigned them each a color: red, blue, yellow, and green – in that order, just like Simon. I started at zero degrees longitude and went east from the tallest building. Thereafter, each became home to one of the four traditional Kingdoms of life: Red for Animals, Blue for Fungi, Green for Plants, and Yellow for Protista.[98]

Latitudinally, I named the buildings within each Kingdom after a species that belonged there. I was able to fill Animalia most thoroughly, as that had been my prior's specialty, but his peripheral knowledge was enough to provide a decent amount of organization for the other three. Not with the specificity of the Red Quadrant of course, where every building was named for a unique animal to make it easier to remember. Marmot. Glassfrog. Fossa. Sun bear. Okapi. Red-lipped batfish. Long-wattled umbrella bird. Venezuelan poodle moth. Penis snake. Pacu.[99]

---

can't lay claim to any round object in space just because people live on it. That's silly – You ignorant child.

98 Some in academia advocate for five, six, seven, or even eight Kingdoms – Well, we're doing four, because there are four original Simon colors.

99 An easy to remember fish. They have human-looking teeth. See? Now you'll never forget.

As I built, my expanded mind chugged along in the periphery. How would I know where the Chime was located, if indeed it was here? Would it give off a heat signature? Change color? As big as this structure was, I could build forever and never find it.

I hated it when the dredge powered down before I could come up the cord. It was the mental equivalent to trying to stop peeing midstream.

The lid spread open. Eyes greeted me as usual.

"What?" I asked, post-dredge/nectar withdrawal headache already forming.

Save us. Gone is the Bloom of God, the Note of Jecca.

"You literally just stopped me from *trying* to save you, just to *tell* me to save you?" I snapped, petulantly. "You're going to have to up my dose of nectar if you're gonna start interrupting me in the middle of my work. I had something good going down there."

The holes in Eyes' face reconfigured and a wave of crimson passed over their boids. They whispered, *Where is the Chime?*

"Down there somewhere! I'm doing my best." I gestured maniacally to the inside of the dredge where I sat. "Seriously, though, I need double nectar. I'm building a tolerance."

You move too slowly. No more nectar.

This was an affront. I stood up aggressively, but before I could demand to talk to the manager, I went light-headed and had to use the dredge to avoid falling over. "I need the nectar to do my work. I've found a big structure or something down there."

Structure?

"Some sort of Death Star."

Which Death Star?

Now, to my mind there were two Death Stars, but I knew that wasn't what Eyes was asking. "Like, a floating city. Hollow in the middle."

Eyes' posture changed. Back straight. Shoulders back. *Hollow city. Name the hollow city, Ben.*

"There are more than one?" I asked.

Hollow cities. Thousands.

"Thousands?" I was sobering right up and starting to tweak.

Thousands.

It was all too much. I started yelling. "Tell me what the Chime does! What is the Bloom of God?" I'd asked these questions a billion times already with no answer. But then,

To carry us home. Save us.

That was something new. "Get you home?" I said, settling down with this offering of new information. "Okay, look, just, ah, let's get some more nectar in here and I'll get back to work."

Save us and you will absorb nectar.

"No, no, no," I said, wagging my finger at the creature that could crush me in a millisecond. "It doesn't work that way. You got me addicted to that stuff. You can't just take it away cold turkey!"

Save us. Absorb nectar.

I started to shake, or maybe I'd already been shaking. "You listen here, Jezzer—" *Wait,* I thought, *who the fuck is Jezzer?*

Suddenly, the Scythin morphed their body, allowing their back and shoulders to splay out like a fan in the same way the tropical bird *Lophorina supurba* shapes its wings to turn itself into a big black crescent for the purpose of attracting females.[100] Only, I don't think Eyes was trying to get me into bed. This was an intimidation display. Or maybe not, because then the Scythin turned neon red and exploded. Literally *exploded* apart into all their individual boids.

I watched, dumfounded, as they spread evenly into a line that ran across the floor, up the walls and over the ceiling,

---

100 Populations of *supurba* are literal sausage fests, so attracting one of the rare females takes immense effort and these guys put in the work.

then just as quickly, sprang back together. Shock and awe
stuff. It was impressive, and probably would have intimidated
someone less focused on getting their fix.

Eyes returned to their normal, dusky shade of black. *You are
remembering.*

"Jezzer? Is that your name?"

The reflections told you.

"They must have... I guess?"

Jezzer, said Jezzer, tapping their chest. *We are hunger. Save us.
Home.*

Behind Jezzer, the door's sinuous strands stretched apart.
Another Scythin stomped in. Pushed ahead of it was Patton.
Maybe it was the room, or the sobering news that my nectar
connection had dried up, but I saw him clearly for the first
time since I'd started this thing.

His suffering fell into sharp relief. Hunched and emaciated.
Filthy. A hollowness ballooned inside my chest and I could
almost hear the pieces of my heart clattering on my ribs as
it crumbled. In seeing Patton, I saw the consequences of my
decisions reflected back to me. I'd abandoned him. Worse, even,
I'd watched him suffer and then judged him for it. He'd faded
as I'd gorged, beholden to nectar and indifferent to his decline.
And through it all, he'd never treated me any differently. He'd
never fought me, challenged me, called me out for what I was
doing. Ugh, I felt weak, nauseous. I deserved that. I deserved
far worse.

The Scythin prodded Patton in the side and he collapsed
onto the floor.

"Patton!" I cried. He didn't so much as glance in my direction.
I went to step out from the dredge, but Jezzer stopped me. I
called out again.

The other Scythin lifted Patton up from the floor and led
him toward the center of the room. I realized it then, like sun
burning away a quilt of morning fog: they were going to dredge
him. My chest was a lava chamber filling with molten panic.

"Hey," I said, softly, beseeching the Scythin called Jezzer. "He's not a Stringer. You can't put him in a dredge. You can't torture him."

The Scythin emitted a sound no louder than air through a vent. *No. You will.*

CHAPTER THIRTY-FIVE

Naecia was in disbelief when they finally tracked down Aptat and found them still alive. And not just alive, but completely unharmed. Only the carapace gave any hint that it had just been in a small nuclear explosion, with a few nicks and inconsequential burn marks. There had been some grumbling among the ship's crew that they ought to just rescue the rare elements and leave Aptat on the float – especially now that all the guush had been wiped out. The argument had merit, but the prospect of galactic annihilation made for strange couplings, and the stringhunter had done as they'd asked without trying any sleight of hand. For the time being, Aptat – and especially their suit – were assets. If Naecia was able to get the Switch working, they were setting themselves up for a conflict with the Scythin, and the indestructible carapace would be essential.

The drone was a misshapen ball of polymers, having just narrowly escaped vaporization at the edge of the blast radius. Similarly, the coil of caridianite had melted onto its spool into a lopsided, globular chunk that looked like a meteorite. It nevertheless remained elementally sound.

Perhaps feeling sanguine that they'd actually been plucked out of space rather than left to drift until the day the Universe finally went to holes, Aptat agreed to help Naecia work the caridianite back into shape. Using a combination of the magmafier and the ship's modest machining hardware, they were able to melt down and extrude the blob back into wire.

Over the next cygie, Naecia installed the fresh wire into homemade receivers appended to the axon diadem and connected it to the machine's data output. She added some leftover caridianite to the interferometer prongs at the top of the machine to boost its fidelity, thus enhancing its ability to quickly gather particle data for cataloguing.

She found herself in a bit of a trance as she went through the repetitive exercise of layering the wire around the prongs, and, as she did so, thoughts of the lanky Earth pilot drifted into her conscious mind. *E.* Naecia vowed that if they got out of all this alive, she'd find out about the woman who had conspired with the scholar to commune with the Oblivion Fray.

If they got out alive. The first of many *ifs* that stood between now and being able to save her family, who didn't even know they were in danger. She took hold of the puzzle amulet at her neck and pretended to feel her brother's touch. What she knew – or thought she knew – about the Scythin, seemed to make every *if* more insurmountable.

The theory, of course, was that the Scythin were extra-dimensional. Captain Arrohauk had captured the closest thing to any evidence of this on her scopes with the formation of the Arusne Supervoid and the concurrent disappearance of the *Timelance*. The Chime was the device – or so it went – that made it all possible by somehow drawing the dimensions together, at which point the *Timelance* could slip across.

The consequence of this was the creation of an artificial void – a vacancy in space with no stars or matter. It would make a cold spot many tens of millions or billions of gilleys wide. No one knew exactly how large a void – Arusne had only been one gilley – but there were plenty of others in the observable universe with which to compare. Some were big enough to swallow not just a galaxy, but entire superclusters. Thousands, even millions of galaxies, all at once in a single moment. Every time the *Timelance* crossed from one dimension to another was a passive act of galacticide. But it was powerless to do so without the Chime.

Now it was *her* galaxy under threat – the tiny bit of Universe that contained everything Naecia had ever known or loved. And its survival hinged on the Chime's whereabouts remaining safely buried within the brain of an affable but clueless Earth man long enough for her and her compatriots to find him, erase his mind, and kill him, just to be sure.

There was no telling what weaponry the *Timelance* had, assuming they could even find the ship. Attacking it head-on was out of the question. If things ended up going bad, they could always fire the dilaceration cannons as a final resort, but better to try another tack first before picking fights with spaceships of unknown capability.

She would wait for a successful test of the Switch before proposing her plan.

Naecia worked nonstop until she'd used up every bit of the caridianite. Completed, the Switch was an odd-looking contraption, a black box with a golden crown. Festooned in the highly conductive wire, the machine's processors would theoretically be able to scan and catalogue every particle of the ship, down to the motes of dust that traveled through the nav system's holographic projections.

She brought it online, then transferred the processors to the ship's power. The screen on the side flicked on. "Let's see if this thing can see us," she said, initiating the machine's cataloguing function from a connected data pad. The lights flickered.

"Did the lights just go off?" asked Oush.

"Yes, Oush. Good observation," said Aptat. "Naecia: did your little machine just pull enough power to interrupt the flow of energy from the reactor?"

"A quintillion superpositional bits will do that," she answered. "Here, look."

The screens on the machine and on the pad showed a simple outline of the *Silent Child*. She transferred the image to one of the big displays. Below the outline, data began populating into columns, going exponentially faster as it went. At the same time, the ship icon started to fill in. After a few cycliseconds it had gone from empty black to glowing orange. "Hmm," she said. "That was fast."

"That's it?" asked Izairis.

"What did it just do?" asked Oush.

"It scanned and catalogued all of the matter on the ship."

Aptat pointed to the columns on the display. "Why are those numbers changing?"

"Well, because matter is always changing," answered Naecia. "We are breathing in the air, converting and exhaling it. The cells inside our body are dividing, dying, growing cyclisec over cyclisec. The ship's battery levels oscillate. Dust drifts from one place to the next. The machine is reflecting the current state of matter at every moment. Whatever that state is when we trigger the drive is the state that will be reproduced."

"How do you know we'll be reproduced in one piece and not jumbled all together into some gruesome mixture of people and spaceship?" said Izairis.

"Ah, yes," said Aptat, stiffly slapping a leg. "The classic teleportation mix-up."

Naecia tapped the pad and gestured the data up onto the large holographic display. "Look, matter is all about location and number. Change the location and number of electrons, protons, and neutrons, change the matter—"

"This isn't helping," said the ex-nun.

"Somewhere in here," said Naecia, approaching the display, "are the numbers that represent the locations of the particles that make you. Not just within your body, but within the ship." She pinched the screen on the pad, expanding the display to show hundreds of columns. "Let's try to find Izairis. Everybody, hold still. Izairis, walk in a circle around the machine." Izairis gave an easy shrug and began a slow lap around the Switch.

Naecia scrolled through a menu. "I'm looking for large, wholesale changes. With everything else being static, I should be able to find Izai – *ah*." She zoomed back in and focused on a column that looked no different from any of the others, except that the raw data was changing as Izairis made her way around the Switch. "There you are," said Naecia. "Now stop."

Izairis did and the numbers settled back down.

"See?" said Naecia.

No one looked terribly reassured.

"Look," she said. "If it doesn't work, we have a fortune in salvage and can run away as quickly as you like. We'll sell it and get rich and then one day, we will all simply cease to exist when the Scythin recover the Chime."

"Isn't that how all life ends?" said Aptat. "You just cease to exist?"

"Aren't you immortal?" Naecia responded.

"If no one kills me first, yes. Of course, how does one prove immortality? Forever has no endpoint. So, I suppose I'm immortal in the sense that I will live until I die."

Naecia donned the reconfigured axon diadem and established a link to the machine. Aptat seemed to start, causing Naecia to look up, but the stringhunter quickly regained their usual buoyant affect. "Are we leaving forthwith?"

Naecia surprised herself with the answer. The Switch Drive was ready. There was nothing to further tweak or refine. It was *go* or *not go*. "We are."

"Now?" asked Oush.

Naecia mumbled in the affirmative, then, "Which direction did the Earth man's voidscull container go?"

Aptat brought up a map showing the voidscull's trajectory before it entered bulkspace, a simple straight line headed out from the *Silent Child*. "It was aimed here," said Aptat, circling what seemed like a random spot of black. "This is where the Scythin broadcasts originated from. I don't think they're moving around. They're waiting."

Naecia's eyes flicked to the scale on the map. "So that's where we'll go," she said. "*Also…*"

Aptat looked up from the nav where a macro display of the galaxy's Dasma Arm appeared. "Also what?"

"Also," said Naecia, rocking her head side to side, "I think we have to do it twice."

"Twice?" asked Oush. "I'm starting not to love this."

"Same," echoed Izairis.

"According to the Earth scholar Payne-Gaposchkin, the protoparticles that make up thought mass are chiral – the literal reverse of each other. Unsuperimposable…" She glanced around at their blank faces. "Point being, the drive is going to bind us to these Fray particles at a distance. If we use the drive once, then the resulting "us" will be the polar opposite of what we started out as. It's probably best to limit our time in that state. This is why we have to unmirror–"

"What does that even mean?" asked Oush. "How will we manifest when we get to the endpoint? Will we turn inside out?"

"Another great question, Oush," added Aptat. "Will I regain ownership of the *Silent Child*? Will the rest of you go back to being merchandise?"

"What if we all become the opposite of who we are now?" asked Izairis. "Aptat becomes a good person and we become evil? Oush shrinks to the size of a boblet."

Naecia filled her cheeks. Any of them could be right. But it was wrong to assume that chirality would manifest in any one way. It didn't automatically mean *behaving* in the opposite. It could simply mean *being in a state of chirality* while behaving in the exact same way. "I think we just have to do it and find out. We'll execute the Switch twice."

Naecia checked the particle catalogue, adjusted the axon diadem, and glanced to the map showing their best guess

as approximate location of the *Timelance,* plus or minus ten
million mylics.

"Here we go," she said, shutting her eyes and opening the
circuit between the machine and the axon diadem.

Her mind blanched supernova white as nearly eight-
hundred exapids of data passed through it. Then it was over.

CHAPTER THIRTY-SIX

".different any feel don't I .happened Nothing." said Aptat, looking at their hands.

Nothing had happened. No portal had opened. No tunnel of stars had gone shooting by. There had been so sensation of movement, no change in orientation. Naecia knelt down to the machine and checked the readings to make sure there were no obvious malfunctions.

".work didn't this that now ,So." said Izairis, *".have may we friends nun on money spending days our out Live .salvage the sell and somewhere get we suggest I"*

".creamery paste-blem own my run to wanted always have I." said Oush.

Aptat seemed surprisingly sullen that it hadn't worked. Naecia was at a loss. She'd done everything according to her priors, building on their work with better equipment and more advanced technology. There had just been a malfunction. She would fix it. A full dismantling of the drive and rebuild. *".down shut a for redundancies these remove to need I."* She gestured to the tool kit. *"?grippers the me fetch you can - Izairis"*

Izairis checked through the kit, found the tool, and tossed it over. Naecia plucked it from the air and bent over to loosen the bolts around the first power redundancy.

"!STOP ,on Hold," shouted Aptat.

Naecia froze, *"?it is What"*

".lefty a You're"

"?so ,Yeah"

Aptat stomped a foot and made a drastic, open-handed *Ta-dah!* gesture to where Naecia was touching the machine. She followed their gaze down to where she was holding the grippers. With her *right* hand.

They exchanged a glance. *"!shits Eleven,"* said Aptat, spinning to the nav display.

"Wait," Naecia asked, her heart pounding. *"?work it Did"*

Aptat threw out the hologram, showing them presently within a gilley of the *Timelance's* estimated location. *".HyRope Naecia ,travel instantaneous invented You've"* They sounded genuinely impressed.

".it rediscovered only I," she said truthfully.

".different any feel don't I," said Oush.

".same the feel I ,Yeah," said Izairis.

Naecia consulted the data pad and then the hologram showing all the columns of data. She set it side by side with the original readings. *"Look."*

Each bit of data had changed to its opposite. *".be should it what of opposite the that's importance of anything about out find we before jump second our do to best Probably"*

Oush very slowly pulled out the front band of his pants and peered inside.

".two number Switch," announced Naecia. *".goes Here"*

Again, no one felt anything, but this time they knew what to look for. Naecia tossed the grippers from her right hand to her left. She removed the diadem and shut down the drive. "That was strange." She checked the nav. The nearest stellar body was a double star called Effelox Binary some four gilleys distant.

Aptat sauntered to the machine, heels clicking, and patted it reverently. "This technology is worth more than every bar of guush ever forged, you know that?" they said with a wink. "I'm tempted to steal it from you."

Naecia tried to project a face that treated Aptat's comment as only a joke, even though she knew there was truth in it.

"Escaping now is a reality, Naecia," said Aptat, seriously. "I'll take you back home to Drev for your family. Then we can go anywhere. Far."

"*You'll* take *me*?" she snarled.

"Poor phrasing."

Naecia had been so focused on getting the drive to work and on finding the Earth man that she'd failed to consider that she now had a way to safely escape with her family. All she had to do was say the word. So, why wasn't she?

"I guess I don't want to leave knowing that an entire swath of the Universe is about to be erased. All the people dying because they couldn't get away. And how far away would be enough for us to be safe if we did leave? Is it one galaxy over, or ten, a hundred? I don't like the idea of the Scythin just wiping people out like that. If we have a chance to stop it, shouldn't we try?"

"And what exactly about your particular experience inculcated you with such noble ideals?" said Aptat.

"You don't agree?"

"I understand self-interest, darling, in case that hasn't been made clear to you now across multiple scenarios."

"You don't mind knowing that you might have prevented trillions of deaths but chose to do nothing?"

"All of those trillions will die anyway. And there are trillions of others, living in a trillion other galaxies. And that's just this dimension."

"Immortality might not be the boon you think it is," Naecia answered.

"Explain."

"The Dasma Arm is the place you know. Given enough time, you'll find yourself in the company of the Scythin again. Or maybe not. But – maybe they'll trigger the Chime and you'll cease to exist without knowing why. Maybe you'll just glimpse the darkness and know in that last moment what had happened – that they'd finally caught up to you. Well... that sounds like torture to me. Living all of those eons and just knowing it was a matter of time until they crossed your path – and that maybe you could have stopped them."

"Are all Scellans so optimistic? I didn't think I could be any more depressed, but you're a real gravity well."

"Sorry for bringing a little conscience to the conversation," she said.

"Fortunately, I lack a conscience. My mind is unchanged."

"I'm not trying to change your mind. I'm just trying to understand it," she said. "Let's have a look at those Vortu suits in case we're lucky enough to have actually landed somewhere near to the *Timelance*."

Leaving Izairis at the ship's console, Naecia and Aptat headed down to the cargo deck where they'd stowed the salvage from the *Terror's Glaive*. Naecia ran her fingers over the pieces of equipment that Aptat had cut out of the ship, still piled in nets and strapped down. Vortu engineering was of the conventional sort, but different enough to be interesting. Her idea of a fun time would have been tucking into one of the hulking components and dissecting it down to the last diode. Another time maybe.

Aptat found and unstrapped the boxes that held the voidsuits. Together, they unfolded them from inside and began the tedious exercise of checking seals. Naecia watched Aptat work. Focused. Efficient. Mind seemingly on nothing but the task. *Seemingly.* She would love to know what was going on inside it. Her own mind was full of questions and she opened her mouth only to remember being nearly choked out the last time she'd broached the subject of Aptat's past.

"Go ahead, then," Aptat said, scanning a wrist connection on one of the suits, then looking up. "What is it you want to know?"

Naecia swallowed the question and shook her head.

"No, it's fine, really. We'll all be dead soon and so this may be our one chance to really get to know one another," said Aptat, holding up their hands. "Look at us. Sitting here like a couple of besties. Circle of trust down here. Ask me anything."

"You know what I'm going to ask," she said.

"I do. But you have to ask it."

"Who else was here? In this ship with you. There was another person, wasn't there?"

"Mother."

Naecia shivered. "Mother?"

"Mm."

"I thought you were... assembled?"

"Is gestation of offspring a prerequisite to motherhood?" asked Aptat.

"I'm not sure what you're getting at."

Aptat sighed. "When I was floating in Earth's orbit, biding my time as I lured Ben out of hiding, I watched a lot of television – uh, the human term for entertainment feeds. Most of the programs were squarely in the *Housewives* franchise. It's this show where very shiny homestead caretakers become intoxicated and yell about each other into a camera and proceed to do surprisingly little caretaking of their various estates. I found it highly addictive, but did manage to pull myself away in order to vary my programming intake. I took a liking to their children's stories – primarily because the parents always seem to die. Anyway, one of these was a tender tale called *Pinocchio*. A childless old man named Geppetto builds a puppet out of wood and the boy comes to life. Geppetto is every bit the boy's father even though the boy was not realized as part of a biological process."

"I wasn't meaning to suggest otherwise," said Naecia, actually feeling a bit bad. "What happened?"

"I killed Geppetto."

Naecia froze.

"'Mother' was *her* word, not mine. Unlike Pinocchio, I wasn't created for my companionship. My purpose was… different."

Naecia put her head down and went back to work on the seals, dragging over a second voidsuit, then flicked her eyes up again.

Aptat nodded tightly and continued, "I was an implement."

Naecia crinkled her brow.

"A tool, simple as that. Something to be used by another to achieve an end." They sniffed. "Oh, these suits stink." They threw one aside and picked up another. "Anyhow. Mother was a dealer. A schemer. I was built to be her unquestioning accomplice. Sometimes I might be a decoy. Other times even her double. Her backup. Her leverage. I was whatever the situation called for. She arranged bigtime deals and I was the one that made sure they went down how she wanted. She might lull the other side into a false sense of security because she was only one person. When they dropped their guard, I would appear and flip the situation. We were unstoppable – especially with the suits. Never saying a word, just doing what the suit allowed me to do. She got rich that way. Bought this ship. Would have been richer too, had she lived longer."

"Where did your armor come from?"

"Stolen. Only pair ever made."

"She have one too?"

"*Had* one."

"Sounds like you guys had a good thing going," said Naecia. "For criminals."

"Oh, *she* did for sure. Me, not so much. While she searched for the next scheme, I lived inside my vault."

"In the cabinet?" said Naecia, gesturing to the deck above. "Where the suit goes?"

"Mmm-hmm. I waited inside the vault until she was ready for the next deal. Only then was I ever spoken to. To receive my instructions."

"Wait," said Naecia, pushing one suit aside and dragging over the next. "How long did she keep you in the vault?"

"On average between sixty and ninety cycles galactic. Sometimes a year or more."

Naecia sprang to her feet, her sense of justice flaring. "A year! Imprisoned in that little cabinet?"

"And I don't require sleep. How about that? I experienced every cyclisecond. Felt every moment of time fully. Of course, that was all I knew. I'd been born in that vault. It was where I'd been when my core was first ignited. From my perspective, that was life. Only once she started getting me out to run our operations did I see the larger world. That made it harder to go back in."

The horror of living inside a stand-up vault and never even having the temporary escape of sleep was unfathomable to Naecia. It made her own captivity seem like hardly a trifle. "How many times did this happen? How many times did you have to go back in?"

"Hundreds. Naturally it became unbearable the more I saw of the world. I very quickly went from assuming life was one way to realizing it was the other way. Mother had designed me with a robust neural processor in order to pull off our schemes, and so I ended up doing a lot of living inside of my own mind. It's what kept me from decohering, to borrow a term from myself."

Naecia saw the odd transposition of their situations. Stringers wanted out of their own heads. Aptat had retreated into theirs in order to avoid going mad.

"I created my own world up here," said Aptat, putting a finger to their skull. "Forged my own plans. Figured things out for myself."

Naecia shook her head, still finding it difficult to process the torture Aptat had undergone. "I would have screamed until she was forced to deal with me."

"Perhaps I would have done the same had I been made with a voice."

"What? You couldn't speak?"

"*Silent. Child,*" said Aptat, raising their brow.

Naecia raised hers back.

"This ship was called the *NineBlades* when Mother ran it – an obvious reference to the dilaceration cannon, and a subtle giveaway about the ship's armament that I never cared for. I changed it once she'd been relieved of command. Anyhow, Mother gave me everything but a voice. Once I was free, I bought myself a vocal organ, had it installed and changed the name of the ship."

Naecia shook her head and exhaled. "Wow."

"Don't get the idea that it was all bad for me. It wasn't like I took nothing from our partnership. Other than the questionable blessing of life and this smokin' bod, Mother gave me two extremely valuable gifts. First, a stunning clarity of vision. Second, a key to untold riches, a secret only few others were privy to at the time: Stringers. Thanks to her, I got my start."

"You don't appreciate the irony of this?" Naecia said, feeling any empathy for the stringhunter beginning to gutter. "Being enslaved only to become a slaver?"

"Not especially," said Aptat. "I rather found it to be a natural progression."

"That's sick."

"Depends on one's perspective, wouldn't you say?" They chuckled. "You know, there is an odd sensibility among some species – one that you seem to share with humans for instance – to see every person's story as an arc or a circle where, for some reason, they *grow* as life grinds them down, become wise and forgive. As if adversity is some kind of fertilizer for the soul. It's like this fiction they put in their television shows – now those are sick – a million different angles on the theme that suffering is redemptive. Would you believe that some of them actually *worship* that idea? Perverse, in my opinion. Yet there is a bias to only tell those stories, I think. People love a redemption story and so those are the ones we hear." Aptat tore out a piece of bad seal and set the suit aside. "I believe the opposite outcome is far more prevalent. Suffering begets suffering. I'm not the exception, Naecia, I'm the rule. That vault wasn't a forge from which my soul was going to emerge, enlightened. It *cast* me. I didn't escape from Mother wanting to change things for the better. What does that even mean, *better?* Better for whom? A life ground down grows hungry. All I knew is that I wanted to thrive, to get what was mine. And the more I see of the Universe, the more I am convinced that my way of doing things is the only way. To turn my wounds into treasure."

Naecia remembered the carapace's control code. "*Aureate cicatrix?*" she said. "A gilded scar?"

"Scars are reminders, yes? My scars remind me that I have only one interest going forward: Aptat."

Naecia rolled her eyes. "That doesn't seem like a life worth living. Being devoted entirely to your own self-interest. Actually, I don't think that even makes sense. You need others to be happy."

"Years in a box will change that perspective," said Aptat. Then they stopped checking the suit and looked hard at Naecia. "I would kill you and take everything you owned if I felt it was in my self-interest, and your wise strategic actions thus far tell me you understand that. Don't let happy myths about trial and redemption cloud the reality of the way things are. The Universe is life and death. Everything else is a nudge in one direction or the other. In the end, we only have ourselves."

CHAPTER THIRTY-SEVEN

They didn't have the exact location of the Scythin ship. There were no heat signatures – assuming the *Timelance* even had a signature – anywhere close by nor hits from mass scans of the local area. Either the *Timelance* wasn't within range of the *Child*'s instruments or it was immune to them. Whatever happened, they weren't going to have a technological advantage, of that Naecia was certain.

"Guess I'll give them a ring?" said Aptat.

"We're ready," said Izairis.

Aptat see-sawed their head side-to-side in an equivocal "we'll see" sort of way. "Okay, well, I hope they aren't super keen when it comes to forged neural diaries and coherence receipts."

"Hey," said Izairis, crossing her arms. "They won't suspect anything. I know what I'm doing."

"She does," said Oush, who had Izairis to thank for being captured himself.

"I'll do an all-directions chirp," said Aptat, issuing the command. "We've obviously done business before. They'll identify it."

Everyone flinched when the return chirp came through the com. There was no light delay at all. It had come from somewhere extremely close.

"I don't see anyone out there," said Aptat.

"A commercial rig mining comets?" Oush suggested, though

they all knew nobody would be drilling in such a remote spot.

Izairis, who had subtly commandeered some of the ship's duties, pushed the display large and swept the starfield with the conventional scope.

Aptat pressed their lips together and said crisply, "Well, let's just see who seeks to parley, then." They brought up the transmission ID and telemetry. All blank except for the basic directional information. Aptat gestured to Izairis. "Put visual on these coordinates."

They watched as the ship's central camera panned the ecliptic. Then it stopped. "It came from that way," said Aptat to a screen of black, salted with stars. "Whoever it is, they're pretty well hidden. Ahem." Aptat tapped the com. "This is the stringhunter *Silent Child*. To whom am I speaking?"

"You have a very nice com voice," said Naecia. "Polite."

"You know, I appreciate that," Aptat said, casually leaning back to address her. "I do try to keep a sense of decorum. In my mind, it's what's really missing these days, especially amongst stringhunters. The truth is you never know how a pleasant disposition will–"

A deafening noise, low frequency and full of gain, blasted from the com. Aptat gestured down the volume. "This is them. Let me run it."

Several wavelengths graphed across the display, then faded along each row into words as the ship translated.

Aptat.
Bringing yourself within our capture radius.
An interesting decision.
Your Stringer works slowly.
How did you come here?
Time is running out.
Exit the area or be eviscerated.
We are hunger.

"Everyone be calm," said Aptat.

"We are calm," said Izairis.

"Right. Here goes," said Aptat, clearing their throat again and speaking a message into the com, which the ship translated into Scythin tones, "I'm sure you've discovered by now that I was telling the truth about the Earth man's knowledge of the Chime. I can hardly be blamed for his unevolved human brain. Hopefully the leverage I sent along has helped his motivation. Nevertheless, I come bearing tidings of good news... for the both of us." Aptat paused long enough to make sure the others knew it was for dramatic effect. "There is another." Then, turning to the group. "See if that gets them tweaking, eh?"

The response came fast, noises like metal slowly twisting. The ship translated:

> *Another Stringer.*
> *Who knows of the Chime?*
> *The Note of Jecca.*

"Yes, I have captured another Stringer who won't shut up about the Chime. Though if I'm being honest, I wasn't the first to pick him up," said Aptat, adding some flair to the story. "See, there was this ice pusher just outside of–"

> *Have you dredged?*

"Uh, short answer: yes. I knew I'd be bringing him to you, and while I normally don't mine the merch, it seemed prudent under the circumstances, and well–"

> *Transmit documentation.*

"Of course," said Aptat, business-like. "I'm sending through the neural diary and coherence log. You'll find it all in order."

Izairis scoffed. "Why would you say that?"

"Say what?" said Aptat. "I thought I played it right."

"'You'll find it all in order'?" said Izairis, mockingly repeating the words. "You wouldn't say something like that unless you had some hesitation about whether or not it *was* actually in order. An honest trader would just say 'here it is'. You're blowing it."

Aptat spun around, shooting a finger back at Izairis. "Leave the negotiations to the professionals, okay?"

"Oh, yeah, I remember your last negotiation," rejoined Izairis. "Two dead Stringers, your ship hijacked by the Vortu, and you having to rely on a third Stringer you nearly got killed to unfuck it all."

"How did you ever get into nun school with a mouth like that?" asked Aptat, in a calm, admiring tone.

"Hacked their system and clicked "Accept" on my application, how else?"

"Hmm, of course," Aptat answered, pushing through the counterfeit documentation on Oush. "Well, if we aren't vaporized in the next twenty seconds, maybe–"

Send the Stringer.
Now.

"Wow. Okay, alright, let's slow down and talk price. You are looking at the profile for Oush-Sadicet Ciksever, a weapons specialist hailing from the moon towers of Ryjenn." Aptat threw a wink at Izairis, who had diligently woven facts about Oush's actual past into the forged profile. "This one is only two-deep on the cord with even better coherence – and work ethic – than the Earthling. Once you have him dig through all the boblet chatter–"

Enough.

"Oh-kay."

The price is: send the Stringer or be eviscerated.

"Yes! Fine! Deal. Calm down. Do I come to you, or you come to me? I don't have a visual."

Silence. Naecia shifted nervously. The others were doing the same. The com squawked and a translation appeared on the display:

Look again.

Aptat scrunched their brow and turned to the others, who were just as mystified, then minimized the com feed and expanded the visual.

Like ink bleeding through paper, the *Timelance* materialized, filling the screen before them.

CHAPTER THIRTY-EIGHT

The Scythin pushed Patton up the platform and dumped him into the dredge.

"Patton, shut your eyes!"

Bad advice, said Jezzer whisperingly.

The second Scythin did something to the dredge.

"What're they doing?"

Anxiolysin.

Anxiolysin. I remembered Dekies threatening Naecia with it. Some sort of drug that makes you pay attention. "I'm trying to save you guys! Why are you doing this?"

Death comes, said Jezzer, now forcing me slowly back into the dredge. *Save us.*

"Save you? Save you from what?"

Save us. We are hunger.

"Wait a minute." I looked Jezzer over, at the increasing ashiness of the armored plates, their mottled edges. "You're sick, aren't you?"

The boids shifted and a dull green coursed over them. *Hunger.*

"I want to help you – you don't have to do this to Patton. Please!"

Jezzer knelt down on the side of the dredge, leaning directly over me and whispered the words like a breeze through chain-link, *You... do this... to Patton.*

"You're making a huge mistake, Jezzer. What if you kill him? I told you I'll quit if that happens."

Jezzer turned their head to the second dredge, where an orange glow haunted its interior. *You should begin.*

Holy shit! They were going to leave Patton in the dredge for as long as it took me to find the Chime. Oh God, oh God, oh God, oh God. Focus, Ben. Focus.

Jezzer said there were thousands of these city structures. The Chime is inside one of them. *It must be the one I'm building, right? Must be. Has to be. Oh God, I hope it is.* That must be why it imprinted on the cord. My prior wouldn't have imprinted a bunch of red herrings, would they? They couldn't have known to even think of such a thing, surely? Was the implantation of false reflections even possible?

Shit, it was hard to concentrate without nectar.

I dialed in, letting the first few shapes come to me. I latched onto them and dropped into the depths of my psyche, where I quickly found the floating city. The Blue quadrant, or Kingdom Fungi, was the least developed, probably because I had the hardest time retaining the fragments and modules that went there. Where Animalia was fully built out and Protista and Plantae were modestly arranged, Fungi was a wasteland. So, naturally, that was probably where the Chime was hiding.

I need more nectar.

I placed myself in the fungal quarter and summoned pieces that belonged there. It was a little difficult to keep it all in order because my knowledge of Kingdom Fungi was so limited. Thanks to Patton – *oh, Patton, my friend, forgive me* – and his underground, drug-farming Aunt Lisa, I was able to round out my organizational system with the names of the magic mushroom strains he liked to bring along to spice up our fishing trips. He considered himself a pothead more than a psychonaut, but the monotony of fishing often required more colorful stuff. *Liberty caps. Flying Saucer. Philosopher's Stone. Florida White. Wavy Caps. Blue Meanies. Blue Ringer. Blue Foot. Pajaritos. Golden Teacher.*

The Blue Quadrant, Fungi, was thusly organized according to fungus drugs.

I pulled back from Blue and felt for missing pieces. Reflections streamed up to me and I placed them into the structure. My pulse quickened as I gathered and ordered a series of clusters for Yellow, threw them where they belonged, connecting here, lengthening there. I was racing now. Within seconds, I collected the parts for a huge energy generation module constructed from one thousand, three-hundred and nineteen separate reflections, and fit it precisely where I knew it would go. I built feverishly, forgetting to breath. I was a termite, an ant, a bee, conjuring the hive.

And then it went warm. No, hot. The entire superstructure glowed, forcing me to avert the gaze of my mind's eye.

I heard the blood swishing through each ear. Cheeks flushed. I saw the build as if I was looking at it through a window. But I saw more than that. I saw through it. I saw it moving and working. Functioning. *This place. The Chime is here. This place. This place called–*

"Aszerat!" I cried out, blown free of my trance. "Aszerat!" I yelled again, pounding the glass. *Aszerat.* I screamed the name over and over. The lid opened and I flew past Jezzer and over to the neighboring dredge.

Aszerat? Jezzer questioned.

"Yes! Whatever the fuck that is. Get him out!" I hammered on the glass. "Patton!"

Jezzer calmly disengaged the machine and the lid's segments opened.

Patton's eyes were wide and dull. Short breaths hitched through his clenched teeth, his chest rising and falling like a machine caught in a loop.

I reached in and lifted him out – oh, he was so light. His legs buckled. "Help me get him up! He needs tube food, he needs nectar!"

Jezzer just stood there.

"Aszerat is as big as a fucking moon, and if you think I'm gonna dig around for one more second trying to find the Chime in there, you got another thing coming, mother*fucker*! Find it your goddamned self!" I held Patton under his arms. "Let us out!"

Jezzer's boids fluttered in a way that portrayed bemusement and gestured the big door open. Walking backward, I dragged Patton, arms burning, back aching, to the great rotunda, through a patch where the Scythin had resumed their swarming. They stopped, watching curiously as one human dragged another back to their prison cell.

Jezzer sauntered some distance behind, seeming unfazed by Patton's condition or my threats to leave the Chime buried.

"I got you, buddy," I said. "We're together now. I'm so sorry, I'm a piece of shit. I'm never going to leave you again. Remember Pickles? He's in there waiting for us. We should go ahead and crack those open, huh? It's over now, Patton. It's over. I'm sorry." My voice cracked. Patton's body felt like... a body. Was he still there? Had the dredge eaten his brain?[101]

We got to the enclosure and I pulled him inside, right to the middle. Sitting with Patton's head in my lap, I screamed, "Jezzer! He needs the nectar!"

Jezzer appeared at the opening of the membrane, gestured nonchalantly to the floor where the tubes appeared. "You better not be fucking with me," I said, grabbing the correct one – *I think* – and pushing it onto Patton's rightmost umbilicus.

He went bow-shaped and flopped out of my lap, arms spread in a swan dive and feet *en pointe* as every muscle in his body fired. His head was thrown back, sinews and veins in his neck popping through the skin. I'd put in a fair time on the tube and don't think I'd ever reacted like this.

"What the fuck is happening to him?" I roared.

---

101 Chipmunks, tree kangaroos, and the great tit (*Parus major*) definitely eat brains.

Jezzer was watching the mists where, for the first time since we'd arrived, the full Scythin horde weltered in fervid murmuration; cycling through forms of colossal crawling beasts and swelling leviathans.

I understood it. Something about my knowledge of this swarming language taken from the same behavior in birds made it less alien. I couldn't translate what they were saying to each other exactly, but the sentiments were unmistakable. Excitement. Anticipation.

I watched even as the membrane drew closed, holding my neglected friend as he absorbed nectar into what was left of his body. A moment later, Jezzer broke off in a dead sprint for the perimeter, disaggregating halfway into multicolored boids that tumbled into the circling mass. The swarm pushed around the perimeter, moving faster than I'd seen it do yet, transforming from one thing to the next at a pace that defied the laws of momentum and inertia.

A churning circle of boids emerged from the mist, its diameter steadily narrowing. Colors flashed across them in sync to an unheard beat. It continued inward toward the center of the great rotunda, swirling faster and faster like the footprint of a tornado with a constricting aperture. I tightened my hold on Patton as the vortex passed by our enclosure with a sound like living thunder. Out in the center of the floor, they seethed, moving so quickly that what I saw in one second had changed by the next. It was as if they were orbiting an object of such immense gravity, that they would inevitably be swallowed by it.

But then, as if released from the bindings of whatever had drawn them to such a fevered gyration, they spilled apart and tumbled away. And I saw then what had been at the middle of it all – or *became* the middle. It was something I hadn't seen before.

Here and there, the spilled boids coagulated back into individual Scythin, with the twenty-six Queens rebuilding themselves closer to the center, where a new Scythin stood. Through moving gaps in the gathered many, I could see this individual was no different from the others, but for an empty chasm running down the center of their chest. A new Queen. The twenty-seventh.

Shit was fixing to go down. I didn't know what, exactly, but it had the same feel as in Kung Fu films when the one guy gets a bloody lip and he wipes it, then looks at it, and you just know he's about to whip everyone's ass.

Not that I knew what was coming or had any way to stop it.

I checked Patton, who snored peacefully, and then watched the churn begin anew. Back into the mist they went, boiling, forming, cycling through whatever it was they cycled through. And when nothing else came of it, I did what one does in such situations – shot drugs into my tummy tube.

CHAPTER THIRTY-NINE

"So. They've got a dilation cloak," said Aptat as the *Timelance* coalesced fully into view. "A second bit of theoretical tech come to life today. Wonder what other sorcery we'll be treated to."

Aptat had always made the point that the Scythin were *different*, unlike anything found in the known universe. At this moment, that assessment seemed rather like an understatement. Naecia was captured by the scale of the *Timelance*. Gargantuan, it was more a thing than a ship, carrying with it the physical manifestation of *presence*.

Massive spire-like fins bisected a huge ring at various intervals around its circumference. Their top points leaned inward over the center point of the ring, while the far ends opened wide at their nadir below. They were set into a large gouge in the outer edge of the ring, suggesting to Naecia that they were movable, able to slide into different positions around the circumference. Inside the ring was a central spindle, whose shape mimicked the larger profile, with smaller spire-fins and all. The base of the spindle twisted to a jagged point far below the rest of the ship. It was easy to guess that this was the business end of the vessel – the *lance*, as it were, in *Timelance*.

In light of its appearance, the fact that it also had a dilation cloak – an artificial gravity generator with the ability to pull the background starfield into the foreground for the purpose of concealment while somehow managing not to crush the ship itself – was hardly shocking. They were here now, showing themselves. Defiant. If there was a God of Armageddon, this was its ship.

Place the Stringer inside the voidscull.

Aptat watched the display intently. "Voidscull on the way, guys. Suit up."

Oush went to where they had laid out the Vortu voidsuits, modified in anticipation of conflict with various armaments. Naecia counted off the steps of their plan in her head. Oush would be the bait. He'd go across in the voidscull and hopefully dock somewhere near to where they were keeping the Earth man. Location was important. She would need to know where to focus her mind when she tried to put the *Silent Child* inside the *Timelance*.

Oush donned his voidsuit and Aptat helped Naecia into hers, which was tailored to fit her smaller frame, while retaining its potent fragrance. They'd taken out some excess length and changed the locations of the utility mounts so they could be accessed by her smaller hands from within the suit. It was still baggy. Catching her reflection in the ship's polished steel walls, she looked like a shriveled medji fruit. She did not smell like fruit.

Naecia and Oush each carried a blunderbuss at their hips and a dozen Vortu grenades over their chests. The only other weapon – the only *real* weapon – they had was Aptat, fully back in deadly carapace.

The voidscull arrived, settling into the bay just below the deck. Aptat triggered the console, which then split apart to expose the fairing-end of it. "Oush, your ride is here."

"We're really going to do this?" said Izairis, though it sounded more like a statement that one says only to see how crazy it sounds when spoken aloud.

"No matter how it goes," said Naecia with forced confidence, "we're sure to give the Scythin a surprise."

"Yes, maybe they will simply faint from shock," said Aptat.

Oush climbed up and wedged himself inside the voidscull.

Naecia looked in after him. "First thing you do if you find the Earth man is administer the Amnesplid. Do it before anything else," she said, handing over a small ampoule of liquid.

"I know," he answered, taking it.

"You can't kill him until his mind is erased."

"I *know*, Naecia."

"Travel safely," said Aptat, knocking heels to attention and giving a salute.

"Suck a farglack's scrotal teats in ascending order of size," said Oush, returning the salute as the fairings closed. The scull descended below and exited the ship.

"Hmm, scrotal teats. Did not know that about farglacks," said Aptat.

Naecia immediately went to the Switch Drive and opened the conduits to the ship's power. "You think they'll fire on us now or wait until Oush gets there?" she asked of the room.

"I think they'll wait," said Izairis. "We don't pose an obvious danger to them right now."

"I suppose they'll want to make sure we sent over the actual merch first," said Aptat. "Or maybe they'll see us not running and figure we're up to some funny stuff, which we are. Either way, they're going to shoot at us."

"Agreed," said Naecia. "As soon as they have Oush, they'll fire."

Aptat stood beside Izairis while the voidscull, invisible against the black, made its way toward the *Timelance*. Aptat hit it with a beam of infrared in order to trace its course.

Naecia brought the Switch to full power. The ship's data began to populate as before. She was perspiring, and the smell of her own sweat mixed with the Vortu funk produced a sickly mélange. Gagging slightly, she put on the axon diadem.

They watched on the display as the voidscull flew below the outer ring of the *Timelance* and toward the inner spindle.

"He's almost in," said Izairis.

"Oop," Aptat exclaimed, pointing at the display. "There it is." Long, horizontal gaps opened along the *Timelance*'s outer circumference, and a powerful, magnesium white light beamed from within. "Pretty sure that's a weapon."

Izairis began counting down. "Voidscull makes contact in *ten, nine, eight…*"

Remembering that they had to conduct two switches in order to reverse the resulting chirality of the first leap, Naecia concluded that she'd take them to a spot of vacant space above the *Timelance*. She'd put them there first, and then into the larger ship with the second switch.

Six, five…

"Count faster," said Aptat.

They couldn't engage the drive until they knew exactly where Oush would make contact. Naecia's fingers hovered over the pad, waiting for the moment to dump the ship's particle data through the doorway of her mind.

The *Timelance* grew bright with malevolent energy.

Four, three…

A ring of pure light.

The voidscull was nearly in, heading for a spot just off-center of the inner hub. It was close enough, they couldn't wait any longer.

Two.

Naecia thought of a place and opened the gates.

Her eyes flicked to the display, which had altered in orientation, just in time to see a burst of energy explode outward from the entirety of the *Timelance*'s circumference. An expanding, ring-shaped laser, like a ripple of water, except more murder-y.

Naecia instructed the drive to re-catalogue for the second switch.

"*?up shoots that laser a have they if Wonder.*" said Aptat.

".bulkspace through leave just they'll that worried more I'm," said Naecia. Her data pad blinked. *".go we Here"*

Thinking about how to communicate with the Oblivion Fray was more challenging this time. How do you articulate the inside of a place you've never been? So, she described it in her mind. *.alive still is he if .man Earth the and Oush both to possible as close as .Timelance the within fit will Child Silent the where place A*

She opened the dam.

The vacuum of space was replaced by a cavernous rotunda, its circumference several mylics across. *Inexplicable.* She'd put one ship inside of another. An accomplishment she might someday look back on with great admiration, assuming she lived to look back on anything. Right now, she was just freaking out.

The view through the display was confusing. A great swirling mist raked the perimeter. Otherwise, there was no movement. Dark hunks of *something* lay across the floor.

"What is that?" she asked, moving close to the display.

"I'm not going to hang around and find out," said Aptat. "Let's go. Doors down! Izairis, you know what to do!"

"I've tried hailing Oush," said Izairis. "He's not responding."

"We'll sort it," said Aptat, mask closing over their face. "We'll make for his beacon."

Naecia removed the diadem but left the drive running, so that all the data would be aggregated and ready for their escape switch. It would be a drain on the ship's power, but they couldn't risk the time needed for another spin-up. A quick glance to the data aggregation display showed a surprising–

"Helmet," said Aptat.

"Right." Naecia pulled on the oversized and stinking Vortu headpiece. The visor was streaked with wear and Vortu grease.

"Shall we, then?" Aptat said in the way of someone proposing a garden tour capped off by cups of fragrant jha and dew-sweetened petal-cakes. Naecia admired the stringhunter's bewildering embrace of whatever was in front of them. Ideally, she would have a similarly carefree approach to life if there wasn't already so much to feel doom about.

Aptat trotted to the door as it pulled wide, and they lit down the ramp together. The edges of the room were obscured by the mist, which had begun to evaporate. Behind it were bodies and... pieces of bodies? Naecia wasn't sure what she was looking at. "Are they dead?"

"Passed out from surprise," said Aptat, taking off at a trot. "Just as I predicted."

"Oush, check in!" she said. No response.

"Up ahead," called Aptat, pointing.

It was hard to miss. Across the rotunda was a towering organic structure, like a giant seedpod that had grown up out of the floor. A huge, milky white-blue taper stretching all the way up to the apex of the vast space.

Aptat put increasing distance between themselves and Naecia, being faster and of bespoke origin, and wearing an augmented suit, and also not being encumbered by the rubbery dead aromatic weight of the second-hand Vortu toilet garb.

Naecia moved as best she could. The suit was rubbing her skin off at the armpits. Their vector took her past what she could only describe as piles of Scythin, who looked as if they'd literally fallen apart. She was left with an uneasy feeling, like they weren't dead, just dormant.

Far ahead, Aptat arrived at the soaring organo-structure. "Oush's beacon is coming from inside this thing," they said. "It's made of something I've never seen. Like twice-hardened rhyconin." Naecia saw the flare of Aptat's magmafier. "Watch our backs, Naecia, I don't trust these chunks to not snap out of it."

CHAPTER FORTY

"Benbenbenbenbenbenbenbenben."

It was Patton, trying to shake me back into the waking world. I didn't want to be in that world. I wanted to be in nectar world. My eyes cracked open. "Ben!" he yelled, kindly slapping my cheeks.

His face came into focus. He looked... *great?* "Patton?" I rasped, "I thought you were..."

"Food tube, bro. Stuff's stronger than Grease Monkey Indica."

I sat up, wiped my eyes and looked ahead. Was there a Vortu lying in our enclosure?

It groaned.

Patton helped me up. "Yeah," he said, acknowledging our new cellmate. "Another voidscull showed up in here and that old Vortu came charging out. Then it fainted. I think I did too."

"Back away from it," I said, scooting a retreat on my butt tube.

"You think it knows Kung Fu?" asked Patton, assuming a vaguely martially artistic stance. The Vortu began rolling side to side, grunting. I pulled Patton away. Then it reached up and popped off the helmet.

"Oush?" I exclaimed.

"We're rescued!" cried Patton.

"Not quite yet," said Oush, pointing to the outside. "We need them to get us out."

A silhouette materialized. "Aptat?"

The membrane brightened with flame.

"Wait," I said, "how did they get past the Scythin? How did you get in here? Where *are* the Scythin?"

"I don't know," said Oush. "Let me ask." He put the helmet back on and com'd the others, then answered, "They say the Scythin are asleep."

"No, no, they don't sleep," I said, peering through the membrane. I could make out some small boid piles on the floor just outside the mist. "I've never seen them sleep."

Oush shrugged.

"How did Aptat get here?"

"Long story. Here," he said, casually withdrawing a small ampoule filled with liquid from a pocket. "Naecia solved faster-than-light. Problem is it makes us all sick. Deadly sick. Take this. It needs time to work. Quickly, please." He cracked the end off of it, handed it to me, and repeated, "*Quickly.*"

I was coming down from the nectar and things were still confusing. "I need to drink this?"

"Drink, stab, doesn't matter."

"What about me?" asked Patton. "I need one too, right?"

Oush's face went blank for a moment – like he'd had a lapse of some sort. "Of course," he answered. "Uh, Aptat has extra doses. There was only so much and... honestly, we weren't sure we'd find you."

"No offense taken," said Patton, actually meaning it.

I stared at it.

"If you want to live, you'll take that right now," Oush repeated, forcefully.

I'd already abandoned my friend once. I wasn't going to do it again. "I'll wait until Patton has his," I said, offering back the tiny vessel. "Unless we can split it?"

Oush's eyes grew wide and they shifted nervously to the

fissure Aptat's flame had begun to create in the membrane. A noise came out of the helmet. Oush held it up to his face and spoke into the neck opening. "We're fine," he murmured. "Under control. Someone's being a little stubborn." Then, to me: "That was Naecia. It's her machine that will get us out of here. She insists you take this. It's dangerous to go without."

Even in my drug-marinated state, alarms were going off. I stepped backward. "You guys must have used the machine at least once without the medication, before you could have known you'd need it, right? Doesn't sound so bad compared to what Patton and I have been through here. I'll deal with the sickness."

"Yeah," said Patton. "He's been throwing up this whole trip."

Oush snatched the ampoule from my hand and launched himself at me. We pounded the ground. The snap of a rib cracked in my ears. As if triggered by the impact, the floor opened and the food eel unfurled itself from within, then slithered aimlessly away.

Oush weighed a ton even without the Vortu suit. I held his arm back with both of mine, dodging locks of his golden mullet, as he thrust the ampoule down toward my neck which made me start to think the stuff wasn't actually for motion sickness. At the same time, his weight threatened to suffocate me. I really started to worry when the skin of his face opened and blood poured out.

"What the fugggggllg," I gurgled.

Patton rammed him from the side. Oush only cantered some and ignored the insult. Patton came again, and this time Oush tossed him to the ground. Patton was right back up, jacked with super strength from drugs. I was stronger too, but not enough to get the large, hemorrhaging pro wrestler off of me.

"You idiot! You need this to live!" he cried.

"It doesn't—" wheezing, water-boarded with blood "—feel that way!"

Then his other hand was on my neck. Choking. My tongue

flopped out. I could sense the inner walls of my throat touching.

Patton appeared again, this time from behind. He flung a loop of tubing around Oush's neck, and pulled back as hard as he could. Oush barely seemed to notice, just gritted his teeth and pushed himself down heavier upon me, at once choking me out and trying to stab me with the very-obviously-bad-thing-that-was-not-medicine.

Patton rolled away, long end of the tube still in hand, and stretched it through the narrow gap in the food eel's face, cinching it in place.

Oush slowly pulled away from me as the tube tightened. His hands went to his neck, dropping the ampoule to the floor. I skittered away and over to Patton, as the eel dragged Oush flopping along the circumference of the enclosure. "Help me," he hissed, while trying to get his hands under the rubbery garrot. "Help." His bronzed face went purple as an eggplant and soon he stopped flailing. His arms fell heavy to the floor. The eel continued stubbornly on, dragging the huge, dead, bemulleted assassin.

"I killed a guy with the poop tube!" exclaimed Patton.

I didn't love the idea of someone dying, but: "He was trying to kill me, right?"

"Totally," said Patton, yanking a comically huge gun from Oush's belt and using the handle to smash the ampoule.

A hole opened in the membrane. Aptat had gotten their fingers through and was now tearing at it. Their mask appeared, opened, and Aptat looked inside. Their eyes flicked to Oush, still being dragged about, a smeared trail of his own face blood left behind. "Oh. That didn't go at all like we'd thought." Then to me: "Hi, Ben. Patton."

"Did you come here to kill us?"

"That depends," said the stringhunter, grunting as they peeled away more membrane.

A tiny Vortu appeared behind them. "Oush!" It was Naecia. Then she saw it. "You killed him?" she screamed, insisting her way through the hole and running to the wrestler's side as his body languidly made the rounds.

"He fucked around and found out," said Patton, with a shrug.

"Did you take the Amnesplid?"

"Was that the stuff Oush tried to stab me with?"

"It was the medicine you need to travel FTL."

"Uh, no," I said. "First of all, he didn't have enough for both of us, and also, it didn't seem like it was really anti-nausea medication. More like anti-life medication."

"You moron. Here," she said, going into a pocket and taking out another ampoule. "I have an extra." She gestured to Patton, who looked to me. "Aptat has another."

At that moment, all I could think about was her face from so long ago, when I'd mentioned the Chime as we had departed the *Silent Child*. The absolute horror written on it. She had another angle, I just didn't know what. "No, I don't trust you," I said.

"Time to go," said Aptat. "These things are starting to move around out here."

Patton slapped away the ampoule and kicked it into the food eel's lair below the floor.

Naecia screamed, "We came here to rescue you!"

"It doesn't feel that way. If you're actually here to rescue us, go ahead and do it."

"What happened to Oush?" asked Aptat.

"He was trying to kill me!" I said. "But you wouldn't know anything about that, would you?"

"Would you believe me if I said no?" they said, gesturing for us to exit the enclosure, which we did.

The Scythin were in a state of disassembly that I didn't understand. I'd never seen them stop moving. Some boids were completely still while others only lolled side-to-side. In certain places, they'd begun a slow coalescence, tumbling lethargically into groups. Whatever Aptat and the others had done to get them into this state, it was wearing off.

Aptat started off at a trot. "Oush was supposed to erase your mind first, and only *then* kill you."

"What?" I exclaimed, while trying to keep up. "Why?"

"The Chime," Naecia said, struggling to move in the baggy Vortu outfit. "It's bad."

"How bad?" I asked.

"Destroys-the-galaxy bad," she said. "We couldn't let you find it."

"So you were gonna kill me?"

"Erase your mind and then kill you," said Naecia, breathing heavily. "The only way to be sure. It wasn't personal."

I was speechless.

Aptat accelerated some. I glanced up ahead and saw what I'd been too distracted to notice before, off in the distance.

Patton said it before I could form the words: "Hey, is that the *Silent Child*?"

It really was there. A spaceship as wide as a football field, sitting inside the *Timelance* like it was an aircraft hangar. "How–?"

"We'll explain later," said Naecia. "You haven't found the Chime yet, have you?"

"Uh," I said, dragging along. "Kind of?"

"Where is it?" she asked.

"Some place called Aszerat," I answered.

"Did you tell them?"

"Maybe?"

"Fuck!" She punched awkwardly at the air to both sides.

"I thought I was saving them!" I said. "They're sick or something!"

Naecia shouted in frustration. "Where in Aszerat?"

"I don't know yet!"

"Meaning they don't know. Good," said Naecia. "We have to get there before they do."

"I got dredged too! I don't know anything…" reported Patton from the rear. I gave him a quick glance. He'd remembered to grab Pickles.

CHAPTER FORTY-ONE

Naecia wasn't really thinking about the chunks of Scythin that had begun to assemble around them into larger creatures. She was working through the question of why they had come apart in the first place. It was like Aptat had said: they'd gone to sleep. And it seemed their loss of consciousness had coincided with the moment of *Silent Child*'s arrival.

Her hypothesis was as obvious as it was wondrous. The Switch had reconstituted the *Silent Child* using the substance of the Fray, which was formed of consciousness itself. Every last thread of it had been sucked out of the *Timelance*, including that of the Scythin, Oush, Ben, and Patton. Thankfully it had only been temporary, and they hadn't turned into unthinking meat shells, though she would have preferred that for Ben. It seemed that the Fray behaved much like spilt water and the Switch like a sponge. When touched to the water, it absorbed all that surrounded it. Once pulled away, water seeped back in to fill the void. Why it had seemed to affect the Scythin more profoundly, she couldn't say.

"We have to go faster!" yelled Ben, yanking Naecia out of her thought.

He was limping quickly along. Far thinner and dirtier than he'd been back on the *Child*. That, and the two friends seemed to have sprouted synthetic tails.

Most of the chunks had now joined with other chunks to form full-sized creatures. Big, wicked-looking things that flashed with bursts of color. They continuously changed their configurations, with each individual morphing back and forth into confusing shapes.

"This is what they do before merging," yelled Ben. "That's bad. They'll destroy the *Silent Child* in seconds."

"The ship is too far for you all," said Aptat, glancing back to where the reassembled Scythin were already proceeding into the mist. "Ben: do you know how to stop them?"

"They'll determine their form through murmuration," he said. "It's a mass flocking behavior seen in some animals – like birds. It's how they communicate when in the group."

"And?" asked Aptat.

"They need to be in contact with some minimum number of other individuals in order to stay in-pattern. The only way to delay them from merging is to disrupt the murmuration. But I don't know how to do that."

Already the flocking had begun, and a leathery tumult of bodies began swarming.

Aptat spun around. "You get to the ship! I'll go ask them to kindly delay their ceremony!" Aptat plucked four Vortu grenades from Naecia's suit and galloped away.

Ben and Patton didn't hesitate in making for the ship. Naecia, already exhausted from making the journey across the rotunda, and burdened by the Vortu suit and ordnance, only lost ground. Her spiracles snapped open and shut as she panted along. Condensation obscured the already soiled mask. Sweat ran into her eyes, blurring the image of the ship ahead. Soon, she was stalled and lost, pivoting haltingly in search of it. She tried removing the helmet, but it had become stuck. Through the visor came a blob of yellow with a face in the middle of it.

"I'm only doing this 'cause I know you're trying to save the galaxy," said Patton, grabbing hold of her arm. "And that, in my mind, is enough to offset you trying to kill Ben. But just barely."

She was too breathless to say anything and allowed the Earthling to tow her along.

"Naecia, hurry!" Izairis urged through the com.

Naecia checked behind. Even through the foggy visor, she could see colossal black shapes converging in the mist. Then, an explosion, and another. Smaller pieces of Scythin scattered out over the floor.

"Almost there," said Patton. And then she felt the relief of the ship's ramp below her feet.

"Izairis," she said breathlessly over the com. "Prime the ventral thrusters, now." The *Silent Child* couldn't be in physical contact with the *Timelance* when they engaged the Switch or they'd take the whole wicked thing with them. She had noticed when they'd arrived that her data pad had begun populating with so much more information than usual. That was it. The Switch was cataloguing the entire *Timelance*.

"Primed!" shouted Izairis. "Ramp coming up. Hurry!"

"No, wait!" cried Naecia.

CHAPTER FORTY-TWO

In European starlings, at least, the magic number was seven: the minimum number of flocking-mates that any single bird needed to monitor in order to remain oriented within the rest of the group. It was how giant swarms of them seemed to move together in coordinated shapes and directions. In all the time spent with the Scythin, it was one thing I'd become absolutely sure of. When they acted in concert, or made group decisions, it was done through murmuration. Day to day communication was conducted via other morphological gymnastics and color changes.

I rushed back to where Patton, clutching Pickles in one arm, was dragging Naecia up the ramp with his narco-strength. "What are you waiting for?" I screamed. "Let's go!"

She wrestled with her helmet, and finally ripped it off, revealing a face striped in sweat-soaked hair. "Aptat is still out there!"

"Yes, they are!" I yelled. "Fuck Aptat!"

"They are distracting the Scythin, just like you told them to do!"

"Good! Great!" I said. "And now we have a chance to feed them to the Scythin! How do we make this ship go?" I looked to the bridge. "Izairis, do you want to wait for your kidnapper to return safely onboard?"

"Not especially," said Izairis.

Naecia yanked herself away from Patton. "There they are," she said, pointing out across the expanse. "Hit the thrusters, Izairis. Just get us off the deck. Leave the ramp down." She trudged the rest of the way inside.

I gazed out across the rotunda just in time to see the Scythin converge from four consolidated groups into two behind Aptat, who was galloping toward the *Child*, articulated arm spitting out dozens of rounds per second. Not that it had any effect. I couldn't believe we were about to let the fucking kidnapper back on the ship.

"Are we really going to let that asshole back on board?" said Patton, echoing my sentiment.

"I guess so," I answered, glaring at Naecia, who had put some doodad on her head. *Is that the axon diadem?*

Thrusters fired and we hovered up from the deck of the *Timelance*.

"There's nowhere to go!" I yelled.

"Just let me know when Aptat's inside!" said Naecia.

"Why?" I said, to no answer.

Aptat came nearer, but so did the beast. Two masses slammed together, becoming one thing – a thick, flexible, snake-missile that charged from behind with the rage of a harpooned whale. Aptat tossed another grenade over their shoulder, which the goliath easily dodged. I cheered the move, rooting for the Scythin in this particular conflict.

"Say when!" Naecia screamed.

Aptat leapt from twenty feet out and made the ramp.

I turned to Naecia and dryly said, "when."

Suddenly the ship was decompressing. Air blasted out the ramp into hard space. I grabbed a railing and screamed silently as the air was sucked from my lungs. Aptat marched right by us and over to the ship's console. Then the ramp was closing and the cabin repressurized. I exhaled and checked on Patton, who was flat against the ramp, one hand in a foothold, the other clutching Pickles to his bosom.

"*!happened just what me tell Someone,*" I asked. "*?we are Where*"

"*.Aszerat from two about and Timelance the from gilleys two about .Oh,*" said Naecia.

"*?Gilley a is fuck the What ?what Two*"

"*.years light Earth two than less little A ?remember .years light Galactic*" answered Aptat.

"*Holy-*" Patton began.

Naecia removed the axon diadem.

"What did you just do?" I asked.

"Check the map, guy."

I did. There was the *Silent Child*, sitting outside of a star system with two stars in it. They were labeled "Effelox Binary". We'd jumped another two light years and I hadn't even noticed. Shown in an orbit much farther starward was a notation pointing to an expanded view of what looked like an asteroid belt that said: EFFELOX FREE CITIES. There were thousands of spherical satellites. Just like Jezzer had said.

"Aszerat's in there?" I asked.

"It is indeed," said Aptat wistfully. "A city of pure commerce. Buy, sell, trade, steal."

"Sounds like your kind of place," said Izairis.

"Hmm, yes," Aptat confirmed.

I shook my head, still disbelieving. We were trillions of miles from where we had been only a minute before, and now suddenly within striking distance of Aszerat. "What about the *Timelance*?" I asked, already noting the first chills of drug withdrawal. "They know where we're going. Can we get to Aszerat before them?"

"We're already there, practically speaking," said Aptat, "and approximately four gilleys ahead of the Scythin as we speak. We made the trip instantly. A conventional craft, even assuming light speed travel, would be almost four Earth-years behind."

"You're going to tell me the *Timelance* is not conventional?"

"You know that as well as anyone by now, I think," said

Aptat, flicking one of my tubes. "No, it is not. It travels through the bulk, at faster than light speed, relative to us, but still not instantaneously."

"The bulk?"

"Yes, the space between dimensions."

"Okay," I said, my mouth feeling noticeably drier and my head beginning to pound. "How soon will they get here?"

"About three cygies – ur, cycles-galactic. About twelve Earth-days. Plenty of time for you to locate the Chime and dispose of it."

I gagged on a gout of bile, stopping all but a tiny squirt of it from exiting my mouth.

"Though," said Aptat, considering my condition, "I'm afraid some of that time will have to be spent getting you and your mate back into fighting shape."

CHAPTER FORTY-THREE

Patton and I were full-on space junkies. Aptat had plenty of stuff on board in the way of pharma, but nothing that could help us manage our return to sobriety in a gradual or incremental way. Our last dose of tube food had been some pure, uncut stuff, producing both transcendent sensatory ecstasy and residual hallucinatory effects, along with bewildering healing powers – mainly for Patton.

Patton remained as strong as he'd ever been, despite his own bout of withdrawal. Aptat was shocked to learn that the Scythin had dredged him. Apparently, dredging a non-Stringer was akin to running an engine at top revs with no oil. His mind should have burned right out. But after checking Patton's coherence with the axon diadem, Aptat was left to conclude that years of drug abuse had actually primed his brain for the onslaught, making it more flexible and elastic – allowing the trauma of dredging to be absorbed where a more sober mind would have shattered.

Aptat's medical bay – if you could call it that – had only a single bed, and into that, Patton and I were tucked, newly beardless.

Detox was like being on the food tube in reverse. At first, my dreams and sensations were as vivid as they had been when I was tripping balls, but there was an entropy to them.

Colors bled to grey; sounds receded, tastes went bland, and smells dulled, leaving behind an empty, metallic ring in my ears, rust in my mouth, and ozone in my nostrils. Then, there were the splitting headaches – magnitude eleventy migraines. Sleep was hard to come by, and when it did, it was only with the assistance of Aptat's modest pharmacy.

One day we woke to find that Aptat had removed our tubes. And that, oddly, had brought with it another type of withdrawal. They'd been so important to us, we'd become so used to them, that it was like having a limb removed. I suffered the weight of finality that I would never again receive nectar.

Worse than all of that though, was the crystalline hatred that I had for myself. I was weak and selfish, and yeah, I had been addicted to cosmically powerful drugs, but I'd known what I was doing. And Patton just... let me do it. It was the worst part about having him as my closest friend. That he let me be myself when he deserved so much more. Sure, he'd sort of barged through the door and invited himself along for our misadventure, but I should have known – okay, I *did* know – that he'd refuse to be excluded once I'd told him about my internet connection with Earthrbro_99. He was unflappingly loyal. And having no illusions about who he was, I'd let him in on it anyway. Because I'm selfish.

I'd said I was sorry a million times, and Patton's response was always the same: *It's okay, no worries.* He wasn't being obtuse or passive aggressive. He truly meant it. But his lack of anger, or even the faintest expression of hurt at my betrayal cut the deepest, because it meant he hadn't expected more of me. And that told me everything. It was the clearest picture anyone had ever shown me of who I really was.

I wished for the chance to start over from the beginning, to recognize this friend whom I'd always taken for granted. To make it better. But life wasn't a game of Simon. There was no starting over.

* * *

Reflections of my third prior began filtering in, indistinguishable from everyday thoughts or ideas; just as those of my earlier priors had done throughout my life – though those two had largely gone silent. It was like the dredgings aboard the *Timelance* had pushed away the earth and rocks above a rich deposit of oil, leaving it free to geyser upward.

I was no longer assembling Aszerat – or maybe I was – but the process was so effortless that it felt as if I was merely observing it in my mind's eye, taking a tour of the place. Aszerat was nearly planet-sized, and with no mantle or core to get in the way, it had considerably more square footage. Why had nearly the entire planetoid been imprinted on the cord if the Chime, or the Note of Jecca, whatever that was, occupied only a tiny spot somewhere deep within? Could one purposefully preserve concepts, ideas, or places on the rope of sentient matter just by thinking about it hard enough?

I made some deductions. First, the Chime couldn't have been lost. It had been stolen and intentionally hidden.

The reflections of Aszerat were all the same. They lacked any individuality that would come from moments of genuine interest. Instead, they felt imprinted through repeated and dogged effort, something I didn't realize was possible. But there was no other explanation. My third prior had retraced ground throughout Aszerat – or perhaps studied the blueprints – in order to strengthen the imprinting of the entire place, thereby diluting the potency of the Chime's actual location. And why would someone do that? Unless... unless they knew what they were... understood that their knowledge would survive their death and be accessible to the next person.

"So you think someone was intentionally trying to hide the Chime from the Scythin?" asked Izairis, swallowing a mouthful of some green space-lasagna. As it turned out, Aptat had been holding back on the *Child*'s food stores. But now that the Stringers owned it, it was Aptat who ate the pemmican.

"Absolutely," I answered. "You don't lose something like that by accident. That'd be like Patton losing Mr Pickles or Aptat misplacing their carapace."

"Maybe someone wanted the Chime for themselves," said Aptat, breaking off a piece of the hardened space bread. "It's the only thing in the Universe more powerful than the Switch."

"But to what end?" I asked.

"Power, of course."

"You think someone broke into the *Timelance* and stole it from the Scythin?" I chortled. "And who would be capable of that? I'm interested in your theory."

"We stole you," said Aptat.

I scoffed. "You had a technology that they don't possess, which was only invented..."

"Four days ago," said Naecia, absentmindedly playing with her puzzle amulet.

"So maybe it was an inside job?" said Aptat. "It only takes one with ambition."

"You misunderstand them. First of all, ambition for what? They're already the most powerful species in the Universe. Second, the Scythin are communal. The only hierarchy I saw was between the queens and all the rest—"

"Did you say, *queens*?" asked Aptat.

"That's just what I called them because they reminded me of these *Azteca* ants. Anyway, the queens looked a little different from the rest, but they didn't treat the others as subordinate, nor were they really elevated above the others. Everything on the ship was entirely equal and co-dependent. Didn't you think it a little strange that none of the individuals tried to fight us until they'd merged into one creature?"

"I was running for my life at the time," said Aptat. "But the thought had crossed my mind."

"My point is that one of them wasn't going to break away and steal the Chime so that they could *become* powerful."

"You think whoever took it was trying to stop the Scythin, not to gain power themselves?" said Naecia.

"I do."

"But then, why hide it? Why wouldn't they just destroy it?" asked Izairis.

"Maybe it's not so easy to destroy."

"Throw it into a star," said Aptat. "Works with most stuff."

"I've thought about that," I said, grunting as I shifted to relieve the pressure emanating from the sutures in my ass. Aptat had graciously 3D-printed small hemorrhoid pillows for myself and Patton. "This might sound crazy," I continued, "but we can't assume a star would have done the job. These guys are extra-dimensional – you saw the material the *Timelance* was made of. Ever seen anything like that? Any of you? Do you know what the melting point of that stuff is? Sounds crazy, but maybe launching the Chime into a star wouldn't do anything more than keep it warm. Look: if a star would have worked, it would be in a star. I can't think of any other reason why it would be at Aszerat other than to bury it where no one would ever find it. I'm the guy on the cord with this person and even I can't find it."

"So, what if we *do* find it?" asked Izairis. "Apparently we can't shoot it into a star…"

I'd thought about the answer. Still felt weird to actually say it. "We use the Switch to hop to one of a trillion galaxies and shoot it into a black hole."

The galley went quiet.

"And… it can't be me who does it. Or Naecia. Or Izairis," I added. "The location information has to be fully extinguished. We've got to leave a dead end. A non-Stringer has to do it." I was looking right at Patton.

He uncoiled from his usual hunch. "Me?" he asked, face brightening. "I get to do it?"

The others audibly scoffed, and understandably. I'd just proposed handing the future of the galaxy to a guy in a shark-tooth necklace. Yes, he still had it.

"That's a little much, if I'm being honest," said Aptat. "With all due respect, and no offense intended, Patton is an idiot."

"Idiot savant," said Patton.

"With all due respect, and no offense intended, Aptat," said Naecia, "I don't trust you not to sell the location information right back to the Scythin."

"Guys!" I barked. "Patton is the only one of us whose consciousness has an expiration date. It's gotta be him."

"Think about what you're saying," said Naecia. "None of us can know where he goes. If we do, then the purpose of having him act alone is defeated. He would have to take the *Silent Child* himself–"

"Oh, nononononononononono," said Aptat, tick-tocking a finger.

"You don't even own it anymore," said Izairis.

"Temporarily," insisted Aptat.

"Listen," I said. "Naecia's right. None of us can know where he goes. We'll have to be in the dark. Aptat, you need to teach him how drive and Naecia has to show him how to use the Switch. Then Patton has to leave by himself and dispose of the Chime – once we have it in hand, of course."

"Can I be taught how to do all of that?" asked Patton with a sense of wonder.

"Sadly, yes," sulked Aptat, closing the mask over their face. Then, in metallic robot voice, added, "Unfortunately, it's all quite simple."

"We should go to Aszerat," I said. "Maybe being inside the real place will jog something loose. Even if it doesn't, we can all try looking."

Patton winced as he shifted in his seat.

Aptat angled a thumb at the both of us. "Your wounds have not yet healed. Your stomachs and anuses have newly regrown tissues. A rupture of either would be bad. Not to mention your withdrawal from chemical dependence."

I felt my stomach again and shifted on the hemorrhoid pillow. "I'll manage it now, so long as Aszerat has toilets."

CHAPTER FORTY-FOUR
THE INSTRUMENT MAKER

On the night of the Procession, all present are rapt. The Instrument Maker ascends to the dais and bows. The children have been fitted to their ukelaklavas and are well rehearsed. All the Instrument Maker needs to do is call for the first notes to be played. And so she does.

The carriage notes of the exposition assert themselves, cut the silence, demand attention.

And then, three hundred and one instruments, held in hands tiny enough to play them, fill the waiting air with sound clear and gentle; the notes so soft they ask permission to be heard. The song is a cycle that follows the spin of their world, with each new segment teasing out a subtle change in the music to reflect the passage of time and permanence of the past. No segment will be repeated once played.

A crescendo is coming, planned to coincide with the Procession of the Moons and their arrival at center zenith high above. That the audience ignores the progress of the satellites is a testament to the music, for in following the moons, they would be able to predict the arrival of the climax. By avoiding the sky's natural clock, the triumph of the Instrument Maker's song may wash over them fresh. The music lashes at the notes that will tell them the climax has begun, feinting inward, then pulling back just when they think it must surely be time. The arrangement is all they had hoped and better. Here they touch perfection. Three hundred and one children bringing the music to life, six hundred and two hearts announcing themselves.

Another ascending chorus comes, coaxing a ripple of euphoric paresthesia over the skin of all who hear. It is at this moment the sky changes, as if the music itself had summoned the heavens, imploring it as witness to the sound. Only it is not the moons that have changed but their backdrop. Far away and coming fast.

CHAPTER FORTY-FIVE

Rather than switch from the outer belts of Effelox Binary to Aszerat and draw attention to ourselves, we cruised in on conventional power, which was fast enough, considering our head start on the *Timelance*. It gave Naecia and Aptat time to show Patton the workings of both the *Silent Child* and the Switch Drive so that he would be able to execute the final leg of the plan.

A month ago, I'd watched Patton eat Doritos from between couch cushions. Now he was learning to fly a spaceship.

Using the ship's scopes, I studied the real Aszerat against the blueprint in my mind. It was terribly surreal to gaze upon something I knew intimately but had never directly perceived. It was as if each of my feet stood in a different timeline: one in the present, the other three lifetimes ago.

There had been some changes to the city since my third prior had imprinted it. Some of these were readily apparent: external changes like docks and communications towers that hadn't been in the reflections. Aptat pulled up current maps that were publicly available. Much of Aszerat was private space, which left a goodly amount of the city's volume blacked out from view.

In preparation for operation Find Chime, I brought everyone in on my organizational system. Patton wore a proud grin as I explained the Simon-based quadrant system, and he beamed with joy upon learning that our focus would be the

Blue quadrant, named for Kingdom Fungi and sub-divided by various psychotropic strains of mushrooms, the names of which I only knew because of him. He had the layout down almost before I'd finished going through it. The others weren't so enthusiastic. To be fair, the totality of my plan was to rush into a city to hunt down an item I couldn't describe, using a map organized like a salad bar for spirit guides.

Blue Quadrant was the size of Shanghai with the density of Mumbai. It could take years to find the Chime without knowing more. Before we arrived, I decided to take a final trip down the cord to see if there was anything I'd missed.

I crawled back into the dredge and triggered the lid. It abruptly stopped closing, and suddenly Naecia was there, sitting on the edge looking down at me with her default level of contempt. I could tell that she didn't even want to address me – to dignify my existence with the acknowledgment of communication.

When it was clear she wasn't going to speak first, I broke the ice, "Anything I can help you with?"

"We almost stopped you." Blunt.

"Okay."

"When did you figure out the Chime was inside Aszerat?"

"Maybe about a day before you rescued-slash-tried-to-assassinate-me?" I guessed. "Tough to say. I'd sort of lost track of time." I displayed my wrist to show off the Timex whose battery I'd killed playing with its Indiglo® technology while in captivity.

She glanced off, clearly frustrated at missing the window to erase my brain and murder me. "And you told them about it as soon as you found it, didn't you? Didn't bother to hold onto the knowledge or at least delay giving it to them?"

"I *thought* I was saving them. *And* I was addicted to nectar. *And* they were torturing my friend, so yeah: I told them it was in Aszerat."

She shook her head and tightened her mouth. The spiracles on her neck flexed open then shuddered an exhalation. "He's *one* person. You put unknowable trillions at risk of extinction by giving up that information."

"I'm sorry for not knowing that the Chime was a weapon of mass destruction. No one bothered to tell me that during my welcome tour of the *Silent Child*. You want to blame someone, blame Aptat."

"I do," she said, refocusing her gaze squarely with mine. "But I blame you too."

"For what?"

"For existing."

"Great," I said, gesturing to the glass. "Do you mind? I need to see if I can find the specific location of this thing so we can grab it before all of the death happens."

Naecia took hold of the lid and leaned in, voice soft. "Don't get stupid down there. Unfortunately, you can't die until we have the Chime. Make sure you come back with all your coherence." She stood from the machine. "Your friend is still here. He'd miss you if you went away."

I closed the lid and, feeling some relief, realized that I quite preferred having my brain dredged to any further berating by Naecia. I dialed in, quickly pushing aside any flotsam-like reflections of Mr Bugs or Mr Watches, and dove for the depths of Aszerat.

It floated there, in the soup of my consciousness, much like the real Aszerat floated in space, looking a bit like a spherical pinecone with all of its monster radiation shields cantered to the dueling stars. My version was a three-dimensional blueprint drawn in glowing blue and purple and amber. I pushed into the Blue Quadrant and floated about through great halls, bays, and power systems, hoping to feel some tinge of familiarity or pull in one direction or another like a hillbilly using dowsing rods to divine water and witch a well.[102]

---

102 You and Patton tried that last summer – *And we would have found water too if the cops hadn't showed up to lecture us about "private property"*.

I didn't feel jack shit.

I swam into the deepest, darkest crannies of Blue Quadrant, down a sewer passage in *Golden Teacher*, into every utility closet lining the halls of *Wavy Caps*. I went through the low-ceilinged ducts of *Pajaritos*, zig-zagged the maze-like power corridor of *Philosopher's Stone*. As detailed as the schematics were, they still rang hollow.

I exploded the view on one of the large residential units, breaking its components into chunks of reflections, then slid them away from each other to get down to the smallest building blocks of memory. I picked one, a simple, bluish, rectangular polyhedron, squared off at the top and rounded near the bottom. I drew it longways through the lid to check the glimmers.

They were still blank as ever.

I repeated this over and over: at a section of the docks, a navigational outpost, even some type of space laser things set out on huge arms that extended beyond the habitable space. The fragments were all the same as they had been since I'd been building Aszerat: full of glowing blue or purple glimmers, capped at the top with a single layer rimmed in bright amber.

And then I laughed. The answer. I was right there. How could I have missed it?

I pushed my mind up the cord where I might find scrap reflections floating around from Bugs or Watches. I grabbed the first one I saw, a neon blue roughly hammer-shaped polyhedron packed with *very detailed* glimmers about Strepsipterans, which are these tiny bugs that live inside wasp assholes.[103] I pushed through the very graphic, and disturbing, description of Strepsipteran reproduction, all the way to the glimmer capping the top. Blue. Just like the rest of it. No outline drawn in another color.

I repeated this a dozen times. Bugs and watches, all one color. No amber cap. I dropped back to Aszerat. Every reflection, not

---

103   Oh, this one is really gross. See, the male just stabs – *Nope. Stop.*

just those in the residences, or in the energy corridor, or the cargo bays – had a single, square, amber-framed glimmer. I'd never thought twice about it since every one of the millions of reflections within Aszerat had the feature. Never did I suspect it was anything more than some default color scheme. Now, I was convinced that it was anything but. It felt genuine, as if it had been imprinted from direct experience. I flew back up the cord and punched open the lid like a drug addled space vampire startled awake from cryosleep.

"It's a door!" I blurted across the deck.

I explained as best I could that, for whatever reason, the third prior hadn't been able to imprint information about Aszerat in the same way as Bugs and Watches had during their lives. Naecia and Izairis, too, verified that they did not have anything but monochromatic reflections, through which the glimmers – though they both called them "moments" – were layered. I tried to articulate my feeling that this third person was somehow hamstrung in what they could get to stick. Almost like the act of imprinting had been done through effort rather than experience – except when it came to the location of the Chime. There was something more *original* or *genuine* about that glowing amber square on the endcap of every reflection… and I wasn't entirely sure that it was because of any intent on the part of the imprinter. After all, it was my working hypothesis that they were trying to hide the Chime, not give it away.

Nevertheless, whatever quality we Stringers held for snooping around in the memories of our forebears had steered me to somewhere in the Blue Quadrant, and – if I was reading this unintentional hint correctly – it was somewhere up high, behind an amber door.

There were two cygies – eight Earth days – left before the earliest that the *Timelance* could arrive when we got to Aszerat. Obsessed, I'd gone back into the dredge again, pounding

through the upper floors of the highest buildings in the city's
Fungal district until Naecia finally made me stop. The axon
diadem showed my coherence plummeting each time I entered
– a sign that my brain was finally wearing out. I hadn't slipped
the cord like Naecia, but I'd lost almost ten percent of whatever
it was coherence measured. The dredge was no longer giving
me anything new anyway. The trail had gone cold.

On the way into the city, Izairis scanned fugitive encryptions
floating out from the docks in the upper longitudes of Fungi
and was able to parse them for analysis. She discovered that
the city's security protocols were based on the same encryption
language as the outer docks – she just couldn't break it. We
were going to need free rein of the city if we were going to
ransack both its public *and* private areas for the Chime. She
volunteered to go into the dredge in order to try and learn
a few tricks that would enable her to crack the ciphers. This
turned out to be fruitful because her first prior was a forger in
every sense, including code and cipher smashing techniques.

The rest of us had also been working away – well, mainly
Naecia and Aptat – to modify the coms on the Vortu helmets
stolen from the *Terror's Glaive*, in order to allow us to talk when
we finally dispersed into the city.

After working silently away on a dedicated terminal for a
day, Izairis stood and stretched. "We're in," she said, grinning
from ear nub to ear nub. "I was able to capture the entry codes
and reproduce them."

"Brilliant work," said Aptat. "I have a whole closet full
of raw media devices we can fashion into transmitters for
whenever we come to a secured area–" Izairis stepped into our
Vortu sewing circle and handed out small rectangular cards,
"–Oh. You've already… Okay," said Aptat, taking one. "And
these are?"

"Security cards," Izairis answered, handing the last two to
myself and Patton. "Once you are in proximity to a sealed passage,
you simply hold the card up to the receiver, and it should open!"

I shared a questioning glance with Patton, and then Naecia. "What?" Izairis said.

"It's just that... these are tangible media," said Naecia diplomatically. "Can't we just throw the signal through the helmet coms so we don't have to stop at every door and swipe a card?"

Izairis tightened her lips, then calmly said, "We'd have to broadcast that signal from here and through the helmets, which could be unreliable or dangerous. Not only are there all sorts of interferences between the ship and wherever we end up, but we'd be advertising ourselves."

I shrugged, still bewildered by the shockingly prehistoric tech. "I mean, it's a hotel key," I said. "We have these on Earth."

Izairis made an emphatic gesture toward her crotch that I don't think she learned at the convent.

We coasted toward the docks near the center latitudes of Aszerat. My nerves, by now, were frazzled from the combined effects of the dredgings and detox – not to mention the anxiety of the Scythin's imminent arrival. All of those things were enough to make a person crack, and yet what really did it was the fact that our chances of finding a galaxy-annihilating relic came down to whether or not a floating space city had any better security than a Hilton Garden Inn.

CHAPTER FORTY-SIX

Sitting in the captain's chair, Aptat projected a map of Aszerat over the deck and the Blue Quadrant was divvied up.

"Naecia and I will take the northern latitudes," said Aptat. "Patton and Ben, the south. Izairis, you'll have the center strip along the equator so you can be close to the ship in case anything goes down."

Naecia knew there was far more ground than they could ever cover, but what other choice was there? They would get through as much as they could each day, then return to the ship for rest, and head out again and again until they found the Chime. Maybe being inside Aszerat would jostle more clues out of the Earth man's brain. If they were still empty handed when the Scythin showed, they all agreed that the only rational choice was to run.

Aptat gave each of them a handful of registered guush micro-billets in case they needed to bribe anyone or purchase emergency supplies, making sure to record the allocations in the ship's ledger against any future profits.

The size of the city came into stark relief as they approached the docks. "How are we supposed to find anything in there?" said Izairis. "It's massive."

"How many amber doors could there be?" said Ben, his optimistic tone betrayed by a grimace.

"In case anyone was wondering, I'm still fine to run away," said Aptat.

"Of course you are," said Naecia. "Just remember who owns the ship."

"Yeah, I meant to ask about that," said Ben. "Why doesn't Aptat own the ship anymore?"

"Stuff… happened," said Naecia waving her hand in the air as if to erase any request that she repeat the story.

"Yes," said Aptat, coming to attention. "And if I recall correctly, the deal was that those shares would be returned to me after I obtained the caridianite from the *Terror's Glaive*, which I did."

"If *I* recall correctly," responded Naecia, "it was to keep you from murdering all of us while in your carapace. Unfortunately, we still need you in your armor. I'll be happy to return your shares once we're done here and can part ways."

"All I'm saying is *that wasn't the deal,*" they hissed.

Naecia gave a dismissive shrug. "Anyway, as I was saying: The Scythin will tear Aszerat apart until they find the Chime, and they will do it far quicker than we will. They know what they're looking for and they don't need…" she fumbled with her security card, "…whatever these are to get around."

"Try or die," said Patton with a fist pump.

Aptat spun in the captain's chair. "Try *and* die, I fear, is the more likely outcome."

The ship coasted gently into the port, and the deck echoed loudly with the metal clank of docking clamps.

Aptat's helmet closed, and they headed for the ramp. "*Shall we?*"

The others wore their Vortu helmets, which was how they would communicate. Otherwise, their dress was uncoordinated. While Ben had been dredging, Patton had designed matching tracksuits for them both that Aptat graciously printed on the ship's fabricator. They were powder blue with bright red and orange lightning-bolt accents, and words that went across the

front in glittering yellow. Patton's said PATTON. Ben's said I'M
WITH PATTON.

All but Aptat carried Vortu blunderbusses, accepting the
stringhunter's assurance that the citizenry of Aszerat would be
far too busy gambling, scheming, and being intoxicated to pay
any mind to the weapons – or the tracksuits.

"These are too much," said Ben, pulling on the fabric of his
zip-up.

"No, no," said Aptat with a hand wave. "Your costumes
won't turn any heads in this place. But humans would be new
to Aszerat, so best to keep your helmets on."

"Com check," said Naecia.

Izairis gave a thumbs up, "I hear you."

"Check," said Ben.

"Down to clown," said Patton.

Aptat's mask shut over their face. "Let's go."

They split up as planned, with Naecia and Aptat headed toward
the city's crown. Just off the docks was a station with tube-
like transways that ran throughout. Technologically speaking,
Aszerat was a mix of old and new, with most of its outward
infrastructure design of similar construction to that of the
Pangemic planets. Being so distant from her home system,
Naecia'd never expected to venture as far out as Effelox Binary
and see it for herself. Now with the Switch, she supposed,
what was distance anymore?

They pressed through throngs of people making their way
into the city. Naecia was taken aback by the diversity of species.
Vask was nominally diverse, but no one was journeying into
the Pangemic system from faraway stars to be a steam farmer.
Effelox Binary was the functional center of a larger cluster of
stars, making it a hub for all of the surrounding worlds. But
to think that Aszerat was only one of six thousand such cities
boggled the mind.

Her eyes were keen for the color of amber and suddenly it was everywhere: on placards, across rows of gambling machines, video displays, items for sale in the shops that lined the place. Amber wasn't a color she'd thought of as that common, but now that she was on the lookout, it was ubiquitous, just not as a colorful frame for doors. Seeing the city from space, Naecia thought she'd appreciated the magnitude of their task. Being inside it, she feared becoming paralyzed by hopelessness. She kept walking, afraid that if she stopped, she might sit down and never move again. So she kept going. For now.

They located the transway for the northern latitudes and boarded. Aptat stood, one hand gripping a handhold. Elsewhere, other obviously engineered persons and robots did the same, while the more traditionally organic lifeforms strapped in.

Naecia focused ahead, careful not to get lost in the passing blur of the city outside her window. It was only a few seconds before they burst through the underside of the city, crossing a vector of open space below civilization that would take them in a straight line from the equator to the top of the sphere. The transway tube ran out in open space for a short while until they ascended through the city's nadir up in the higher latitudes.

The shuttle slowed into the northern station where the two of them debarked. The entire trip had taken only a few cygments, just long enough to listen to the audio tour of Aszerat she'd downloaded to her com.

Aszerat was the twelfth of the Effelox Free Cities to be constructed, starting nearly a thousand galactic years prior. Built to offer a no-consequences getaway for the system's growing population of workers, tycoons, and "security" syndicates, its offerings were primarily of drink, pharmacy, flesh, and entertainment. Its heart and soul remained with those first wild occupants and the city managed to keep a reputation in line with those early times. The seedy underbelly of the Effelox system had risen from the streets and transways of Aszerat and still thrived there today.

Aptat walked briskly out and into the crowd before Naecia had even unstrapped, saying through the com, "I'll work out West from here, you take the East."

"Okay."

"Get up high as soon as you can. Work your way down. Limit the amount of traverse."

"Right," she said, watching Aptat disappear.

She found the nearest lift, housed in a building occupying four hundred and twenty-one floors. Stepping in, she said, "Four twenty-one." The doors closed and the floor felt like it was shot up below her. Everything on Aszerat was twice as fast as she was accustomed to. She stood in the corner, giving her two surfaces to lean on.

The elevator spoke as it ascended. *"Peba Unin Tower features the most exciting choices in entertainment. May I interest you in a brief sojourn before you arrive at your floor? Casino, brothels, level two-ninety. Playhouse, restaurants, free combat spectating, level three twelve. Organic grocers, scholars' library, level three fourteen. Grappling bouts begin in a half cygment on level three fifty, with tickets—"*

"Shut up," said Naecia. The lift obliged. She thought about Oush, the grappler, and his unlikely murder at the hands of Patton, who seemed to be full of surprises. They'd known Oush was taking a great risk by venturing to the *Timelance* alone but had never countenanced that he might die at the hands of the yellow-maned drug sponge.

"Map," she whispered into the helmet, calling up a three-dimensional model of the city in the upper left corner of the Vortu visor. She traced her eyes over the buildings, most of them connected near their top floors by walking paths or transways. The visor followed the direction of her eyes, and she sketched out a few different lines through the geography, trying to plan the most efficient route and erasing them each time. "Clear," she said, frustrated.

How do you find something you can't describe? If the Chime could do what they'd hypothesized, it held the energy of a million stars. Something like that couldn't be hidden in a locker. Naecia was of the mind that it would be left in plain sight, disguised as a larger thing, like a generator, a hydration plant, or scrubber. And if it was set up as a piece of equipment, it would probably be wherever they kept the decommissioned machinery. A big, dark room somewhere – not in the fancy top floors of Aszerat's tallest towers. They weren't thinking strategically. Look for an amber door? The plan was stupid.

Patton's voice blasted through the com, "Hey, did you guys know there's a food court in here?"

Naecia sighed angrily. "Stay on your local channel, Patton!"

"I found an empanada place. I mean, they look like empanadas."

Naecia growled through the com and the Earthling fell silent.

The lift stopped. The doors opened to an unobstructed view of space through a panoramic window that spanned half of the building's top floor. Feeling a bit of vertigo, Naecia stabilized herself on the wall before stepping out. She walked to the glass, placing hands on a small railing that followed the curve of the building, and looked out over the strange city. Above where she stood, even farther out into the black, was the edge of one of the orb's huge radiation shields, canted at an angle toward the dueling stars around which they orbited, a few million mylics distant.

She chose a corridor perpendicular to the one by the windows and followed it. Soon, she was at a plain metal security door upon which the building's logo was painted. Locked. Reluctantly, she slid Izairis's security card from a pocket and waived it near the panel on the door. It immediately flew open with a whoosh.

"Okay," she said at the phenomenon of something working as it was supposed to.

She continued on like this, proceeding blindly across the upper floors of the building through service passages where the only interactions she had were the glances of maintenance staff or the occasional resident. In her helmet, they must have thought she was just another dilettante, drunk on shots of Moonspike after gambling away her daily allowance. Fighting the ever-present weight of hopelessness, she kept moving, and covered a considerable amount of ground, personally checking thousands of doors across dozens of buildings over the course of the cygie, with none of them rimmed in amber.

This went on until time had run nearly out.

They were all getting anxious. They'd only covered about twenty percent of the Blue Quadrant's upper floors and were close to collapsing from exhaustion. All except the stringhunter, of course, who didn't require sleep. Nevertheless, Aptat had become increasingly chatty about making the call to run, and Naecia had no doubt that they would have already done so if they had the permissions to unclamp the *Child* from the docks. She held a seed of remorse for using her leveraged ownership of the ship to hold Aptat hostage, but it was the only way to ensure they weren't all abandoned. Plus, restraining the freedom of a slaver didn't really knock the needle of her moral compass.

She was near halfway down her slice of latitudes at the end of the third cygie, jogging along a heavily cabled passage through which the city's solar energy flowed.

"Hey Ben," it was Patton. Using the all-channels broadcast again.

"Hey: *Brown Dwarf*," snarled Naecia. "Get off the com unless you find something. Are you – are you eating?"

"Yeah, the empanada place," he answered.

"You're making me want to barf, man, geez," said Ben.

"Have you even been looking for the Chime?" Naecia said.

"Anyway, Ben," he swallowed loudly, "this thing reminds me of LEGO-Kong. Remember LEGO-Kong at your place?"

"Yes, Patton. I think that's what it is."

"I mean, it's roundish, with like, all these layers. I swear even the space-fins are the same."

"What do you mean by 'fins'?" It was Aptat.

"Whatever the big panel-things are on the outside. The fishy-fin things."

"Radiation shields," said Naecia. "Shut up now."

"Yeah, we put 'em all over LEGO-Kong. Made it look like coronavirus. Not exactly, but if you squinted. You know, all spikey?"

"What in the galactic fuck are you talking about?" said Izairis.

"See, we had this pandemic and–"

"Hold up, hold up," Ben cut in.

"What is it?" asked Naecia.

"Patton, you're a genius."

CHAPTER FORTY-SEVEN

As the famous philosopher Céline Dion once said, *it's all coming back to me.*

"The radiation shields!"

"What are you screaming about?" asked Naecia.

"Everyone get to a radiation shield," I said. "If I recall right, there are seventeen in the Blue Quadrant. I'm flagging them on our maps now. Find the closest one and go."

"Who would even think to hide something there?" asked Aptat. "Are they even accessible?"

"Each one has two columns usually built into an adjoining structure that lead up into separate compartments within the shields. There should be a lift or a ladder for us to access the shields themselves. Check both compartments." I was already breathing heavily as I trotted to the nearest transway. "I assembled some of these inside the dredge."

I leapt into a transport for the short jaunt to the nearest shield, where a building had been constructed around one of the huge columns. It made so much sense. The shields weren't livable space, but they were the tallest structures on Aszerat. My nectar-less brain had gone back to thinking inside the box again. Thankfully, Patton's brain could never be hemmed in by walls.

I sprinted out from the transway and took the elevator to the top floors, then used my hotel card to get through a maintenance corridor that led to an access portal for the column. There was a plain door in the wall. Keycard. The area behind the door was closet-like, small, with a ladder built into the far wall. I took hold and gazed upward. The top of the column was far enough away to be obscured by darkness. I stuffed the keycard into a cargo pocket in my hideous light-blue pants and began upward – and outward – from Aszerat.

I knew the blueprint cold. There would be another door high above, with access into the actual body of the shield. My palms sweated as I climbed, making each handhold more precarious. The environmental systems weren't cycling the air with as many exchanges as down in the common areas. I wondered when the last time was that anyone had come through. A few hundred feet up, I arrived at a smaller door, hatchlike, just over my head. Holding onto the ladder with one hand, I retrieved the hotel card and waved it over the panel. The latch clicked and the door popped open by half an inch. I pressed it up and inward with the top of my helmet until it fell back against a bulkhead.

It was dark. I turned on the helmet lights and shot them through the hollow body of the shield.

Empty. No door. No amber paintjob. Disheartened, I reminded myself that there were sixteen other shields. It would just be inside one of those – or perhaps in the next compartment over. I went back down, took a transway to the building that held the second column and repeated the trip.

Again, nothing.

I chinned the com. "First shield empty."

The others checked in as they found their way up into the shields, with all relaying the same result. Patton and I crisscrossed the southern half of Blue Quadrant, ascending columns in *Blue Meanies*, *Laughing Gym*, *Cubes*, *Landslide*, and *Teonanacatl*. All dry holes.

Exhausted, we reported our lack of progress and waited nervously for the others to do the same. One after another, they did, until all seventeen shields had been accounted for. No amber door. No Chime.

I crumpled in the base of the last column, dismayed, smelling like a Vortu's taint.

"Maybe the Chime is somewhere else," said Naecia. "If anything, we've proven it's well hidden. I... I think we should go."

If Naecia was willing to give up, then maybe it was time.

"Heading back," said Izairis.

"Same," said Patton.

"Aptat?" said Naecia. "Where are you?"

"Squaring some old accounts. You never know who you'll run into!" they said. "Be on my way shortly."

Aptat continued talking but I wasn't hearing the words. Head down, arms wrapped around my knees, I imagined my blueprint of Aszerat. I rotated it like a globe, reexamined the Quadrants, counted shields. Seventeen shields. Two columns each, placed at alternating latitudes and longitudes, with smaller ones at the poles, and long, wide ones near the equator. The pattern was the same all the way around, with the western-most, zero-latitude shields slightly overhanging the neighboring quadrant. *Overhanging the neighboring quadrant!*

"I'm so stupid!" I leapt up, punched through the door to the external corridor, and started running. "I'm heading into Red Quadrant."

"I thought you were sure it was in Blue?" said Naecia.

"*Fungus,*" added Patton unhelpfully.

"It *is* in Blue," I said, rushing to the transways. "There's one shield fin that overhangs Blue Quadrant, but the supporting columns are in Red."

"Do it, but hurry," said Aptat. "We see any hint of the *Timelance*, we're gone."

"Except me, I'll stay."

"Thanks, Patton. I know."

* * *

Sparklemuffin[104] was among the tallest buildings in the Red Quadrant of Aszerat, one of the first I'd explored so long ago inside the Scythin dredge. The lift ended several thousand levels up in an otherwise featureless space not so different from the basement of an office building where you might find HVAC and water mains. I'd never been in this room – *my prior* had never been in this room; I knew these things in my soul. And yet I felt closer to the Chime than I'd ever been.

I skittered up the column and reached the top, sweating like a pig.[105] I unlocked the hatch with my hotel key and opened it.

The smell that poured over me was like that from a decades-old bug collection. Dry and musty, with a light organic funk. Decay, yes, but old, dusty decay. Unpleasant. Not enough to completely turn the stomach, but highly dead.

I climbed through the hatch and stood on the metal floor inside the shield. Aside from the light that came up from the column, it was pitch black. I chinned on the helmet lights, which cast a white beam down the shield's inner length toward the distant bulkhead. Unlike all the other shields, there was dust. And the smell. Something had been here. I lowered the hatch door back down into the floor. The latch clicked, and a row of amber lights came on, illuminating its perfectly square outline.

I recognized it immediately. Not just because it matched the marmalade-topped reflections of the Aszerat I'd built, but because it was yet another example of my living room sculpture manifested in real life. A grey door framed in amber singles – my secret LEGO cookie cabinet. The Chime's final resting place. It had been spelled out in plastic blocks atop my coffee table for the past year.

Ignoring my sudden desire for a cookie, I cast the helmet

---

104 Australian peacock spider. *Maratus jactatus*. The most fabulous of all spiders.

105 Hmm, pigs don't really sweat. Now, horses? They sweat. Better than being a stork, though, who shit on their legs to keep cool.

beams far into the darkness. The smell was considerably stronger now, and my footfalls kicked up clouds of dust that lay in a heavy scrim over the floor. It was like churning up silt in a pond with a casting reel – one little dab of the lure on the bottom and the whole thing goes murky. I tried to be gentle with my steps to not kick so much up. Didn't work.

The space tightened farther in, following the shield's arched shape. A glint of light reflected from up ahead. I stopped and tried to find it again with the beam. Another glint, this time from a different spot. Panning the helmet, I followed along a span of material, something that stretched from the wall on one side of the space across to the other. Another step. Another glint. Keeping the light steady, I paced forward, tracing the sinuous strand from within the darkness to the wall high above my shoulder, where it terminated.

There was no mistaking the black resin. It had covered every inch of the *Timelance* and the voidscull before that. Hardened Scythin space mucus. More of the stuff stretched across the floor like black glass, solidified after being strewn while molten. I had to duck beneath a thick cable of it, then step over and slip through a gap between two more spans.

A few paces revealed an explosion of it, flung out over the floor and the walls, long black veins unspooled. Dust was fully in the air now, reflecting the helmet's light back to me, leaving only the visor's periphery marginally clear. My throat and lungs thickened with the stuff. I kept coughing it out.

Despite the suffocating particulate, the smell, the confusion, I only moved faster. Closer and closer toward the thing I'd always sought, an object that someone else, long dead, had hidden away. I was compelled by something stronger than instinct to retrieve this thing that meant life to some, nonexistence to trillions.

I came to a place that no longer resembled the interior of the radiation shield. It was Scythin by all measure, but also different from the *Timelance*. The strands of resin radiated from a single point just up ahead, desperate volleys that weaved a funneled web. Like long-fingered hands reaching out. Final gasps.

I waded through the dust, waving it away, dodging strands of Scythin glass. Then, something familiar. Embedded in the structure of the shield was the distinctive bow of a voidscull. Jutting up from where the wall met the floor, it appeared to have pierced the heavy structure of the shield, melding both together in a moment of relativistic alchemy. Only by its shape was it distinguishable from the surrounding surfaces, which had been coated in layers of the sinuous exudate that originated from inside. A black shadow beckoned from the gap between the fairings, drawing me in.

Gently moving anomalies peppered the periphery of my vision, gliding past and disappearing into false distance. I took them for motes of dust at first. But gradually they assumed colors I recognized, and I saw them for what they were: Reflections. Filtering into my present awareness from a place deeper than I'd ever been. Without the dredge as medium, they were no longer presented as intricate geometrical shapes with layers to dissect, but as flakes of snow, with orange, violet, and aqua flurries falling toward an invisible horizon. I was remembering.

I angled the beam between the fairings, and the flurries fell harder, tiny fragments of memory pouring up from the past. And suddenly *I* was the one fleeing the *Timelance* decades ago. *I* was the one absconding inside a voidscull to the floating world called Aszerat in order to conceal the Chime. *I* was the one seeking to end the drawing together of dimensions so that they might be crossed, destroying unfathomable life in one so that mine might continue in the parallel. *I* was the one who trapped my people within this alien dimension to die.

I shook my head. "No, I'm Ben," I declared aloud, publicly reasserting my identity.

I stepped squarely before the voidscull, allowing a strip of light to fall upon what sat inside, and glimpsed a slice of the traitor's mask. Slowly, through the drifting dust mixed with memory, I reached out to the fairings, placed my fingers into the crack, and touched the inner edge. Both halves slammed open, revealing the long-dead stowaway. The final resting place of the being whose consciousness I shared.

My third prior. A Scythin queen called Jecca.

I stumbled backward over the hardened entrails, my gaze locked upon the desiccated husk of the fugitive. Collapsing down against the far wall, memories boiled up from their abyssal reach, swallowing me entirely into the world of the Scythin, making me witness to an understanding.

Ancient, inviolable, they were the first juggernaut.

A thing that roiled, inexorable, through the skins of infinite worlds.

Immune to consequence.

Oblivious to suffering.

Unconsidering.

An apex unmatched.

The ultimate creation.

The testing blade.

Set free across spacetime.

Life without bounds.

Unbridled *being*.

Coursing through membranes meant to hold others.

Original and continuous.

Feeding on the flesh of thought.

One and all, at once.

I saw the world of Jecca, played out in reflections imprinted on the cord that we shared. Then, a change of scene.

A whirling vortex in a mist of others. Communing. From

their hearts the Twenty-Seven draw forth metallic prongs, each the same but different, then at once strike them upon the surface in a ring above the spire. A chord resonates in a language that speaks to the Universe, with each prong contributing its distinctive tone. Twenty-seven Notes resonate to twenty-seven tilting fins at the edge of the ship's body, drawn wide. A carnivorous flower. The Bloom of God. A chord amplifies from this stellar mouth, a thundering radio burst, calling to stars and roping them in upon the frequency's wavelength. Fuel gathered, the singing Notes are touched to the spire itself, drawing the stars inward, weaving their fissile bodies together, directed to a pinprick in the dimensional fabric. Spacetime itself shudders. The needle hooks the weft of sentience and the void itself is pulled taut.[106]

The ship spins like a top, drawing the galaxy inward by the warp of thought, as if it were the cloth upon which the stars were sat. The Scythin devour the raw matter of consciousness as their ship spools it up. And as that which holds everything together feels their dominion, all begins to burn. The fire that birthed the Universe reignites at the galaxy's edge and collapses inward, this time bringing death. Imbalance invites the dimensions to communion, and the gate is open. The ship slips through and is gone. All consumed in the vacated dimension, only cold remains.

For a moment my vision cleared and I was back in my own head. The Chime wasn't one thing, it was twenty-seven things. The things the Queen Scythin carried in their chests. Tuning forks of death. *Notes.* And what they did – if I understood the visions correctly – was worse than anything Naecia had suggested. The Oblivion Fray was their sustenance, their energy source, and their ticket to other dimensions. The collection of it set fire to the heavens, evaporating trillions in an ineffable horror too momentous for human brains to

---

106 Ben, it's the Oblivion Fray. They can touch it.

fathom. The Bloom of God was all consuming, leaving only abject nothingness behind – a void where even the idea of existence becomes vapor. Whatever force had spawned the big bang, the Scythin could summon it. In reverse. With a musical chord.

I tried to get up, to dive into the tomb for the prong embedded in Jecca's body – the Chime – only to discover that my limbs had gone numb. Like a fainting goat, I was paralyzed.[107]

A blanket of white drew down – not in front of me, not between myself and Jecca – but in the world of my mind. The blizzard of reflections came together, erasing everything I saw, everything I thought. And I was shown a new imprint, not from Jecca – *through Jecca* – the entire story of Jecca's *first* prior.

And my fourth.

---

107 Okay, there's a lot going on right now, and I hate to interrupt, but it's important to clarify that the goats aren't actually fainting. It is a condition called myotonia congenita, which is a stiffening of the muscles based on a chloride channel disorder. They remain conscious the whole time. Carry on.

CHAPTER FORTY-EIGHT
THE INSTRUMENT MAKER

Black becomes violet becomes burning pink and orange – the sky of dawn in the center of night. Those gathered into the amphitheater see it as well, though they are too mesmerized by the transcendent notes and the imminent crescendo to care much for the phenomenon happening above. An aurora, perhaps, come to join the stars in audience to the numinous sounds of the Procession, nothing more.

The Instrument Maker continues in spite of the anomaly. Being the director of the music, she is not swaddled in it as those who have come to watch, and views the change with greater concern. But what is there to do except continue? To give melody to the thing that has come.

Great white spanners blow on the night wind, then in an instant change direction and become incandescent. The orange horizon brightens yellow, yellow sears white. A great flaming arc appears in the sky, burning away the black ahead of it. All in the space of a moment's fraction.

She understands, as does everyone who sees it, that it will be death by fire. A cleansing flame sent from somewhere far away. An erasing conflagration meant to leave nothing behind. Not the town, not the moons, not the planet.

At some point the music stops. Sound and time cease.

Thought and existence evaporate. And at the penultimate moment when she is still something, before all is ash, and then the ash too is obliterated, the Instrument Maker's thoughts are of a single ukelaklava sitting in the dark of her shop. The three hundred and second. Made for a child who will never be born to play it.

CHAPTER FORTY-NINE

Naecia leapt from the tube and ran to the port where the *Silent Child* was docked.

Izairis nearly collided with her as she crested the ramp. "The Switch!" she yelled. "It's gone!"

Naecia knew immediately. "Aptat," she snarled.

"But–"

Naecia opened the com. "Where is it, fucker?"

"I gather from your tone and word choice that you have discovered that the Switch has been transferred from the *Child*–"

"I can't believe you!" Naecia screamed. "Where is it?"

"This… searching about for something we can't identify. It was a stupid plan."

"I know," said Naecia, "It's all we've got!"

"Well, I came up with a better plan the very moment I heard our destination was Aszerat."

Her blood ran cold. "To steal the drive and abandon us?"

"I told you that Aszerat is a place of commerce–"

"You *sold* it?"

"Of course not – well, a small, non-controlling interest in the technology – how else could I have purchased a second ship?"

"You bought another ship!"

"I couldn't sell the *Silent Child*, could I? You own it along with Izairis and whoever stands to inherit Oush's estate, may he rest in... whatever."

"We were going to give it back as soon–"

"Yes, yes, promises, promises... Here we are, a place of commerce, graced with a revolutionary new technology. And here *I* am, a connoisseur of opportunity. I told you what I would do if I had the chance. And my dear, you should have listened."

Naecia closed her mouth and gritted her teeth. Aptat had said exactly that. If presented with the chance, they would take the machine. What Naecia took for boastful hyperbole from the flamboyant stringhunter had been the pristine truth. She'd ignored it. And what was worse, they'd had two chances to abandon Aptat and both times it had been she who had overruled the others, insisting that they be brought back on board. Right now, Aptat could be floating in space where the *Terror's Glaive* had exploded or shredded to pieces on the *Timelance*, but no – they were right here, because she had continually intervened, always believing she could manipulate the kidnapping, stealing, scheming stringhunter to her advantage.

"Do you remember, Naecia? When I said I was just waiting for the right moment? I told you what I would do, and you ignored me. Pretended I was more like you, even as I tried to convince you that I wasn't."

"It's mine," she growled.

"Oh, now, please, let's not demean ourselves with falsehoods," said Aptat. "It was never yours! You happened upon it. And then I happened upon you. Explain the difference, please. *Morally.* I'm fascinated that you subscribe to the notion that anyone should be governed by anything other than consequence. Should I let you keep the Switch Drive because it's 'yours'? Just because you assembled the pieces according to directions authored by somebody else? Utter nonsense, all of it. And even assuming some construct of ethics to which you and I had tacitly agreed, you broke it first when you didn't immediately sign the *Silent Child* back to me after I salvaged the *Terror's Glaive* for the caridianite you needed."

Naecia sneered. "You would have done this anyway."

"Of course I would have! Which brings me back to my first point about the idiocy of moral codes."

Her first thought was her family back on Drev. "So... you're just going to leave us here to die? Eventually–"

"I know it all. You explained, remember? The big, bad Scythin will destroy this galaxy and the next, erasing them methodically until, at some point through some collision of chance, I too, am erased. There are trillions of galaxies in this dimension and the Switch Drive can take me to any of them. Running was always the better option."

"What about your *investors*?"

Naecia could hear Aptat smiling. "Oh, they have no idea what's coming. Once they're torn apart by the Scythin and/ or evaporated by the Chime, their shares will revert to me. But really, will anyone care? I'll be a billion gilleys away by then."

"Where are you?"

"On my way to fetch you."

"I thought you were going to abandon–"

"Your words, not mine. I wouldn't leave the machine's great architect behind! We're partners again!" The com went dead.

Naecia immediately selected Ben's channel, "Ben? Ben. Come in."

"Anything?" asked Izairis.

Naecia shook her head. "Ben? If you can hear me – Aptat stole the Switch Drive. They are on their way to abduct me in order to run it. We don't know where it is. Come down as quickly as you can." She dropped the link. "SHIT!"

"You should run, Naecia," said Izairis. "Hide."

"Hide? Fuck you."

"O-kay, just trying to be supportive," answered Izairis, calling up the display.

"Sorry," said Naecia.

"You're under a lot of stress. Anyhow, more good news. The *Timelance* has emerged from bulkspace just outside the belt."

"Shitfuck." Naecia looked around desperately for anything that might help them. The power connections for the Switch had been sabotaged beyond use. "Izairis, can you ping Aptat's com and find out where they are?"

Izairis played with the interface on the ship's console. "Huh," she chuckled. "No. They've frozen us out. But…" She pointed to the display as a small green blip appeared. "They still have their security card."

"Those are traceable?"

"Of course. So that we could find each other," she said. "Eighty-fifth degree of Blue Quadrant and moving south at pace. Must already be in a transway."

"Alright," said Naecia, checking the level on her Vortu blunderbuss. "I'll be right back."

She took the ship's lift to the third deck. Just off of the galley, around a wall that curved outward and into one of the ship's "wings" was the door to the second room that she'd only known about from schematics. Even then, every detail had been blacked out. It was easy to assume that it had once been Mother's. Naecia made a perfunctory check on the lock, keying in her access code as an owner of the ship. It didn't work. Aptat had somehow set additional security on the door. *Fine.*

Leveling the blunderbuss, she stepped back, twisted the barrel to narrow its shot aperture, and fired. The blast obliterated the door and the recoil flattened Naecia. Sucking in a breath, she pushed up onto her elbows, and twisted toward the weapon laying behind her. She considered it with bewildered respect for just a moment, then retrieved it and entered the room. "Lights."

No lights. The room must have been entirely walled off from the ship's systems. She turned on her helmet beams and scanned about. It was simple quarters: bed, cabinets, storage lockers, a head. The furthest wall was taken up by a vault – same as the one on the command deck below. Even through a heavy layer of dust it gleamed. "Mom's old hiding spot, eh?" She approached the vault, then halted, remembering to check in. "Izairis. Aptat update?"

"Sixtieth latitude, Naecia. What'd you find?"

"Can you break into the second living quarters up here? I think it's cordoned off."

"Standby."

The lights came on.

"That was easy," asked Naecia.

"Aptat had a tiny patch on it. I just rammed it with the ship's computer. You should be good."

Naecia went to the vault. "Do you see the carapace vault on your display?"

"It's here."

"Can you open it?"

"Standby."

Cyclets passed. Naecia impatiently toed the vault.

"Okay, I'm in."

"Great."

"It says 'currently configured'." Said Izairis. "You want me to try a reset?"

"Who is it configured for?"

"Profile says *Mother*."

A shiver ran head to foot. "Yes, reconfigure."

"I don't have all the permissions for the suit, so I can't completely wipe it," said Izairis.

"Wait, the suit is actually still inside, then?" asked Naecia.

"Showing it is from where I'm sitting," said Izairis.

"That sneaky little worm." Aptat had killed Mother but kept her suit, the sick bastard. Probably to keep it out of anyone else's hands. "Open it."

"Yep."

The doors opened. The smell was worse than a nest of post-molt colon queevils.

The suit was there, identical to Aptat's, and closed everywhere except for the four segments of the mask, which revealed the melted and charred remains of the one called Mother.

Naecia grimaced. Gagged.

And then she was angry. More deception from Aptat. They had never let on that they still had it. Even when the Vortu had threatened to destroy the entire ship and they could have used it. Even when Aptat gave up ownership of the *Silent Child* in order to get their own suit back. Was keeping the second suit hidden that important?

"Izairis, open the suit." The suit opened and the body – what was left of it – slumped out onto the floor. Naecia nudged it to the side with a boot. It moved easily. After so long a time, there wasn't much left, with all of Mother's liquids long evaporated away. At the base of the suit, where the heels of the boots met the floor of the vault, were black stains where she had leaked out from it. The arc of her liquification reached across the floor.

"Izairis, I'm going to send a chirp from my com." She bit down on her cheeks.

"Got you."

"Will the suit talk to it?"

"I think so, but again, without a hard reset, it'll be more like you're just visiting."

"I'm used to that." Naecia threw off the Vortu helmet, grunted, and stepped into the ichor-stained mobile sarcophagus. "Where's Aptat?" she asked.

"Thirty-fifth latitude."

Damn if these transways weren't quick. "Okay, Izairis. I'm inside. Yuck. Pair me."

"Hold on. Your com isn't exactly new tech."

"It's newer than this suit."

"That suit is still a hundred galactic spins more advanced than your com. Stop talking."

"Sorry."

A few seconds later. "Try now."

She knew from Aptat's suit that the power augments had operated with a type of anticipatory intuition of movement based on the slightest twitch of muscle. Supposing that Mother's suit operated in the same way, Naecia began to lift a leg to step out. Instantly, she felt the suit kick in to boost the movement. She did the same with the other, and exited the vault entirely. She held up her hands and closed them, the suit processing and then assisting the movement – all except for the non-existent middle finger on her left hand. That finger on the suit remained permanently straight, even when the rest were closed.

Then, two words came together to form an intention in Naecia's mind. *Protect me.* And the mask snapped shut.

CHAPTER FIFTY

What made Jecca decide to leave the *Timelance* and cripple their own species in the process? What was the thing that penetrated their mind enough to change it? How can something incapable of understanding anything beyond its own limitless power be made to question its purpose? Now, the answer seemed obvious: introduce a sensation it had never been forced to experience, a feeling against which it believed itself immune: *pain.*

Jecca had shown me their prior, the life and death of the Instrument Maker. Their experience had been indistinguishable from hers; so that in the final moment, they had perceived the Instrument Maker's death as their own. I knew this as absolute truth: I had felt Jecca's horror as they'd watched the Bloom of God swallow the sky through her eyes.

As with my recent priors, the Instrument Maker had become more insistent over time, bombarding Jecca's mind with the reflections of her life, her music, her child – and her death that had come at the tolling of the Scythin's terrible chord. At first, Jecca denied and ignored. But the break in their reality couldn't be undone – the Scythin had experienced absolute terror and soul-piercing anguish, sensations that their kind simply did not feel. And so the fractures spread.

Jecca had always eaten the fruit gathered by the Bloom of

God, the food of thought that fueled the Scythin. Now, it only brought disgust.

Reflections came to me of Jecca trying to forget what they had witnessed, experienced. As a Stringer, Jecca *had been* the Instrument Maker when the Bloom of God had brought about her death, obliterating the very galaxy where the cord of Jecca's consciousness had been wound. Memories and lamentations for her seeped into Jecca's being and expanded like ice in a crevice. In the end, it was blunt force empathy that had broken the lone Scythin. And they mourned the lives that would be lost if the chord were ever allowed to sound again.

Jecca's condition deteriorated. They refused to consume, sickened at the prospect of devouring consciousness that might have once been hers. Jecca struggled to wall off their mind from the others when in swarming behavior. The multitudes had begun to notice Jecca's reluctance to give them complete access to their thoughts, as was the Scythin way. The truth was unavoidable. Jecca could no longer strike the Chime. They could no longer bear to let their species sound the chord. It was no longer beautiful. It was the sound of nothingness.

Jecca was forced to act when the time came for the Scythin to feed and for their ship – it does not have a name – to cross dimensions again. The Notes, the Chimes – great prongs struck in order to play the chord – were indestructible, impossible to cut, disassemble, melt, or obliterate. Jecca searched for places to hide the one embedded within their chest. It would devour a star instantly. Dropping it into open space was too risky – their ship's eyes could find a fragment of slag across half a galaxy. It had to be concealed and forgotten.

Jecca chose one of the myriad floating cities that surrounded the dueling stars of Effelox Binary. They were numerous, immense, and the last place a Scythin looking to hide something would be expected to go for it was impossible to move about unseen in the free cities. Jecca knew all of this, but it was never the goal to end up where people actually lived.

Jecca left in haste, absconding inside an untraceable voidscull while the others exulted in swarming behavior, and set the vessel to emerge from bulkspace into a spot already occupied by solid matter. When it did, Jecca was effectively entombed – becoming one with the radiation shield. They lived for only a short time after, as their entire lower half had melded into the shield, with only the glowing amber of a faraway hatch bringing any light. And there Jecca died; hidden, body moldering, their biology reaching out.

CHAPTER FIFTY-ONE

Mother must have been larger, for the suit fit better than Aptat's had. Naecia stepped out away from the vault, hearing the whine of some joints working harder than others. On the whole, this was good news. She'd half expected it not to work at all. *Power?* she subvocalized through the com.

A display came up in the corner of the mask accompanied by a bar that showed the suit fully charged. "Do I have magmafier?"

"I'm not seeing any operational limits here," said Izairis. "But do you have propellant?"

Propellant? Another bar appeared – this time empty. "So much for that." She stood in the center of the room. *Melee limb?* Another icon showed on the screen and she actually felt the articulated weapon unclick from her back. *Ammunition?* Nothing on the display. *Projectiles?* Nothing again. "Izairis, how do I find out if I'm loaded?"

"The system refers to the ammunition as 'Stings'."

"Okay." That was weird. She subvocalized it. *Stings.* The display appeared along the very top edge of the screen, where she'd look if she wanted to see her own eyebrows, showing four rows of tiny dart-shaped symbols. "Seems like I'm fully stocked. Where is Aptat?"

"Just south of the twentieth latitude."

"Okay, I'm going out." She marched toward the lift, stopping only to punch a hole through the wall just to see if she could, then hopped down to the second deck.

"Whoa," said Izairis as Naecia stalked by. "Where are you going?"

Naecia turned, opened the mask. "We should have left that fucker floating in space."

"Or on the *Timelance*," said Izairis, twisting the knife some. "Nothing to be done about it now. How can I help?"

"You've seen them use the suit. You can't."

"I could say some prayers I learned at the convent," she said. "I don't remember them all, but there's one about asking for strength in fighting the temptation to touch yourself."

Naecia huffed a little laugh through her spiracles. "Why would you want to fight that?"

"I only said it when I was made to," said Izairis, grinning. "It didn't work."

Naecia went to the map on the display and poked a tiny blue dot. "Is this the *Timelance*?"

"That's them. Preparing to enter orbit from the other side of Aszerat. We don't have long."

"Fine," said Naecia. "Get Patton back here and come up with a distraction."

"A distraction? For Aptat?"

"No. For the Scythin. To keep them away from the ship."

"I'll try to remember some better prayers."

Naecia was met by the blare of klaxons and the flashing of lights when she strode down the ramp. An announcement warned everyone to vacate the outermost reaches of the city and to proceed home or to various evacuation centers, due to an "unknown threat". There was nobody around, so that was good. She trotted toward the empty transway station. Maybe she could catch Aptat waltzing out of it.

She wanted to try out her weapon prior to engaging the

stringhunter. *Melee: Cargo box left.* The limb swung around, nearly throwing her off balance, and fired ten stings into the target. "Amazing."

Trying another technique, she pointed a finger at an autonomous mover. *There.* Ten more stings, right where she'd indicated. She nodded stiffly. "Okay, then."

She reached the station and found an enclave tucked into the shadows between rows of gas canisters. Pipes ran from the canisters and into the wall. She ascertained the cutoff valves, spun them shut, then snapped the length of pipe running between them. "Izairis, ETA?"

"Now."

Ding.

It was a blind corner, so she listened carefully, and soon heard the telltale clickclack of Aptat's signature strut.

They marched right past. Naecia pushed herself out – fast – slid to a knee and swung the pipe as hard as the suit would swing it. It clipped Aptat's heels, flipping them over, while their melee limb went live, firing twenty, thirty, stings that glanced harmlessly from Naecia's armor. She ran over and hammered down with the thick pipe, collapsing the stringhunter flat to the floor, and beating them until the weapon finally crimped. Then she was sprinting off as Aptat pushed up from the ground. She slid behind a cargo skiff and tried to get a clear picture of what was happening.

Aptat was upright again. "Hold please," they said through the com. Then there came a noise. Repetitive. Like some sort of… music?

Bum buda-buda bum-bum, bada bum-bum, bada bum-bum.

Bam.

Bum buda-buda bum-bum, bada bum-bum, bada bum-bum.

Bam.

"What is that?" Naecia yelled over the noise.

"*What is that?*" exclaimed Aptat in a tone of great offense. "Just a little ditty by Michael Jackson entitled 'Smooth Criminal' from his chart-topping 1987 album, *Bad*. It went double platinum, Naecia. People's Choice award for Favorite Music Video in 1989."

"I don't know what any of that means! Turn it off!"

"Prepare to be cultured!" exclaimed Aptat while going en pointe and doing a twirl. Then the melee limb swung to life again, peppering sting all about as the soundtrack played.

Naecia burst upright and ran, sliding behind a huge pile of rations boxes.

Aptat sashayed headlong to the beat. "You made a mistake, love."

"Oh yeah?" she snarled defiantly. *Had she?* Probably.

Aptat stood perfectly straight, and executed some quick, Jacksonesque head twitches. "See, I'm sure you've already surmised that I killed the last person to wear that suit. While they were in it."

"Looked to me like an ambush," Naecia said, trying to get control of her breathing. She jumped up from behind the pile, pointed a finger. *Fire.*

The melee limbs on both suits angled and fired, dozens of rounds per cyclisec, that went bouncing off the carapace armor. Naecia closed her fist to stop the volley.

Aptat halted a beat later. "Don't you recognize a stalemate when you're part of one?"

"It's not a stalemate just because one side can't win," she said. "That's you, by the way."

Aptat gave an easy shrug. "Pretty confident."

"You can't operate the Switch Drive without me."

"You can't escape the Scythin without the Switch Drive."

"But I don't need you once I've got it," she said. "You need me."

"I'd love to have you along, if not just to make things easy for myself," Aptat said. "But I will kill you if need be."

"You want me along because you have doubts about whether or not you will be able to commune with the Fray in order to operate the drive."

"Preposterous."

"You wonder if your consciousness is genuine or just an impotent analog," Naecia said. "That's why this isn't a stalemate, Aptat."

"Look who suddenly thinks she's a psychologist to the flesh construct set," they said, throwing their weight to one side and doing a kick with the opposite leg. "Here's a question: Where did Aptat tuck away that Switch?"

Bum buda-buda bum-bum, bada bum-bum, bada bum-bum.
Bam.

Aptat charged again, so quickly that Naecia barely registered the sudden movement before she was flying through another pile of cargo staged for shipment.

Aptat's voice came through the com, now parroting a version of the lyrics, "*Naecia are you okay? So, Naecia are you okay, are you okay Naecia?*"

"I have armor this time," she grunted, rolling away from the spilled equipment. Effortlessly, she picked up a motorized dolly, spun it around, and flung it. Aptat ducked in time to dodge it and burst upward as it came overhead, punching it impressively away. Finishing the move, the stringhunter tilted their head down, grabbed at the brim of an imaginary hat, put one foot up on tip-toes and wiggled a knee.

Naecia tore off again.

"I'm tiring of this and the Scythin really are going to be here very soon," said Aptat, moonwalking after her.

Naecia had already ripped a huge pipe from a rack running coolant, sending a gusher of the stuff skyward. "Sorry to hold you up!" she said, launching it like a spear.

Aptat leapfrogged it with some effort, then sprinted after her. "Do you know how I killed Mother?" they asked, chasing her around a corner, heels clapping to the rhythm of the song's chorus.

Naecia plucked a railing from the wall and swung it. Aptat sprawled, avoiding the hit. "You melted her face with the magmafier," she answered, changing direction.

They sprang up, executed a heel spin. "But do you know how I was able to get her mask open?"

"Oh, so she knew you were trying to kill her?" Naecia drew herself beneath a massive satellite suspended by a crane and directed the melee limb at the straps holding it in place.

"She did, actually, yes." Aptat picked up a canister of gas and threw it like it was a small stone. Naecia narrowly dodged.

Her melee limb fired, breaking the satellite free. Rather than run to escape it, Aptat did a pelvic thrust as the machinery crashed down upon them. That made Naecia stop. The satellite had been as big as some of the ships in dock.

Aptat emerged from an access panel in the side of the wreckage, punctuating their appearance with a *hee-hee!* taken straight from the song.

Naecia began to panic. The simple physics should have turned Aptat to paste, regardless of the suit. She'd underestimated it.

Aptat didn't skip a beat. "Mother believed the suit would protect her," they said, taking dainty steps to avoid the twisted heap and then skating away in time with the song's refrain. "And it would have."

Naecia backed away. "But?"

"I guessed her suit's override code."

Naecia's heart skipped. Suddenly she was prey, scrambling for a place to hide. She tore across the dock in the direction of the *Silent Child*.

"*Courser's quarry*," said Aptat. "Open mask."

Naecia's mask opened. The stringhunter had control of her suit. But two could play that game. Remembering the code for Aptat's carapace, she shouted, "*Aureate Cicatrix*, disassemble!"

Aptat flicked a hand theatrically as if sweeping back an invisible coat or jacket, then made a show of looking their suit over. When it failed to come apart, Aptat said, "Always change your password, Naecia."

Protect me, she thought, and the mask began to close again.

"*Courser's quarry*, override," Aptat repeated. "Pause all carapace mobility; lock out coms."

Immediately, the suit seized and Naecia toppled stiffly to the floor, inert as a child's play toy. Not a single joint would budge. The music cut out.

"Assign carapace functionality to me," Aptat added, sauntering over. "I stand corrected. You were right. It's not a stalemate when only one side can't win." They lifted her up in her paralytic state, and her necklace slipped out from inside the armor. "Oh," said Aptat, seizing the amulet and ripping it from her neck. "You won't be needing this any longer."

She cried out as Aptat launched it through the atmospheric envelope and into black.

They began down the dock. "We're going to leave now, you and I, before the Scythin arrive."

The suit was cast in stone. Sobbing, Naecia struggled to move even though she knew it wouldn't budge. The immobility set her mind aflame. Every decision she'd made had only further empowered the stringhunter, up to and including placing herself quite literally into their arms. She screamed in frustration.

"Now, now."

"I will let the Scythin kill us before I help you escape," she said. "You might as well leave me. Or kill me."

"Kill you?" Aptat scoffed. "So dramatic." They clicked along for another few moments. "You know you're a terrible negotiator? I almost feel bad for you. Almost. Again, you fail to see the angles. Did we get the Chime? No. Are the Scythin going to find it and destroy everything within a million gilleys? Probably. Do I prefer that you operate the Switch Drive? Of course. How do I ensure that you do that? Simple. The first place we go – you do the navigation after all – is Drev, to retrieve your family. Then we flee the galaxy, the four of us carried to safety."

Naecia said nothing. She'd been outflanked at every turn.

"There's a poetic balance between the perfect amount of leverage and consequence, don't you think? You'll of course want to take your time to agree with me, I'm sure; doing so too readily might wound your pride. Believe me, I understand. Very prideful here. *Guilty*."

At bay seventeen they ascended a ramp into a small, well-used asteroid tug. It was a simple box with oversized drive cones on either side, and a big, retractable claw suspended underneath. The name on the side said ODIAT. "Forgive the temporary state of our mount. She's all I could do on short notice." Then, cheerfully: "On the bright side, she's powerful, and with surprisingly few amenities!"

Aptat set Naecia carefully down on the floor of the cramped deck and went to the console. Unable to turn her head, she had very little range of vision, but the Switch Drive was there.

"I'm going to get us out of the city, but we'll need to hurry on after that. The Scythin round Aszerat as we speak." They projected a star map out from the console. "Oh look, there's Drev! Your mother and brother. How many years has it been? You can see them again *today*, in quicker than the spin of a pulsar."

She was crying. All the way. Sucking up breaths of air soured by the coming surrender. Aptat had her cold. Absolutely. Dead to rights. Of course, she would save her family. The ramp began to close. Like the end of a story. After all of her efforts, she'd failed. It was over.

Aptat came up alongside her, opening their mask, looking down with a sharp-toothed grin. "This situation here? This would be checkmate."

And then their head exploded.

CHAPTER FIFTY-TWO

The forced reminiscence complete, I stood, finally, and stared at the hollowed out and desiccated corpse of Jecca, the one who had awakened to the world beyond the Scythin and fled. Taking an ashy breath, I reached into the cavity of their chest, through flaking tissues that crumbled beneath my probing fingers. And then, something solid. Non-biological. I lodged my fingers in the center gap between the tines and pulled. A loud crunch sounded, along with a billowing of evaporated flesh. And again. Until it came free. And then I had it. The Chime. The Note of Jecca.

It was as long as my arm, a *perfect* object. Simple. Beautiful. Three-quarters of its length were a symmetrical pair of parallel arms, flared to sweeping and poetic swirls along the outer edges. A cosmic tuning fork. I wanted to hear it.

I heard something else. A voice in my ears. I fell back into myself, as if disconjured from a spell, seeing my surroundings as they were. The voice was urgent, panicked.

"Attacked...

"Switch Drive...

"Aptat...

"Stolen...

"Return."

"Wait, wait," I said, rushing into the present. "Izairis?"

"Yes, it's me. Please come. Also, the *Timelance* has taken an angle for orbit. We don't have much time.

"I have the Chime! Everything we thought is true. It's really, really, bad. Hello?"

Nothing. Then:

"Hey dude, it's Patton," said Patton.

"Is everyone there?"

"Uh, not really."

"Where's Naecia?" I started awkwardly down the ladder with one hand holding the Note, which had to weigh about thirty pounds.

"Uh, she's adjusting her armor," Patton said.

"*Armor?* What?"

Patton responded, "Long story but I'll try: Aptat stole the Switch Drive and tried to kidnap Naecia, but Izairis was able to trace them to this other ship because Aptat still had their hotel key. I just went where she said they would be and sort of shot Aptat in the face with a blunderbuss. So, we're not really doing the team thing anymore."

"I... what?" Maybe my head was still foggy from being inside Jecca's for so long. "Aptat's dead?"

"Yeah," said Patton, "turns out you can't trust kidnappers."

Izairis came in, "Ben: Aptat moved the drive to a new ship – the *Odiat*, bay seventeen – it's already been wired for power. Naecia's working to get it free, but we need more time than we have."

"We'll just take that ship."

"It's registered to Aptat. We can't fly it."

"The *Silent Child*?" I asked.

"Power connections sabotaged."

"How close is the *Timelance*?"

"Entered orbit. They'll be at the docks soon. I don't see how we avoid them at this point."

I tilted my head back and stared up at the door to Jecca's resting place high above, wondering just how we would avoid certain slaughter now that we – *that I* – was no longer needed by the Scythin. They'd rip Aszerat to pieces. I felt the Note, heavy in my hand, warm where I held it. I let it tip forward, until the corner of one prong tapped the wall of the column. The result was a tone pure and clear, like a swallow of cold water down a parched throat.

"What was that?" Izairis asked once the sound had faded.

"That was… the Chime," I said, still marveling at the beauty of the sound. The Scythin would surely recognize it. "Hey – can you record?"

"Of course. Go ahead."

Standing precariously on the ladder, I lifted the Note up again, higher. "I found the Chime," I declared, then struck the prong against the wall. This time, it rang like cathedral bells, with resonance enough to shake a star's iron core.

"Ouch," said Izairis.

"You get all that?"

"Yes."

"Good. Find a way to get that recording deep into the city so you can broadcast it. Maybe they'll follow it – give us the time we need to get out of here. Grab whatever you need from the *Child*. I got a feeling that's where they're headed first."

"Okay, alright. We'll come up with something. What are you going to do?"

"Save us," I said.

"I'll hold my breath."

"You shouldn't."

I raced the rest of the way down the ladder to find the once bustling city of Aszerat a ghost town. And silent except for a threat announcement playing on a loop. I took a lift to the transway and headed back West, my mind churning the whole way. I ran through the sequence of what was going to happen. The Scythin's arrival at the docks was imminent. Naecia wasn't going to get the Switch Drive unmoored from the *Odiat* in time.

I got off the transway at the food court closest to the docks.

The air was still a thick mélange of all the different dishes on offer, all left sitting on trays and heating racks. My stomach had the nerve to grumble.

"We have visual!" shouted Izairis. "*Timelance* has placed itself in geosynchronous orbit outside the docks."

"Fuck. Okay," I said. "Are there any voidsculls coming across or anything?"

"Nothing yet."

"Hey here's a crazy idea," I said, casting about for a temporary place to hide the Chime, "but couldn't we just fire the Switch Drive and... take all of Aszerat with us?"

"Don't you think I thought about that, already?" Naecia spat through the com. "We can't bring up the *Odiat*'s reactor, and even if we could, we're talking about a city the size of a moon. It wouldn't be enough power for the aggregator to assemble all the particle data. We need to get it off this ship and onto something with real power, and I don't know what. It's going to holes, Ben."

"Too late," said Izairis.

CHAPTER FIFTY-THREE

Naecia and Izairis watched the *Timelance* fill the *Odiat*'s passive display. The ship's spiked outer ring was so large that it resembled a floating city unto itself. As such, it had to remain distant or collide with Aszerat. It was still close enough that they could see the thing that came out of it.

"Are they, uh…" said Naecia, feeling her stomach drop, "… how?"

Izairis stared. "There is nothing I know that could explain that."

They watched as a thick, serpentine braid of glowing Scythin flesh threw itself directly into the hard vacuum of space and spiraled toward the docks. Razor-like fins tipped in orange and magenta twisted down its length from behind each of its four blunt heads.

"Help me uncouple this thing," said Naecia, lifting a corner of the Switch to access the main power connections. The task was easy in Mother's carapace. Aptat's parting gift had given her full access to the suit. *Courser's quarry.* She'd regained control when Aptat's neural signal ceased. Patton had now saved her twice.

Izairis rushed over. Naecia said, "The thick one. It's got eight compression latches." Izairis snapped them open, one by one.

A tremor made them look up to the port feed right as

the Scythin worm-missile plowed through the docks with the momentum of a runaway barge, peeling away the superstructure as if it were made of solar foil. Moments later a tremor shook the *Odiat*. Once Aszerat's structure had absorbed most of its inertia, the missile disaggregated into a million chaotic boids. The *Silent Child* was enveloped in the blink of an eye, and then just as quickly abandoned. They swarmed briefly before becoming the serpent again, this time with claw-shaped "heads" at both ends. Rather than slithering, each head operated as a massive adze, smashing into the floor and using the leverage to pull the rest of itself along.

It made its way down the dock, falling apart and pouring over the other ships parked there, then reforming and moving down to the next.

"Oh, we are so dead," Naecia mumbled as she watched the ship in bay seven disappear in torrent of boids.

Izairis shut the hatch. It didn't give Naecia any more confidence in their safety. She closed her mask.

"Patton?" she said. "What is your current position?"

"Me and the decoy are just about halfway to the drop zone. Over and out."

Izairis shrieked. Naecia saw the display. They'd reached the *Odiat*. Immediately, the tiny tug was rumbling back and forth in the docking clamps, the sound of snapping metal booming through the structure.

Naecia took Izairis by the shoulders and shoved her inside a blast closet. A hole tore open in the hull behind them. She slammed the closet shut and spun around. The melee limb worked into action, its fusillade sparking harmlessly off the talon-like worm head as it pierced the skin of the ship. She might as well have been shouting insults.

The second head crashed through the ceiling and gashed the floor, knocking her backward. "Patton!" she screamed. "NOW!"

"Now? Now what? I'm still in the transway!"

Naecia rolled away from a boid-tentacle. "Do it!"

"Loud and clear."

A ribbon of color strobed down the tentacle' s length and it coiled like a scorpion's tail, rearing back pre-strike. Naecia cowered, wondering if their plan would work with Patton halfway across Azerat. Then the beast stopped moving, and, not a moment later, spilled into pieces. The boids rumbled away, springing back through the new skylight. Others burst directly through the walls for the docks. Naecia realized she'd been screaming and stopped, breathless.

"Patton's still on the transway!" yelled Izairis from the blast closet.

"I think he's far enough ahead," Naecia said, running over and setting Izairis free. "Depends how fast those things can travel through the city." She looked to the drive. Still intact. Not that it mattered. "Help me get this thing up. We need to find power."

"Nice outfit." It was Ben. Standing where a wall used to be.

"Ben!" said Naecia, opening the suit's mask. She looked him over. "Where is the Chime?"

"Hidden."

"Where?"

"I can't tell you."

"None of us can know, remember?" said Izairis.

"But you know," said Naecia.

"I'm going to fix that," Ben answered. "Look – there's a massive power corridor right behind those walls across the dock."

"How do you – oh right," she said. "You built this whole place in the dredge."

"Yeah. I've already switched off the breaker. The rest I'll leave to you. I don't really do engineering."

"Even if I can get power to the drive, the Scythin are here," said Naecia. "And even if the machine can assemble a reliable particle catalogue, they'll effectively be a part of Aszerat at that point. We'll just take the Scythin with us wherever we go!"

Ben shrugged. "If it comes to that, we'll take it, I think. It would separate them from the *Timelance*. At the very least we could switch ourselves far enough away that they would never be able to find it, much less reach it. They can't destroy the galaxy without that ship."

"Yeah, but they'd shred Aszerat and every person in it," said Naecia. "Us included."

"You're the one always talking about saving uncountable trillions at the expense of a few, right? Sucks to be the few." Ben leaned backward and glanced down the dock. "Look – I'm still going to try and get them out of the city. They're searching for me, remember?"

"They'll catch you, Ben. Or they'll kill you. Neither of those things can happen."

"First step is escaping with the Chime," said Ben. "It's here. Hidden. Tell Patton it's in a place that will remind him of Saturday mornings. He'll figure it out." He paused, furrowed his face. "Hey. Where is Patton?"

Izairis stepped forward. "The city's PA is locked down hard. Only the emergency announcements are coming through. We couldn't throw the recording to somewhere else."

"So…" his face was suddenly distressed.

"We turned a Vortu helmet into a transmitter and Patton is bringing it to the far side of Aszerat," said Izairis, taking Ben by the shoulders. "Your plan worked, Ben. He started the transmission and the Scythin just fell apart and went after it."

"It wasn't my plan to have Patton be a sitting duck!"

"I don't know what a sitting duck is," said Naecia, "but he's buying us time. What's the rest of your plan?"

Ben looked at Izairis. "I need you to teach me to fly the *Silent Child*."

CHAPTER FIFTY-FOUR
PATTON GETS A CHAPTER

Patton belted the chorus to *Enter Sandman* by Metallica as the transport zipped across open space.

"Patton!" It was Naecia "NOW!"

"Now? Now what?" he said, checking his surroundings. "I'm still in the transway!"

"Do it!"

Alright, alright. "Loud and clear." He lifted the Vortu helmet and checked to make sure he pressed the correct switch. Izairis had helpfully marked it for him. *Idiot Savant.*

Ben's voice played from the helmet's speaker and across an all-channels frequency, *I found the Chime*, followed by a loud strike of sound. Patton flipped the switch again to end the transmission.

If the ploy worked, the Scythin would be on their way to kill him forthwith. Now he just had to stash the thing.

The shuttle pulled into the transway station behind the docks in Green Quadrant, which was on the opposite side of the sphere from Blue. He leapt off with his gear and scanned around for a place where the transmitter would be safe – at least until the Scythin found it. No one was strolling about on account of the invasion in progress, so Patton had free reign of the place.

He found himself in a wide-open section of the city – though it was hard to think of it as a city. It was a planet as far as he was concerned, even if there was no dirt. The area beyond the docks seemed half shopping mall and half park, with flower-framed walkways and strangely shaped ponds with strangely shaped fish peeking up to consider him. He wished Ben were here to say something about them. He'd probably make all sorts of smart observations; explain what those extra fins are for and how they could manage to swim with so many facial penises. Ben was great that way.

With the goal being to plant the signal as far away from the Blue Quadrant as possible, Patton picked up the pace. Ahead, a large corridor like an airport terminal split off in three directions. A high-end spaceship showroom with large, scale models on display, drew him down the right-most branch. He'd come to understand the value of guush over the last few days, his experience sharpened by the many foods he'd sampled. The metallic jingling in his space pants felt a whole lot less rich as he gazed upon the models in the showroom window and their manufacturer-suggested retail prices.

He stopped inside the abandoned shop, promising himself to only linger briefly. All sorts of ships were on offer, from little shuttle things labeled "Effelox System Sprinters", to big, fancy "Galax Cruisers", to nasty looking "Interceptor/Pursuit Sloops", that looked a lot like updated versions of the *Silent Child*.

At the center of the showroom was a full-scale replica of a two-seat cockpit for one of the sprinters and, never passing up the opportunity to be inside an awesome place, Patton sat. And it was *very* awesome. There were all sorts of different colored buttons and knobs and touchscreens. He was very excited to find that it actually had a steering wheel and rejoiced. Because what was the point of racing if you didn't have a steering wheel?

He set the decoy into the co-pilot's seat and lifted the Vortu helmet from off his head, then indulged his fantasy of piloting the craft on a quick, imaginary joy ride, complete with vrooming noises and laser effects, and just the right type of girls who would be impressed with all of that.

He dropped his hands from the wheel, then leaned over and turned the helmet transmission back on so the Scythin would continue their pursuit for it. The sound baffled him. The Chime sounded, like, well, a chime. A really big chime. But still. If there truly was a sound evil enough to destroy the galaxy, wouldn't it be something like post-*Black Album* Metallica, or Justin Bieber? This was a... a doorbell. He sighed. From the bathrooms to the pending End of Everything, outer space had so far been one disappointment after another. Spaceship showroom excepted.

He considered the decoy, sitting next to the helmet. "Okay, man. Time for us to part ways. Give 'em hell, buddy." He tapped the jar of pickles lovingly as one might a small pet; then, as it was arguably a poignant moment, gave the lid a try. It turned with a satisfying pop-hiss.

Patton selected the center pickle as one does and held it in his mouth while resealing the lid. Then holding it aloft, said, "To me and you, Ben," and took a bite.

He set the Vortu helmet, still broadcasting, over the top of the jar, and strapped the pair snuggly into the cockpit-replica. His internal sense of time, which was admittedly not good, began to insist that now was in fact when he should stop dawdling.

He left the spaceship store with a few souvenirs and jogged back to the transways. There were ten tubes that made the center-crossing transit. Several sat empty. He stepped into the one furthest from the one he'd rode in on and wondered: Would the Scythin take the transways? Would they need hotel cards to do it? He chuckled to himself as the doors closed, thinking about a tube full of extra-dimensional Scythin galaxy murderers reading the newspaper or doing Sudoku as they waited for their stop.

Over the last few days and several spilled drinks, Patton had learned how quickly the transways accelerated. He dutifully strapped in before the thing really took off. The center-crossing transways were a special type of fast. Satisfied at a job well done, he relaxed and let the acceleration press him into the seat.

All said, it had been a great adventure, even if they were eventually killed. But he did have one regret: that circumstances hadn't allowed he and Ben to share the pickles together. Patton had technically broken their promise, but he figured Ben would allow it since it had been in furtherance of saving the galaxy. Alas, there would be other pickles and Ben surely would have approved of the use. *Just imagine the look on the Scythin's whatevers when they realize they were chasing a jar of pickles!* Soon enough.

Seeing the ride as the perfect time for a nap, Patton closed his eyes.

He had only just taken up his sword in what had the makings of a promising Viking dream, when a vibration shocked him awake. He was still in the transway, still alone, still alive. He rotated his head to the side, looked across to the other tubes. Half had been reduced to drifting glass.

CHAPTER FIFTY-FIVE

Back inside the *Silent Child*, Izairis put her finger to a random spot on the console map. "Go."

"That's it?" I asked. "That makes the ship go?"

"Yes," said Izairis with a note of light condescension.

"What if I want to tell it to do a certain maneuver, or take evasive action, like a barrel roll?"

Izairis drew a squiggly line on the map, then looked back up at me. "Then you say go and the ship will go. *Or.* You can describe for the ship what you'd like her to do. *Run away. Dock at that restaurant. Hide on that asteroid. Match orbit with that passenger ship. Shoot at those bad guys.* I've authorized you as a pilot. She knows your voice."

"Okay," I said, beginning to feel confident that I could actually do this. No harder than telling mom's minivan to park itself. "What weapons does she have?"

"Big one is the dilaceration cannon. Takes a while to charge, so after you leave you might say something like 'Ship, charge dilaceration cannons'. There are also your standard fissile/ fusile projectiles," she checked the inventory, "of which you have one. So. Good luck."

"Fissile like nuclear?"

"Like thermonuclear. Oh, Naecia wanted me to give you this," said Izairis, presenting a small object. "We had one more. Aptat still had theirs."

"Wow," I said, taking the ampoule. "Yeah, okay. Smart." There had been a tiny moment, just a millisecond where I thought maybe Naecia had offered a gesture of friendship or good luck after all we'd been through. Nope. Just a mind-erasing tonic.

"Amnesplid," Izairis explained. "If it looks like they're going to capture you, drink it and also stab yourself somewhere."

Ugh. Yeah, okay. "Where should I stab myself?"

"Doesn't really matter, as long as you do."

"Don't worry," I chuckled. "There won't be any need, because you three are going to leapfrog them to rescue me."

"*Yeah*," she drew the word out, "that's a tight move, Ben."

"Naecia thinks she can do it if you all can pull enough power. I trust her."

"As do I. Still..."

"I'll have enough of a head start. I'm not worried."

I was *very* worried. I prayed Patton had been able to draw the Scythin into a crisscross of Aszerat. Once they realized the Chime was a fake, they'd be super pissed and head back our way. In the meantime, two things had to happen. First, I had to fly the *Silent Child* as far away as possible. The Scythin, having been duped once, would return to the *Timelance* and give chase. Then Naecia had to use the Switch to move the entire city, which meant plugging the machine into the city's main power. Even though I'd located a conduit, I didn't even know if such a thing was possible.

Then – and this is the part at which Izairis had rightly directed her doubts – assuming they *were* able to pull enough power, Naecia would to try to jump Aszerat, the entire moon-sized city, to the exact point in space where it would subsume the *Silent Child* into its vacant middle, all before the *Timelance* caught up with me. I would quickly dock – effectively becoming part of the city – and she would engage the drive one last time to get us as far away from the *Timelance* as possible. At that point, we would proceed with our plan to have non-Stringer Patton dispose of the Chime, and also explain to an entire city of millions that although they were now in a new galaxy they'd never heard of, their lives had been saved.[108]

"I gotta go," I said, having a hard time believing that I was really leaving.

"Yeah," Izairis said, keying in a combination. "I'm removing the docking clamps. Tell the ship to maintain static."

I hesitated, momentarily forgetting the instructions she'd already given me on how to do that.

"You just talk to her."

"Ship, stabilize yourself when the clamps let go." A metal echo sounded from below and the ship micro-adjusted itself to remain squarely in the berth.

"You'll need to work on your brevity," she said. "Now go."

"Good luck, Izairis. Look out for Patton will you? He's gonna be torn up that we didn't get to say goodbye."

"You'll see him soon, Ben." And then she was gone down the ramp.

I sat in the captain's chair and surveyed the control screen which showed a map of Aszerat, my current location, and the stars beyond. "Fly out a little bit and turn around."

The ship pulled back from the dock and pivoted toward the black. Just off to the left sat the shadow of the *Timelance*. I was banking that the Scythin were so unflinchingly communal that none of them would be left on board to chase me. Or if there were, that they'd be fine allowing me a head start. Aptat had explained that while both the *Silent Child* and the *Timelance* were bulkspace ships, the Scythin ship could walk down the *Child* if it wanted.

I set the ship to accelerate continuously to just below my personal explosion point and tapped the hot pink button that made it all go.

---

108 Now that I've heard the plan all laid out, I'm betting all my guush on the Scythin – *Can't say I blame you. Except that it was all your idea.*

Boy did it.

My vision shrank to a pinpoint at the end of a long tunnel as the blood was wrung out of my brain. I did some Lamaze breathing to keep the lights on, then pulled my eyes up to where we'd tagged the *Timelance* on the holographic display. Little blue dot. Still showing locked in orbit with Aszerat. Either they were waiting for everyone to board before giving chase, or they'd figured out that I didn't have the Chime. And unless they'd gone surfing in the bean dip, there was no way they could know I'd left it behind.

"Take us into bulkspace, same course," I said.

The ship obeyed and the starfield on the display scrolled upward, overtaken by black, as we slid between dimensions.

It was weird to have nothing more to contribute to our effort. The move had to be made to draw the Scythin off, but at the same time I wanted to be with the others. I knew my presence there would have little utility, but it still felt wrong to be off and away from them while the threat was so real. I let out a slow exhalation. It was all just mental masturbation at this point – there was nothing more I could do for them. My only job was to keep running.[109]

---

109. Okay, rewind for a second: *When* were we masturbating, again? Did I miss a sesh?

CHAPTER FIFTY-SIX

Naecia found the power corridor and the conduit that Ben had mentioned behind the wall facing the docks. It branched through at even intervals that corresponded with each of the berths and she spent a few seconds evaluating their output before deciding they couldn't supply enough power to move the whole city. They would need to splice into the power that came straight from Aszerat's reactors. That was the main conduit back behind the wall.

She tasked Izairis with moving the drive from the *Odiat* down across the docks and into the electrical space. Patton appeared shortly thereafter, spouting about a "Pickle Gambit" and how the Scythin were in for a rude awakening, but was persuaded to be silent and help Izairis.

Naecia was glad for the suit as it mostly alleviated the need for large cutting tools. Izairis had helped her siphon fuel from Aptat's suit, and now she had a working magmafier. Which was helpful because the primary conduit was thicker than her leg.

The torch made quick work of severing the massive cable, then it was about unspooling the smaller component wires and splicing them to the Switch Drive itself. In order to do that, she had to rig up entirely new contacts on the drive end. The present ones were far too small to couple with the secondary cables, so she had to fashion sleeves that would go from small to big. Eight connections to build from scratch and almost no time.

Izairis and Patton were able to winch the drive onto a dolly and wheel it down into the energy corridor. The added benefit of the location was that they were largely hidden, so long as the Scythin didn't start opening doors. Thankfully, those leading into the electrical maintenance area were marked NO UNAUTHORIZED PERSONS.

"How long did it take you to cross, Patton?" she asked while slicing insulation from around an unneeded cable on the other side of the conduit.

"A little less than two hours one direction, but I think the Scythin move faster than the transways. When I saw them coming the opposite direction, it actually overtook one of the transports from behind. So, call it ninety minutes from now?"

"Hundred cyclets give or take," said Izairis.

"Ping his helmet," said Naecia.

Izairis used her com to try hailing the helmet sitting atop Pickles on the other side of the city. She shook her head. "It's gone."

Patton mimed pouring out a drink onto the ground. "Respect."

"Yeah," Naecia said, accepting the shortened timetable like just another piece of bad news they'd grown accustomed to. "Here, take this." She handed Patton and Izairis each a piece of the thick, flexible cable insulation. "I need six more of these, exactly the same. Tools are there. Can you do that?"

Naecia was already onto the next thing, which was to concentrate the amount of conductive wiring coming from the cables into a size that could connect with the drive. There were many problems with this, but the main two were potentially fatal. One, the reduction in wire diameter could create too much resistance and fail to provide enough power for the drive to work, or second, the sheer amount of current coming through would simply overload, discharge, and bake them all at temperatures rivaling the surface of Effelox. The only saving grace was that the drive pulled the power quickly. Hopefully it could eat as fast as it was fed.

The strands of conductive media were finger-thick and Naecia was using all of the suit's augments to bend and twist it. Still, it was taking too long. Her mind replayed an image of the many-headed Scythin snaking back toward them. "Fuck!"

"What?"

"Izairis, this is taking too long." She looked up from a bouquet of golden wires. "Even if we had twice as much time, we couldn't finish this. There's no way this will be done right. We're talking about running one percent of the power in this place through that." She gestured derisively at her machine. "Ideally, you'd build models and mockups and run simulations."

"Naecia, I get it, but—"

Naecia sprang up. "The fucking thing is homemade! I built it out of stolen scrap!"

"We have no other choice!" screamed Izairis, leaping up in kind and sending her robes billowing. "We get power to it and fire the thing! Sometimes you get killed when you do crazy stuff trying to save the world!"

Naecia looked over the parts and equipment laid out before her and took a deep breath. "Okay, new idea." She went to the base of the drive; a heavy, brushed ring of metal, and clinked it with a driver. "In here is where the main power is divided and capacitated. There's a good bit of resistance provided, which means that if we get rid of it, I won't have to run as much of Aszerat's power into the machine. It'll be unprocessed and unstable, going straight into the works. The power usage is still immense, but the switch is instantaneous. I'll just have to time it right."

"I don't know what any of that means," said Patton.

"It means that you two need to remove the base plate. Inside the collar, you'll find four large resistors. Pull those out. I'll do the rest."

"Aaaaaaaand, what does a resistor look like?" asked Patton.
Naecia glared at Izairis.

"I got him."

Naecia made some rough calculations to figure out the
largest amount of power she could run to the machine in the
shortest amount of time, then isolated four cables the size
of her arms and began capping off the excess. When Patton
and Izairis had finished removing the resistors, Naecia began
making the connections. "Patton – go check the monitors. See
if you can find out where the Scythin are."

He saluted and trotted toward the doors at the far end of the
corridor that led out toward the transway station. He stopped
before pushing them open and turned back. "You guys feel
that?"

Glove, Naecia subvocalized, causing the armor around her
fingers and hand to split along the bottom and peel backward,
exposing her skin. She put it to the cold floor. A low vibration
left no doubt. "We're too late."

Somewhere, an explosion went off. "Izairis, where is Ben?"

As the rumble grew steadily louder, Izairis called up a map
on a data pad connected to the *Odiat*'s nav. "Not showing up.
He's in bulkspace."

The noise increased to a tectonic rumble – like an avalanche
pouring through the guts of Aszerat.

"They're at the docks!" Patton squealed.

Naecia fumbled with the cables, trying to force her makeshift
connections beneath the drive, but the fit was imperfect and
kept slipping. Finally, one twisted in as it should, locking
soundly. Then the next. Outside, it sounded like the Scythin
were tearing the city in half. If she could get the final two
connections in, they could fire. Naecia reached to the other
side. Third connection made. One more.

The sounds of metal being twisted and torn boomed through
the corridor.

The carapace's augments ground loudly as she worked to

force the final coupling. "Patton, go to the breaker!" she yelled over the noise, pointing to an open metal cabinet near the end of the corridor. "When I say flip it, you flip it!"

Patton threw on Izairis' helmet and ran down the way.

The walls shook. The coupling snapped into place. Naecia leapt up and pulled the axon diadem tight to her forehead. "Where is Ben?" she asked again.

Izairis consulted her data pad. "Here! He's out of bulkspace!"

The ground roared. "How close are they?"

Izairis showed her the dock feed on the pad, just as the Scythin wave crashed through it, cutting another gouge through the substructure in the direction of the *Timelance*.

"As soon as they're off city, we're going!" shouted Naecia, preparing her mind to receive and transmit an unthinkable quantity of data.

The boids leapt from the docks, through the atmospheric barriers, and into open space where they formed the many-headed razor worm. The last of the Scythin debarked and it was completely silent.

"Flip it!" shouted Naecia.

Patton did.

The lights flickered and died. Dim emergency lighting sprang on.

The machine's display remained dark. "Oh no! No no no!"

"What happened?" called Patton from the breaker.

"They must have severed the power!" cried Izairis.

Patton threw the switch over and over as Naecia slumped and removed the diadem. She shared a somber glance with Izairis, then went to an access port between the corridor and docks, opened it, and ducked through. They were shrouded in darkness, but there were lights further down the dock.

She sprinted to where the Scythin had launched themselves, and nearly fell in. A chasm had been made in the very structure of Aszerat as if it had been no more than soil before a plow's blade. It was as wide as a ship and just as deep. A canyon of engineering and utility infrastructure ripped to shreds by an inexorable force. Flashes of light arced where the power coming from the city's reactors had been severed. Naecia stepped out toward the edge of the docks and watched the behemoth streak toward the *Timelance*.

Patton caught up, panting. "They're going to catch him."

"I'm sorry, Patton. I am. But he doesn't have the Chime," said Naecia. "It's still here. We have to keep it from them. They'll be back for it."

"He left it here?" said Patton. "Where?"

"I don't know," Naecia answered with a shrug. "He said you would. He said it was a place that would remind you of Saturday mornings."

"What does that mean?" asked Patton. "Saturday mornings? Is there a dispensary here?"

"You better figure it out," said Izairis, running up, checking the pad again.

"We have to tell him we lost power!" said Patton, pivoting anxiously. "He's sitting out there waiting for us. He has to know that we're not coming!"

"Coms are dead," said Izairis.

Naecia tried her implant and shook her head. "Signal is too weak for mine – I need a relay and there's no power." Not being particularly good when it came to expressing emotional support for others, she moved awkwardly to embrace him, but was saved when he collapsed to sit on the floor. Izairis knelt and tried to give him comfort.

Naecia gestured to the canyon of wreckage. "We have to get the Switch to power, somehow. But there's no way over that."

Patton reached into one of the large cargo-pockets on his tracksuit and withdrew a shining white disc. He twisted the center portion forcing variously shaped metal keys to emerge from its circumference, then tossed it onto the floor.

"What's that?" asked Izairis.

CHAPTER FIFTY-SEVEN

I brought the *Child* out of bulkspace so that the others could find me. The nav showed the blue dot of the *Timelance* just getting underway from Aszerat. A few seconds later, it disappeared into bulkspace.

I tried hailing Naecia and Izairis but got only static in return. Either they were still trying to get the Switch to work or they were already dead.

"Okay guys," I said, doing my best to envision Naecia triumphantly firing the Switch Drive and leap-frogging the *Timelance* to rescue me. "Anytime now." The external cameras showed only stars, but I concentrated hard, willing the interior of Aszerat to surround me. My eyes flicked to the map. The city remained static.

"Hey there, folks. It's me, Ben. From Earth. I'm not sure how long I've got before the *Timelance* gets here. They're in bulkspace, so, you know, matter of time." The energy left my voice there at the end, as my mood turned sullen. I looked outside. I checked the display. The lights seemed to dim, but it was just my subconscious draping the pall. As I watched Aszerat stubbornly holding its spot among the Effelox Free Cities, I knew the range of my possible outcomes was narrowing. Would the Scythin try to torture me for the Chime's whereabouts?

I reached into my pocket for the ampoule of Amnesplid and

considered the liquid inside against the light of the display. The more time that went by, the longer Aszerat sat in its orbit, the more likely this little vial of brain eraser became my future. The thing that would cut the string, protecting the next person from the curse of knowledge. Knowledge that could spell the end of everything they ever loved or ever knew. I was glad that it was me who was having their brain erased as opposed to someone who had more to leave behind. I hadn't made much of a mark on the world, never did anything remarkable except to exist as I was made; and then, always fighting it. Never accepting it. Always searching while the other people in my life were living. That's what I should have been doing too. *Living.*

Ugh, pathetic. Even my internal dialogue is a pity party.

"Ben here," I said, noting a quiver in my voice. "I hope you guys are okay. I'm just plugging along. *Timelance* is still MIA. Uh, MIA means *missing in action*." I wanted desperately to stop babbling. To die with some dignity, if that were possible. "Anyway. Hope you can get here soonish, heh-heh." I stared again at the ampoule. "I don't really want to have to drink this little guy."

The *Timelance* appeared.

For just a millisecond the orientation threw me off. It was *in front* of the *Silent Child*, pacing my speed. I keyed the com with a shaking finger. "So, I've got an update for you: the *Timelance* is here."

No response.

"Alright, well. You guys make your Switch and get out of there. Patton: I love you. You're the best friend anyone could ever have had. And I was a shitty one. You deserved better. You have the biggest heart of anyone I've ever known. I'm so sorry. Please get away. If you can, get word to my parents that I love them. Maybe leave out the drugs and the butt stuff."

I killed the transmission and focused back on the display.

What the hell was the *Timelance* doing? Clearly, they weren't going to try and kill me just yet. Which meant they were going to see if I had the Chime. *Then* they would kill me or torture me. What an endgame: death, or torture *and* death.[110] As for right now I could only guess that they were going to take me alive – trail me until the reactor ran out of fuel or until they decided to board the ship. I was nearly out of options.

I tapped the big screen on the console and brushed through the menus until I found the weapons system. I had that nuke. And I had the dilaceration cannon. Aptat had used it on the *Terror's Glaive* and chopped the thing to bits. *Oh, shit, I forgot.* "Hello?" I said in a vaguely ceilingward direction, "Uh, *charge the dilaceration cannon.*"

Instantly, the menu showed the cannons powering up. Slowly. Next, I scrolled through and found the missile. Maybe I could fire that first and then the cannons right after?[111]

I tapped the missile – there was only the one – highlighting it in white. "Shoot that ship in front of us."

I leapt in the chair as the missile launched from the *Silent Child* toward the *Timelance*. A direct hit, but no explosion. Nothing. "What happened?"

The display put up a schematic, showing the route the missile had taken, which was directly through center mass. "Why didn't it explode?"

MISSED.

"What do you mean, missed?" I yelled. "It was aimed right at it!"

¯_(ツ)_/¯

"Can we fire the dilaceration canon?"

SURE.

"Great, let's do that one." My mouth went dry.

---

110 Yeah, I ran the simulation too. Bad news: we die.

111 Wow, are you sure we don't have a war general as a prior, because you're really acing the strategy portion of the test – *You're just gonna run out the thread aren't you?*

OK.

"Target the *Timelance*," I said. The ship complied. It almost felt too good to be true. With them flying out in front of me, it was a pointblank shot. I couldn't miss. They were sitting ducks.

"Friends?" I said into the com one last time. "This is it. You there?"

I waited two more seconds then gave the order. "Fire!" Nine planar lasers, white as the sun, sliced the void into ten vertical stripes of black, cutting through the *Timelance*. A direct hit.

I blinked away the afterimage and refocused on the display.

The ship was still there. In one piece. Bewildered, I mumbled to myself. "Did we fire the canon?"

YES.

Did we hit them?"

NO.

"What happened?"

The display played it back in slow motion. The dilaceration cannons fired perfectly – all nine of them, straight through the *Timelance*. It should have been sliced ten ways. Why wasn't it? "Replay slower," I said, and the display showed the lasers firing again, right through the ship. "Slower! Like a million times slower! Focus in on just one laser. *Jesus*." The display was now focused so near to the *Timelance* that I could see the familiar, sinewed patternization I'd come to know from being inside it. "Play."

This time, when the laser cut through, it was the skin of the ship that moved first. It *anticipated* the weapon, collapsing in on either side of the path of the incoming laser, creating a channel through which it traveled. A nanosecond later, the rift closed, showing no evidence it had ever been there. I didn't have to look at the other eight lasers to know it would show me the same thing.

"Son of a bitch," I sighed, slumping down into the chair.

Blinding lights appeared on the Scythin ship's outer ring. I didn't know, but I knew. I was about to get smoked. I stood, puffed up my chest, and yelled at the display, "BRING IT ON, YOU WINDCHIME PLAYING MOTHERFU–"

Twin sickles of light pulsed out from the *Timelance*. The *Silent Child* only shuddered. I wasn't dead. Had they fired a stun gun? An electromagnetic pulse? A warning shot?

Emergency icons and status reports filled the displays. "What happened?" I asked. As if in answer, a simple animation appeared on the display, showing the outline of the *Child*. Then it showed the wings separating from the body and floating away. "The wings are off?"

YES.

The engines dropped to zero. Made sense – they were in the wings. Auxiliary power came on, but it was the bare minimum. Lights and life support, best I could tell. Gravity systems failed. Amongst the warnings were those showing steam lines venting into space, and the ship began to tumble as a result. I held the captain's chair as long as I could, but the ship's multiaxial rotation sped up and I flew out of it.

They'd only maimed the ship. They meant to board, or to take the piece of the ship containing me with them.

Disoriented, I flew about the deck, sliding across the floor, then rolling up the walls and ceiling. I smashed a display with my ass, then rag-dolled the console before shooting across open air and whacking Aptat's carapace vault. I wrapped my arms over my head as I proceeded back along the wall and floor. One solid hit to the head would kill me. I couldn't die while I still knew where the Chime was – and more importantly, the identity of the person who was going to find it: Patton.

I slid like a hockey puck over the center of the deck, one hand over my head, the other down a pocket trying for the ampoule. I got it out just as I shot from the floor to the ceiling, smashing my face. Stars lit my vision. Blood from my nose and mouth spilled into air.

I spun into the middle space, flailing for a handhold, one eye obscured by the blood trailing up from my nostrils. I wiped at it, tried to orient myself. My jaw felt like it'd been ripped from my face. I'd be pulp before too long. I wasn't going to get another chance to use the Amnesplid. I went to break it open, only to find I was no longer holding it.

One-eyed and drifting across the deck, I cast about until I spotted a shining constellation floating nearby. Shards of glass, perfect little spheres of liquid, and a pair of teeth.

A loud noise. An echo of metal. The ship instantly ceased tumbling and I pounded the deck, still miserably alive, still knowing where the Chime was.

I stood, dizzy, weak from the pummeling, and made for the distant wall, toward the black smudge I hoped was the neural dredge.

Other sounds echoed through the structure of the ship. I tapped the panel on the dredge and slid the power to maximum, then laid down inside with a grunt. The lid closed.

Fragments of the past presented themselves in jewel-like reflections. I felt my chest heaving. *Stop being a little bitch, Ben.* I didn't want to die, or have my brain wiped, or whatever it was that happened when you slipped the cord. But I was tired – or more, weary. And while I wasn't at peace, a part of me looked forward to it – the quiet – even if I would no longer be there to experience it. Just knowing that quiet would come… it settled my heart.

I didn't know how many Stringers there were in the galaxy. Thousands? Millions? But now, at least, some other person born after my consciousness ceased would be spared a lifetime of questions. No bugs. No watches. No Chime.

I focused on the reflections and got on the cord. Pushing the memories up through the lid in order to go deeper, I flew past drifting glimmers of one man's peculiar thing for insect privates, and the passionate, yet boring, ephemera of another person's affection for horological curios. Then, to Aszerat, the sprawling and tedious work of the one who had come three lives before me – Jecca, without whose sacrifice none of us would have ever lived. I spun the massive architecture round like a globe and let go.

The blue and purple and amber city expanded in the centrifuge of my mind. Sections disaggregated into clusters of fragments, layers I'd built from the afterimages of flashing reflections, slid apart into their smallest components – the building blocks of imprinted recollection now free to drift forever.

The dismantled city expanded as it shrank into the distance far above me, until it looked like the remnant cloud of an exploded supernova, and then that too became a dot and went away.

I had been tipped backward from a precipice of hard consciousness and now fell, aware enough that this was the thing that had happened to the one with the neck holes, though I no longer remembered her name. Slipping the cord, they had called it. It was not blackness as I had guessed it would be. Hardly so. It was bright, sour acid green or yellow, with lighter areas, spread out like strands of yarn pulled wide, weblike and soft. Then, as sparks that drift upward from a dying fire, an unexpected sprinkling of reflections appeared.

In the twilight of my thereness, I reached for one and considered the glimmers within it. An Instrument Maker, eyes laid brightly upon a gift she'd made for someone she would never meet.

Either my grasp faltered or there was nothing more to hold onto after that. I perceived acceleration until I no longer did. I was warm and then I was neither warm nor cold. Neither fearful nor hopeful. I became aware of a consciousness held within a single human mind, coursing toward the Oblivion Fray, unraveling.

There was a person who had once explained the thing that happens now, but I can't remember what it was.[112]

---

112 *The Universe takes you back.*

CHAPTER FIFTY-EIGHT

Naecia sprinted along the docks pushing a dolly that carried the Switch Drive, a length of stolen cable, Izairis, and Patton. The suit made the task easy, but distance was against them. The souvenir that Patton had taken from the showroom on the other side of Aszerat wasn't just a "cool ashtray" as he'd first assumed by its shape, but a key fob for a Galax Cruiser parked in the Red Quadrant in berth number five-hundred and eighty. They'd just passed number sixty.

"I'm getting some connection still from the *Odiat*'s nav," said Izairis, scrolling through her hand pad. "Spotty."

"Where's Ben?" asked Patton, twisting around from his place at the dolly's bow. "Can you see him?"

Naecia clicked along, panting lightly, her spiracles snapping open and shut to the rhythm.

Izairis messed with the pad. "Uh."

"What?"

She spun the display to Patton. The two dots were right on top of each other.

"What does that mean? Is he caught?"

Izairis pressed her lips together and took back the pad.

Patton gazed at her like someone who'd just been informed their parents were dead. Saying nothing, he faced ahead.

"Look!" said Naecia. The next sector over was lit. It had power.

They found a transway that ran the city's perimeter along the docks. She pushed the cart and its passengers inside. "Berth five-eight-zero!" she shouted. Then: "*Timelance?*"

"Still out there."

Naecia pushed the dolly into a gap in the seating reserved for cargo and triggered a short wall to keep it in place. "Could be very soon that they realize he doesn't have the Chime."

"Oh shit," Izairis exclaimed, holding the data pad for them to see.

The blue dot on screen was now traveling in the opposite direction, leaving the pink dot of the *Silent Child* behind. "How did it do that without a braking deceleration? It just... changed direction."

Izairis looked on. "I don't know why we keep acting shocked."

The transit slowed and pulled into the station serving the five-eighties. They tore out from their straps. Naecia got the dolly. "Go!"

Patton and Izairis sprinted from the transway, saw that they were at five-eighty-five, and ran back down the dock. Naecia soon came up beside them, her legs moving at three times their clip even with the extra burden of the Switch on wheels.

She had never seen a galax cruiser. Most of the craft on the routes around and between Drev and Vask were utilitarian beaters, only as large as they needed to be. Still three births away, the ship was unmistakable. A titanic silver-bronze teardrop of gleaming technology with few other visible features or inclusions. No other obvious weapons systems, arrays, or coms. All likely hidden away behind panels or otherwise internalized. A solid second place for the strangest ship she'd ever seen.

Patton raised the fob and called ahead, "Open!"

A section of the skin of the cruiser pulled wide like a theater curtain, but without any wrinkles, seams, or hinges. It just changed. A ramp scrolled down from the opening to touch the deck as Naecia got the dolly to it, and she continued up and in. She caught the name of the ship embossed in small, nondescript type along the side of the door. *Stellarcade*.

Patton burst in after, shouting orders to the ship, "Lights! Nav! Reactor!" And it was working. Displays warmed to life across gorgeously burnished surfaces. Status holograms projected up and spun lazily in the air.

"What kind of power does it have?" asked Naecia.

Izairis shoved Patton aside and pushed the holograms around until she found the ship's specifications. "Oh, she's a big girl. She can put out as much as we need by herself, but she's plugged into Aszerat as well." She rotated an ethereal dodecahedron navigating through the other menus. "Back there," she said, pointing to a bank of ports along the far wall where custom features might be added to the ship. "Access points."

Patton went along and opened the electrical ports. Naecia rolled the Switch Drive into position. "Couldn't you have stolen the dock key as well, so we didn't have to move the entire city?"

"I didn't know I was stealing a key at all," Patton said defensively. He held up the fob. "This was just a souvenir."

"Well," Naecia huffed, yanking a heavy cable from one of the ports, "now you get to take an entire city and a couple ten million people as a souvenir instead."

Izairis transferred the navigational profile from the *Odiat* to the *Stellarcade* and projected the map over the deck just in time to watch the *Timelance* disappear from her screen.

"It's in–"

"Bulkspace," said Naecia. "I know."

"It took them a quarter cygment to get out there. So that's how much time we have left."

"Great," said Naecia, forcing connections yet again, all the while going through the same mental observations she'd had before. The likelihood of catastrophic death, needing to pee.

The suit wasn't equipped for it. Maybe Mother had had the bladder of an urplorp heifer.

Izairis expanded the map so the local region of the Dasma Arm showed across the deck. Then, surprisingly, they were ready. The *Timelance* was on its way but had yet to appear.

Naecia broadened the field of stars with a series of gestures that at first let them see the entire Dasma Arm of the Galaxy, then the Galaxy itself, then clusters of galaxies and so on, until the deck was filled with a chunk of the Universe a few billion gilleys wide. "I guess we could go anywhere," she said.

"We're not going to get Ben?" asked Patton. "If the *Timelance* is headed here, we can leapfrog them now and go get him."

"Patton," said Naecia. "This–" she gestured to the drive with its ad-libbed electrical connections and gargantuan power requirements, "–setup is not good. To get wherever we're going, we've got to engage it twice without blowing ourselves up. Adding a trip to go get Ben means two more hops. It's just... we're talking about the survival of everything."

Izairis was at the com. "I've hailed the *Silent Child* over and over, Patton. It's there. The coms are on. No one is answering. It's in free float. The *Timelance* had it. Ben isn't there any more..."

"I know," Patton answered, taking a seat and buckling himself in, even though the Switch produced no momentum.

Naecia shared a somber glance with Izairis. She turned to the map and walked across the deck and selected a nice looking, elliptical galaxy. "Guess here is as good as any," she said. "Ready?"

"Yes," said Izairis. Patton said nothing.

Naecia donned the axon diadem and triggered the machine. They all watched as the particle data for the Stellarcade and the entire city of Aszerat filled the screen. Then, just as it finished, Naecia told the Fray where she wanted them to go.

They didn't explode. She quickly thought of their final destination and initiated the second switch.

The holographic map remained up across the deck, only filled now by different stars. And no blue dot. They'd made a trip of a billion galactic light years instantaneously – and dragged a few million people along for the ride.

Smoke began to pour from the base of the machine. "Izairis, kill this circuit!"

Izairis did as instructed. The smoke and heat faded. Naecia toed a cylinder at the base of the Switch. The shrouding sprang open to more smoke and a smaller flame, which she readily blew out. "So, this is why we normally have resistors." Naecia removed the diadem and quickly powered down the drive, then disconnected it from the ship's massive power plant. "I'm sure we can find replacements nearby."

"What now?" said Izairis.

"This place is going to be chaos, and really fast," said Naecia. "Patton, you have to go find the Chime. Right now, before someone else does."

"Sure, no problem. I'll just stroll the grounds and hope it turns up."

"You're the only one of us with a fully functioning brain, surprising as that is, so figure it out." She turned to Izairis. "We have to come up with a way to explain to Aszerat that they've been relocated."

"Right. Can we do it in a way that doesn't get us murdered?"

"We can try."

CHAPTER FIFTY-NINE

"Okay then, let's begin: Name?"

"I don't remember."

"Place of origin?"

"I don't know."

"Your earliest memory?"

"Sitting down in front of you."

"Lying on the ground, looking up at the sky."

"I've never seen the sky."

"Parents?"

"People who love you?" I felt alone.

"Dreams."

"Is this a dream?"

"Life."

"Am I alive?"

"Wonderous. Joyous. Pallid. Neutral. Indecision. Magnificent."

"Wonderous. But only because it's the first."

"Fire or Ice?"

"Neither?"

"You are walking on a beach."

"There is sand on beaches, right?"

"Purpose?"

"Whose?"

"A terrifying thing."

"This moment."

"A terrifying thing."

"Not knowing."

"Your first memory."

"Waking from death."

"Your first memory." Faster.

"Waking from death."

"Your first memory!"

"Light!"

"Your first memory!"

"You want me to say something else. There is nothing else."

"Your mother singing after you woke up in the morning."

"Someone sang to me?" I could feel my eyes welling.

"Sing a song of sixpence."

"I don't know."

"Pocket full of rye."

"What do you want me to say?"

"Four and twenty blackbirds."

"I don't understand."

"Baked in a pie?"

"Pie?"

"Petals unfold."

"Are you still talking about the pie?"

"Petals like a flower."

"Have I ever seen one? A flower?"

"The Bloom of God."

"I don't know what that is. Who are you?"

"A friend."

CHAPTER SIXTY

The room was magnificent. Really big. Bright and new. Lots of different people around. Very diverse. And smells. Nice smells. All different types of smells. It seemed like a place you would want to be. It seemed like the best place in the world. *I wonder where this is.*

I was seated at a small table, though I didn't remember sitting down. There was a black ring about the size of – I felt my head – *my head* laying across from me.

Who am I, again?

I laughed a little bit. The idea that I wouldn't know who I was. *Ludicrous.* It'll come back to me in a minute. Just a minute. I'll, uh, remember. Just sit here and enjoy the sights. The nice smells. I'm me? Remember? My name is…

Markhamishgabbyrobbysnehaamyjennykurtpaulahmed timjeromenicholas…*shit.*

Don't panic.

I looked around. I didn't recognize any of it. At the same time, I couldn't imagine a place that I *would* recognize. *Panicking. Need to get up and walk somewhere.*

A person with a large pile of yellow hair arrived with a tray of nice smelling… food? Yes. It was food. See? I know the basics. They scooted the black ring to the side and set down the tray. This was the type of person you'd describe as sort of a man-guy.

"Hey there, buddy. How you doing?" he said, grinning widely.

Hmm. Friendly. "Me?" I said.

"Yeah, you, funny guy. Who else?"

"Where am I?"

"This," he said, pausing reverently, "is the food court."

"The what?"

"Hey, this is hard for you, I know. But guess what? You're doing better. This is the first time you've sat still while I went and got us food. You know how many times I've had to track you down after you've wandered off?"

"Track me?"

"Friendly reminder," said the man-guy, reaching across the table and into a chest pocket I didn't know I had in a hideous blue zip-jacket I didn't know I owned. "If you do wander off again, don't lose this. It's how I find you." He held up a white, rectangular card, then shoved it back in my pocket.

My eyes drifted to the tray.

"Oh, you like those, do ya?" he said, lifting a platter and setting it in front of me. "Those are empanadas. Of course, here they call them 'zorch latkes' or something, I'm still working on the language to be honest. *Effelox Universal* they call it. It's mainly grunting and orgasm noises."

"Empanada," I said, hoping the word would ring a bell. It didn't.

"I figure if anything will get you remembering, it's those. You hid the Chime in the refried beans! Can you believe that?" He laughed to himself. "They're not actually beans I don't think, but it's what they got out here."

"Who are you?" I asked, sniffing the empanada. "Chime?"

"I'm Patton, and you, for the millionth time, are an Earth man called Ben. You're The Shopkeeper. You're kind of a big deal around here." He smiled and popped an empanada.

"Okay," I said, biting into one of the hot, pillowy, half-moons. "Mm, good."

"Yes, *good*, Ben. We've been eating here for like two weeks, ever since we got you from the *Silent Child*. You lucked out, man. The Scythin just ditched you 'cause you erased your brain. That was a solid move. Only choice you had."

"Do I have amnesia?"

"Yeah, it may be a little more than that," he said taking another bite and filling his cheek with food. "We'll go through it all again. *I* think the repetition is helping. The axon diadem shows you at almost to one-tenth of a percent of coherence!" He patted the black ring sitting at the corner of the table.

"I don't remember anything though."

Patton considered the tray. "I'm glad I got thirty-two of these. This usually takes a while."

"What does?"

"The whole story. I tell it to you every day, but I don't mind. It's epic! You and me, we got abducted. You got super addicted to nectar and we pooped through tubes. I killed a guy with one – it was justified though because he was trying to kill you." Another bite. "Defense of another. Universal law."

I stared at him.

"Sorry," he said. "I get a little ahead of myself sometimes. I just want you to know what you did. For everyone. You saved the world. The Galaxy. Probably even more than that."

I ate more of the empanada. It was good. I chewed and let my eyes wander. The "food court" filled the space of a sphere, with level upon level of places where an incredible variety of people – and other things – were eating and talking. I brought my eyes back for another bite just as a shiny robot thing walked up. Its head split open and there was a beautiful person inside with purplish skin. They looked at me judgingly, then turned to the man-guy, Patton. "Does he remember anything?"

I answered, "I remember my name because he just told me. It's Ben."

"Ben, I'm Naecia. Nice to meet you again."

"She tried to kill you once," said Patton, like it was no more than a bit of interesting trivia.

Naecia threw her arms out, helpless against Patton's unfiltered candor. "Really?" she said.

"Really?" I asked.

"It was justified at the time," said Patton. "You got past it."

Naecia rolled her eyes. "Patton: we're going to take Mom and Aeshua out to see some more investors. Do you want me to wait for you?"

Patton dismissed the notion with the wave of an empanada. "No, no, you and Izairis got this. She and those nuns are top schmoozers. I'm not great with corporate types."

"We agree on that," she said.

"Plus, I need to go look at sprinters so I can get my racing team put together – oh, Ben, you can help me pick out color schemes. I was thinking–"

"So we're off, then," interrupted Naecia.

"Right," said Patton. "See you guys at dinner."

"Dinner," she said, clicking away in the elaborate armor. "Ben, maybe you'll remember me tomorrow."

"Bye," I said.

"You *will* remember, dude," Patton said, taking my hand. "I *believe* in you."

"I forget things even when you tell them to me? I can't learn?"

"Well, you have a tender brain right now, but last week your coherence was half what it is today."

"A twentieth of a percent?"

"Exactly! Promising!"

Didn't sound promising.

Nevertheless, Patton went on to retell the whole story of the Shopkeeper and the Pipefitter. I'm the Shopkeeper because I used to work in a tiny shop that sold items that caused something called "fish" to snag themselves and become food; and Naecia is the Pipefitter because she was a person who fit pipe together. He started from before our abduction all the way up until he found the Chime in the beans. Afterward, some Aszerat gangsters had come for their piece of the Switch Drive, but Naecia politely explained that the person who had sold it to them – a no-good, scheming, meat-robot opportunist called Aptat – had never been the rightful owner. When the gangsters didn't like that explanation and tried to take it by force, she converted them into ex-gangsters. She was already building quite the reputation for herself on Aszerat.

Patton retold the part about our interlude on the *Timelance* with a level of editorial distance that wasn't present for the rest of the story. He plainly reported what had happened to me with the nectar addiction and the daily dredgings, while saying little about himself. Curious, I pressed him. He couched it in as favorable terms for me as he could, but it was impossible not to see the truth. Engulfed by my addiction and obsessed with my search for the Chime, I'd left him to languish, even to die if it came to that. He blamed the nectar, but there was a note of hurt in his voice that made me think I'd more willingly surrendered to it than fought it and lost.

After everything, there had been more than enough guush – that's what they call money here – from the first investors for Naecia to purchase a 'galax cruiser' called the *Stellarcade*. She renamed it the *Electra*, after the aircraft flown by her third prior, some famous Earth pilot named Amelia Earhart. It was currently the only ship in the universe with a Switch Drive. And while the drive was a revolutionary technology, it was also a potentially cataclysmic one. For one, it rendered borders meaningless, which was problematic for a whole host of reasons, or as Patton explained it, 'the machine could be used to put everyone up everyone else's asses'. So, as of right now, Naecia wasn't selling. Just offering services as an instantaneous transporter/courier and occasional do-gooder. *Anywhere in the universe in no time.* The slogan was a work in progress.

Something nagged at me. "What'd you do with the Chime?" I asked.

"Well, we tried your plan first," he said, taking a sip of a thick, grey drink. I couldn't help but grimace as he gulped at it. "Farglack scrote milk, dude. Don't knock it."

"My plan?" I asked.

"Oh yeah. It sounded pretty good, too. So, I left Naysh and Izairis here, took the ship out to a black hole of my choosing, and droned it in."

"And?"

"Well, see, it ate it."

"That's good, right?"

"No, no, Ben: *The Chime* ate the black hole."

"Holy shit."

"That's what I said."

"How did you destroy it?"

Patton glanced around the room like he hadn't heard me.

"You didn't, did you?"

He leaned over and lowered his voice. "Before I tried to chuck it, we did some analysis on it."

"What kind of analysis?"

"*Scientific* analysis," he said. "It's over sixteen billion years old."

"So, it's old, who cares?"

"Our Universe is only fourteen billion years old, Ben. It didn't come from this dimension. And it doesn't seem like anything in this dimension can kill it."

"What did you do?"

"Well–"

"You hid it somewhere, didn't you?"

"What else was I supposed to do?"

"Where'd you hide it?"

"Obviously, I'm not going to tell you or else you'll have erased your brain for nothing. But Before Times Ben would have been able to guess it. Don't worry, though. I knew a good spot."

"What if they find it? The *Th-Th*ythin?" I asked, lisping the last word. I reached up to my mouth and felt around.

Patton cringed. "Yeah, you knocked a couple of those out somehow. I'd hate to see the other guy!"

I glared.

"It's not a big deal. They've got all sorts of doctors and stuff here. They'll mount a railgun on your head if you want them to. Teeth are nothing. Once you're feeling more yourself, we'll work on that grill." He smiled, truly satisfied with his answer.

"The *Th*-Scythin?" I prompted.

"Well, we knew they'd left you on the drift and so we took the *Electra* to find you after we moved Aszerat to a safe distance across the universe, repaired the Switch, and ditched the Chime. We also wanted to see if they'd buggered off, which they had. Poor guys. Running around the galaxy trying to find the unfindable. They were spotted a handful of times across the Dasma Arm. There's even been rumors about the ship just falling apart right in front of people. I don't even know if it still exists." His eyes went wide. "Hey? You want to see the one you found?"

"I found?"

"Yeah, this one Scythin was stuck in a radiation shield with the Chime. You climbed up there and got it. It's on display in Aszerat's main port as sort of a memorial to what happened. Very creepy." He began gathering the empanadas into his arms as I looked on, strangely.

"Hey?" I said.

"Yeah?"

"My parents…"

"That's a tough one, Ben. You don't really know them anymore. Maybe we'll work on your coherence and see what happens. Who knows, you get up to one or two percent some day and maybe go visit."

"But they probably think I'm dead."

"You kind of are dead, to be honest."

"Yeah, but they don't know that!"

"They don't," said Patton. "Look, I took care of it like you asked."

"What do you mean you took care of it?"

"Well, you know, we got over near Earth and I just made a call."

"You called them?"

"Nah, nah. I'm not an idiot. That'd be way too traumatic for them. I thought about sending a letter, but I didn't have their address. I figured the library did, so I called Ludlow the Librarian and just asked him to write a little note on our behalf and mail it to them. He's good people so he said no prob. I shot a photo for him to send along so your parents would know you were good."

"Wait, you had a stranger send a picture of me... with a note... to my parents?"

"Ludlow may be Wiccan but it's not really fair to call him a stranger. Here, look." Patton withdrew a rectangular thing with a screen on it. The picture was of a person I assumed was me, looking confused and disheveled. Probably exactly how I looked right now.

"Patton," I said. "What did the note say?"

"I just told them that you are safe and being treated well and that when the time was right, we'd be in touch."

"They'll think I was kidnapped... they'll think the librarian did it!"

Patton stared at me, gears turning. "I had not considered that possibility, Ben. Does have the ring of a ransom note, doesn't it? We should probably go straighten that out." He shrugged. "I'll get a bag for these. Oh," he said, "check your ear there. Might jog some memories."

I reached up and felt my earlobe. "Ah!" I gasped. "There's something stuck in it!"

"That's the *Alpha-Boom-Train*, Ben. It's a fishing fly. You *made* that. Big deal where we come from." He went off for the bag.

I was still unclear on the whole "fishing" thing. I tilted the shining empanada tray up toward my face. "My" face. Could have been anyone's face. The fly was a bright, flamboyant little thing. A spark of life stuck in my ear. Exquisite. Detailed and expertly crafted. Something that must have taken years to learn how to make, regardless of what knowledge I'd once had in my head that informed how I made it. There was a lot I could say about the little piece of art, but none of it came from anything I'd known before, suddenly springing to awareness in the food court. No memories kindled. No emotions swelled within me.

In the end, everything Patton had told me was just a story. And not my story. It was, and would always be, the story of the Shopkeeper and Pipefitter. The Shopkeeper was another guy who used to live in the same body who ended up doing some regretful stuff and some pretty amazing stuff from the sound of it. But I was never going to think of that life as my own. Whatever that guy had held in his mind, whoever he'd been, was gone. Utterly and completely. It was all just a thing that had happened. I was the next guy. We just looked the same.

ACKNOWLEDGMENTS

I have a wonderful group of friends and family who I can always count on to read my novels and give me straight ahead feedback. Those who braved the waters of *Stringers* were my wife, my Dad (first place ribbon, quickest beta-reader out there, helped un-meh a few things), old and dear friend Matthew Pierce, Marith Zoli, Gabriela Houston (*The Second Bell*), R.W.W. Greene (*The Light Years* and *Twenty-Five to Life*), fellow flash writer Michael Carter (*Boneyard*), who made sure my fly-fishing stuff was accurate ("Ask two fly-fisherman the same question, you'll get three different answers"), Noelle Salazar (*The Flight Girls*), and Dan Hanks (*Captain Moxley and the Embers of the Empire* and *Swashbucklers*), who I personally insult in Chapter Thirty-One. To my wife – thanks for the support and encouragement. It meant everything to me. But most of all, thanks for "dick-knuckle" which I used in Chapter Eight.

It was my Agent, Hannah Fergesen at KT Literary, who suggested that I submit *Stringers* to Angry Robot, so file any complaints with her. In the space of a few days, Hannah helped me shape the story's opening chapters into something that had real life to it. Her suggestions altered the course of the story and improved it immeasurably. I'm fortunate to have an agent who will pitch a book like this (and likewise a publisher who read a proposal heavy on bug sex and went, "Yeah, that").

I love working with the genuinely great people at Angry Robot. Eleanor Teasdale, Sam McQueen, Caroline Lambe, and my editor Gemma Creffield, who again guided a book of mine through the final process. I am continually wowed by her ability to latch onto a story and see it with clearer eyes than me as well as her patience for my next level neuroses. Andrew Hook is a fantastic copy-editor and I'm so glad he put his eyes on this. The cover process was great because we always get there despite my bombing them with my nectar-fueled concepts. Kieryn Tyler delivered an absolutely stunning design. I love it.

Thank you to all the drunks in the Transpatial Tavern for your support, enlightenment, patience, and advice.

I want to make sure to acknowledge all the passion, time, and effort put in by people who love books and help to raise their profiles, especially those by publishers outside the big four (three? Two?). Book Sellers (like Kel in Indiana, Hey!), book bloggers, booktubers, bookstagrammers, and booktokers are all part of a hugely important ecosystem for authors and publishers. I see the work you do and hope many others do too. Thank you.

Google: thanks for all the animal facts. I did double and triple check my data, so I apologize if I got anything wrong and to any animals whose reputations were sullied by the publication of this book. I promise it was intended as a love letter to the Animal Kingdom.

Metal bands I listened to while writing this book in no particular order: Hail Spirit Noir, Anaal Nathrakh, Spirit Adrift, Tides from Nebula, Volbeat, Zeal and Ardor, Genghis Tron, Pig Destroyer, Weekend Nachos, Killer Be Killed, Insomnium, Spectral Wound, Ghost, Sylosis, Amorphis, Cadaver, Stagnater, Carcass, Tribulation, Gojira, Carpenter Brut,[113] Malevolence,

---

113 Synthwave, but whatever.

Borknager, Desolated, Wrought of Obsidian, Royal Blood,[114] Jonathan Hultén,[115] Alterbeast, Skeletonwitch, Ringworm, Pale Flag, Ulcerate, Power Trip, Crypta, Opeth, Mastodon, Windrose, Nervosa, Dying Fetus, Metallica,[116] Ensiferum, Loscil,[117] The BombPops,[118] Wintersun, Harakiri for the Sky, and many others I was rocking too hard to remember.

---

114 Technically, those guys are just rock – *Technically, you can shut up.*
115 Okay, also not metal. He's like more folk chanting in a forest.
116 Pre-*Black Album*. ;)
117 That's not even music! It's like listening to space.
118 The Bombpops are *Pop*-punk, it's in the name for fuck's sake.

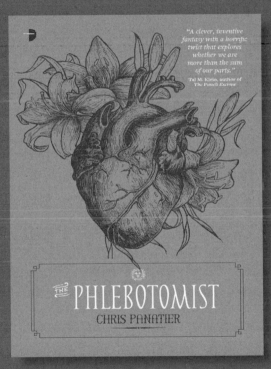

CHAPTER ONE

HYPOVOLEMIA
A state of decreased intravascular volume, including as a result of blood loss.

The sun was barely up, but the hour didn't keep folks from scrambling in to sell their blood. Early bird donors packed into lines that stretched to the entrance, their collective anxiety like a vapor that flooded Willa's nostrils when she walked in behind them. After so many decades on the job, she could almost discern the iron tang of it. That they were a mixture of types was obvious by their dress, with some low- and midbloods sprinkled in among the usual O-negs. Willa double-checked the time in case she'd somehow arrived late and glanced around for the station manager. "Claude?"

"Over here," he called, rounding the corner from the big freezer.

Willa held her arms open toward the growing mob.

"Price boost," said Claude.

"Again?"

"Check your PatrioCast," hollered Gena from down at Stall D. "Came down thirty minutes ago."

Willa slipped on her reading glasses and brought up the alert screen on her handheld touchstone:

▽ **PATRIOCAST 10.19.67** ▽

Residual ionizing radiation since Goliath causes latent spike in chronic diseases

To answer demand, Patriot offers the following incentives for units donated above the Draw. Valid through 10.21.67:

ONEG: +40.75

OPOS: +34.64

ANEG: +18.75

APOS: +16.67

BNEG: +5.7

BPOS: +5.13

ABNEG: +1.71

ABPOS: +1.45

▽ *Patriot thanks ALL DONORS. Your gift matters!* ▽

Patriot called it the Draw, but the people called it the Harvest. It came every forty-five days, a reaping of blood from every person sixteen and up. But it wasn't the Harvest that had Donor Station Eight packed to the gills. It was the chance to sell. For those feeling blooded enough to give beyond the minimum, Patriot was a willing buyer – that was the Trade.

Willa hung her jacket and donned her black lab cloak, then brought Stall A online. She buttoned the cloak and pulled its hood snug to her head as the various scanners and probes hummed to life. Each stall had two lanes, corral like, so phlebotomists could handle a pair of donors simultaneously if they were dexterous enough to manage. Willa was.

All of Patriot's collectors carried the title of "Phlebotomist," a point of unvoiced contention for Willa, since she was the only one who'd ever actually been a genuine phlebotomist. Sure, the others could pull a blood bag, spot-check it for authenticity, and drop it in the preservation vaults, but they wouldn't know the cubital vein from the cephalic. Especially Gena. Decades before the world went sideways, Willa had been trained in the old ways of venipuncture. Not that it mattered. True phlebotomy was an antiquated practice, irrelevant, like driving a car, another thing she used to be good at. The new ways were undoubtedly more efficient. It was for the best, after all. People in the Gray Zones needed the blood.

Willa's first two donors, a man and a woman, stepped into the lanes and lowered their shoulder-zips, exposing ports in their skin onto which blood bags were connected through a small siphon and needle junction. She quickly removed and processed the man's bag, then turned to the woman.

The man interrupted, "I got extra," and presented a second full bag from a satchel.

"Where'd you get this one, Tillman?" Willa asked. He was in so often that his sourcing had to be black-market. Most likely blood muggings. The cash-for-blood trade had created an unseemly underground economy, and it was booming.

"It's mine, *reaper*," he answered with a devious grin.

He knew that she had to take the blood if it scanned clear. It was company policy to accept any blood offered, so long as the phenotype, or blood type, matched the donor's profile. That didn't guarantee it was actually the donor's blood – far from it – but it gave Patriot a veneer of deniability if they were ever accused of being a market for questionably-sourced product. She ran it over the needle probe, which analyzed for phenotype, as well as other immunoreactive antigens and antibodies, the organism of origin, diseases, and the percentage of red blood cells in eryptosis, or cell death. If the readings were off, the bag would be rejected.

The probe cleared the unit and she dropped it curtly into her booth's cooling vault. Tillman smirked and scanned his touchstone for credit. "See you tomorrow," he said.

"You'd better not," said Willa.

She rotated to the woman. "Sorry about that, ma'am."

The woman was rough, wearing her thirty or so years like fifty. She held her sleeve open loosely, eyes drooping. Willa sighed and reluctantly removed the blood bag from her port. "Ma'am?"

The woman's eyelids fluttered as she struggled to say something. Her head flopped forward and she collapsed against the stall, her thin legs and arms in a tangle.

"Claude! Gelpack!" Willa rounded her station into the narrow corral. "Ma'am?" She tapped the woman's cheeks.

When Claude arrived, Willa traded the woman's blood bag for the gelpack, a small syrette filled with carbs and epinephrine used to jumpstart folks who sold more than their bodies could give. She broke its cap, pushed the two tiny needles into the skin on the inside of the woman's arm, and squeezed the contents into her basilic vein.

Claude looked at the woman, shaking his head. "Crazy. An A-neg in here trading like a lowblood."

Willa applied a small bandage over the wound and gave a touch of pressure. "How do you know she's A-neg?"

"Just a hunch." He leaned into the stall and scanned the bag on Willa's console. "Mmhmm. A-neg."

"The incentives are too high, Claude."

"I hear you, Willa Mae, but…" he dropped the bag into her vault and took the chance to whisper "…what can you do? Rules are rules." He gave a helpless shrug.

Willa helped the woman to a bench along the wall opposite a screen tuned to the Channel. She let her eyes blur over it while the stranger went in and out of consciousness on her shoulder. Back before the war, before Patriot, the medically recommended wait between donations was fifty-six days. This was to ensure that people fully recovered between donations. The absolute earliest that the human body could replenish a unit of blood was twenty-eight days, with many people taking up to three times that. The Harvest had lopped eleven days from the interval, mandating one donated pint every forty-five. If you wanted your government food rations, you showed up. If you didn't, you starved.

The Harvest alone was enough of a strain. But Patriot had gone a step further, offering cash to people willing to sell even more than the Harvest minimum. Of course, people were drawn in. Robots had taken most of the jobs and the Trade was regarded as something like basic income. Except folks were paying for it with the fruit of their veins. It never ceased to amaze Willa how much people could adapt, walking around in a constant state of hypovolemia just to get a little more coin, wearing symptoms so long that they eventually became character traits. Weakness, fatigue, confusion, clammy skin. Eventually anemia or shock ended the cycle. To Willa it was like state sanctioned Russian roulette, and folks were just spinning the cylinder.

Claude looked at her sideways. She was violating company policy by vacating her stall, but Claude tended to give her wider berth than the others. She had quickly worked her way up to Stall A – the equivalent of first chair in an orchestra – and had never relinquished it. Her gaudy production numbers brought her a certain amount of leniency.

The woman's hands lay folded against the bench like possum claws; skeletal and dirty, the dwindling meat beneath the skin a ticking clock. Willa had seen it all before, a cycle of destruction that churned through the districts to touch every family.

The woman straightened as if she'd been suddenly plugged back in.

"Ma'am?" Willa asked with a gentle touch to her wrist.

"What do you want?"

"You passed out. You've given too much."

The woman's pupils tightened on the screen, where a scrolling chyron flashed yet another incentive bump and she sprang from the bench. Willa latched to her arm instinctively. "There's no need. You're A-neg. The price will be the same tomorrow. Please, don't."

"Get off me," she growled. Willa knew it wasn't who the

woman really was, but the Trade had a way of exposing the nerves. Ripping her arm away, she returned to the back of the line.

Willa stepped into her stall and got her line moving. She processed bags, checked for fakes, but her eyes stayed on the woman. In short order, she was next in line, a new bag on her port, filling red pulse-by-pulse. "I'm feel good," she mumbled in anticipation of Willa's objection.

"No, you don't," said Willa. "That's the gelpack talking. It's just adrenaline. Please don't do this."

The woman leaned heavily on the side of the stall. "You haffto I got kids."

She was technically correct. Willa did have to. Grudgingly, she removed the half-full bag and processed it. It was a brutal thing, the blood trade, but here she was stuck on the receiving end of it; a cog in a runaway machine.

Just before close, a notification glowed orange on her display. She deactivated her stall, sending glass barricades across the lanes and flagged Claude in Stall B. "Coolant."

Claude summoned Willa's donors to his line and they grumbled their way over.

Willa angled a panel open and dipped her hand into her cooling vault. Her toes curled anxiously inside her orthotics. It was warming. "How much room do we have in the big cooler?"

"Topped out after lunch."

She had almost fifty liters. Blood couldn't be transfused after four hours in warm conditions due to bacterial proliferation. It would go bad long before morning if she couldn't get it cooled and her pay would be docked. "I'll call a technician."

"Good luck with that."

Willa tapped the support button and sat helplessly as donors side-eyed her from the long lines in front of Claude. *Sorry* she mouthed.

Closing time came with no technician responding. Normally, all of the vaults would be taken to the distribution hub after hours, but with no way to cool hers, it had to go now. She wheeled the vault, about the size of an old hotel refrigerator, from under the console and unhooked the cables from the processing interface. Having taken all of the extra donors, Claude's line was still out the door.

"I'm taking this to SCS," said Willa.

"Sorry, Willa, I'd do it, but…" The station supervisor couldn't leave with donors present and Patriot didn't turn away willing supply.

"I know," she said. "When you're done… do you mind… can you fetch Isaiah from school?"

"Sure. He's at the same spot?"

"He is. Thank you, sweetheart."

"My pleasure," answered Claude, swiping blood bags from the donors nearly as fast as she.

Outside Station Eight the sky was purple on one side and orange on the other, with clouds like gray icing layered between. The type of weather Willa described as *soon-to-be*. Mid October cool, soon-to-be cold. She shivered preemptively and hailed a taxi drone.

Drone rides were an absolute luxury in the blood districts and Willa felt guilty in summoning one, even if it was necessary to help her ferry the vault. After half a minute, a taxi drone in mustard yellow broke from the low-hanging clouds.

The sight of a drone descending from the sky to land right in front of you was something Willa would never get used to, even though they'd been around for decades. They seemed alien. Aside from helicopters, things that could fly were supposed to have wings. And drones were *not* helicopters.

To Willa they looked like flying gumdrops. Aside from some aerodynamic ridges that pinched out from the sides, they were rounded at the edges and slightly narrower near the roof. The motors were mounted in an array around the top rim, giving them a crownlike appearance. They were called "ducted fans," though the term meant little to Willa. They resembled giant rolls of toilet paper with propeller blades tucked snuggly against the inner walls. Independent articulation allowed them to control not only lift, but direction and altitude. With small alterations to the blade shape over the years, they were hummingbird quiet. Another eerie feature.

The taxi landed and the door swept open from the bottom. *Welcome aboard CROW FLIES*, it said.

"Patriot Distribution, SCS," said Willa. "Quickly please."

We will arrive at Patriot Distribution, Southern City Segment, in two and a half minutes.

Once she'd buckled into the bench and secured the vault to the cargo clip against the wall, the drone lifted off. A screen around the inner perimeter created a false three-hundred and sixty degree window, interrupted only by an actual window, set like a porthole in the door. She'd flown in plenty of drones but, much like their appearance, she had never gotten used to them – how they felt, how they took away all control. She longed for the solid predictability of a steering wheel and the responsiveness of an accelerator. Before the war, before the Harvest, before Patriot, when the asphalt was still good and cars could be afforded, Willa owned the roads, collecting tickets like blue ribbons. Speeding – her one real vice. But that was then. Nowadays, a car would appear every so often near the business district, but only the rich had money for such extravagances.

The drone traveled through the early evening glow in electric silence, toward the rough geographical center of the Southern City Segment. This was one of four such segments that made up the city, along with North-by, Crosstown, and Eastern. Each had a distribution center that collected the day's take from the donor stations in that segment. Totals from each were then shipped by transport drone to Central City Collection – CCC – downtown. Set in the middle of an urban forest, Triple-C was a sprawling complex that Patriot media proudly termed "the Heart" because it was the central hub for the circulation of blood to the Gray Zones. *From our heart to yours*, so it went.

Willa put her hand to the side of the vault, anxious over the precious cargo warming inside. Her anxiety was double since she didn't know when the coolant had actually gone out. It was possible the entire load was bad, and a single day of lost pay could break her.

The drone settled and Willa quickly unclipped the vault. *You have arrived at Patriot Distribution, SCS,* said the drone. *Will you be needing continued service?*

"No, thank you," she said, her heart already pounding like a countdown.

Have a most pleasant evening, then.

"You too." She rolled the vault onto the concrete apron in front of the building. The drone sped away.

Set off from the more densely populated residential areas, SCS Distribution stood alone at the center of a magnificent hexagonal concrete expanse, surrounded by a wall with trees stretching up behind it. A single road led out and into the blood districts. As far as she could tell, the place was empty. No people or other drones. Just a speedloop tube descending from the building's outer wall and into the ground at the far side.

The transports had not yet taken to the sky, and until they'd all departed, she had time to deposit the vault. She wheeled it heavily to one side of the huge polygonal building where a cutout in the thick concrete had a processing interface that looked like an old automated teller machine.

Willa's orthopedics slipped on the moist concrete as she struggled to roll the cooling vault to the connection point at the far end of a ramp.

Her bangs wicked away beads of sweat as she wrangled the vault. *You're too old for this.* Finally, with her legs about to give, a loud click signaled the vault's successful connection to the interface and it absorbed into the building. She rested against the wall for a moment, letting the cool cement sooth her nerves. Above, the blood transport drones began to filter from the building. They were wider and shorter than human transport drones, more utilitarian, and less refined – shaped like giant cigar boxes with ducted fans powerful enough to carry up to six cooling vaults apiece. Their only embellishment was the phrase BE A PATRIOT illuminated on their bellies.

She felt for her touchstone at the end of its lanyard and navigated to the screen that would register if the blood had gone through. It still read 00.00. She'd gotten the blood to distribution but wouldn't receive credit if it had spoiled. Holding her breath, she watched the numbers and willed them to change. They had to change. They had to. Afraid to blink, her eyes started to burn.

… 47.52 liters

Relief. A stay of execution. Only two and a half liters rejected.

She exhaled and stood up. Aside from the exiting parade of blood drones, she was alone. The air smelled like rain. She pulled up the hood on her reaper's black and began walking. Maybe she'd get home before it really came down.

She stopped after only a few steps, thinking that she'd heard something like a distant mosquito. It became more pronounced, a high-pitched whining that seemed to emanate from the squadron. One of the drones had fallen below formation. Even if it cleared the wall, she could see it wouldn't make it over the trees. A tick of panic came at the loss of such a large amount of blood, especially after she'd exerted so much effort to save a single vault. She briefly envisioned herself running underneath to try and catch it. Much as she disliked the Harvest, the Gray Zones needed every drop. Willa drew up her touchstone and alerted Patriot Emergency.

The motors on the drone struggled as it sank, with one exploding in a torus of glowing shrapnel. It hit the compound's outer wall and smashed to the ground, sending prop blades into the hull and gashing the steel. Vaults tumbled onto the pavement as the twisted carcass came to rest. Willa felt herself drawn through the debris field, but stopped short of the drone, still showering sparks. Calm down, she thought, there's no one in there.

A metal ring rolled lazily to her foot where it toppled over, and silence returned. She took stock of the scene and began toward the wreckage, careful to avoid the red slick of donor blood that would soon coat the asphalt. But as she neared the drone, her stomach twisted.

There wasn't any.

She triggered her touchstone's light and flashed it over the ground. Not so much as a drop of red, and no bags whatsoever. Had they remained inside the vaults through the crash? Had they all somehow held? Their poly construction was strong, sure, but those fan blades... it seemed impossible. Nearby, a dented vault laid open on its side, one wheel still spinning. She knelt to look inside.

Suddenly a white light blanched her vision. Willa turned into the beam eyes closed, her touchstone held aloft. "Willa Mae Wallace!" she yelled. "Station Eight, SCS."

The light descended from the sky and settled nearby. She cracked an eye just enough to make out the shape of a Patriot security drone silhouetted against the backdrop of the outer wall.

"Step inside, please," came a voice.

Willa took a final glance at the carnage and headed for the drone. When she was clear of the glare, the door opened to reveal a nice-looking man standing inside. He was in his early forties with a tanned face and a full head of brassy hair. His beige suit set off a bright pink tie and matching pocket square that immediately made Willa think of country clubs – if those still existed someplace. Her eyes were drawn to a gold pin in the shape of the letter "P" with the stem plunged through an anatomical heart that rested against his lapel.

"Yes, well, the newer insignias are terribly bland, are they not?" He spoke as if already in mid-conversation. "I suppose I flout the corporate message by remaining loyal to the original logo after a rebrand."

"I've seen you at our station before, I think," Willa said, "but I'm afraid I don't recall your name."

"Jesper Olden." His voice had the velvety timbre of wealth. "Patriot security. Please, step in from the cold." He took her hand and helped her inside.

"You don't look like security," she said, forgetting herself, then quickly added, "I mean – my apologies, it's been a long day. You just don't see people dressed like you many times in the year. Especially not out in the districts."

"No offense taken, Ms Wallace." He tapped the control screen. "We should have you home in fewer than two minutes."

"Oh, you don't have to do that, sir, I'm OK walking." But just like that, Willa felt the drone lifting off.

"Nonsense. We don't need you getting hit on the head by a defective drone." He gave a tepid chuckle. "Think of the liability."

Willa smiled weakly. Liability? The court system had long ago been largely dismantled, now used only to settle financial disputes among corporations and wealthy individuals. Regular people didn't meet the net worth threshold to utilize the system. His choice of words was perplexing. Maybe he was just using outdated vernacular as a matter of habit. Perhaps he was so out of touch that he didn't even consider how ridiculous the reference had been. He stared blithely out the window and Willa decided that must be it.

"Well," she said, "thank you for the ride." She stepped to the opposite side of the passenger compartment and took a seat. Relief was immediate. She'd always stored anxiety in her feet.

Olden considered the viewscreen. "Ah, there they are. The diagnostics on the crashed drone, see?" He gestured to some figures that Willa couldn't make out and gave the rest a cursory review. "Did you hear or see anything odd? Did you note anybody in the area before it went down?"

"I didn't see anyone else," she affirmed. "It just fell, that's all." There had been at least one empty vault in the wreckage but she had a gut feeling she wasn't supposed to have seen that.

"No one saw you there?"

"Not anyone other than you, Mr Olden."

"Wonderful. I appreciate the effort you made to get your take processed, especially this close to our Patrioteer conference." Willa knew about the conference, an annual two-day meeting for upper management to do whatever it was upper management did. Jesper played with the screen. "Let me credit you, let's say, five hundred as bonus for your effort. Is that fair?"

"Oh, Mr Olden, you shouldn't do that," she protested, uncomfortable accepting unearned lucre.

"Don't be foolish, Ms Wallace." He tapped in the amount. "That drone could have killed you."

"It was nowhere near–"

"Willa. May I call you Willa?" he said without really asking. "I insist on it. Patriot insists on it." He brightened. "You could buy Halloween candy this year. Five hundred would cover the entire segment, I'd bet. You'd be royalty."

"It's too much, Mr Olden, I'd prefer you didn't give me any money." The amount was more than a week's pay, and easy money came with strings. Aside from that, Halloween hadn't been observed for at least twenty years.

"And I'd prefer our drones not endanger top performers." He tapped the display. "Now let's not have any further discussion of the matter. *With anyone.*"

"I'm just happy to do my job."

"I assure you, Willa, we appreciate it." He flattened his suit jacket. "Ah, here we are at your stack. Do you feel well enough to return to work or will you need some days off?"

"I'm fine," she said as the door opened. "I'll be there tomorrow."

"Lovely, then. A good evening to you and to Isaiah."

She shivered at the mention of Isaiah. It always surprised her when Patriot managers voiced little details about her life that she considered private. She halfway assumed that the executives received prompts from their implants whenever they spoke with low level workers to make them seem more relatable or friendly. But she never got used to hearing strangers mention her family members out of turn.

The drone lifted away and her touchstone signaled the arrival of the money. An influx of five hundred would have had her rejoicing and thanking God out loud if she'd actually earned it. Entering her apartment stack, it felt like a chain.

She greeted Isaiah with a suffocating embrace that made him lose whatever game he was playing on his old viewer and he grumbled an objection.

Claude, who had come over to keep an eye on Isaiah, politely passed on a dinner invitation. She couldn't blame him. He was a station supervisor and didn't have to eat from The Box like everyone else. The Box – a literal box of prepackaged food – was provided by Patriot to residents of the blood districts who maintained one-hundred percent participation in the Harvest. The idea had been sold as a way to streamline subsistence programs. Instead of going to the store and picking out groceries for yourself and your family, the government picked them for you. Processed mystery meats and condensed dairy, sickly sweet canned fruit cocktails, powdered grains. On lucky weeks, a handful of oat cubes or tea. Many lowblood families relied on The Box completely. With her job, Willa leaned on it as a supplement, but few were able to live entirely Box free. She'd pass on it too if she could.

She and Isaiah ate genmod pasta prepared with a splash of black-market vinegar, topped with the last of some dehydrated poultry cubes that she'd managed to stretch over a full week. She stirred her bowl until they puffed into something that resembled the meat they had once been, and took small bites, chewing deliberately to make it all last. Isaiah devoured without ceremony.

A thought occurred to her, curiosity in the wake of her encounter at SCS, that she might tune to *The Patriot Report*. The show, which aired in place of the local news, touted Patriot's blood collection statistics and good deeds. Willa considered it a painfully tacky program, tortuously drawn out to thirty minutes in length, and cast in the mold of an old lottery-drawing segment complete with a shiny host yammering on through billboard teeth. The company served a vital role but bragging about it in such an ostentatious fashion left a bad taste. The fringes of the country were at war. People were suffering.

Swallowing her disgust, she turned it on, drawing Isaiah to the screen like a moth to a porchlight. Another reason she rarely watched anything.

"Isaiah, please," she said, yanking him back a reasonable distance. "It's nothing good."

Tanned darker than a roast turkey, the host was flanked by two scantily-clad assistants who held up digital posters announcing the statistics for every precinct within each of the four city segments. Willa did a double take. Setting her dinner to the side, she paused the screen and quickly added the figures. Southern City Segment was reporting a full take, highest in the city.

Impossible. With a crashed drone – carrying what were most likely empty vaults – SCS should have been dead last. They were either mistaken or they were lying. She reached for something to write with and jotted down the numbers, thinking she'd discuss it with Claude, but her pen scratched to a halt. Jesper had been clear. She couldn't tell Claude, couldn't tell anyone.

For more great title
recommendations,
check out the Angry Robot website
and social channels

www.angryrobotbooks.com
@angryrobotbooks